Praise for *Tidewater Bride*

"A powerful tale that brings history alive."

Urban Book Reviews

"Frantz weaves suspense and romance beautifully in this enjoyable inspirational historical."

Publishers Weekly

"The well-researched descriptions of the colonial era draw the reader in, and it is a treat to be introduced to such thoughtful, complex characters. This novel is a sure winner for any romance fan."

Historical Novel Society

the SEAMSTRESS *of* Acadie

Books by Laura Frantz

The Frontiersman's Daughter
Courting Morrow Little
The Colonel's Lady
The Mistress of Tall Acre
A Moonbow Night
The Lacemaker
A Bound Heart
An Uncommon Woman
Tidewater Bride
A Heart Adrift
The Rose and the Thistle
The Seamstress of Acadie

THE BALLANTYNE LEGACY

Love's Reckoning
Love's Awakening
Love's Fortune

the SEAMSTRESS of Acadie

A Novel

Laura Frantz

R
Revell
a division of Baker Publishing Group
Grand Rapids, Michigan

Published by Revell
a division of Baker Publishing Group
Grand Rapids, Michigan
RevellBooks.com

Printed in the United States of America

Library of Congress Cataloging-in-Publication Data
Names: Frantz, Laura, author.
Title: The seamstress of Acadie : a novel / Laura Frantz.
Description: Grand Rapids, Michigan : Revell, a division of Baker Publishing
    Group, 2024.
Identifiers: LCCN 2023017867 | ISBN 9780800740689 (paperback) | ISBN
    9780800745660 (casebound) | ISBN 9781493444793 (ebook)
Subjects: LCGFT: Christian fiction. | Romance fiction. | Historical fiction. | Novels.
Classification: LCC PS3606.R4226 S43 2024 | DDC 813/.6—dc23/eng/20230417
LC record available at https://lccn.loc.gov/2023017867

Scripture used in this book, whether quoted or paraphrased by the characters, is taken from the King James Version of the Bible.

This book is a work of fiction. Names, characters, places, and incidents are the product of the author's imagination or are used fictitiously. Any resemblance to actual events, locales, or persons, living or dead, is coincidental.

Published in association with Books & Such Literary Management, BooksAndSuch .com

Baker Publishing Group publications use paper produced from sustainable forestry practices and post-consumer waste whenever possible.

24 25 26 27 28 29 30   7 6 5 4 3 2 1

To readers everywhere who've embraced my novels.

Thank you for journeying to Acadie with me.

I hope we have many more historical adventures to come.

Learn to do well; seek judgment, relieve the oppressed,
judge the fatherless, plead for the widow.

Isaiah 1:17

Historical Note

The history of the Acadians began in 1604 when French settlers crossed the Atlantic to Acadie, now present-day Nova Scotia, Canada, where they became prosperous farmers and fishers. Though the bountiful land they lived on was contested by the French and the British, the Acadians declared themselves neutral. They spoke French but traded with the British and tried to maintain peaceful ties to both nations, including native tribes like the Mi'kmaq. However, Acadie passed back and forth between British and French control until 1755, the time of Le Grand Dérangement, or The Great Upheaval, when the British began to forcibly remove the Acadians from their homeland.

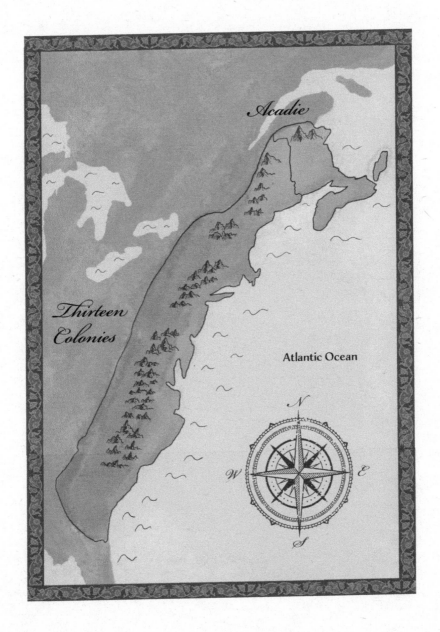

Glossary

aboiteaux—a dike that keeps seawater out
Acadie—French name for Acadia, present-day Nova Scotia, Canada
adieu—farewell
Anglais—English
au revoir—goodbye
Baie Française—French Bay (renamed "Bay of Fundy" by the British)
bel homme—handsome
bien-aimé—beloved
bien sûr—of course
bienvenue—a welcome or kindly greeting
bof—okay
bon—good
bon courage—be brave
bonjour—hello
bon sang—for goodness' sake!
bonne santé—good health
chère—dear
défricheurs d'eau—water clearers
Dieu—God
eau—water

fais de beaux rêves—sweet dreams
fête—party
française—French
frère—brother
gâteau—cake
grâce au bon Dieu—thanks to the good God
héritages—heirlooms
ici—here
jardin—garden
jolie—pretty
Le Diable Blanc—The White Devil
Le Loup—The Wolf
l'étoile—the star
médecin—doctor
merci—thank you
merci pour tout votre aide, pour toute votre bonté—thank
    you for all your help, for all your kindness
miam—yum
Mi'kmaq—Canadian Indian tribe
mon ami—my friend
mon cher—my dear
Noël—Christmas
objet d'art—piece of art
poutine râpée—potato dumpling with pork
quoi—what
ravissante—ravishing
rivière—river
sabot—wooden shoes
s'il vous plaît—please
sœur—sister
très belle—very beautiful
veillée—evening gathering

Prologue

Have your musket clean as a whistle, hatchet scoured, sixty rounds powder and ball, and be ready to march at a minute's warning.

Major Robert Rogers, founder of American Rangers

LAKE GEORGE, PROVINCE OF NEW YORK
WINTER 1753

He was numb, the wind-whipped snow driving icy shards into his exposed skin, the grip on his rifle weak. All the while a fire burned in his mind, driving him forward as he half clawed up the frozen mountain. He was no longer the commander of the Ranger Corps scattered in the valley below but a boy bent on saving his own life all over again.

Strange what came to a man when thirty-odd years flashed before his eyes. The thwack of Pa's axe. His little sister's gap-toothed smile. Chilled pewter mugs of cider atop a trestle table.

Winded, he pressed on amid snow blindness as other images assailed him like arrows. Mam's gathering basket that bore the scent of herbs, rosemary and rue foremost. Her candlelit profile as she read aloud to them at night, eyes closed in weariness between words strewn like bread crumbs in his consciousness.

For I know the thoughts that I think toward you . . . peace . . . not evil . . . to give you an expected end.

And then calamity had struck on the heels of those words as if to refute them, consuming all that he knew in a few smoky, charred moments, leaving a black footprint on the frozen ground.

They'd said Indians weren't winter raiders. An outright lie.

Gripping a brittle mountain laurel, he pulled himself up with his free hand. He tightened his hold on his gun while battling his way forward even as his shoepacks slid beneath him. Each harried second brought the fear his chest might explode from the pressure of his climb. He was all that was left to carry on his family name. Blackburn. A fine Scots name that needn't die on this whitewashed mountain.

He wanted another, better kind of life. As he thought it, that stubborn childhood vision slammed into him like the knifelike wind, his breath powdering the air in front of him as snow thinned in a scraggly stand of pines. The mountain suddenly gave way to a wending river . . . a blooming orchard on one side of it . . . a handsome house up a greening hill. Clear as a painting on a parlor wall. He'd first encountered the vision soon after that fiery day he'd lost his childhood. A fancy? It revisited him only when he hovered between life and death. It returned now with all its color and clarity, something not even a blizzard could obliterate.

He looked back, his trained eye detecting a flash of motion just below. Abenaki? French militia were not far behind, yet the encroaching darkness was in his favor, silvering the snow and forming a hazy wall that pushed the enemy back.

He had in mind more than survival. If he got free of this present danger, he vowed to go in search of that other, peace-laden place.

Almighty God, help me.

1

It was a Fine Country and Full of Inhabitants, a Butifull Church & abundance of ye Goods of the world. Provisions of all kinds in great Plenty.

Lt. Col. John Winslow

ACADIE
DECEMBER 1754

Sylvie Galant took a deep pine-scented breath. Atop the snowy bluff overlooking Baie Française, the sharp afternoon air cut into her lungs yet cleared her head after so much time indoors. Cold seeped through her shoepacks though her head and shoulders were warm, wrapped in a black wool scarf brightened by a red stripe, her mittened hands snug. She'd always found the snow enchanting. It lay like white silk shot through with silver thread and had the power to shut them in for days. Weeks.

Her delight dimmed as her gaze rose from the shimmering, silver-blue bay to a ridge crowned by the new, star-shaped Fort Lawrence, a blight upon the pristine landscape. Its British flag snapped about in the raw wind as if defiant, its parapets and ramparts blurred white by weather. Fort

Beauséjour, the French garrison she was in service to, stood just as stalwart, a mile of frozen marshland between them. Beyond its walls stood a church—some called it a cathedral—its unfinished, snow-topped spire giving an illusion of rustic grandeur. Its familiarity gave way to a niggling worry.

On the tip of this exposed bluff, was she watched by any at the English fort?

The climb to the top through thick forest left her heart beating hard beneath her loosely laced stays. This was her private place where few trespassed, her father's land. Taking her eyes off the two forts, she sought the seat that nature had made from an oak felled by a lightning strike when she was just a girl. Smoothed by time and weather, it made a comfortable rest. She brushed the snow off, her woolen petticoats an ample cushion. She craved quiet. Peace.

But oh, the churning in her heart.

Snowflakes swirled, adorning her garments like exquisite embroidery and turning the near woods into a glittering blur. Still, she spied him. Only a Mi'kmaq would be out in such weather. Her heart gave a leap, and she shot up from the stump in case he missed her and took the trail she'd come up through the Galant orchards.

"Bonjour, frère!" she called, her voice thin on the wintry air.

"Ma chère sœur!" he returned, quickening his step. He caught her up and swung her round in his hard, bearish embrace.

"Is it truly you, Bleu?" Laughing, Sylvie sank back into the deepening snow when he set her down, her wet skirt hem dragging. "I feared—"

"Never fear." His smile broadened, banishing her unease for a trice. "Hudson's Bay Company has kept me well occupied since autumn."

But not only Hudson's Bay? She studied him, her beloved

half brother, the cause of many a hope and prayer. His remarkable eyes—Acadie blue, Père called them—were the one feature they shared aside from their black hair. "I suspect it is not trading that keeps you but a sweetheart in the wilds."

"A paramour?" Bleu's deep laugh erupted, shutting down the notion. "I fear my many adventures snuff any courtship."

"Would that you wed and stay closer to home."

"Home? Where is my home?" He blinked, snowflakes rimming his long lashes. "Not only on the shores of Baie Française with our swelling clan. I am half my mother's people, remember."

None could forget it, looking at him. He was a striking mix of heritages, both Indian and French. Their father's beloved Mi'kmaq wife lived on in Bleu. And he was continually on the move across the vast French frontier—wood ranger, trapper, trader, voyageur, mariner, marksman, interpreter, warrior. Some even whispered spy and a leader of the French Resistance.

Her hopes stood on tiptoe. "You are home for Noël."

He nodded and glanced at the forts across the water, the lilt of his voice belying his dark look. "And what a celebration it shall be, eh? I have brought supplies that cannot be had with the British blockades. Cloth and spices and such."

"Oh?" The haversack on his back looked hopelessly small.

"I've cached them for now," he said, gesturing to the woods.

"Dare I ask if you remembered your sisters?"

"Did I?" He winked. "Only the finest for the mademoiselles Galant."

"So it has been a lucrative trading season?"

"At York Factory especially." His restless gaze returned to the landscape. "Why are you here alone?"

"I always come alone."

"With all the unrest, it is unwise." His eyes held a rare rebuke. "You never know when les Rosbifs are about."

She almost smiled at the sobriquet. Did these arrogant English soldiers care to be called roast beefs? Better that than les grenouilles—frogs—which she'd heard flung at the French firsthand, and even at Acadians, her own neutral people.

"I want neither frogs nor beeves here." Even imagining it seemed to sully so hallowed a place. "I like to think of the English coming no farther than the bridge at Pont-a-Buot."

"Pont-a-Buot, oui. I hear English soldiers congregate with French soldiers at the tavern there."

She nodded. "So Pascal says. He has dealings with the tavern keeper." Her middle brother's fascination with Fort Lawrence concerned her, though his business there was lucrative enough. "Selling spruce beer and cider from our orchards keeps him busy."

"Your orchards, you mean. The finest cider apples to be had."

"Merci." Orchards were a woman's domain in Acadie while the men minded the cattle and fields and tended the dikes. "I have saved you an entire barrel of L'Epice apples and another of Fameuse."

"And I may have brought you some seed." His smile reassured her of a promise kept. "The one variety you lack. Pomme Grise, no?"

"Oui." Her brows arched in delight. "All your lengthy rambles are forgiven, if so. Marie-Madeleine and I have even cleared ground in preparation. Once the snow melts . . ."

His wry chuckle doused her excitement. "The Mi'kmaq predict a heavy season. Seldom are they wrong. The beaver and muskrat have built especially large houses and their fur is heavy."

She shivered. "Remember the winter of '45? So bitter our cider froze and Père had to chop it with an ax?"

"I've not forgotten it. It curtailed my rambles, as you call them." He looked heavenward as snow swirled harder. "We might not see the ground till May."

Five more months. The time stretched long, fraught with a thousand uncertainties. But suddenly all that mattered was that Bleu was here and Noël was before them, the most joyous celebration of the year.

Smiling so wide her frozen face hurt, she said, "Come, Mère has made a fine soupe de la Toussaint and Père has just finished cider-making, his best yet. It is not frozen, so you may drink to your heart's content."

2

They [the Acadians] are found retreated to small portions of land, although their concessions are large.

Governor Joseph de Brouillan

Together they turned toward the only home Sylvie had ever known as the storm strengthened, whipping her skirts and shawl about like the fort's flags. Heads bent and arm in arm, they made their way down the bluff to the lowlands. There, a commodious house sat back from the bay, nestled in trees, its gable roof tiled, its twin chimneys puffing thick smoke.

Laughter bubbled from inside, sneaking past stone walls a foot thick as Sylvie and her brother passed outbuildings and mounted stone steps to the wide front door. Stamping their feet at the entrance brought the door open, and Marie-Madeleine stood facing them, her rapturous expression amusing.

"Bleu!" she bellowed, throwing herself into his embrace.

"Is this my wild apple?" He pulled his face into an exaggerated scowl as if doubting it, making her giggle into the folds of his fur coat.

Sylvie moved past them, into the center of the house redolent of sautéing cabbage and onions and baking bread. Mère scurried past her, intent on Bleu, while Sylvie went to warm herself at the large slate and fieldstone hearth, removing her damp scarf and gloves. Rows of wooden shoes—sabots—in various sizes were lined up near the dog irons, and she exchanged her shoepacks for these, her stockings still dry.

Giving the kettle a stir, she checked the bake oven next and found the wheaten loaves nearly done as more greetings were exchanged at the door. With twilight overtaking the last of day, Père and her brothers would soon appear, raw-cheeked and ravenous. As she thought it, she heard their familiar stomping outside.

Soon they'd all gathered around the long table that dominated the large chamber serving as kitchen, dining room, and sitting room. Chests of all shapes and sizes stood against white, plastered walls, and decorative shelves displayed possessions both pretty and practical. A maple syrup sugar mold. Clay pipes. A mint-green cup and bowl. Marie-Madeleine's latest drawing of her dolls. Even Sylvie's silver-plated embroidery snips dedicated to her sewing.

She glanced at the finished stack of men's shirts by her sewing chair near a south-facing window. Mornings were devoted to these while afternoons allowed her to help Mère about the house. The cold brought a reprieve of sorts. The stone cellar was half full at midwinter and fragrant with wintering apples. Countless tasks kept them well occupied while they dreamed of spring.

But spring was the farthest thing from Sylvie's mind as they sat down together as a whole family again, her heart so full her mind was empty. There was little talk, only the contented clink of cutlery and murmurs of appreciation as dishes were passed and savored.

Once Mère and Marie-Madeleine cleared the table after

supper, Sylvie peeled apples for breakfast and listened to the men. With Bleu home, the usual quiet pipe-smoking about the hearth gave way to more spirited conversation and long-awaited news of the outside world.

"As for elsewhere, French traders have been granted licenses to move inland and trade furs in Rupert's Land," Bleu was saying between draws on his pipe. "There is little war talk there. All is commerce from sunup to sundown."

"I wish I could say the same here." Père leaned back, his own pipe smoking furiously. "With new British forts—and English soldiers—trying to gain ground and encroach upon us, we hear little but war, war, war."

"Still, the French have won a string of victories, no?" Lucien leaned back in his chair and looked satisfied. "And they recently built Forts Duquesne, Machault, Presque Isle, and Le Boeuf."

"I am impressed you can name them, but . . ." Pascal frowned as he whittled with a small, sharp knife, fragrant shavings at his feet. "For all we know, they have since fallen to the enemy. News is slow to reach us in Acadie."

"True." Bleu got up to dig through his haversack. His gray wool justaucorps hung above it on a peg by the door, his beaver hat with it. Sylvie watched as he untied the bag's leather straps, heightening her anticipation. The promised goods, cached, could be gotten on the morrow if the snow was not too deep. "I have brought the latest reports from the enemy den, Halifax. Israel Putnam and his militiamen encountered me and my compatriots near there. We kindly relieved them of their papers rather than their scalps."

"Putnam is not my concern." Père looked at Bleu, eyes sharp, pipe aloft. "What of William Blackburn and his Rangers?"

The sudden hush in the room boded ill.

"Blackburn is said to have spent considerable time cooling his heels at Fort Saint-Frédéric after seeking refuge with the French in a blizzard." Bleu spread copies of the *Halifax Gazette* on the hearth's flagstones. "Once he was released in a prisoner exchange, he was granted a new commission, approving the expansion of his unit and tasking it with protecting British interests in Nova Scotia."

"Grave news, indeed." Père picked up one of the English papers, news of the coming war with France in boldface. "So he is at large again somewhere on the frontier?"

"Who can say?" Bleu shrugged. "He is unpredictable. Not even his superiors know what he is doing much of the time. He is always on the prowl, striking when least expected and refusing to wear the British uniform."

"I suppose he has now returned to New England to recruit more men after the Battle on Snowshoes," Père said.

Sylvie looked up from her apple peeling. "What kind of fool wages war on snowshoes?"

"None but Blackburn could have achieved it," Bleu said with a wry smile, sitting back down. "It seems he found himself cornered near Lake George on a scouting expedition and walked into an ambush."

"It is the stuff of legends," Pascal murmured. "Pont-a-Buot Tavern talks of nothing else."

Another hush ensued as her brothers nodded—all but Bleu. The tightening of his jaw told her he was no bystander.

Père continued in low tones. "As I recall hearing, Blackburn led his companies on snowshoes, some three hundred Rangers—"

"Less than two hundred," Bleu amended quickly, "while Fort Carillon's commander sent out a combined French and Indian force of more than seven hundred men."

"Oh?" Père studied him, understanding dawning. "If you were there, then you tell the tale."

Bleu hesitated, his gaze on the fire as it sent a spark past the dog irons and burned a tiny hole in the newsprint. "Outnumbered, Blackburn walked into an ambush and fought valiantly with his Rangers till dark. Much of their powder was wet and the muskets misfired. Still, there were many dead on both sides, and he lost the most men. An Iroquois warrior boasted he had killed him, but then we learned of his escape."

Caught up in the tale, Sylvie leaned forward. "Escape?"

Bleu nodded. "A wounded Blackburn climbed up the west slope of the nearest summit in the dark. He knew it well, make no mistake, but most men would have perished. French militia and Abenaki pursued him as far as they could. It was I who found Blackburn's buckskin coat with his commission in his pocket."

Lucien let out a puff of triumph. "An undeniable defeat."

"Defeat?" Dark amusement rode Bleu's features. "I would not call sliding down a near vertical mountain a thousand feet to a frozen Lake George without so much as a coat to cushion his descent a defeat."

Sylvie could not keep quiet. "And he lived?"

"He not only lived, he then put on his snowshoes backwards to appear that he had gone another direction, thoroughly confusing his pursuers."

Père shook his head. "Mon Dieu, deliver us."

"What happened to his coat?" Sylvie asked to their answering laughter. She was forever mindful of garments, in this case even the enemy's.

Bleu shrugged. "It was last in Father Le Loutre's possession, a trophy of war."

Lucien perused one of the papers, brows knit. "It says here there is a bounty on Blackburn's head, the highest ever made by French officials."

Sylvie shivered despite the warmth of the room. She'd heard too much of these Rangers and their leader. William

Blackburn sounded much like Bleu, fearless and inspiring fear, not even the wilderness his master.

"What of you, Pascal?" Bleu's eyes bore a harsh glint. "Is it true Fort Beauséjour's commandant is pressuring you to join the militia?"

"True enough. But how can we possibly do so when we Acadians declare ourselves neutral?"

"I am confident the English will fall before the French," Père said. "And there will be no need for Pascal to take sides nor be called away from his work here at home."

Lucien turned toward him. "But what if there is to be a war, as many predict?"

Sylvie wanted to cover Marie-Madeleine's ears. Mère shot a warning look at the men as she distracted her youngest daughter with a question. "Now, shall we serve molasses bread or apples?"

"Molasses bread," Marie-Madeleine answered, licking her lips as she fetched the coveted jug.

The men's voices rumbled on until Bleu stood and returned to his bulging haversack. "Though I have been away, I am not deaf or blind to your lack," he said. He began with Mère, handing her several packets.

She took them, eyes widening in appreciation. "Dried mushrooms and artichokes? From France?"

At his nod, Sylvie's anticipation heightened. Marie-Madeleine abandoned the molasses bread for a bountiful supply of blue silk ribbons.

"The color of your eyes," Bleu said.

"And yours," she returned with a laugh. "Does that mean you will wear them too?"

With a growl, he drew out a larger, thicker bundle, his attention swiveling to Sylvie. "While you sew your fingers to the bone for Fort Beauséjour's officers, do not think I want you clad in rags."

Suddenly aware of her humble garments, she took the offering, wondering what lay beneath the sealskin covering. All eyes were upon her as she opened his gift. A collective gasp went up from her mother and sister.

"Lyonnais silk," Bleu said as proudly as if he himself were the maker.

"But—" Sylvie exclaimed, eyes and hands caressing the sumptuous, pale yellow fabric with its vivid patterned fruits and flowers. "I've not seen officers' wives in so fine a cloth!"

"Princess Sylvie," Père said with a wink. "I have always thought you were meant for finer things."

Flushing at the familiar if misplaced sobriquet, Sylvie raised grateful eyes to Bleu.

"For your wedding gown, mayhap," he said. "A garment to be handed down to a daughter and a granddaughter . . ."

"Oui, oui," Pascal teased as Lucien got up to add another log to the fire. "If Fort Beauséjour's good doctor has anything to say about it."

Titters went round the circle as the blood rushed to Sylvie's cheeks. "Shush. How can I possibly be a fit doctor's wife? I quail at the sight of blood."

"See?" Père winked again. "She *is* a princess."

"Speaking of Dr. Boudreau . . ." Lucien said, sitting back down again. "When will you have the spectacles he recommends for your work?"

Folding up the silk, Sylvie did not answer, wondering whether to style the gown robe à la française, while Dr. Boudreau poked at the edges of her consciousness.

"Sylvie has garments to deliver when there is a reprieve in the weather," Mère remarked briskly. "She can see the doctor then."

Bleu continued withdrawing items from his pack. "If tomorrow allows, I shall go to the fort and escort you."

Sylvie merely nodded as Marie-Madeleine served molasses

bread. She'd tied a blue ribbon in her dark hair, which Bleu pulled at mischievously as he continued his gift giving. Père exclaimed aloud over a new hunting knife, while Lucien and Pascal made much of their new flints and axe-heads. Mère seemed delighted with the promise of not one Hudson's Bay Company blanket but two, both with indigo stripes, still cached in the woods.

Sylvie looked to the silk that shone gold in the firelight, its embroidery a sewing feat. With so much of winter before them, it was the perfect time to fashion a new gown.

3

[The mantua-maker's] business is to make Night-Gowns,
Mantuas, and Petticoats, *Rob de Chambres*, &c for the
Ladies. She is Sister to the Taylor, and like him, must be
a perfect Connoisseur in Dress and Fashions; and like the
Stay-Maker, she must keep the Secrets she is entrusted
with, as much as a woman can.

R. Campbell, *The London Tradesman*, 1747

Two days later the weather cleared enough to journey to
Fort Beauséjour. At first light, Père shoveled a path to
shore, where a number of Galant vessels waited. Baie
Française glistened, so salty it never froze even when the land
was locked in winter's icy grip. Bleu loaded a caribou-skin
canoe with Sylvie's stack of finished shirts before helping
her into the boat, where she sat without taking up an oar.
Bleu had no need of help, cutting through the water to the
far shore like Sylvie's scissors sliced silk.

As they drew nearer, Sylvie could not master a flinch.
Voyageurs and soldiers stood about the dock, loading and
unloading vessels, many of them familiar. She was never
comfortable on this side of the bay, never relaxed her wary

stance. She leapt to shore, eyes on the snowy trail that would take them up to the fort's star-shaped walls.

Bleu secured a sled and heaped their goods atop it, including some of his own trade items, intent on the fort. Like an ox he was, his sheer strength a marvel. With leather straps about sinewy shoulders, he started pulling the sled up the hill after exchanging a few greetings with those he knew. Sylvie trailed him in snowshoes, an unwelcome reminder of Blackburn's Battle on Snowshoes. She was soon out of breath, but Bleu never slowed his easy stride, only looked over his shoulder now and then to ascertain she followed.

When the fort's parapets appeared, she chafed, a sense of foreboding overtaking her. She could not foretell the future, but lately when she encountered it her emotions grew dark. Here the Troupes de la Marine under their commandant, Jean-Baptiste Mutigny de Vassan, kept watch night and day for any English, who seemed to creep ever closer.

Once through the sally port, Sylvie freed her shoepacks from the leather thongs that tied on her raquettes before going into the quarters reserved for trade. As usual, hot tea was served, chasing the chill from their bones and their garments. Sylvie kept her eyes down, letting Bleu do the talking. It would not do to invite men's notice with her attention. In a fort full of soldiers and few women, she was as tempting as a freshly baked tart, Mère oft said.

Still, men took her measure. She was known as the seamstress. The blue-eyed daughter of Gabriel Galant, head of a large lowland clan. Sister to the renowned Métis—Bleu—one of Abbé Jean Le Loutre's most respected associates.

Beneath her lashes, Sylvie eyed the tall, thin priest in the corner with cold loathing. This was no holy man. How could he be when inciting his Mi'kmaq converts to attack the English? And not just soldiers but all Protestant settlers coming into Acadie? The cathedral in progress beyond fort walls was but a front for his devilish schemes, some said.

With a word to her, Bleu left the room with Abbé Le Loutre. Sylvie's spirits sank as she savored her tea. Before she could ponder the implications of their meeting, a door opened and a humbly clad woman entered. Maidservant to one of the officers' wives? Sylvie had no wish to leave the hearth's leaping fire, nor had she finished her tea.

"Mademoiselle Galant?"

Sylvie forced a smile. "Oui."

"Can you spare a moment to meet with my mistress?"

Sylvie gestured to the stacks of men's garments Bleu had hauled uphill. "I am awaiting payment for my work."

"I have already told the quartermaster you are needed elsewhere." The insistent edge to her tone brought Sylvie to her feet. "This is far more important than officers' shirts, mademoiselle. You will be well rewarded."

With a nod, Sylvie traded the fire's warmth for a cold walk down several wooden corridors to a more comfortable chamber filled with thick rugs and paintings and fine furnishings. Only a few officers' wives were willing to live at the fort. Sylvie credited whoever this woman was with an intrepid spirit.

Someone speaking rapid French preceded another door opening. The officer's wife? A tall, slender woman with mouches on her chin and cheek came in with a rustle of lutestring. Sylvie noted all the little details and embellishments of her glossy, rose-colored gown as the maid made introductions.

"Ah, the humble Mademoiselle Galant." With a gesture to a trunk along one wall, Madame Auclair summoned her maid to fetch the fabric. "I have seen your fine stitching and am in need of a gown for a Noël ball. Surely you must be bored with men's garments. They seem beneath your skill."

Sylvie smiled. "I can sew those in my sleep, I sometimes think."

"Exactly. But can you produce a quality gown like the one I have in mind? In so short a time? I have plenty of thread as well as ribbon and lace for trim."

"I can get up a dress in a few days' time usually, but a simple one, not a ball gown. My mother sometimes assists." Even as she said it, her spirits sank. Her own gown must wait. Besides, where would she wear such sumptuous silk? Her Galant clan—and her fellow Acadians—would say she was proud when in fact it was only that Bleu was generous. "Someone else must be assigned my shirt work."

Madame Auclair smiled. "My husband is second in command here at Fort Beauséjour. I will arrange for your work to be given to someone else." She went to another trunk and brought out an abundance of lace and ribbon, the finest Sylvie had ever seen. French-made, no doubt.

Sylvie reached into her pocket and withdrew her ribbon measures while the maid went to retrieve a dress she could use as a template.

When she'd returned, holding a small, elaborate case, Madame said, "This is newly arrived from France in the style of gown I have in mind."

The maid lifted something from the case as if it was an objet d'art and presented it to Sylvie. A fashion doll? She'd heard of these exquisite creations, often replicas of their owners. Green glass eyes stared back at her, the painted features so like Madame Auclair it was almost eerie. Touching the curled hair, Sylvie found it as soft as her own.

"Guard it." Madame looked at her intently. "The Pandora has come all the way from Paris despite . . . um, international difficulties."

Staring at the wax doll that was sure to make Marie-Madeleine forsake her homespun ones, Sylvie wondered how such a luxury would survive a downhill march in the snow and a water crossing, not to mention her sister's inquisitive nature. Carefully she returned the treasure to the maid and began applying the measuring ribbons, memorizing the numbers as she did so. All the while she remembered the words she'd just read about mantua-makers in the *Halifax Gazette*.

She must learn to flatter all Complexions, praise all Shapes, and, in a word, ought to be compleat Mistress of the Art of Dissimulation. It requires a vast Stock of Patience to bear the Tempers of most of their Customers, and no small Share of Ingenuity to execute their innumerable Whims.

Doubts assailed her. Could she get up such a fine gown in so short a time?

Finally all the measurements were double-checked, though Madame Auclair seemed somewhat dubious that Sylvie could keep all the numbers in mind. She also seemed bereft to be parting with the Pandora, clearly a coveted possession.

"I'd like you to apprise me of your progress. Either send word to me here or come in person," she told Sylvie before asking her maid to serve tea. "For now, you must sit and tell me of yourself—your sewing history and habits."

Madame gestured to a linen-clad tea table by a window that overlooked the fort's parade ground. The curtains were partially drawn, but Sylvie could still see soldiers milling about, some shoveling snow, others managing artillery, and a few managing livestock running amok.

Tamping down her unease, Sylvie tried to remember her manners, surprised Madame wanted her company. But in a fort overfull of men, why wouldn't she? Sylvie stifled a smile at something Bleu had said. *Some of the fairest belles have the emptiest heads.* But Madame did not seem cut of the same cloth.

The maid brought scones, butter, even jam. Sylvie's mouth

watered. She had not thought to pack victuals. Bleu always carried jerked meat anyway, something she had had so much of she could do without. A scone was a wondrous thing, surprisingly more English than French.

Watching her discreetly, Sylvie followed Madame's every move. Serviette in lap. Teacup near the table's edge. Her hostess poured from the porcelain pot effortlessly, nary a drop spilled. As Sylvie took the first sip of a delicate tea she'd never tasted, Madame seemed to read her mind.

"Pekoe." She smiled rather wistfully. "While scones are decidedly an English invention, tea is most certainly not. We French have been drinking it for ages."

Madame was gentry French, then, enjoying such delicacies. Pushing past her shyness, Sylvie took a scone and attempted conversation. "I've mostly had green tea, not black."

"Ah, known for its medicinal benefits. Though you hardly need it, for you seem bonne santé to me." Adding a generous splash of cream, she stirred her tea with a silver spoon. "Now, tell me about your sewing."

Nearly squirming beneath Madame's keen eye, Sylvie searched for a beginning. "My mother taught me my stitches when I was very small. Alphabet samplers and hemming garments and sewing on buttons. Then, when I was ten, I went to live with an aunt in Louisbourg on Ile Royale and attended the convent school founded by Sœur de la Conception."

"Ah, of course, the school for proper young ladies. But I thought they only accepted daughters of officers from the garrison there."

"My aunt was wife to the etat-major. Since they had no children, she enrolled me as her niece." Could Madame hear the sadness in her voice? Aunt Lisette—her father's sister—had been one of Louisbourg's brightest lights. Beautiful and accomplished, she'd succumbed to a fever when Sylvie was thirteen. "After her passing, I returned home."

"A sad circumstance. But you learned embroidery and other sewing techniques while in Louisbourg, no?"

"A great many, oui. I've since been charged with making all the garments for my family. We have a herd of sheep and also grow linen from flax we spin."

"'Tis a wonder you have time for such tasks. Your stitching on my husband's shirts is what caught my eye, especially your monogrammed embroidery on the officers' garments. You don't just sew, you go beyond and create beauty amid simplicity."

Flushing, Sylvie thanked her. "I can always see how a garment can be made better, even smallclothes."

"I think your talents are wasted on men. Leave them to the tailors. You were made to create finer things for those who can truly appreciate them."

"You mentioned a ball . . . here at Fort Beauséjour?"

Madame's green eyes glittered. "A Noël ball at Pont-a-Buot. We have extended an invitation to the officers and their wives at Fort Lawrence to join us. Since our men fraternize at the tavern dividing our territories, perhaps it is time for the ladies to meet there also."

Sylvie could not imagine it with tensions so high. "Have they accepted this gracious invitation?"

"Not yet." She lifted slight shoulders in a shrug. "But one can hope."

Hope? Abbé Le Loutre, Bleu, and the Resistance would think that more laughable than laudable. The English, Bleu said, would not make peace till they'd taken every arpent of Canadian land.

"It's a goodwill gesture to show that we have much in common and might live in harmony." Madame took another sip from her exquisite cup and began to talk about the coming ball as excitedly as if the French king himself might be in attendance.

4

The winter is agreeable in that it is never rainy nor filled
with mists, nor hoar frosts. It is a cold which is always
dry and with a bright sun. One never sees a little cloud in
the sky. . . . One goes from eight to fifteen days, and even
three weeks, without seeing it snow, during which time it
is always good weather.

Nicolas Denys, French fur trader and explorer

Will you say a prayer, mon cher frère?" Sylvie eyed
Baie Française warily as she clutched the Pandora's case. "That the canoe will not sink?"
Bleu chuckled then grew serious. "Not on my watch, ma
chère sœur." He seemed to take extra care as he secured
Madame's meticulously wrapped silk for the gown with all
its embellishments at the canoe's bottom. "Your talents are
no longer secret." He studied her intently as if reconciling
his sister with that of a mantua-maker. "Soon every madame
on both sides of the Missaguash River will be clamoring for
your services, no?"

"That would depend on the quality of this gown when I
am finished," she returned, sitting down in the canoe yet still

eyeing the water warily as if it might rise up and consume the Pandora.

To her dismay, the wind shifted, creating lacy swells that smacked the canoe's leeward side as they reached the midpoint of the bay. Always chary of the water even on the best of days, Sylvie held the Pandora as she would a newborn baby. Cold bit her nose and cheeks, her scarf loose about her head. Bleu paddled furiously as if evading some unseen danger, his beaver hat pulled low against the fretful wind.

It seemed odd to return without a stack of government-issued cloth for officers' shirts. Who would assume the task in her absence? Granted, there were new people moving in and out of the fort every day with a variety of skills. She would not give herself airs and imagine she alone could ply a needle. Still, Madame's regard warmed her even as the weather worked to turn her to ice.

Once blessedly beached and out of the boat, Sylvie all but ran toward their front door while Bleu stowed the canoe and unloaded cargo. Never had she been so glad to be home. She spied Marie-Madeleine watching from the window as the setting sun stole the last of daylight, ending their eventful day. She was unprepared for the questions certain to pepper her from all sides once she crossed the threshold.

Père and Lucien were still stamping the snow off their boots just inside the door. Pascal, she recalled, had gone to the fort the land route, driving their cattle on the hoof to be butchered and salted there once they were sold.

Marie-Madeleine rushed Sylvie before she'd even removed her wraps, her wide eyes on the Pandora case she'd carefully set on a bench. Sylvie felt a protective qualm yet didn't want to deny her little sister something so lovely, if only to look at.

"Have you brought me something from the fort?" Swiping at her flour-smudged cheek, Marie-Madeleine stood on tiptoe in anticipation. "So jolie a case!"

Sylvie hung her scarf and cape on a wall peg, realizing she'd forgotten to bring her sister something as was her custom, if only a sweetmeat from the fort's sutler. "It belongs to Madame Auclair at Beauséjour. You may open the case and take a look if your hands are clean."

Clearly intrigued, Marie-Madeleine flew away to wash. Père and Lucien chuckled as she rushed past, casting querying looks at Sylvie before following her into the main room.

Mère greeted them with a smile, the mingled aromas of the kitchen and bake oven like her loving embrace. "At last everyone is finally here but Pépère and Mémère," she said of her parents, who lived farther down the bay.

"The weather is about to take another turn, and they cannot chance it," Père finished for her, sympathy on his bearded face.

"Perhaps by Noël. I worry so about Mémère, especially with her rheumatism and this snow."

Père sent her a reassuring look as he added another log to the hearth. "We chopped enough firewood for them to last through an eternal blizzard."

Chuckling, Bleu and Lucien sat upon a long bench facing the hearth, trading their damp shoepacks for their sabots. Yawning, Sylvie wanted to join them, but her sister showed no such weariness. Eyes adance, the supper she'd helped prepare a memory, Marie-Madeleine watched, transfixed, as Sylvie placed the case on the dining table.

"For now, I have no more sewing of officers' shirts," Sylvie said, still uneasy about her new assignment. "I've instead been charged with getting up a gown for the wife of one of Fort Beauséjour's officers."

"Oh?" Mère never ceased slicing bread. "Someone of note has taken notice of your sewing? I am only surprised it has taken this long."

Sylvie began undoing the silken ties of the case, anticipating her sister's grand reaction. As expected, Marie-Madeleine gasped, her hands covering her open mouth as Sylvie took the Pandora out carefully, aware of a few details she'd overlooked. The tiny slippers with diamond-dusted buckles. The miniature fan that lay at the case's bottom, along with a bergère hat adorned with a finger-sized feather and silk roses no bigger than buttons.

For once, Marie-Madeleine was speechless though Mère was not. "Oh! I have never seen such extravagance!"

"Madame Auclair is quite fond of it. This is but one miniature gown. The Pandora has many."

"Mademoiselle Pandora . . ." Marie-Madeleine's gaze left the doll briefly. "Is that her name?"

"It is the name for dolls like her. They wear the most coveted of fashions. See this ball gown? Madame Auclair has given me silk to make one just like it."

"May I hold her?" Marie-Madeleine asked.

"Are your hands clean, petite sœur?"

She held up freshly washed hands, then gently took the doll, admiring the lace petticoat before lifting it. "Oh la la! She has on clocked stockings with lace garters, even an embroidered shift!"

"She also wears stays. The smallest stays I've ever beheld."

Marie-Madeleine's inquisitive fingers moved to the coiffure in examination. "Her hair feels real, as real as my own."

Mère chuckled. "You remind me of a doctor with your probing of Mademoiselle Extravagance." Her attention swung to Sylvie. "Speaking of surgeons, did you see Boudreau?"

"Not this time. He was at Fort Lawrence consulting with the English surgeon about some matter."

"So, your spectacles must wait." Mère sighed, the matter long unresolved.

"It would be nice to have them as I get up this gown,"

Sylvie admitted. "Perhaps Père could fetch them next time he is at the fort."

"'Tis not Père Dr. Boudreau wants to see but *you*."

Warmth flooded Sylvie. She stared at the Pandora, but 'twas Bernart Boudreau she saw, with hair the deep russet of an orchard apple and a rather unbecoming cleft chin. Though French, he had come to the fort two years prior from the Royal College of Physicians in Edinburgh, and he had no wife, a malady many unwed women wanted to remedy.

"I shall be too preoccupied with Madame's gown to return to the fort," Sylvie said. She dare not devote any time to anything but the elaborate project before her. "First the silk must be carefully washed to make it more amenable to handling."

"I wish you had your spectacles." Mère began stuffing the poutine râpée with salt pork to boil, unwilling to let the matter rest. "The winter days are short, and firelight is a far cry from sunlight."

"I must go to Beauséjour day after tomorrow," Pascal said from where he sat by the fire. "I will see if Boudreau has returned."

Sylvie felt stark relief. While she found the doctor amazingly knowledgeable, his attentions were disconcerting. Was he aware that Père had set considerable hectares of land aside for her and her future husband, a generous dowry that had gained her several would-be suitors? But none of them, even though they were Acadian, stirred her, and she was no surer of Bernart.

She watched her sister handle the doll as if fearing it were glass and might break. How could a girl of eight do any harm? Leaving her alone, Sylvie began helping Mère with supper preparations, her own stomach rumbling in anticipation.

"You'd best begin the gown." Mère's chiding reminded

Sylvie of how much was at stake in so short a time. "You can work in the parlor, where all is clean and quiet."

"I shall." Sylvie felt the mounting pressure of her task. "But for now I just want to be simple Sylvie Galant, poutine maker, not seamstress to a fancy fort madame."

"Once the other ladies see that gown, you will no longer be sewing men's shirts," Mère said. "Unless you wed the good doctor and sew his."

5

The coasts are as rich as ever they have been represented; we caught fish every day since we came within 50 leagues of the coast. The harbour itself is full of fish of all kinds.

Governor Edward Cornwallis

The needed spectacles arrived with Pascal a few days later—along with a note. Sylvie looked up from her fabric cutting when he held both out to her. After setting her scissors aside, she took the case that held her spectacles while pocketing the sealed paper.

Too many eyes pinned her, and Bleu's droll amusement was rattling enough. "Let me see you wear them." He crossed his arms, a study of patience while the note burned a hole in Sylvie's pocket. "Are they a proper fit?"

Self-conscious, Sylvie withdrew the spectacles and slowly put them on. The pinch to her nose made her want to sneeze. She blinked, disbelieving. Could her vision truly be sharpened?

"Steel, tortoiseshell, and glass," Pascal elaborated. "London made."

"The cost?"

"He refused payment."

"Oof!" Her head came up so fast the spectacles nearly flew off. Adjusting them, Sylvie stared at him through the round lenses. "But why?" As soon as she voiced the question, she was sorry.

Bleu winked, his hearty laugh bringing Marie-Madeleine into the parlor. "Because he is a smitten suitor from all accounts . . . and that note you pocketed so hastily no doubt bears proof of his ardent devotion."

"Shush," Sylvie said. She took up her scissors again as Pascal left for the barn and Bleu gave their sister a coveted sweetmeat.

"Candied lemon peel?" Marie-Madeleine looked as pleased as she'd been disappointed when Sylvie had returned empty-handed. "My favorite. Merci."

"So how goes the dressmaking?" Bleu asked after sending Marie-Madeleine to the cellar for cider.

"Slowly," Sylvie confessed. "My nerves make me hesitant."

"Are the spectacles an improvement?"

She squinted through the lenses and examined her stitches in bewilderment. "No."

"No?" He scoffed and took them, then put them on and proved such a spectacle wearing the spectacles that she giggled as wholeheartedly as Marie-Madeleine.

"You look quite studious," she said, still giggling.

"They seem naught but clear glass. A courting ruse, perhaps." Returning them to her, he looked over the parlor table, examining the silk and all the furbelows strewn across it. "At least Mère will be appeased. She is not helping you?"

"Her hands are full of spinning and the stillroom. Even now she has gone with Lucien to take a tonic to Pépère, who is suffering the gout."

"I am sorry to hear it. Mère's stillroom remedies are without equal. He should be well by Noël, no?"

Ah, Noël. The very word filled her with joy. A dozen different images warmed her heart at the mention. Soft, scented candlelight and days-long preparations for the réveillon, the festive dance and dinner redolent of spices and delectable, flaky-crusted pork pies. French carols filled her head like a symphony. There was snow, always snow, the icy flakes sifting down like the fine sugar atop the fried croque-cignoles, the pastries Père was so fond of.

"Oui, by Noël, so we hope," she finally replied. "Lord willing."

Bleu turned away to tend the parlor fire that Sylvie had neglected, pausing to take the cider their sister brought. As Sylvie cut the last of the silk to the smoke and snap of oak rekindling, Marie-Madeleine sidled up to watch, clearly itching to handle the Pandora that rested in the open case.

"So jolie a doll needs a name," Marie-Madeleine said, gravely serious.

"She is Pandora, no? I think the English call them Fashion Babies."

"The English?" Marie-Madeleine screwed up her face as if she'd bitten into a worm-ridden apple. "I shall call her Aliénor."

"Très belle. Like something from a fairy tale."

"May I play with her?"

"I fear not." Sylvie smiled apologetically. "She is made more for admiration. And I need my eye on her as I get up this gown. But if there are any scraps left over, I might adorn one of your dolls."

Tired of hovering, Marie-Madeleine left to go in search of Bernadette and Maryse, a worn pair of dolls made from castoff fabric but nevertheless beloved. Reassured she was alone by the ring of Bleu's axe as he chopped firewood beyond the back door, Sylvie took the doctor's note from her pocket.

The paper was no ordinary rag linen but fine foolscap, almost soft to the touch and affixed with a charming blue fleur-de-lis seal. Unfolding the note, Sylvie realized she'd never seen the doctor's handwriting before. It scrolled across the page like a black wave, smacking her with its intimate salutation.

Chère Mademoiselle Galant,
  I regret that I was called beyond fort walls and unable to ask you this in person. Thus, I write to request the pleasure of your company at the fête to be held at Monsieur Casey's at Pont-a-Buot the Saturday before Noël. Weather permitting, I am wondering if Pascal might accompany you. I look forward to being your escort upon your arrival. There is no other mademoiselle who comes to mind so frequently and with such fervor. I remain your devoted doctor-servant.

Yours entire,
Bernart Boudreau

A fête with the doctor? Held at a mysterious tavern she had only heard of but never set foot in. How had this happened when she'd always treated him like she did her brothers? Had he taken that familiarity as flirtation? She swallowed, the flutter in her stomach cresting to queasiness. The kettle in the kitchen across the hall hissed, but she hardly heard it.

Pocketing the paper again, she looked down at her simple woolen dress with the customary red stripe. With no time to sew a suitable party dress, how could she possibly go?

Bleu's gift lay hidden in her dower chest Père had hand carved. Three drawers high and decorated with white flowers on a blue background, it bore her initials. She went to it and opened the drawer where the silk rested, realizing it even outshone Madame's fabric. There she secreted the doctor's note before shutting the drawer again.

The parlor clock struck four. She removed her spectacles, set them by her shears, and hurried to the kitchen to take the kettle from the hearth. Cups were snatched from a shelf and arranged so that Bleu and Marie-Madeleine could join her for the usual pine needle tea Père preferred, an old Mi'kmaq recipe. She carried them to the table on a tray alongside a plate of cinnamon pastries made from tourtière dough.

She didn't even have to call for her siblings. Marie-Madeleine never missed teatime, and sharing it with her oft-roaming brother made it a special occasion. She even propped her dolls up beside her, the miniature wooden cups Pascal had whittled for her in their laps. Bleu entered next, taking Père's chair to one side of the hearth while Sylvie and Marie-Madeleine sat upon the bench. For a few moments Sylvie savored their being together like the humble repast before them—as much as her fretful stomach would allow.

Bleu winked at her, a prelude of what was to come. Cupping his tea in one dark, callused hand, he took a sip. "Do you care to divulge the contents of that note?"

Sylvie nearly squirmed on the bench. "I do not."

"What note?" Marie-Madeleine asked, cinnamon-sugar on her lips.

The silence stretched long, begging for a reply. Her sister was as dogged as Bleu, holding her with those Acadie blue eyes, demanding answers.

Sylvie took a steadying breath. Why had she hoped to keep it a secret? "Dr. Boudreau has invited me to a fête."

"Oh la la!" Marie-Madeleine said, the sudden stars in her eyes an indication of how she felt about the matter. "Dr. Boudreau is bel homme!"

"I am not surprised, Sister." Bleu drained the last of his

tea from his cup. "Just don't wear your spectacles or that woolen dress."

Pretending indifference, Sylvie finished with tea and made ready to resume her work. "I am not certain I shall attend. I cannot get up two gowns in so short a time. Also, another snow may fall."

"You are meant to go." Bleu took out his pipe and began filling it with tobacco. "Boudreau must have heard what a splendid dancer you are at clan gatherings. Time for a little merriment, no? We have had enough war clouds on the horizon."

Sylvie smiled as Marie-Madeleine cleaned up the cups and crumbs, only to frown as she returned her attention to Bleu. "Madame Auclair from the fort said something about inviting Fort Lawrence's officers and wives to Pont-a-Buot for a fête, but I never dreamed I would attend."

He lit his pipe, and a haze of smoke began spiraling around his head. "I, for one, would not mind seeing you merry. And with such a renowned escort besides."

She studied him, noting his faintly mocking tone. Père had not shown any signs of displeasure or caution when he learned the doctor fancied her. But Bleu was cut of a different cloth. He was a merciless judge of men.

"You have no reservations?" she asked.

"If so, I would have already told you . . . and Boudreau."

"I have not given much thought to him as a suitor," she said. "Nor have I encouraged him."

"You have encouraged no one in all your five and twenty years."

She smiled ruefully. "I have found no one worthy . . . yet."

And now her peace-loving, practical self had been turned on end with a bit of ink and paper.

There is no other mademoiselle who comes to mind so frequently and with such fervor.

Fervor. It sounded like *fever*, for it contained heat. Why could she not get that word out of her head?

"He could have his pick of any woman in Acadie," she said, returning to her sewing in the parlor.

Bleu and Marie-Madeleine followed, sitting by the parlor window as if watching for Mère's return. Bleu continued to smoke and said nothing while Marie-Madeleine played with her dolls and eyed the Pandora, the snip-snip of Sylvie's scissors the only sound other than the pop of the hearth's fire.

6

Love is often the fruit of marriage.

Molière

Mère's arms were akimbo, her stance stubborn. "I shall sew you a gown."

Sylvie looked up from finishing a difficult sleeve. This was not what she wanted. "But all your other tasks—"

"It is time your sister helped more about the house. Besides, it is winter. Far less to do now than in other months, aside from readying for Noël."

"Suppose you take all that trouble with the Lyonnais silk and rough weather prevents me from wearing it?"

"Then there will be other occasions to don such a gown." Mère was already at the dower chest, opening the drawer. "You must not disappoint the doctor."

If Sylvie had any doubts as to her mother's feelings about the matter, Mère's insistent words erased them. Ever since he'd heard the news, Père went about whistling, a new vigor to his step. Though he said nothing, she saw a telling light in his eyes when he looked at her. Was he already envisioning grandchildren?

The weather glowered. Sylvie anticipated an imminent blizzard, though Pascal was confident he could escort her when the time came, snow or no. And so Sylvie and Mère sewed, sharing scissors, needles, linen thread, beeswax, and an abundance of pins in what felt like a race to get the gowns done.

As the days passed, Sylvie stitched with more confidence, now at work on the pleated back, her tiny stitches hardly showing. Soon she would be sewing the gown's hem, no small feat given the quantity of fabric. She sent Madame word of her progress by way of her brothers, though she would need to go to the fort for a fitting.

While she and Mère stitched, they talked of many things. A cousin's twins newly born at Louisbourg. Another British fort raised at Lawrencetown. The cost of goods at Fort Beauséjour. All the calving in their swelling herd. Lucien's ongoing repairs to the aboiteaux and how much salt hay remained to feed the livestock. They lingered longest on the spring garden, having inventoried their seed.

"Tell me again of how you met Père," Sylvie said, rethreading her needle. Though she had heard the story countless times, she never tired of it, and Mère seemed to add a new detail or embellishment with every retelling.

"It all began with the aboiteaux, as you know. Your father was a young widower on the lowlands adjoining ours. His Mi'kmaq wife had died in a raid by English soldiers soon after Bleu's birth. Do you recall her name?"

"Aroostook." Sylvie had always thought the name lovely. "It means beautiful, clear water."

Mère nodded. "As it was, my dear father needed hands for the dike building. My older brothers, Etienne and Marc, had recently lost their lives in Old Sough while fishing that spring." She paused as she always did as if to honor their memory. "In exchange, I was to care for Bleu while your father and mine built the aboiteaux together. Being the youngest in our family, I had little experience with infants."

"Bleu was only a few months old, no?"

"He was still a lap baby, barely weaned. His Mi'kmaq aunts wanted to take him and raise him as their own, but your father would not allow it. Bleu was all he had left of Aroostook."

"And so, after a fashion, Bleu became very attached to you as his caregiver."

"Not only Bleu." Mère chuckled. "Though he was nearly two years old before your father approached me with an offer of marriage. He'd tried my patience waiting but wanted me to mature and be confident of him and what our life would be like."

"You were fond of him from the start."

"He was handsome, like Bleu. And he was a kind, loving father. I had other suitors, but I was particular . . . like you." Mère gave her a pointed look. "Till Dr. Boudreau."

"I would not count Dr. Boudreau a suitor, Mère."

"Oh? He is more than the provider of your spectacles, is he not?"

Sylvie wrinkled her nose where the spectacles rested. "For now, he is simply my dancing partner—if weather permits."

Mère shrugged lightly. "Le trois fait le mois."

The old saying failed to reassure her. How could the weather on the third day of the month predict the weather for the month? A ludicrous superstition, she'd always thought.

"It was sunny if cold on the third of December," Mère said as if the words carried the weight of Holy Writ. "Père recorded it in his journal."

Sylvie finished a seam. "I am openhanded about it all."

"What do you mean?"

"I scarcely know the doctor. What if he is a bad man? Suppose he has some hidden habits that would—"

"Bon sang!" Mère laughed, the fine lines about her eyes creasing. "Only Dieu is perfect. Boudreau is a skilled physician of noble lineage—a descendant of Charles de Saint-Étienne de La Tour."

"But can he dance?" Sylvie mused, half teasing. "Will he step on my toes? Perhaps I should wear my sabots."

They laughed, twittering over their sewing like birds till Marie-Madeleine came round. She eyed the Pandora atop the near table, and Sylvie read the question in her eyes before she asked it.

"Go ahead and hold her if you like," Sylvie said, swallowing her reluctance. "She'll soon return to Madame."

Marie-Madeleine's alarmed cry brought Sylvie's head up. "Aliénor is missing a buckled shoe!"

With a tsk, Mère looked on as they examined the Pandora, one leg sporting a clocked stocking and silk garter but no shoe. Suddenly they were a-scramble, on all fours, searching like Cendrillon for her glass slipper.

What would Madame say if the shoe stayed missing?

Near tears, Sylvie realized the long days and late nights were taking a toll. Down on the floor, she felt a headache beat against her temples even as her back pinched. Poor Mère. How did she feel working tirelessly on so difficult a gown for a daughter who had reservations about even attending the fête?

At last Marie-Madeleine gave a triumphant shout and held up the lost shoe. Grabbing her, Sylvie squeezed her hard for one grateful moment, then glanced at the mantel clock as it ticked on incessantly and seemed to grow louder. How much time remained? Five days? Could they finish? The sooner the Pandora returned to Fort Beauséjour, the gown safely delivered, the better they all would be.

Mon Dieu, help me.

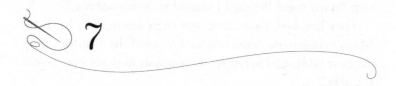

7

Oh, how fine it is to know a thing or two.

Molière

The weather stayed clement if clear and cold. At last, both gowns were finished, and the Pandora was safely returned during a final fitting. Madame Auclair expressed great delight over her finished gown, and few alterations were needed. When Sylvie thought it prudent to tell her she would also attend, Madame's brows raised and her expressive eyes snapped.

"Ah, Dr. Boudreau is full of surprises. It is he who advocated most for this party. And now to think he will be escorting Mademoiselle Galant!"

Once they were home, Pascal brought a report that Pont-a-Buot hummed with activity ahead of the festivities. "Since the fête will last late into the night, I've reserved a room for us at the tavern should that be needed. The dancing could well last till dawn," he said, adding to Sylvie's jitters. "Several Fort Lawrence officers and their wives have decided to accept the invitation, so it should be very entertaining, to say the least."

"Perhaps this bodes well for us all," Père said, ever optimistic about Acadie's future. "It is time the French and English made peace and accepted our Acadian stance of neutrality. Can we not all live together in harmony?"

"Ask Abbé Le Loutre that. He will tell you no. So will the officers at Beauséjour." Bleu paused as he mended a shoepack by the fire. "The English want to establish themselves here as they have in the American colonies. The French have but a fragile foothold in comparison, and their territories are already being renamed by the enemy, a portent of what is to come. Two years ago there was no Fort Lawrence, no boundary line at Pont-a-Buot."

"Still, one can hope for peace." Père rubbed his brow as if he had a headache. "And pray."

"There will be no peace until every Acadian signs an unconditional oath of allegiance to the English Crown," Bleu countered. "Which will then cause the French to be in a fury."

"Tensions are high," Mère said, putting a final flourish on Sylvie's gown. "Suppose a fracas breaks out at the tavern? You know how surly these soldiers become when they've drunk too much."

"Rest assured, I will protect Sister with my life." Pascal took a seat on the bench, his back to the fire. "And besides, Bleu will be patrolling the area, guarding against anything untoward."

So Bleu would be on hand? Sylvie felt relief and trepidation in equal measures. The English hated Bleu as much as the French hated Blackburn and his Mohegan and English Rangers. Bleu was known to be one of Acadie's foremost Resistance fighters along with his Mi'kmaq followers, striking terror in the hearts of both the French and English, especially English settlers who encroached on Acadian lands.

Though her family rarely spoke of Bleu's activities and long absences, he was always uppermost in their hearts and minds in the ongoing fight for Acadie's survival. But how confused he oft left Sylvie. She loved her brother, but she was not at all at peace with his methods or his ruthless associates, especially Le Loutre.

Sylvie's thoughts scattered like autumn leaves. The latest trouble had been last fall when the Resistance raided a new English settlement farther across the bay. The ransacked village was abandoned, the soldiers and settlers fleeing to Halifax.

"All will be well at the fête." Sylvie forced a levity she was far from feeling, looking to the gown that Mère was gathering up.

"Let us go upstairs for a final fitting," Mère urged, leaving the men to their talk.

Up the wooden steps they trod, Mère's arms upraised so as not to drag the dress through any dust or catch it underfoot. Rarely did they come upstairs. This was Père and Mère's domain. Sylvie and Marie-Madeleine had simple sleeping closets in the family sitting room while Pascal and Lucien shared a room off the kitchen. How fitting, she'd often thought, for her ravenous brothers.

A squeak on the stair made Sylvie turn to see her sister trailing, dolls in arm. "I must see you in your dress before the doctor does."

Again, that subtle quaver in Sylvie's stomach flared. She wanted nothing more than to return to the way things had been before Madame required her services and Boudreau asked to be her escort.

"You will be the belle of the fête!" Marie-Madeleine told her. "I wish that I could go with you."

"Someday, perhaps. For now you must dress your dolls in the caps and fichus I made them from Madame's scraps of fabric."

Mère draped the gown over the bed, looking weary but

pleased as they busied themselves with all the underpinnings and then the gown itself, which gave a rich, silken rustle. Turning before the looking glass, Sylvie realized her mother had stitched a great many hopes into the making of it.

Marie-Madeleine reached out a hand to touch the lustrous embroidery. "You rival the Pandora!"

Once the gown was pinned and in place, Mère stood back to admire her work, snatching at a stray thread here and there. "Now for your great-grandmother's pearls."

Marie-Madeleine was already at the jewelry box on Mère's dresser. "Tell us again about Morven Ross, Mère."

"Ah, Clan Ross." Mère looked less weary at the mention. "Your maternal great-grandmother arrived on Acadian shores when she was but ten years old. Her father was a lord and a gentleman, one of the Covenanters exiled for his faith rather than killed. He arrived in Acadie with little but his family and the jewels. What he didn't sell he saved to be handed down as heirlooms. Morven was his only daughter."

"How I wish I had met her," Marie-Madeleine lamented. "And when she grew up she met our great-grandfather, the handsome Paladin Amirault."

Clearly enjoying the moment, Mère watched her youngest daughter sort through the case's treasures. "She had no dowry but was a learned lady who knew how to read and to write, which is how their courtship commenced. She taught him to do both."

"He paid her in apples from his orchard. And kisses." Marie-Madeleine held up a string of pearls. "And she wore which of these necklaces on her wedding day?"

"The garnet necklace and earrings," Mère replied with a smile as if she hadn't told the tale a hundred times before.

"I prefer the Jaquin pearls over the Persian pearls," Sylvie said.

Dutifully, Marie-Madeleine brought the Jaquin strand.

Mère shook her head. "Fond as you are of the pearls, I believe something altogether more eye-catching like garnets is called for."

Back to the jewelry case Marie-Madeleine went to retrieve the garnet necklace. It sparkled like red fire against Sylvie's pale skin. Though cold about her throat, she had to admit it paired beautifully with the colorful floral embellishments on the gown.

Looking perplexed, Mère said, "How shall we arrange your hair?"

Sylvie studied her reflection. She would not go bewigged and powdered like the officers' wives. No beauty patches would adorn her, nor a plunging décolletage. Mère had ensured her bodice was modest, sewing in a lovely lace frill. "As simply as possible."

Her sister's eyes rounded in dismay. "You cannot wear your usual braid!"

"Of course not," Mère replied, lips pursed. "Your hair must be pinned up, to better show the girandole earrings."

Sylvie stayed firm. "Please, no earrings. The necklace is elegance enough."

Oddly, Mère did not argue. Did she sense Sylvie was one step away from refusing to attend? And yet Pascal had given Boudreau her word. The doctor had even arranged for a sled to be waiting at the dock upon her arrival to transport her to the tavern.

"Turn around one more time," Marie-Madeleine pleaded, hands clasped together in childish enchantment. "I want to remember this moment forever."

Sylvie smiled and turned in a slow circle, glad to grant her wish. Oh, for a little of her sister's joie de vivre, her ongoing ability to embrace the new, never thinking beyond the present moment.

If Marie-Madeleine was sunlight, Sylvie was snowmelt.

Slow to thaw and ever cautious, Père said, the future forever in mind. Was it because she had grown up pressed between two warring powers and her sister was too young to understand the continual volatile threat?

The gown was unpinned and removed, then hung in a corner of her parents' bedchamber. Sylvie was glad she did not have it near in her sleeping closet, a continual reminder of what was to come. She would rather face a mountain of linen to sew into soldiers' shirts than a roomful of dancing strangers.

8

There are no secrets that time does not reveal.

Jean Racine

The next day, Sylvie stood by the west window that overlooked the courtyard, their well at the center, the barn just beyond. Behind the barn stood the apple orchard and the trail that led to her beloved bluff lookout. As she stared at it with wistful longing, a burst of snowflakes hit the glass, hurled by a windy fist. The pewter sky seemed poised to unleash a fierce winter's storm. Never had she been so glad. Her soul sang with the possibility.

The house was blessedly quiet. Mère had taken Marie-Madeleine to adorn the church for Noël while Père and her brothers, all but Bleu, were tending the livestock and aboiteaux. For once she was alone, minding the hearth's fire and supper.

Earlier, Bleu had brought haddock from their weirs and she'd made a fish chowder rich with potatoes and onions and cream. On the trestle table sat three still-warm loaves of wheaten bread from the bake oven and fresh butter churned at dawn.

She heard the ring of Bleu's axe near the woodshed. A re-assuring sound. When he was home she felt safer. He'd killed a gray wolf prowling near their sheep but two days ago. The pelt would be useful, though she was glad she didn't have to cure it, only endure the smell when Bleu turned tanner.

She lifted the lid on the kettle and stirred the chowder as Bleu's chopping stopped. Turning toward the window, she fixed her gaze beyond the glass on another figure. The Mi'kmaq who stood talking to her brother was one of Abbé Le Loutre's men who stayed near Fort Beauséjour and rarely strayed like Bleu.

She cast about for his Mi'kmaq name. Kitani? He was gesturing now, his handsome features animated but alarmingly so. Intensity emanated from him like the sun's rays. Bleu frowned as he listened. Sylvie had a sudden urge to lighten their mood and take their visitor a mug of spruce beer. Hospitality reigned in their home. Why would a little weather stop her?

Drink in hand, she went outside, her cap nearly taking wing along with her skirts. Seeing her, Kitani stopped his gesturing and his intensity softened to a half smile. Bleu turned toward her, but the storm in his eyes didn't die.

She handed Kitani the mug, his appreciation evident in his dark eyes. "Wela'like."

He took a long sip as she replied in Mi'kmaq, what little she knew. He, being fluent in several languages like Bleu, answered her in French. When she smiled and turned away so they could resume their conversation, Bleu stopped her.

"Sœur, wait."

As the wind blasted them like a blacksmith's bellows, Sylvie winced, raising her shawl from her shoulders to cover her head. She faced them, noting Bleu's eyes roamed the clearing as if he expected English soldiers to materialize before their very eyes.

"Come into the house," she urged, suddenly feeling unsafe. "No one else is here."

With a nod, Bleu obliged, and soon they were at the kitchen table, partaking of the meal she'd enjoyed preparing. Quiet now, the men seemed lost in thought. Why had Bleu sought to detain her outside? She knew his moods, and this one was black.

Bleu looked at Kitani. "Tomorrow night my sister will be at Pont-a-Buot when the English come to frolic with the French."

Surprise flared in the Mi'kmaq's eyes. "How so?"

"Dr. Boudreau has invited her to be his partner."

Kitani responded in Mi'kmaq, his features stern. Sylvie took a seat by the hearth and waited. Something was afoot, even amiss. Would they not tell her?

As she wondered, Kitani smiled, dispelling the tension. "I have heard you dance as well as you sew. Do the English know you speak their tongue? Dr. Boudreau?"

"I only speak French around them, never Anglais."

"But you know the English tongue well?"

"Well?" She lifted her shoulders in a shrug. "My great-grandmother was Scottish and passed her tongue down. I speak it when with Grandmère and Mère but no one else. It is an odd, flat language. I much prefer the musicality of French."

He nodded thoughtfully. "It is good you are so discreet."

Bleu studied her in his penetrating way. "While at Pont-a-Buot, I advise you to keep your English ears wide open while speaking your flawless French."

She stared back at him, his intensity unfathomable. "You mean I am to . . . spy?"

"I am merely asking you to listen. A great quantity of rum and other spirits may well loosen tongues and inflame tempers." Contempt rode Bleu's dark features. "Be aware of what the English say in your hearing. It might prove useful to us."

Us. Meaning the Resistance?

Kitani finished his spruce beer and she lifted the pitcher to pour him more, but he declined with a shake of his head. "No one will suspect you, mademoiselle. You seem French through and through."

"And if things take an ugly turn," Bleu said, "we will be on hand outside tavern walls to spirit you to safety."

His calm reassurance did little to settle her. "Why would any ugliness happen?"

Kitani looked toward the window. "It is rare the French and English mingle except to fight."

She sighed, her dread deepening. "I had hoped this meeting—this fête at so hallowed a time as Noël—was a sign of peace."

"It seems you have Père's high hopes." Bleu let out a breath. "How I hate to disappoint you."

9

The mind grows narrow in proportion as the soul grows corrupt.

Jean-Jacques Rousseau

The day of the fête came. Sylvie, despite her trepidation, had slept well the night before, confident a fresh snow meant the end of the charade, this dreaded fête. But a mocking first light revealed only a dusting. For two hours she endured Mère's playing lady's maid before stepping into the boat that would carry her to the opposite shore, feeling dressed for a performance, ready to take her part in some perilous stage play.

Bleu and Pascal rowed swiftly, the oars nearly soundless in the calm, windless water, the skies above still glowering. She sat up straight, the pinch of new stays not yet conformed to her shape, and focused on their destination.

What if a storm happened in the night and she was snowed in at Pont-a-Buot?

Shush, she told herself. How like Mère she was with her worrying. As it stood, Mère had nearly cried when Sylvie left the house, as if she might not return. Such did little to bolster Sylvie's spirits. Marie-Madeleine, on the other hand, was jumping for joy at the prospect before her.

"I want to hear every detail. What you ate and drank. What music you danced to. Who you partnered with." She twirled about, performing a country dance with quick steps. "I hear the tavern is large and grand!"

True, the tavern keeper, an Irishman named Casey, had a penchant for luxury goods transported on French merchant ships. Rarely had she ventured anywhere other than Louisbourg on Ile Royale. She relied on Bleu to tell her of far-flung places.

They came ashore just as darkness snatched the last of daylight. The tavern was not far, the promised sled waiting. Over the snow they flew, pulled by a sturdy, dark horse that followed the frozen tracks made by other travelers. Sylvie wished she'd brought an apple to reward the sure-footed creature.

A fiddle's lilt reached her, and then tiny pinpricks of gold shone amid the blackened trees. She was unprepared for not just a tavern but a trading post, blacksmith, and what seemed a small village dotting the landscape of Pont-a-Buot.

People in all shades of finery crowded the tavern entrance, hardly mindful of winter. With surprising adroitness, Pascal halted in front of the tavern, then helped her out of the sled while Bleu melted into the forest without an adieu. Pascal left the sled to a stable lad at Boudreau's bidding.

The doctor was on the tavern porch, waiting. Sylvie's smile was tremulous, though a spark of courage propelled her forward as the musicians tuned their instruments. After helping remove her cloak, Pascal slipped past them and went into the tavern to see about their lodging.

"Mademoiselle Galant." Boudreau bowed, then reached for her hand and brought it to his lips, murmuring something about her dress.

Despite her swirling emotions, she could not help but note his own attire. His sleeve buttons winked jade in the candle-light and bespoke a rare elegance, as did the lace-edged cravat about his neck. His coat and waistcoat were of pale green satin, his breeches black. Who had tailored them so finely?

Bereft of her cloak, she felt a chill, which vanished when the doctor escorted her into a crowded room where chairs lined the walls and sand was spread upon the floor for dancing. An astonishing assortment of plush sofas, velvet wall hangings and elaborately framed looking glasses—and even a gilt chandelier—were on display, turning the room into a glittering, multifaceted jewel. No wonder soldiers congregated here.

Madame Auclair saw her straightaway and started toward them. The knot of ladies she'd been a part of watched her go, fluttering their lovely fans and leaving Sylvie with a sinking realization she hadn't one.

"Mademoiselle Galant!" she said, smiling at the doctor while taking Sylvie aside. "You look ravissante!"

Sylvie thanked her and repaid the compliment as every challenging stitch and seam returned to her.

Madame continued to admire the Lyonnais silk. "By Marie Le Borgne in Louisbourg, no doubt. It has the look of her gowns." Sylvie did not correct her while Madame waved her fan about as if to cool her high color. "We arrived early. My husband wanted to make sure all was in readiness. What do you think of the fête so far?"

Sylvie paused, hardly having had time to take it in. "I had not thought to find so many musicians or fine furnishings. Or"—she cast a delighted look at a table in an anteroom—"gâteau."

Did a baker lurk within the tavern kitchen? The festive confection was towering, rivaling the ones she remembered from Louisbourg. Madame laughed and moved on, leaving

Sylvie alone with the doctor, though they were hardly alone. The room was ringed with soldiers in uniform, the French gray and white with blue facings in sharp contrast to the British red.

"I must introduce you to Fort Lawrence's commander," Boudreau said, taking her by the elbow and guiding her toward one tall officer in particular. "Sir, allow me to present Mademoiselle Galant. This is Colonel Monckton, mademoiselle."

Sylvie lowered her eyes and gave a nod. Dark-haired and aristocratic, Monckton wore a black patch over one eye. The officer to his left was older, bewigged, and powdered.

"And this is Major General Winslow," Boudreau continued. He next introduced her to their wives, who nodded politely, their crisp, English greetings making Sylvie smile as if in befuddlement. She must not forget that she knew no English. They likely knew little French, as several interpreters were on hand.

The music began in earnest, preventing further conversation. She'd grown up with the branles and rondes, old dances brought over from France a century before. Often at Galant gatherings the family sang and danced.

"I prefer the circle dances," Boudreau told her with a smile.

As he said it, a chain of dancers formed on the sanded floor. Taking her hand, he led her out to join them. Soon they moved as a group, taking sideways steps to the left and then the right, circling and gliding. The light of appreciation in Boudreau's eyes made her more confident.

He was no stranger to the dance. As one branle faded to the next and the rondes began, he never misstepped.

Winded and exhilarated, Sylvie eyed the enormous porcelain punch bowl. Would they not stop and cool their thirst?

Pascal stood near the tavern's front door. Her thoughts

swerved again to Bleu, and she recalled snatches of their conversation with Kitani. Would the anticipated trouble erupt? An adjoining room revealed men at cards about scattered tables. Their loud talk and laughter suggested they'd been long at the rum, a hastener of spilled secrets. If she kept dancing she would hear nothing of importance, but she could hardly sit down and join their gambling.

At last Boudreau brought her punch. She was able to catch her breath and admire the gowns of the ladies present, though her seamstress's eye dampened her appreciation. How quick she was to detect some flaw! A crooked seam or misplaced embellishment. An ill-fit or poorly boned bodice . . .

Few would argue that Madame Auclair was the belle of the ball. Aside from her gown, she seemed intent on making the acquaintance of the English officers' wives, moving among them and talking at length in their tongue, even laughing. She possessed that sanguinity many lacked. Her husband, a taciturn man, stood by the blazing hearth, drink in hand, and seemed content to simply observe, not converse or dance.

In time Sylvie became aware of a great many eyes on her. Because of her gown or her dancing? Or because Boudreau was her escort? She met Pascal's gaze across the crowded room. Would he not dance? Or had the tavern keeper posted him as guard? Her suspicion was confirmed when a scuffle broke out on the porch and Pascal intervened.

"I should like to attend one of your clan gatherings," Boudreau told her above the music's din. "I have heard you Galants celebrate like no other."

"Oh?" Sylvie met his gaze. Candlelight called out faint lines about his eyes and mouth, making her wonder how old he was. "There is much feasting, singing, and dancing."

"As it should be." He frowned. "I am alone at Noël, far from family."

Alone. Did he mean lonely? She pondered it, a bit shame-faced she'd never thought of how he spent the hallowed day, but reluctant to extend the invitation without Père's prior approval. Or was it her own reluctance that kept her from it? "Our house is larger than most, so we are happy to host clan gatherings."

Even as she said it, her mind swerved to Bleu. Though he'd said little about the man beside her, his silence shouted. Kitani's own reaction when the doctor's name had been spoken worried her.

"Beauséjour does not celebrate in some fashion?" she asked Boudreau.

"A pittance." He finished the drink he held. "Sometimes one needs to be within the embrace of a family, even if it is not one's own."

"Of course. You've not spoken of your family. They remain in France?"

"Lorraine, mostly. Some are outside Paris. Merchants and such."

"But no doctors?"

He smiled. "Only one Boudreau foolish enough to sail for the wilds of New France."

"A bold adventurer, then."

"A lonely médecin who is growing weary of fort life."

His eyes held hers. Fervor, oui. A thousand feelings smoldered in that gaze. Boudreau's singular attention seemed suffocating.

She lowered her eyes, taking another sip of punch. "I am not weary of Acadie. I desire to go nowhere else."

Frowning, he took their empty punch cups to refill them. There was a lull in the dancing as guests formed a line for cake. Sylvie looked toward the stairs leading to the room she wanted to escape to.

"You truly have no desire to see other places?" Boudreau asked as he returned, handing her the punch.

"Why would I? Where else compares with these forests and fields and watercourses?" She kept her tone light though her thoughts were dark. "Why else would the French and the English fight over it so long and so hard?"

"The English mean to win here just as they did in Scotland when I left university there in '45."

"I've only heard of the '15 Rising."

"Because you are too sheltered and have not been beyond New France." He pressed a shoulder against the wall and turned toward her. "The Jacobites rose up against the English king to restore a Catholic Stuart ruler to the throne, but the English, led by the Duke of Cumberland, mowed them down."

"Ah, the English king who is in fact a German." She wouldn't be thought a hopeless rustic. Though her great-grandmother had left Scotland as a child, the woman's descendants were still interested in the affairs of her birth country.

His brow raised. "So you are not ignorant of foreign affairs."

"I hear things . . ." She stopped short of confessing how. If only French officials did not oppose printing presses, forcing them to rely on the *Halifax Gazette* instead.

"Hearing is not the same as experiencing," he said, taking her cup and setting it on a window ledge with his. He took her hands in his, hands that had mixed medicines and examined wounds and treated untold maladies within and without fort walls. "Let me show you the world, Sylvie Galant."

10

Wounds and hardships provoke our courage, and when our fortunes are at the lowest, our wits and our minds are commonly at the best.

Pierre Charron

The fête's cake tasted sickeningly sweet. Sylvie swallowed a bite, expecting it to resemble the Galants' confections. What she truly craved was water from their own well. Pure, thirst-slaking water, not more spirit-laden punch that made her woozy and gave her a headache.

The spirited gaiety showed no signs of stopping. Smoke from the gambling den rolled in like fog to the other rooms, so unlike Père's and her brother's fragrant Mi'kmaq tobacco. She realized at midnight why there were so many musicians. They took turns, clearly determined the dancing should go on till dawn.

She cast a beseeching look at Pascal. He'd spent most of the evening on the porch following the earlier fracas, as the tavern's rooms were overwarm. Sweat lined her brow and even stained the doctor's fine Holland shirt. He'd removed his coat, and she was astonished by his embroidered waist-coat with its frosted gray thread.

"You've a high flush, Sylvie." Boudreau assumed a physician's air. "Let's go outside."

She smiled her consent, yet a chill touched her spine. But with Pascal standing watch, how could she object? By the time they'd wended through the revelers, Pascal had gone elsewhere, though other couples loitered about the tavern entrance. Moonlight silvered old snow, making it seem freshly fallen. The cold was refreshing only for a moment. Sylvie missed her cape but had no idea where her brother had left it.

Boudreau came to a halt by the side of the blacksmith's shop with its reek of iron and ashes. A fire still burned at the forge as if waiting for them to warm their hands, which the doctor did, inviting Sylvie to do the same. The heat stole over her arms and wrists, adding to her high flush and making her grateful for the darkness.

"Careful you don't catch fire to your lovely lace sleeves." He draped her shoulders with his frock coat, which carried the scent of camphor.

"I shan't," she replied, eyes on the tavern in her endless pursuit of Pascal.

Boudreau's voice turned low and silken, his French purer than their drawn-out Acadian patois. "I want to court you, Sylvie."

Of course, she had expected it. Still, dismay made her grit her teeth. "Then you must ask my father first."

"The renowned Gabriel Galant." It was said with respect. For that she was grateful. Not everyone was fond of Père or his success. "I am always ready to venture beyond fort walls, so that shall be my next foray . . . asking your father's permission."

Lacking that, he would not attempt to kiss her, surely. She moved slightly away from him lest he take that liberty, just as someone came out of the shadows. Pascal? The fire flicked light on a scarlet uniform. No, the man she'd seen standing closest to Fort Lawrence's commandant on the dance floor. They'd been introduced, but she had quickly forgotten his name. Bleu wouldn't have been so careless.

"Pardon, Boudreau. A quick word with you, if I may."

With a nod, the doctor acknowledged him, but the officer was looking at Sylvie as if questioning her presence.

"She speaks no English, only Acadian French," Boudreau said quietly in English.

Sylvie stood astounded at his assumption, though she'd never given him grounds to think otherwise. Still, the officer gestured to a spot beneath the smithy eave as Sylvie continued to school her surprise and warm her hands, eyes on the tavern.

Bleu's words came back to her. *Keep your English ears wide open while speaking your flawless French.*

As Kitani had predicted, both men, tongues loosed by spirits, spoke with less discretion than they might have otherwise. She strained to listen. Eavesdropping was not easy for her. Honesty was her hallmark. Though she did not catch every word, the point of discussion seemed to be about a map.

Would Bleu be disappointed?

Their conversation seemed of little consequence. Boudreau was well known to the English. Fort Lawrence's physician oft sought him out to discuss medical matters just as Boudreau sought out their physician, Dr. Wood, the most recent matter being poisoning from bad rations at Fort Beauséjour.

Once the officer strode away, Boudreau returned to her side, looking preoccupied, his brow knotted. All because of a map?

When the silence grew long, she began, "I have not thanked you for my spectacles, Dr. Boud—"

"Please, call me Bernart."

She hesitated, wishing the spectacles had not been so useless. "I used them when sewing Madame's gown."

He smiled, but there was chastisement in his tone. "You need not sew gowns for anyone but yourself, Sylvie. Or shirts, for that matter. Well, perhaps mine. Though where I am going there will be tailors."

"You're leaving Beauséjour?" She felt a little start. He seemed such a fixture there.

"With war on the horizon, who can say where we'll be in future? I am growing weary of the conflict, the escalating warring." He looked at her intently. "'Tis wise to make plans even if they don't come to fruition."

"You wouldn't return to France or Scotland?"

A shake of his head shot down the notion. "New France is where I'll stay. Québec City perhaps. I might work at a hospital there."

She couldn't imagine so large a place as Québec City or Montréal. She bit her lip to keep from telling him she'd read about Hôtel-Dieu, a hospital established by nuns.

Another man emerged from the shadows. Pascal, carrying her fur-lined wool cloak. Sylvie returned Boudreau's frock coat before her brother draped hers around her shoulders, a cue to return to the tavern. His protectiveness warmed her even as she sensed it piqued the doctor. She thanked her brother with a reassuring, relieved smile.

"Are you tired?" Pascal queried. "Your room awaits upstairs."

She hesitated, wanting nothing more than a sound night's sleep, but the doctor interrupted in a cajoling tone. "A last dance before you retire, Mademoiselle Galant, s'il vous plaît."

The next morning Sylvie awoke before dawn, greeted by a cock's raucous crowing instead of the merry snapping of her family's hearth's fire. The cold was threaded with stale spirits, not the familiar aroma of sweet dumplings and coffee. Pascal snored lightly next to her on the narrow bed, leaving her to wonder where Bleu had passed the night. She herself was fully clothed, the pinch of her stays overridden by her fatigue from the fête. Though she could work an entire day without complaint, dancing and conversation and the newness of being here had worn her down.

Where was Boudreau?

The hearth was bare of all but a few flagging embers. She stirred them up with an iron poker and added a piece of wood before passing to the sole window that overlooked the blacksmith shop. Snowflakes pressed against the pane, and the sullen sky seemed ominous, the bay restive.

"Pascal, please awake—we must get home before the weather worsens!" She pulled on her slippers, wishing for her sabots instead. Wrapping herself in her cape, she let out a breath that plumed like a frosted feather.

Within a half hour, they were at the dock where only Bleu was waiting. He simply smiled as they approached and hastened them into the canoe as snow pelted down harder, whitening the muddy pier faster than Sylvie wanted. Would they be caught in the teeth of a blizzard upon Baie Française? As it was, her brothers took advantage of the morning's high tide.

Pascal sat behind her while Bleu took the bow. They were the only ones on the water so early. In such weather, few would be out. Sylvie hunkered down in her cape, drawing it close about her face to keep the wind from snatching it free. But the storm did not keep her brothers from their teasing.

Pascal's voice carried in the wintry stillness. "I am surprised, smitten as the doctor is, that he did not sleep outside your door till you departed."

Bleu chuckled. "You were the belle of the ball, Sister, yet you seem unaware of that fact."

"There were many belles. I was but one."

"L'étoile," Pascal insisted. "None could hold a candle to you in dancing—or dress."

"My brothers are biased," she replied, fixing her gaze on their beloved home across the bay, the twin chimneys breathing fiery sparks like fabled dragons.

"So, how do you feel about him?" Bleu asked.

"He is going to ask Père if he can commence our courtship."

"Your courtship is already commenced," Bleu said with a chuckle. "And that is not what I asked you."

With a sigh, she fell silent. In truth, she felt bewildered. This attachment was happening too quickly for her tastes. She had only just begun to come to terms with the fact the doctor regarded her as more than a patient . . . while she still regarded him as the doctor.

They reached the far shore, and Sylvie felt half-frozen. Pascal helped her out, but she lingered, watching Bleu stow the oars in the now blinding snow. Shivering, stomach rumbling, she looked toward the barely discernible ridge. Was Boudreau back at the fort?

When Bleu turned toward her, she was waiting. "Last night by the smithy," she began through stiff lips, "Boudreau talked with an English officer about a map."

Bleu looked at her through the wall of white. "A map?"

"I heard little else, but a map was mentioned more than once. They did not think I understood English, so they spoke a few feet from me. The doctor seemed disturbed once the officer returned to the tavern."

"Who was this officer?"

"I don't recall his name. He was tall and bewigged and had a mole on his right cheek."

"Ah." Bleu's eyes seemed to bore a hole through her. "Did Boudreau say anything more to you of merit?"

"Just that he is tiring of fort life. He's considering going elsewhere—to Québec City or Montréal perhaps, to work in a hospital there. He blames the hostilities. His mind is clearly on the future."

Taking her by the arm, a preoccupied Bleu escorted her up the slippery path to their front door. Never had she been so glad to get there.

11

Things never pass where you think, nor along the paths you think.

Gilles Deleuze

Noël neared, and with it came a blizzard that cut off any communication with Fort Beauséjour. As if expecting it, the Galant clan gathered early. Their stone house soon resembled the Pont-a-Buot tavern, sending Sylvie and Marie-Madeleine to the root cellar continuously to feed the four thousand, as Père merrily put it. Truly, a miracle of the loaves and fishes was needed as more Galants arrived, laden with baskets of food, their combined laughter and talk spilling out into a world gone wildly white.

Warm and well-fed, all made the most of their time together, singing and storytelling, fiddling and feasting. Sylvie's grandparents, despite their infirmities, seemed at their best, sitting side by side, even holding hands. Fifty-three winters ago they had been married on this land during a snowstorm, a story they recounted every Noël that no one grew tired of hearing and seemed to grow sweeter at every retelling.

Full of hot cider and fried sugar pastries, Sylvie retired to her sleeping closet at midnight with two of her cousins, Lydie and Violette, only to find two babies at the bed's foot. They climbed in carefully, then lay down as the house settled and the mothers came to take the infants to their own makeshift pallets.

Yawning, Lydie turned on her side toward Sylvie, pressed between her and Violette. "I want to hear about the fête at Pont-a-Buot. Was it as exciting as it sounds? You and Dr. Boudreau are being whispered about clear to Grand-Pré."

Sylvie felt her face warm. She stared up at the ceiling, wondering how the doctor fared. Was he lonely, as he said? "The fête? It was . . . crowded and noisy and colorful."

"Come, Cousin." Violette gave a little snort. "Those are not the details we are wanting."

Mimicking Marie-Madeleine at her most theatrical, Sylvie said, "The renowned doctor's genteel waistcoat was a work of art, replete with silver thread, which failed to outshine his glittering sleeve buttons that flashed in the candlelight like fine emeralds."

"Of course you would notice such things, plying a needle as you do," Violette whispered as Lydie laughed. "But we care nothing for waistcoats and sleeve buttons."

Lydie gave a fierce jab to Sylvie's ribs. "I want to know if he kissed you."

Wincing, Sylvie wondered if Boudreau might have if they'd lingered at the smithy and Pascal hadn't appeared. "He only talked about courtship . . . asking Père's permission."

"Of course Uncle Gabriel will say oui." Exasperation edged Lydie's voice. "Boudreau is a catch! Every unwed woman I know covets being courted by so learned a man and one so well regarded."

"And well dressed," Violette teased.

"I have no wish to live at Fort Beauséjour," Sylvie whispered back.

"Surely he would build a house for you beyond fort walls. A family—children—must have orchards and woods in which to run free."

Québec City or Montréal did not fit that description. Though Sylvie had lived in Louisbourg happily if briefly, she disliked the idea of a city or town. So many people pressed together bespoke filth and clamor, a slight to her tranquil soul. She wanted nothing more for her children and future generations than Acadie. There was no finer heritage.

She lay still, pretending to snore, which sent her cousins tittering all over again.

"How unromantic," Lydie said. "If your doctor could see you now . . ."

"He is not my doctor," Sylvie said softly. "In truth, I hardly know him."

Yawning, Violette drew the covers up to her chin. "I want to hear more about your time at the tavern in the morning over breakfast. Every last detail. We have no beaus ourselves yet so must make do with yours."

There was no hoped-for service on the eve of Noël. Their parish chapel remained closed, the itinerant missionary priest unable to venture forth in such weather. Sylvie missed the hallowed candlelight and sacred relics and wondered if Abbé Le Loutre would say mass at the newly built church outside Fort Beauséjour.

Would Boudreau attend? He didn't seem a particularly religious man. She'd even heard him take Dieu's name in vain. It had rankled at the time and now rankled afresh as Père led prayers before midnight and spoke so reverently.

At the stroke of twelve, Sylvie and Marie-Madeleine along with two dozen other children braved the cold, bundling up in their wraps to make their way to the barn. Not wanting to disappoint them, Bleu and Lucien had shoveled a path to aid them, but the snow flew so furiously it seemed a silly task. Giggling behind mittened hands and wide-eyed with anticipation, the smallest of the Galant clan went first, their excitement palpable. Pascal held up a pine torch to light their steps while Marie-Madeleine walked beside Sylvie at the rear.

Only on the eve of Noël did the barn animals talk.

Such a tale had amused Sylvie since childhood. What could a cow possibly have to say to a sheep? A sow to a chicken? If you overheard the animals conversing, it was said they would be talking about your death. Such a melancholy thread in a magical tradition. Of course no one had ever heard the animals talk, but still the Acadians came.

In the barn's earthy, torchlit confines, Sylvie looked at the expectant faces as they watched and listened, some of them holding hands, all of them caught up in the beloved, hallowed tradition. Together they said an old prayer from Provence, carried to their shores long ago.

"Jesus of the crib, give us the virtues of those that surround You. Make us philosophical as the fisherman, carefree as the drummer, merry in exploring the world as the troubadour, eager for work as the bugler, patient as the spinner, kind as the donkey, strong as the ox that keeps You warm. Amen."

A cow in a near stall lowed, startling one of the youngest children and making him cry. Sylvie lifted him up, smiling and murmuring to him till he quieted. His cold-reddened cheeks glistened with tears, and she swiped them away with a mittened hand. When he lay his head on her shoulder, she melted, envisioning a babe of her own, full of innocence and wonder.

But first a husband. Why had she, at five and twenty, been slow to become enamored? Many of her cousins—both male and female, most younger than she—had wed. These children she shepherded to the barn were theirs. Would her children not join them in time?

But Bernart Boudreau as the father?

The longing inside her faded. He was not one of them. Not a Neutral Acadian but a thorough Frenchman. Pondering it, she felt flummoxed all over again. She hardly knew him or wanted to learn more. He was simply the doctor who supplied her spectacles, the one for whom she sewed shirts. If she never saw him again, she would likely think little about it.

Didn't love mean more than that?

12

The majority of the apple trees that were planted in the days of Commander Razilly are still alive and bear fruit every year. In fact, I drank cider made from them this year.

Simon-Pierre de Bonaventure

Sylvie walked with full milk pails from the barn to the house, careful not to slosh the contents and spill the precious cream. It flavored the tea Bleu had brought her along with the fine sugar from Louisbourg. Père usually traveled there twice a year when the tall-masted ships arrived from France, delivering all manner of imported goods. Smuggling abounded too, but Père chose the high road, not wanting trouble with the authorities.

Bleu promised them the goods they lacked once he went again to Hudson's Bay. Usually he would have left home after so many weeks, but something kept him tethered here. There was plenty that needed doing on their two hundred hectares, even in winter. Lucien and Pascal were out mending fences and moving cattle with Père. Sometimes Bleu went with them, but lately he kept to home.

When family or friend happened by, Bleu vanished till he

had ascertained who it was. His caution made Sylvie wonder. Did he have an English bounty on his head like the French did William Blackburn? How bold he had been to go to Pont-a-Buot! Yet few had ever seen Bleu, so he moved in a sort of anonymity around all but those who knew him best.

Sylvie looked at the mountain of firewood he'd chopped since they'd burned so much at Noël. It was nearing Candlemas, another celebration and another clan gathering. No doubt Bleu had that in mind.

She was nearly to the house when he came and relieved her of her pails. The cellar was icy, nearly cold enough to freeze the milk, but he went below without spilling a drop. She built up the fire, hearing Mère and Marie-Madeleine upstairs. Morning sunlight slanted across the rising dough in the long tray atop the kitchen table. A crock of butter and plum preserves tempted at table's end.

Bleu reappeared, shutting the cellar door in the kitchen corner with a resounding thud. How she would miss him and the quiet way he relieved her and everyone else of chores, always seeing what needed to be done and then doing it quietly, never expecting thanks. Even now he remembered her cream, bringing her a little jug of it, cold and fresh.

"I thought you would have gone by now," she told him, putting on a kettle for tea.

"No." He shrugged off his matchcoat and hung it up before taking his particular cup from a shelf. "The trouble is here."

His grave tone—and the slow way he said the words— shook her. She paused from hammering at the sugar lump.

Trouble. Would he not tell her? She barely heard the singing kettle. He took a seat by the fire as she poured them tea then sat down beside him and asked, "By trouble, do you mean Dr. Boudreau?"

"He is but part of the problem. It goes further and deeper."

"You will not tell me."

"I will not burden you."

"Perhaps I should help shoulder the burden." She took a sip, the usual savor of cream and sugar falling flat. "I am no longer a child, though I will always be your younger sister."

He hesitated, gaze on the hearth's fire. "Soon Boudreau will appear and ask Père's approval to court you. That is all you need concern yourself with."

"He has not yet come. I hope the delay means he's reconsidering—favoring someone else." The continual suspense of whether he would appear or not was wearing. "I'm still unsure how I feel about him."

"All the better if your heart remains neutral." He took a drink of tea. "In future, talk to him. Learn what is happening with the English at Fort Lawrence."

"Pretend I am wanting his company?"

"He is pretending to want yours, Sylvie."

She drew up in surprise, feeling decidedly dim-witted. "Do you mean this is a farce, our courtship?"

"I do not deny he is attracted to you. Only a fool wouldn't be. But Boudreau is after something more."

As she opened her mouth to question him further, Marie-Madeleine bounded in, Mère on her heels. Arms full of linens, they restocked the cupboard on the far wall, chattering all the while. Sylvie continued sipping tea, alarm widening inside her, while Bleu looked as serene as Baie Française on a midsummer day.

⌒

When Boudreau came—for Bleu had removed all doubt that he would—what would he find her doing? Sylvie didn't wonder long. A sudden thawing after Candlemas found her outside. Melting snow turned the ground to mush, and she took care that her sabots and woolen stockings would not be soaked after her rounds in the orchard.

Les suêtes had swept in, those strong southeast winds that snapped branches and toppled trees. The air smelled freshly scrubbed though splintered wood littered the ground, and the maiden fruit trees, the smallest in the orchard, had taken a whipping. Sylvie righted and tied and cleaned up what she could, glad for time outdoors, already anticipating the blooms of late spring and then a bountiful fall harvest.

She'd always dreamed of marrying in the orchard, beneath an array of blossoming apple trees, instead of at home or in church. Pale petals would flutter down in the coastal wind, and she'd carry cut apple blossoms for her bouquet. A May wedding—

Hoofbeats ended her musings, replacing them with a hard, cold realization. It was Boudreau, but he had not come just to court her. Self-conscious, she picked a twig from her be-ribboned skirt, hastily shoving a tendril of hair beneath her plain linen cap.

He dismounted at the end of one mature row. She could see him easily through the leafless trees. His horse was a chestnut roan, of Breton stock, she guessed. He approached slowly, the sun shining behind him so brightly she squinted.

Surprise pinched her at how well dressed he was, as if he wanted to please her—or impress Père? Her parents would not approve of her being alone with the doctor. She rued Marie-Madeleine had just left her side to manage the afternoon milking.

"Welcome, monsieur." The greeting sounded flat, so Sylvie smiled. She could not call him Bernart. Not now. Perhaps not ever.

He came to stand in front of her and gave a little bow like he'd done at the fête. Few Acadians bothered with such social

niceties. He was French through and through. In response
she curtsied, and he smiled, reaching for her hand.

"Your father has invited me to supper," he told her, looking as if he'd just won at bilboquet. "He told me to fetch you
from the orchard. Apparently this is your favorite place."

"One of them." She wouldn't tell him about the ridge or
the secret trail leading to it. She'd save that for her true beau.

"I heard the Galant orchards are among the finest in
Acadie. The orchardists especially." He eyed her hungrily,
and she flushed, feeling as ruddy as the Rambour and
Reinette apples that would soon be hanging on the weathered branches.

"I hope Mère has made something you savor. You can
count on plenty of cider, at least."

They walked toward his hobbled horse, which nickered
softly. Before she could protest, his firm hands encircled
her waist and helped her to the saddle. He took the reins
and led her home on foot, making her wonder if he would
brave the dark to return to Fort Beauséjour if supper took
too long.

Or would Père and Mère offer to let him stay the night?

She looked ahead to their chimneys, the smoke blowing
sideways in a puff of wind and wrapping their stone house
like a scarf. Lucien and Pascal were in the courtyard near the
barn, finishing their chores. Dismounting near the front steps
of their house, Sylvie stifled a smile at Marie-Madeleine's
wide-eyed stare through a crack in the door.

Just who was smitten here?

The doctor tethered his horse to the hitch rail out front,
and Sylvie called for Lucien to bring salt hay and water.
Her gaze veered to the bay. Bleu's canoe was missing. Did
that mean he would not return for supper? Her mind took
another sharp turn. Had Boudreau come for Bleu? Was he

secretly aligned with the English and set on collecting a
bounty for her brother?

To Marie-Madeleine's apparent delight, Boudreau bowed
when she opened the door. Clapping a hand over her mouth
to stifle her giggling, she motioned them in and relieved them
of their wraps. "Mère says you and Sylvie can be in the parlor
till supper is served," she told them with the aplomb of a
born hostess.

Sylvie wanted nothing more than to help with supper
and leave her sister to entertain the doctor. Denied that, she
went into the parlor, finding it empty. The largest window
overlooked the bay, offering an expansive view of the steep
rise to the fort beyond it, reminding her the man had come
overland for miles to see her.

"Please, sit down," she urged, sending the still lurking
Marie-Madeleine to fetch him a drink.

"Your home is unlike most Acadians'," he remarked,
looking about the simply furnished chamber. "More commodious."

"Père constructed it long ago. As clan elder, he built it big
for our gatherings." Had they not been over this before? She
took a seat opposite him near the hearth, surprised when
he got up to add more wood to the dwindling fire. "He had
plenty of help from my uncles."

"A far cry from fort quarters." He took an iron poker and
jabbed at the logs till they settled. "So, I have finally met your
sister. But not all your brothers."

The spark of alarm she'd felt flared. "You know Pascal
and Lucien, of course, as they frequently come and go at
the fort."

"Is there not a third?"

She hesitated, knotting her hands in her lap. "That would
be Bleu. He is seldom here." A white lie. She'd last seen him
at breakfast. "He is often in the north . . . and has busi-

ness with Hudson's Bay Company. He most resembles our father."

Mon Dieu, help me. Why on earth had she added that? She was an utter failure at subterfuge!

He took the cider from Marie-Madeleine, thanking her, and she smiled then disappeared. Sylvie looked out the window, wondering how long supper would be delayed.

"Your father is a gracious man. I've had few dealings with him till now."

She looked away from the window to her knotted hands. "I'm thankful he's rarely in need of your services."

"As am I." His gaze slid to her beribboned skirts. He reached into his weskit and removed a black silk ribbon. "A gift."

She took it from his outstretched hand and murmured her thanks. A small gold cross pendant was strung on a dark ribbon and glittered beguilingly in the light from the window.

"Allow me?" he said, taking the gift back and coming to stand behind her.

Everything in her rebelled at this unwanted intimacy, but here he was, carefully tying the ribbon around her neck. As his fingers fell away, she put a hand to the cold pendant resting in the hollow of her throat.

Was this a part of courtship? Even an unwanted one?

Mercifully, Mère's announcement of supper led them to the kitchen, where Marie-Madeleine gaped at the necklace in question. Sylvie sat down in her usual place, somewhat amused that Boudreau took Bleu's. They bowed their heads, and Père said the blessing.

"Bless us, O Lord, and these Thy gifts, which we are about to receive from Thy bounty, through Christ Jesus our Lord."

They chorused "amen," and the meal began. Sylvie snuck a look at the doctor as the dishes were passed, and her appetite fled. She said little, adjusting to the feel of her new

necklace and the man beside her, dismayed at how at ease
the doctor seemed to be in their company. He bantered with
her brothers, laughed at Père's jokes, and even paid Mère
a compliment. Was he ingratiating himself to learn more
about Bleu?

"Your culinary skills are much appreciated, Madame
Galant," he said at meal's end. "The garrison cook is in need
of a lesson or two."

Mère smiled while Sylvie abandoned her supper. Thankfully no one said a word about Bleu.

Père invited Boudreau to smoke in the parlor, and the men
left the kitchen. Relieved, Sylvie began to wash the dishes,
wishing an end to the evening.

Marie-Madeleine dried a plate with a linen cloth and said
in a too-loud whisper, "Did Dr. Boudreau give you that pretty
frippery?"

Casting a look toward the parlor, Sylvie nodded.

"Well, you don't look very happy about it!"

"Shush," Mère whispered back. "You know your sister.
She embraces nothing straightaway like you do. She needs
time to reflect on it first."

"Will the doctor stay the night?" Marie-Madeleine asked,
moving on to refill the salt cellar.

"I think not," Sylvie replied tartly. "A gift is one thing.
Overnighting is another."

"You wouldn't be saying that if you were taken with him."

Mère frowned and pressed a finger to her daughter's lips.
"Courting is not something someone young as you should
contemplate. Now, return the molasses to the larder."

Across the hall, the men were having a robust conversation punctuated with laughter that failed to bolster Sylvie's
spirits. Boudreau seemed to have charmed everyone but her.

When Marie-Madeleine's back was turned, Sylvie mouthed
to her mother, "Where is Bleu?"

Mère's slight shrug ended the matter. Sylvie moved to stand by the window, trying to make out the slightest movement in the twilight.

Father, please bless and protect him. Protect us all.

A quarter of an hour had passed with the women still busy in the kitchen when Dr. Boudreau appeared at the doorway. "I take my leave of you fair ladies with a full stomach and heart."

Obviously enchanted, Marie-Madeleine curtsied, which only widened the doctor's smile. Sylvie bade him good night from where she stood. Was he expecting her to see him to his horse? Père spared her that, and the front door shut with a resounding thud at their exit. With any luck, the doctor would make it back to the fort before full dark.

13

Life is thick sown with thorns, and I know no other remedy than to pass quickly through them. The longer we dwell on our misfortunes, the greater is their power to harm us.

Voltaire

Bleu returned sometime in the night. When Sylvie awakened before dawn to kindle the day's fires, he had already done so and was sitting near the kitchen hearth with a cup of coffee. On such a frigid morning no one else was yet awake. Her relief was so great it propelled her across the room to put her arms about him in a fierce embrace. His rumbling chuckle removed all her angst, at least temporarily.

"So, all is well at present?" He held out his empty mug, which she refilled, the coffee's aroma like ambrosia to her rumbling stomach.

"I missed you at supper," she told him, fetching her own cup from the shelf and adding sugar and cream.

"Alas . . ." He stretched his buckskin-clad legs toward

the fire, his feet bare. "I was busy at Beauséjour, ransacking Boudreau's office."

Sylvie sputtered on her first sip. She coughed, trying not to spill the coffee. "You . . . what?"

"Abbé Le Loutre and I, oui." He took another sip. "A convenient situation with the doctor preoccupied here."

All her angst returned tenfold. "Oh, Bleu . . ."

"Though we found little to confirm our suspicions, we remain confident he is an English spy."

She stared at him, open-mouthed, coffee forgotten. Yet did it not confirm her own suspicions?

He looked into the leaping fire. "We have it on good authority that the doctor is in league with the English at Fort Lawrence. Captain Scott seems to have hired Boudreau as a spy, wanting French maps and battle plans. It is no secret the doctor despises his superiors at Beauséjour, particularly Commander Vergor and Abbé Le Loutre."

Her stomach soured. "What would motivate him to go over to the enemy?"

"Greed. Pride." Bleu gave a slight shrug. "He has openly stated he feels the English have superior military strength, so he is no doubt looking to his future."

"What does this mean for Beauséjour?"

"It makes the fort especially vulnerable and gives the enemy at Fort Lawrence more power to encroach upon French territory with stealth and success."

"Then why would he waste time with courting? It plays no part in his plans, surely?"

"Ah, but it does. Word has already spread that he is wooing the daughter of Gabriel Galant. That alone removes him further from suspicion. He is also able to hear directly from a clan elder like Père the current temper of the people, their thoughts and plans."

Sylvie's mind returned to supper. All the genial talk and

compliments and laughter had been naught but a ruse? Her fingers went to her neck where the ribbon pendant had rested. It now lay atop her dresser. She'd fling it into Baie Française—

"Of course you must tell no one." Bleu's steady gaze held hers. "I am merely telling you because you are involved, however unwillingly."

"Père and Mère do not know?"

"Père and Mère suspect."

"But not our brothers?"

A shake of his head. "The fewer the better. As the saying goes, two can keep a secret if one of them is dead."

She shivered. "What does this mean for all of us who live in the shadow of Fort Lawrence?"

"We of the Resistance feel the English will soon deal a vicious blow to Beauséjour and all Acadie. We know not what that entails, but we are working relentlessly to find out. Rest assured, we have our spies, just as the enemy has theirs."

She fell silent, digesting the news, forgetting to start breakfast. "Did you make a mess of Boudreau's office?"

"Just enough to crack his composure and leave no doubt he is being watched." Bleu's satisfied smile held no warmth. "We also took maps that may have been intended for the enemy."

She studied her brother, certain that he was at great risk. "Boudreau asked me about you quite smoothly when we were alone in the parlor before supper. I was evasive, but I sense he is very aware you might be near and is wanting to collect any bounty upon your head."

"Of course. Such a reward would feather his nest far more than his doctoring can do."

"If only we could live in peace," she whispered vehemently. "We are Neutrals. We only desire to farm and raise our families and honor God. This we have done for the past one hundred fifty years. We want no war, no forts, no boundary lines. No trouble."

"But trouble is what we have, mon cher, and it is going to get worse before it gets better."

Bleu slipped away like he had come, silently and without adieu. Sylvie felt more melancholy than usual at his going. She thought he might tell her goodbye, at least, since they had had so many secret conversations. Besides, why would he leave after warning her of trouble?

As the days ticked by, she entertained a horrifying possibility. Perhaps Bleu had not simply gone away like before. Perhaps he was . . . dead.

What if Boudreau had come upon his ransacked office and felt Abbé Le Loutre and Bleu and their compatriots were behind it? Was the doctor not only a spy but a murderer? She'd not seen him since he'd joined them for supper, as he'd been confined to the fort with an attack of grippe. Winter was a hard time with men cooped up like chickens, illness rushing in like the tide and refusing to ebb.

Mère sent a basket to Boudreau by way of Pascal. Sylvie had helped her fill it with kitchen delicacies and stillroom remedies. Though it was a customary kindness, Sylvie felt they were feeding the enemy.

"I doubt a doctor of his standing will appreciate our herbs and simples," Sylvie said.

"If he wants to get better, he will forgo the foolish bloodletting and such and rely on these," Mère replied, always at odds with anything other than nature's bountiful provision.

Pascal brought back the empty basket and a load of Holland cloth from the fort's sutler to be made into officers' shirts. No more gowns for officers' wives were needed at present, and Sylvie was glad, for as the weather turned clement she was more outdoors than in.

Now March, it was warm enough to churn butter on the house's wide front stoop overlooking the bay. Sunlight warmed the stones behind Sylvie and beneath her bare feet. Her sabots were not far. The warmth soaked into her pale-as-milk skin, making her drowsy. She wanted nothing more than to curl up like their barn cat, Papillon, who was asleep in a circle of sunlight nearby.

"Sylvie . . ."

She started, eyes flying open as she leaned back against the house. "I—you caught me napping—"

Boudreau chuckled, taking a seat on the step and facing out toward the bay as she drew her feet beneath her petticoats. She did not see his horse. Had he walked all the way? "I've come to thank you in person for the basket you sent."

She put a hand to her throat. Would he notice she wasn't wearing his necklace? As for the basket, it had been Mère's idea. "Are you recovered?"

"At last. But two soldiers lie buried and another three are still in hospital. If it were Hôtel-Dieu they might have a chance, but here in the wilds . . ."

While at the fort she'd seen the exterior of the hospital, a small, rude structure barely big enough for a dozen men. "I'm sorry to hear it," she said, the memory of the fort's burial ground outside Beauséjour's walls always sore.

"As a physician it grieves me." He seemed earnest enough, looking at her with sorrowful eyes. "Pray for their souls."

"Of course."

"Do you pray for mine, Sylvie?"

She took the lid off the churn and set it aside to peer at the milky ball of butter within. "I do pray for you." She wouldn't tell him what she prayed for, namely that any evil intent of his would be thwarted, exposed, and come to naught.

He stared down at his boots, expression rueful. "I confess I do not pray. I have, for the most part, given up on God."

Yet another strike against him. She was hardly surprised. What most surprised her was her almost indignant response.

"You have given up on God, on prayer?" Her quiet query was impassioned. "How is that even possible? God is everywhere, all around us. In the sunlight, the sea, all of spring."

"You have a little of Abbé Le Loutre's fervor."

She sensed this was no compliment. Le Loutre, like many priests, was as political as he was religious, more outward show than adherence to Christ. "Our heavenly Father opens believing eyes to the good all around us. The beauty."

He turned toward her again. "I see good in you, Sylvie."

She felt a flash of impatience. She had little time for the ruse of courting in broad daylight, especially with chores waiting. Though if she was truly fond of him she would not care, as her sister had pointed out. The butter could fail to separate or turn rancid and she'd shrug it away.

"But I do not see much good in others," he murmured.

There seemed a shadow about him today. Being a traitor carried a taint, no doubt. Or had his ransacked office left him feeling haunted? Hunted?

She called for Marie-Madeleine to come and help. Again, her sister made much of seeing the doctor, even pressing a hand to her forehead and complaining of a pain, which made Sylvie and Boudreau laugh.

"Alas, I brought no headache powders," he said, palms outstretched.

"Entertain our guest while I put the butter away," Sylvie told her, wanting to flee.

When she returned and Marie-Madeleine went with Mère into the stillroom, she and Boudreau were alone again.

"Will you walk with me?" Boudreau stood and held out a hand. "In your orchard?"

His touch was hardly the rough-hewn, gritty grasp of her father and brothers. This was a man more at home with a medical book than an axe. They walked toward the pruned trees, past his horse hobbled there, which accounted for the stealth with which he'd surprised her.

"Have you given any thought to coming with me to the city?" he asked as they passed down a row of full-grown trees.

"Did you tell my father about that when you asked his permission to court me?"

"No. The matter is between the two of us."

Père would not approve. Besides, they would have to be married to go to the city, and they had just begun courting. Only it was naught but a sham courtship—

"But before we wed I want to spend more time with you and your family. Meet the relatives I have not yet met."

Stunned, she gestured toward the water. "My grandparents live farther down the bay. But in truth, I am related to half of Acadie."

He smiled and turned toward her, slipping an arm about her waist while holding fast her other hand as if they were about to dance. "You won me over at the fête with your fine stepping and your gown. I had not thought to find such costly fabric in your possession. How did you come by it?"

Sylvie hesitated. Would his every question circle back to Bleu? Feeling ensnared, she echoed the words of Madame Auclair at the fête. "From Marie Le Borgne in Louisbourg."

Father, forgive the lie.

"Fit for Québec or Montréal. You were meant for grander things, Sylvie." His eyes, warm and cold by turns, further unnerved her. He seemed to possess the smooth subtlety of the snake in Eden's garden before the fall. Inwardly she recoiled while outwardly she let him lead her in a rondel over the uneven ground.

They stopped at the farthest edge of the orchard. She tried to step back, to no avail. Though slight, he was stronger than he looked. His arms tightened about her and then his mouth was on hers. There was no tenderness in it, just a swift, forced, clumsy kiss. When he released her, she worked to hide her disgust—and her heartache.

In a trice he had stolen what belonged to the man who would win her forever, her future husband—whoever that happened to be.

Her gaze ricocheted past Boudreau's shoulder to the woods. Bleu stood there long enough for her to see his displeasure. In a blink he was gone, melting into the forest, just as Marie-Madeleine's strident voice reached her.

Shame lit a fire in her face. She spun shakily round in the direction of the house to find her sister approaching, a croque-cignole in hand. For the doctor, no doubt. Never had Sylvie been so glad to see her.

Boudreau chuckled as Marie-Madeleine presented the pastry then curtsied prettily. After thanking her, he took a bite as Sylvie put her fingers to her lips, which seemed almost bruised.

"Père welcomes you to take supper with us, Dr. Boudreau," Marie-Madeleine announced. "I hope you are fond of fish."

14

Tears are the silent language of grief.

Voltaire

A lengthy stretch of sun brought the orchards into bloom earlier than ever before, the swelling buds bursting into blossom against bright blue skies. L'Epice and Fameuse were Sylvie's favorites, thriving in the clean salt air. In the middle of the orchard stood the Ancient, planted by her great-grandfather Galant, its trunk as thick as four men. Boudreau had commented on it during his visit the month before, but she'd not seen him since.

Bleu had again disappeared, carving a hole in her heart. His increasingly long absences left her pondering why. Did he mean to protect them from his whereabouts and activities so if English authorities pressed them for information, they could gain nothing? She sensed he was fully engaged with the Resistance in a fight for not only his life but theirs.

"Ma chère sœur."

At the beloved voice, Sylvie whirled around, light-headed with relief. Bleu stood at the end of a row of yearling trees, barely visible through their leafing branches. She moved toward him, wanting to shout the news of his homecoming, but he put a finger to his lips like Mère did with Marie-Madeleine, who was busy sowing seed with her in the herb garden near the stillroom.

Quietly, Sylvie and Bleu embraced. When she stepped back, she saw an angry crimson line from his left brow to his jawline.

He did not miss her wince. "It will soon be a scar, Sylvie."

"Oh, Bleu. I have prayed for you night and day, but it has still not kept you safe."

"Your prayers likely kept me from further harm."

She stepped closer and examined the wound, which looked as if it might fester. "Mère has salve in the stillroom. Come, let me tend to you."

"I cannot stay long." He looked around, his heightened wariness chilling. "I only bring news."

They moved toward the house as chickens strutted about the cobbled courtyard and a rooster crowed. Mère and Marie-Madeleine had just gone inside, so Sylvie and Bleu passed into the stillroom and shut the door. Potent with dried herbs, the shadowed room bore numerous shelves. Sylvie searched for what she needed even as she steeled herself for whatever Bleu might tell her. After taking a small crock, she began blending essentials.

He took a stool, watching both her and the door. "First, tell me what has become of you and Boudreau."

"He has not been here for a month or more. Pascal brought word he is busy tending to the hamlets outside Beauséjour." She added crushed rosemary to the salve and mixed it with a wooden spoon. "There has been much sickness there lately."

"You are no fonder of him than at first?"

She began applying the salve as gently as she could. "How can I be fond of a man who may be a traitor?"

"I doubt you would care for him if he was the archangel Gabriel. He is not the man for you."

She smiled fleetingly, imagining Boudreau winged. "Have you brought any *good* news?"

"No." He stayed stoic as she finished with the salve. "Soon the English will renew their attempts to force Acadians to swear allegiance to their king. When that fails, they will begin to disarm them from Port Royal to Ile Saint-Jean and Ile Royale."

"But we need our guns to hunt—to keep our livestock safe." Her mind spun with all the implications. "To defend ourselves against enemies who would do us harm."

"It is but another strike in a long volley of them." His tone was grim and exacting. "I am here to tell Père to hide his weapons. Secret them where the enemy cannot find them."

She wiped her hands on her apron. "What comes next?"

"Our spies report the enemy has ordered New England troops to sail north in transport ships. Ranger companies like William Blackburn's will soon arrive. Together they will attempt to take Beauséjour once their numbers are such that we can form no resistance."

"Beauséjour is undermanned. Boudreau has said so."

"It will be the first to fall if they succeed. The English want to make an example of Chignecto especially. It's of strategic importance as it removes the obstacle preventing them from advancing west." He crossed his arms. "'Those of the Chignecto district who have been most rebellious shall be removed the greatest distance,' so an intercepted missive says."

Sylvie stared at him in horror. "There is no rebellion among our people here or anywhere. Only among the Resistance."

"They pass lies like beaver pelts to justify their evil ends."

She sank down on the stool opposite him. "What do they mean by 'the greatest distance'?"

"I know not . . . yet."

"Perhaps they mean to push us west toward Québec City or Montréal. Will you warn Père about all this?"

"As clan elder, he must know and then alert all the others."

She nodded, breathing in the solacing herbs that for once failed to soothe. Tears blurred her vision, and she tried to blink them back. "He is in the dike lands with Lucien and Pascal repairing the aboiteaux, but he should return by supper."

"I am sorry to grieve you so." Bleu looked toward the window, his profile stark, his features tense. "How I wish to make you smile with some trinket or more silk. But now is not the time for merriment."

15

It is such a secret place, the land of tears.

Antoine de Saint-Exupery

As May's apple blossoms scattered to the winds, Sylvie sought her path to the overlook above Baie Française. Had it only been December when Bleu found her here in a swirl of snow? Today she stayed back from the steep bluff, not wanting to look at the feuding forts on the opposite ridge. An ancient, moss-covered rock backed by pines proved a fine seat and left her feeling, for just a moment, elevated above her troubles.

Bending her head, she tried to gather her tangled feelings into a prayerful plea. Did Dieu side with the English or the French? Would He allow her people to be bullied by both nations when they had tried to remain neutral and live honorably? Her heart was overfull, words eluding her. Love your enemies, Mère said, and pray for them. But that seemed too simplistic for a time of war, a possible battle over the very ground she sat upon.

And what abundant ground it was. Soon bayberries would overflow with fruit and spice the air as golden heather adorned the beaches. Wild roses were already showing in pink bunches, and there were wildflowers at her feet. She reached for some bluets and daisies and began weaving a crown. Marie-Madeleine delighted in wildflower crowns. She had been understandably moody of late, her joie de vivre traded for a toothache.

Perhaps Sylvie herself would wear a wildflower crown on her wedding day as well as carry apple blossoms for her bridal bouquet. Such turned her thoughts to Boudreau, absent for weeks. If his false pursuit of her had done anything, it had made her consider a marriage contract and the kind of groom she wanted. And he was opposite the doctor in nearly every way.

He must be a man of integrity. Of faith. Kind yet strong, self-assured and self-controlled. If she had her druthers, he would not be petit but tall. Not russet like Boudreau but dark like Père and Bleu. Capable of removing the taint of the doctor's unwanted kiss.

Her shudder gave way to a sigh as the wind freshened, toying with her linen cap and the fichu about her shoulders. She raised her gaze from the almost finished flower crown, eyes on the great blue bay she knew by heart in any season. In autumn and winter it was gunmetal gray, in spring and summer robin's-egg blue—

She shot to her feet, the flowers falling to the grass. There marring the water sailed not one or two vessels but an entire English fleet. It was as Bleu had warned in the stillroom. The New England troops had come, including William Blackburn's dreaded Rangers. Stretched taut in the wind, Union Jack flags marked more than thirty transports, including sloops and schooners and frigates. Their names eluded her at such a distance, though their portent did not.

Weak-kneed and trying not to weep, she took the trail that led her home, forgetting Marie-Madeleine's flower crown.

These ships—more ships than she had ever seen at one time—signaled something imminent. They were too close to French territory, too near Fort Beauséjour, which was lauded the strongest of all the French garrisons. How many soldiers could be aboard so many ships? Far more than Beauséjour could boast. Even Abbé Le Loutre's combined militia and Mi'kmaq were said to number only a few thousand souls.

By the time she reached home, her breath was ragged, and she realized she was not the only one who'd seen the fleet. Mère watched from the window, her face disfigured with alarm, while Père and Pascal and Lucien stood silently on shore. Though the ships were still quite a distance away, the names of some were now visible.

Mermaid. Siren. Success.

Her stomach cramped. The trouble was indeed here.

16

Better keep the devil at the door than have to turn him out of the house.

Scottish proverb

From the quarterdeck of his sloop, *Constellation*, William Blackburn lifted his eyes from the vast blue bay the British called Fundy to the ripening grain fields of the Acadians, backed by thickly forested lowlands and bluffs. Slanting rays of sunlight heightened every hue and detail of what seemed an earthly oasis, the water's blue not only beguiling but blinding. He'd expected Acadie's many charms to be exaggerated, not understated, but the poetic prose had utterly failed to paint it properly. Slightly slack-jawed he was. Little wonder England was determined to wrest it from the French and Indians for good.

Nova Scotia hugged the east coast, not unlike New England, the territory he knew best, with its secluded harbors and deep woods. He'd heard the French-held islands farther north were mostly rock, good for privateering and fishing and little else. But Acadie was a treasure waiting to be won.

"'Tis remarkable ground," the ship's captain was saying.

"At least in summer. Winters are brutal. The wind pierces like a sword."

"Weather is a fearsome enemy this far north," Will replied.

"Even in New England, aye." The captain took out a brass spyglass and passed it to Will. "I'd like to hear more about your time on the American frontier, Major, though you are unquestionably more a man of action than words. Perhaps one day you should publish an account of your exploits and how you cheat death at every turn."

Will felt a sting of surprise. Had the captain heard his journals were soon to be published? Once, all those pages seemed a more alarming foe than French and Indians, weather, and disease combined. But what else was one to do when held by the French for an unending winter? In hindsight he thought differently about being closeted with pen and ink, hunched over a ream of paper, resurrecting those exploits. So much stillness and reflection had opened a window into his own soul.

"Providence more than my own wits has kept me alive, Captain," Will finally said, looking through the spyglass to the fort called Beauséjour. "Let that suffice."

"At least I delivered you safely here, though I cannot say, given the conflict, I'll see you safely home."

Will ignored his strangely ominous tone and returned the spyglass. The voyage from Boston had been unremarkable, rough weather aside, with no French ships sighted. Secrecy shrouded their cruise. He was not privy to British Colonel Monckton's orders, just his own. He was charged with reconnoitering the land before him and obtaining intelligence about the enemy—their strength, situation, and activity—as only men accustomed to the backwoods could do.

For now, he relaxed his near constant vigilance and savored the sight before him. For years he'd heard about the

Acadians' impressive aboiteaux, their abundant farms and fisheries and cattle. He'd noted the swelling number of English settlers moving north from the colonies and elsewhere to come here. Monckton had even dangled hectares of land in front of him as a reward for his involvement.

But would the English win? Or would the French hold their beloved ground?

Will slapped at an insect stinging his neck, only to find a hundred more swarming him as he walked across Fort Lawrence's parade grounds to the commandant's quarters. Though it was only May, summer's heat seemed to throb within the high palisade, magnifying the sweat, offal, and rankness of men and livestock. It made him long for the frosts of autumn or the slow-blooming sweetness of early spring.

In minutes he'd traded the fort's parade ground for the heaviness of tobacco smoke and spirits in a bombproof casemate. A guard had been posted, and after presenting his papers, Will entered the room to a volley of words uttered like an expletive. A knot of officers turned toward him as the door closed and an equerry made introductions.

Colonel Monckton stopped speaking, his vehemence fading. "At last, Major." With an air of authority, he introduced Will to the other men. "I doubt we could make as many inroads as we're about to without you and your Rangers." He went to a sideboard and poured Will a drink. "Though we are warring with the French, we do profess a certain fondness for their wines, brandy foremost."

A low ripple of assent rounded the room. Will accepted the finely fluted glass, so at odds with their coarse surroundings, and took a drink as another man, slight of build and clad in civilian clothes, entered.

"And here is Dr. Boudreau from Fort Beauséjour. He has

been supplying us with maps and all manner of intelligence gleaned from French officers, who remain ignorant of his doing so."

Will met the man's lackluster gaze. A spy? Common enough on both sides if the price was high enough. What had enticed the Frenchman to betray his own people?

"The doctor will apprise you of the foremost leaders of the Acadian Resistance—the rebels you will undoubtedly bring in as prisoners," Monckton continued with a smug confidence.

A hefty order by a man who oft complained the Rangers were little more than savages, citing their refusal to wear the British uniforms as proof. Will schooled his dislike for the commandant's arrogance if not the task before him.

Boudreau gestured to a map spread upon a table anchored by irons. Finished with his brandy, Will looked down on the intricate black-inked rendering of Nova Scotia that could have been made only by one who knew it well.

Monckton came to stand between him and Boudreau. "You'll start across the isthmus of Chignecto here." His callused thumb traced a path toward the bay's western shoreline. "You'll not only reconnoiter for the enemy but bring in any deserters as well, both army and navy."

Boudreau reached a pale forefinger to another marked location. His French accent was slight, making his words more understandable. "Here is the home base of one of the most troublesome leaders of the Acadian Resistance. A warrior by the name of Bleu from the renowned Galant clan."

Will committed the details to memory, knowing it mattered little. These rebels never stayed long in one place. They were on the move and in league with the Mi'kmaq from Nova Scotia to Newfoundland and deeper into the Canadian interior, as relentless as Rangers.

"Bleu Galant works closely with the rebel leaders Beausoleil and Surette." The doctor's voice thickened with disgust. "A den of vipers, all. I have made attempts to locate him at the Galant habitation without luck. He is as elusive as he is dangerous. He and his compatriots are responsible for the recent raid and fall of Lawrencetown, though they have done more damage elsewhere and are poised to strike at new English hamlets along the Bay of Fundy at any time."

"What of Fort Beauséjour?" Will said. "Who is the English's most formidable adversary there?"

"Within the fort itself there is the parish priest, Abbé Le Loutre, who is the true commandant of Fort Beauséjour, not Vergor, whose incompetence bodes well for us."

"Vergor is but Le Loutre's minion," Monckton confirmed.

Boudreau nodded. "Le Loutre is rabid to incite the Acadians to take up arms against the English at all costs, even withholding mass when it suits him. I have heard him say openly from the pulpit that the English are responsible for the death of the Christ."

A lunatic priest, then. "You are not Acadian?" Will asked.

"I am French, but not a Neutral," he replied with a mocking smile as the officers chuckled. "Most definitely not a Neutral, though I have attempted to court one of the comelier Galants with as little success as apprehending the Resistance fighter."

With a grunt, Monckton poured himself more brandy. "We are still trying to decide who among the English here at Fort Lawrence is spying for the French," he said, looking toward the closed door. "Once we discover them, they'll meet with a traitor's death."

With a little bow, Boudreau set down his empty glass. "For now, gentlemen, I must bid you adieu until I have intelligence worthy enough to visit you again."

Stars glittered in the Acadian sky like jewels Will had once seen on ladies' dresses at a colonial ball, only those gems were a decidedly poor imitation. As he sat outside his tent at the edge of the English encampment, wind rolled over him and rifled a grove of nearby willows, cooling his heated face. Peace was in this place. Peace he'd not felt on the ship amid so many men, nor in Monckton's company upon his arrival yesterday at the fort. In a war-torn land it seemed odd to experience peace on contested ground in Fort Lawrence's forbidding shadow.

Before dawn he'd forsake any tranquility and be on the move. He'd already discussed tomorrow's reconnaissance with his men, consulted maps stolen from Fort Beauséjour, and spoken with scouts. As smoke from a near campfire stung his eyes, he looked up at the moon, wondering how many Acadians did the same and if they knew what was coming against them.

"Pardon, sir." The respectful address turned Will's head. "Your dog friendly?"

"If you are, aye." Will looked down at his faithful companion lounging in the grass.

The lad approached somewhat warily, toting a basket. He tipped it toward Will, firelight illuminating a great many apples. "Winter keepers. All Acadian fruit. None finer."

Will reached inside his linen shirt, then tossed the lad a guinea before choosing a large scarlet apple and taking a bite. Still crisp and honey sweet. None finer, aye. "How is it you're peddling Acadian fruit if you're English?"

"My family helps provision the fort here. We're from a near village that chased out the Acadians. Their orchards are now ours." Dropping to his knees, the lad rested the basket on the ground. "And who are you, if you don't mind my askin'?"

"A Ranger from New England."

"Blackburn's Rangers?"

"The same, aye."

Astonishment washed his face. "Wait till I tell my pa! He knows all about 'em."

Amused, Will swallowed another bite. "Seeing as how I gave you a guinea, mighn't you have an extra apple for Major Blackburn himself?"

The boy began sorting through his wares, obviously intent on the biggest. "When you give it to the major, tell him Ezra Johnson wishes him all the best in his mission against the French and Indians." Handing over another apple, the boy looked around. "I'd best get back to my pa. He don't like to go lookin' for me."

Will tipped his cocked hat, and the boy ran off, lightning in his heels.

Laughter lurked around the tent corner. "So, Major Blackburn, with all due respect, it seems you are already in disguise and we've not yet set out."

"Show yourself, Captain," Will replied. He tossed the second apple to the figure who stepped into view.

"I confess apples are the furthest thing from my mind." Sinking to his haunches, Hugh Sterling bit into the fruit. "I thought you'd be abed. Tonight's the last sound sleep we'll get for some time."

"The stars win." Will looked upward again, the apple core discarded. "I had plenty of sleep on the *Constellation* . . . and plenty of time to give thanks I'm not a naval man."

A grim chuckle. "Ships come by the name 'coffins' deservedly. Let's hope our return to New England is swift. I have no desire to winter here. Garrisons are sickly places in the snow, be they French or English, and summer is little better."

"Which is why I remain outside fort walls. I prefer a seen enemy to one unseen."

"The spate of dysentery, you mean? Well, there are plenty

of both here." Hugh took a wary look around, lantern light glinting off his coppery hair. "The Resistance foremost."

"We've just arrived and already I'm wondering our true intent. Both Governor Lawrence and Colonel Monckton are notably closemouthed about the Acadian problem, as they put it."

"Not only Lawrence and Monckton. With all due respect, you yourself said little on the voyage here and even less since we arrived."

Will glanced at him, a spare shadow whittled down by the wilderness, as he continued.

"Granted, you're never full of wind like most officers. But in all my years serving as your adjutant, I've never seen you so . . ." The unfinished sentence hung in the air bewilderingly.

"So . . ." Will echoed.

"Fashed." Hugh expelled a breath. "Could it be because you're becoming widely known and the French now have a price on your head?"

Will shrugged. "Mayhap time is running out. Every foray seems a greater risk . . ." He left off, unable to dismiss the internal ticking of some unseen clock. "As the French say—a deux digits de la morte." *Every moment within two fingers of death.*

"You are seldom unsettled. That doesn't bode well for the rest of us." Glancing over his shoulder, Hugh studied the torchlit fort that had assumed the air of a powder keg about to ignite. "We are here to harass and rout the French and their allies, leaving the Acadian Neutrals be, or so we were told. Have those orders changed?"

"There's rumor of forcing Acadian allegiance and depriving them of their weapons."

Hugh paused. "Forcing and depriving mean untold trouble. We have the added disadvantage of not knowing this territory and are at greater risk of becoming prisoners of the French and Indians."

"If so, we can expect no mercy."

Hugh took out his pipe and began filling it with tobacco, a habit he indulged only when vexed. "A duplicitous business, all."

"Be especially wary, Captain." Will looked up at the stars, struck by how fiercely Orion glittered. "And not only of the enemy."

17

If you suppress grief too much it can well redouble.

Molière

June began with ripples of unrest and then a tidal wave of rumors. Sylvie kept close to home, having heard how many English soldiers had disembarked from the transports and were now crawling over Acadie like a plague of ship rats. Undaunted, Père and Lucien and Pascal continued their normal tasks, but their long expressions pulled at her and it seemed they became increasingly brooding.

One sultry dawn, when the men were not far in the fields, Sylvie came out of the barn from the morning milking and nearly walked straight into a stranger—and a dog. She drew up short, and milk sloshed onto the ground from her twin pails, splattering her sabots.

"Pardon, mademoiselle," the man said in nearly flawless French.

Feeling clumsy, she set her overfull pails down as he approached. With a humble manner so contrary to his imposing stature, he knelt and wiped the creamy milk from her shoes with a finely embroidered handkerchief, leaving her speechless at his gallantry. Then, after going to the well, he drew water and washed out the square of linen as efficiently as Mère would do.

Turning back toward her, he smiled. "I apologize for startling you."

"I was only startled, oui," she said, flushing. "But I would have been terrified had you been wearing a red coat." She tore her eyes from him with difficulty to look at the fierce creature by his side. "He is part wolf?"

"Aye. Sergeant Bonami is a master tracker if not marksman." His subtle teasing both charmed her and made her chuckle. His French—did she detect a slight accent?

Her focus switched to the rifle dangling from his right hand as he removed his cocked hat, a black affair embellished with trade beads. His longish hair was tied back, its gloss blue-black. He wore leggings and moccasins in the Indian style and a hunting frock, more weapons at his waist. Having been raised with so many Galant clansmen, she summed him up in a trice. He wasn't a man of the fields but the forest. And he moved with a lithe athleticism that told of endless trails and unspoken trials, a man among men who made Boudreau seem a mere flea.

His steady gaze held hers for one exquisite, dissecting second. "I am trying to find your oldest brother."

"Bleu?" She felt none of the wariness Boudreau had evoked with his queries. This man was clearly one of the Resistance. "Is he here?"

"No." She swallowed, willing herself to look away from him. "But I shall tell him upon his return your name and reason for seeking him out."

"Have you seen many English?" Intensity tightened his tanned features. "Or heard anything that causes you alarm?"

"We have seen the British ships. We want no trouble, as I'm

sure you know. As Acadians we simply want to live peaceably and stay out of any conflict."

His eyes left her to roam the courtyard and outbuildings, giving her a chance to study him further. He was taller than even Bleu and just as well honed. Whiskers shadowed a strong jaw and turned him more handsome than unkempt. And his eyes . . . When they returned to her, she steeled herself against their clarity and hue, akin to silver sand. She forgot all about the milk and the fact Marie-Madeleine was watching from the kitchen window. It seemed the whole world had fallen away, lost as she was in the force of his presence.

Surely he sensed her flagrant fascination. Squaring her shoulders, she had to almost shake herself free. "Let me fetch you a cup of cider." Without waiting for a reply, she moved toward the cellar, milk pails in hand.

Within moments she was back, having promised to answer Marie-Madeleine's questions in return for her seeing to the milk.

The stranger took the cup and sampled it with obvious appreciation. "From your fine orchards."

His compliment warmed her like the sun on her back. "Oui. I have tended them since I was small. This year's harvest promises to be the best in many seasons."

"Perhaps I'll return in autumn, then, Mademoiselle . . . ?"

"Galant." She lowered her eyes briefly to the sabots he'd cleaned. "Sylvie Galant." Blinking, she looked past him to the trail Bleu often took. "I'm sorry my brother is not here as you hoped, monsieur."

He handed the empty cup to her. "Then tell him, mademoiselle, that Le Loup hopes to meet up with him in future." He took a step back, locking eyes with her a final, spellbinding time. "Merci pour tout votre aide, pour toute votre bonté."

Will reached an unknown Acadian village, torched and still smoking. At the heart of the carnage a church had somehow stayed standing, its steeple pointing proudly amid the char and rubble, its door open as if even the priest had fled. Boot prints marred the earth, likely those of rampaging English soldiers, though he'd heard some Acadians were setting fire to their own habitations to prevent the English from having them.

With a word to Bonami to stay behind, Will went inside the chapel, struck by the carved oak interior. Someone had taken the valuables, as the altar was bare. Oddly weary, he took a seat on a bench. Rarely did he turn his back to a door, but Bonami stood watch and the place appeared entirely desolate. He bent his head, staring at the floorboards, wondering whose hands had laid them, the nails even and distinct. Where had the inhabitants gone? From a distance he'd seen swelling encampments of displaced Acadians around Fort Beauséjour as the English gained contested ground.

He stared at the empty altar, cast back to Ticonderoga and another mass house, as the English derisively called it. Caught in the teeth of a blizzard along Lake Champlain two winters ago, he and a few snow-blind men had had merely frozen juniper berries and snowmelt to sustain them. Their only recourse was to throw themselves upon the mercy of the enemy French or freeze to death.

Hoisting a white flag encased in ice, he and the last remnant of his Rangers surrendered themselves at Fort Saint-Frédéric, whose twelve-foot-thick stone walls and four-storied citadel seemed more mirage in the storm. Coming over the drawbridge and into the fortress, they'd barely escaped a large company of Indians who'd nearly overtaken them.

He'd not known much of the French tongue then, yet the

French officers behaved with striking humanity, even courtesy. When one of his Mohegans died from exposure, they'd performed a moving burial. As other Rangers recovered and were released, the French kept him. He was far less a threat removed from any action than he would be on the field.

In the months that followed, Will had slowly absorbed their speech and made note of their customs. He'd even visited their chapel, to the amusement of the Troupes de la Marine. What was the White Devil, as the Indians called him, doing in a holy place—and the enemy's holy place at that?

He mourned his lost men there. Mourned his family too, the loss that had started him on the rocky path of Rangering. In that French chapel he'd stopped striving, stopped fighting the wilderness and its enemies long enough to ponder and put down on paper who he'd become and what he'd done. And then in late spring, he'd been ransomed in a prisoner exchange with the British and released.

Without a home, he'd soon been on the move again, his Dickert rifle never far. A decades-old restlessness drove him on with the stealth of an enemy, never allowing him rest.

Yet right here in a shell of a place, for a few hallowed moments, came that odd peace, a silken part of the stillness. Amid jagged, broken glass, a starling sang on a windowsill, Acadie's ever-present wind stirring the leaves of the elm outside. With effort, Will made himself move, abandoning the calm.

The calm before the storm.

By dusk he'd skirted Galant land while his men combed the woods and ridges elsewhere for anything resembling the Resistance. Noting a well-trod trail in back of the heavily leafed orchard, Will gained the uplands and a staggering view. By full dark he'd returned to the lowlands again and hid behind a laurel thicket, a cool mist concealing him as much as the surrounding forest. Still, he had an admirable view.

Numerous Galant outbuildings gave the habitation the look of a small village. The courtyard where he'd stood that morning was charming, Old World French, the stone well at its center. Nearby a large barn and stable were a possible cover for Bleu. Three men he guessed were Galants soon returned from the fields for supper—without the brother he sought.

Odd how baking bread smelled the same anywhere. It lent to the cramp in his middle, though he was more vigilant when hunger gnawed at him. Bonami contented himself with a strip of Will's jerked meat, settling down beside him. Silent and unseen, Will clocked the efficient routines of the household as night overtook him.

As dawn lit the sky hours later, an older woman threaded through the shadows to the barn, where a cow bawled as if announcing she was late. Her step was steady, purposeful. Madame Galant? She shooed a jaunty rooster from her path as a young girl in a plain dress and apron appeared next, a long braid a sooty smudge down her back. When she performed a little dance around the well, a striped cat on her heels, Will's mouth pulled in amusement. She disappeared into a henhouse and soon reappeared with a basketful of eggs, dancing her way to the barn before returning to the main house with the older woman, their low voices almost musical in the morning's hush.

There came a lull before the men emerged as the sun broke over the horizon. One younger man went to the water where a canoe waited while the other two—one of them most assuredly Monsieur Galant—walked toward expansive grain fields farther down shore. Nary a sign of the warrior Bleu.

Will's searching gaze returned to the house. Where was the young woman—Sylvie Galant—who'd served him cider? The taste lingered in his memory, rich and sweet. Setting his jaw, he curbed any other thought of her lest emotion overrule his reason. She was simply a comely mademoiselle in the wrong place at the wrong time who had little understanding of British ambitions.

In a quarter of an hour she was walking in the direction of the orchard, her white-capped head bent as if she was lost in thought. Her beribboned skirts were unlike any he'd ever seen beyond Acadie, as beguiling as her bonnet and apron were commonplace and her sabots strange. And though she wasn't smiling, he remembered that smile, her retroussé nose, and her remarkable eyes—a clear, bewitching blue.

He reined in his gaze as she left his line of sight and went into the orchard. Bonami gave a slight whine as Will took a last look at the Galant habitation. The brigand Bleu was less likely to appear in broad daylight, and Will had stayed up most of the night to no avail. Stifling a yawn, he signaled to Bonami and ended his watch, intent on rejoining his men.

The June evening was aglow with fireflies, the tide's return a familiar melody. All seemed calm despite the British ships still at anchor in the bay and gray smoke riding the horizon in various places, feeding Sylvie's fears. Upstairs Père snored, the sound sawlike in the stillness.

Sylvie climbed atop her feather paillasse, weary but wide-eyed. Unusually quiet, Marie-Madeleine lay awake against the wall, sharing Sylvie's sleeping closet of late.

Leaning over, Sylvie kissed her lightly on the cheek. "Fais de beaux rêves."

At that, Marie-Madeleine slipped into sleep, her rhythmic breathing a balm for Sylvie's ragged nerves. Questions darted through her mind like fish trapped in the weirs on the water.

Where was Bleu? Dr. Boudreau? The stalwart stranger she'd served cider to?

Warmth pressed down on her, and she pushed back the

bed linens. She longed for an open window, but the house was locked tight.

Finally she drifted, nearly asleep when Père's snoring was overridden by something as chilling as a Mi'kmaq war cry. Footsteps? Strident voices?

Breaking glass jerked her fully awake. Marie-Madeleine gave a shriek, fisting Sylvie's linen nightgown with both hands.

The stairwell resounded with Père's hurried footsteps as Sylvie peered through the bed-curtain, watching Pascal stamp out a flaming torch that had been hurled through a broken window. But none of the Galant men could stop the tide of English soldiers.

"In the name of His Majesty, King George II, we are here to disarm you and all your household," came a loud shout. "Bring out your weapons, one and all, or we shall further ransack your dwellings."

Their abode swarmed with crimson coats and smoke, the latter promising that while Pascal had put out one fire, others were burning elsewhere. Held tight in Sylvie's arms, Marie-Madeleine trembled so violently her teeth chattered. Her back pressed to the wall of the sleeping closet, Sylvie felt she herself might be sick as the drama beyond the bed-curtain played out.

Would these marauding men poke their bayonets into their very feather beds? They stomped about the room, sending crockery shattering to the floor and overturning all that the family held dear.

Père surrendered a musket, a fowling piece, and a pistol, all ancient relics that misfired. The rest he had hidden. Where, Sylvie did not know.

When the soldiers finished their rampage and departed, there was no sleep to be had that night. Ruination ruled, and righting the mess consumed them till midmorning. The sight of Mère standing over her shattered spinning wheel etched an indelible scar across Sylvie's consciousness, as vivid as Bleu's glaring wound she'd salved.

The English had taken not only guns but goods, even their breakfast, while plundering their chests for clothes and mocking their sabots. Outside, the henhouse was partially burned, the woodshed smoldering. Someone had tried to fire the orchard, but the grass of June was not as ignitable as in late summer, for which Sylvie gave thanks.

Her mind returned to the stranger, wishing he'd been there with Bleu to confront these soldiers. She'd last seen her brother fade into the tree line, his lank black hair waving in the wind, his linen shirt one of her making, his buckskins worn but still serviceable. He was changed, not only wary but weary, and lean as a leather string, a sign he was constantly on the move. Somewhere Bleu was fighting. For his life and theirs.

Père grew more melancholy while her brothers assumed an unspoken defiance. She read it in the jut of their jaws, their usual affability subdued. When Pascal snapped at Marie-Madeleine over some minor matter, she wept as if the world would end, but he did not make amends, as if doing so was trifling given the turmoil all around them.

Soon, fire lit the ridge where Fort Beauséjour held sway, and word came that Commander Vergor had burned the new church as well as all the houses surrounding the garrison ahead of the English assault. Smoke and soot rolled across Baie Française like storm clouds, spreading ash and turning the fleet of warships more menacing.

The Galants waited, breath held. Père assembled their nearest kin and neighbors to the chapel to pray. Word came that Fort Beauséjour had fallen without much fight and Vergor had raised the white flag in surrender.

Mère simply said, "We are in the hands of le bon Dieu, not the English."

Only God, oui. It was comforting in a world turned upside down.

Though it sickened Sylvie to hear it, the jubilant English quickly renamed Beauséjour Fort Cumberland. "After the royal English butcher who gave no quarter at Culloden," Père said in disgust.

Sylvie shivered, remembering Boudreau's mention of it at the fête. How could a man who had committed such atrocities be lauded? It seemed a portent of what was to come.

"What's more," Pascal said, having come from Pont-a-Buot, which was now firmly in English control, "'tis said Abbé Le Loutre disguised himself as a woman and fled with a Mi'kmaq escort when the fort fell." Sylvie's shock turned to contempt as he continued, "And Dr. Boudreau has gone over to the English."

"Good riddance." Père stood and reached for his coat to go outside, as if he were unable to stomach more. "Le Loutre was not content to concern himself with our souls. Pride and ambition were his downfall and now his disgrace. As for Boudreau, he is the turncoat we suspected."

Lucien shook his head. "What is even more laughable is that French officers entertained the British victors at a dinner party the night after Beauséjour's surrender."

Shaken, Sylvie went to a front window overlooking the harbor and the rise where Beauséjour had once stood strong.

In the days following, as the smoke cleared and news grew thin, there came an uneasy lull. Was the new commandant at Fort Cumberland awaiting further orders?

18

You forget that the fruits belong to all and that the land
belongs to no one.

Jean-Jacques Rousseau

Bleu returned with Kitani and a party of Mi'kmaq.
They camped on the edges of Galant land and posted
patrols around the clock. Sylvie felt safer but sensed
another storm was brewing.

"Soon the English will seize your very lands like your
weapons." Bleu stood by the kitchen hearth and told them
the harsh truth late that night. "Your choices are limited.
You can leave with the Mi'kmaq and go west to French-held
territory, or you can flee to Ile Royale or Ile Saint-Jean like
so many."

"The islands are naught but rock." Père gave a vehement
shake of his head. "Little will grow there, and that is why
the people are starving and living in hovels. And don't forget
the plague of black field mice and locusts, followed by their
recent drought."

"And if we stay?" Pascal asked.

"You will be burned out or have all that you own taken by English settlers in time," Bleu said.

Sylvie wanted to cover Marie-Madeleine's ears. For once, Mère seemed to forget to shield her. Marie-Madeleine sat on the hearth, her dolls in her lap, her face expressionless, as if the thought of losing their home was inconceivable. Struck dumb herself, Sylvie pondered her usual tasks with appreciation, realizing with a sense of panic that they might be lost at any moment.

"I choose to believe the best of these English officers." Père drew a deep breath, his muscled chest rising and falling like a swell. "Men like Monckton have allowed us to remain unmolested under an oath of neutrality till now. We dutifully send delegates to Chibouctou—"

"Pardon, Père," Pascal said, "but Chibouctou has been renamed the English Halifax, remember."

Père expelled a breath. "Whatever it is called, we send our delegates regularly to discuss important matters that arise. I advocate for that to continue."

"That is all in the past." Bleu's usual stoicism showed a flash of exasperation. "These new leaders—Lawrence and Cornwallis and others—show no conciliatory attitudes like their predecessors. They have labeled all Acadians the enemy and will treat them as such."

"So with the fall of Beauséjour, we now forfeit all to them?" Lucien asked. "Our homes, our lands and livestock, the very harvest that will soon be upon us?"

"We are prisoners of war, then," Pascal stated flatly.

"All that and more." Bleu's certainty was chilling. "You have little time to waste. Delay might well mean death." He got up from the table and went outside. He didn't stay away from his Mi'kmaq brothers for long, at least of late.

Sylvie followed, wanting a private word with him. Catching up with his long stride near the well, she touched his arm.

"I wanted to tell you about the man who came here shortly before the English arrived demanding our guns."

He stopped and looked down at her in the moonlight, his scarred face making her flinch. Perhaps word of such a stalwart ally might cheer him. In truth, she wanted to learn more about the man who'd appeared without warning and been so chivalrous.

"He asked for you by name." The moment was unforgettable. "He goes by Le Loup. Or perhaps that is on account of his wolf dog. Do you know him?"

Bleu stared at her blankly. Had he not understood?

She stumbled on. "He is tall—taller than you and nearly as dark. He has a most unusual manner—"

"I do not know him, but I know of him." Bleu's hand moved to the hatchet at his waist. "And he is no friend but foe."

The bottom dropped out of her stomach. "An enemy?"

Bleu's eyes were flinty. "What discourse did he have with you?"

Sylvie swallowed, feeling she'd committed some trespass. "He simply appeared when I came out of the barn after the morning milking." The memory of the spilled milk—rather, his kneeling and wiping off her shoes—would never leave her. There'd been a graciousness in that gesture, a courtesy that rang true. In that moment he seemed not foe but friend. "He was pleasant, so pleasant that I offered him a cup of cider."

"Provisioning the enemy," he muttered bitterly.

"How could I have known?" she exclaimed. "Who is he?"

"Le Loup. Le Diable Blanc." Bleu's face hardened. "He is called many names, none of them remotely pleasant."

In the stunned silence, all her misconceptions were righted. "He works for the enemy . . . and he is after you as one of the leaders of the Resistance."

"He seeks me as I seek him, but . . ." He rubbed a hand

across his stubbled jaw. "Le Loup is as elusive as a phantom. He appears suddenly and strikes, conducting raids that make most men cower. When pursued, he leaves no trace yet often takes prisoners wherever he goes. He is so revered in New England it is said church bells are rung at his appearing." He spat into the dirt. "And now he knows I have a lovely sister. Somehow that does not sit well with me."

"Surely this man has a name."

"You have only heard of him till now." Bleu turned away, clearly done with the conversation. "He is none other than Major William Blackburn, founder of Blackburn's Rangers."

The summer harvest commenced without more trouble, making it seem the unrest with the English was a bad dream. Would the enemy be content with Fort Cumberland née Beauséjour and nothing more?

Pondering it, Sylvie worked in the fields alongside her family and their neighbors as she'd always done to thresh the wheat and then the corn. Never had the grain been so rich, so abundant. More than enough to get them through the coming winter and share generously, as was their custom. She could see why Père did not want to abandon it as some Acadians were. Sylvie held on to the slight hope that somehow peace would be reached and they could continue as before.

Though she knew Bleu wouldn't like it, she couldn't push William Blackburn from her mind. He was clearly the enemy, a threat to her beloved brother. To all Acadians. That alone should have deterred her. But this stranger had somehow carved an inroad into her head if not her heart. A dozen little details about him bedeviled her. She wished he had been anything but gallant.

But his was no different from Boudreau's false gallantry,

staged to lure her into revealing her brother's whereabouts. Le Loup—no, le serpent! The man who'd slid down a mountain after fighting a battle on snowshoes. Who had been a prisoner of the French to their ultimate detriment, learning their language and customs and plans. Who could appear and then vanish like a phantom. Who was wholly intent on their demise.

And she had stood talking with him, believing him to be with the Resistance, and even offered him the best of their cider.

19

[The Acadians] must be transported to some place where mingling with our subjects, they will soon lose their language, their religion, and the remembrance of the past.

Governor Richard Philipps

I n early August, Fort Cumberland's new English commandant, Robert Monckton, ordered all Acadian men in the district to meet and hear the reading of the orders of His Excellency the Governor. A fierce debate ensued in the Galant household as to the wisdom of complying. Monckton insisted the governor of Halifax only wanted the people to gather concerning arrangements for the conservation of their farms. Still, every Acadian village hummed with suspicion, and in the end only half of Acadie's men met Monckton's demand. Père went, but Pascal and Lucien did not. As for Bleu, he was again unaccounted for. Sylvie knew he would have advised Père not to go just as he'd advised their family to flee to the Mi'kmaq.

Within hours, they realized Père's folly. The fort's gates were locked, the Acadians who'd gathered there made prisoners. All were declared rebels, their lands and habitations

131

forfeit to the Crown. Mère burst into tears when she found out Père wasn't coming home. At once their very lives seemed drained of strength and purpose, the emptiness profound.

Monckton had ordered the women to provision their men. But what if this was a ruse meant to entrap the women too? Though her brothers cautioned her against going, Sylvie filled a haversack with food, including the first of their apple crop hauled in a cart. Wary, she joined a large group of friends and family intent on the fort, baskets on their arms and backs.

The sight of the former Fort Beauséjour partly destroyed by mortars, as well as the burned church and habitations surrounding it, shook her to her soul. Sylvie traipsed around debris to reach the fort's sally port. There, redcoats took their provisions, making her wonder if Père would ever get them. Though the women left singing the old, beloved songs as if to encourage their imprisoned men, Sylvie's heart stayed at her feet.

Marie-Madeleine was waiting at the window when Sylvie returned, looking older than her years. "Will Père never come back?"

Sylvie bent and kissed her sister's brow but could say nothing encouraging.

"We must pray unceasingly," Mère replied, her voice wavering. "I feel Père and the others will be with us soon."

With so many men now entrapped within fort walls—and not only at Fort Cumberland—morale and cleanliness deteriorated rapidly. Word of similar happenings at other fallen French forts reached the Galants, and the acrid stench of smoke from burned-out villages across Acadie could not be escaped.

"You must hide," Mère told her sons. "At least until the worst has passed. If things become peaceful, you can return. Since you did not go to the fort as ordered, you are now rebels on the run. Le Loup and those like him will hunt you down. You mustn't be here when they return."

"How can we leave you?" Pascal looked near tears himself. "You are alone here with our sisters. Unprotected. These redcoats will take advantage of that."

"God is with us. And I have no peace while you are here." She began packing haversacks for him and Lucien. "The harvesting has stopped as our fields are no longer our own, nor are their yield. There is nothing more for you to do."

"Père's guns are hidden beneath the porch stoop. You and Sylvie know how to use them," Lucien said. "Though I will take one with us to hunt."

"We will not be far," Pascal promised. "We will keep an eye on you."

"If things worsen and we are cast out of our habitations, you must join our Mi'kmaq allies," Mère insisted as they embraced. "Above all else, keep praying—and hoping."

They clung the longest to Marie-Madeleine, who was shaken by great, heaving sobs, and finally left after dark so as not to be seen. In their wake, Sylvie felt a writhing anguish unlike she'd ever known, her mounting fury choking out tears.

⁓

Bonami sniffed the ground at Will's feet as if possessed. Will's company of Rangers, thinned to a dozen for this foray, stood wary and watchful, even winded as they halted their uphill climb in the heat-ridden woods. The shackled Resistance captives, five in number, glowered at him the nearer they came to the fallen Beauséjour.

"Major Blackburn, sir . . ."

One of his Mohegans gestured to a wolf's paw, claws intact. It dangled on a rawhide string from a low branch along the deer trail oft used by Resistance fighters coming to and from the former fort.

A warning? If so, a not-too-subtle sign.

Will took the paw in hand, noting Indian beadwork on the underside. His gaze swung to the woods as that shadowed feeling returned, raising the hair on the back of his neck. "Double the rear and advance guard," he said, tearing the paw free and tucking it into his shirt.

They reached Fort Cumberland at dusk to find it being repaired from the June assault. Here they turned over their prisoners before going over the ridge to Fort Lawrence. They wended through soldiers and camp followers and peddlers, Will's gaze falling on the burned-out Catholic church. Surrounding it were herds of Acadian cattle packed tight into pens to feed the British army. Countless hogsheads of grain lay about while untold quantities were being destroyed that might have fed New England's poor.

Such needless waste turned him surly, as did the knowledge of Acadian men held behind the fort's high stone walls. Men deprived of their weapons. Men who Nova Scotia's Governor Lawrence believed were supplying the French with intelligence, quarters, provisions, and assistance. In the eyes of the British authorities, those at Chignecto and Beaubassin were the worst of the offenders.

The Rangers' arrival at Fort Lawrence was met with muted Saturday night revelry, kegs of rum rolled out. After spending an hour behind closed doors in Monckton's secured casemate, Will retreated to his tent at the edge of camp, hard-pressed to conceal his mounting turmoil. Meeting with the commandant left him feeling flummoxed and fooled, Governor Lawrence's terse words thundering in his head.

These French Catholics must be evicted from these lands at the muzzles of our guns and at the points of our swords.

Will ducked inside his tent as Bonami settled outside. The airless interior lent to his vexation as the latest order ate at him. That elusive peace he'd felt in the abandoned Acadian chapel had long since departed—and a short bark alerted him that any needed privacy was short-lived.

"Major Blackburn." Hugh's rolling Scottish lilt sounded outside the tent entrance. "A word with you, if I may."

"Aye," Will replied tersely, lighting a lantern at the back of the tent as the captain entered.

"Care to join me at cards?" Hugh flashed a deck, reminding him they'd not played since they'd been aboard ship.

"It's not gaming you're after but details about my meeting with Monckton," Will replied.

Hugh's grin was both sly and sheepish. "Both, actually."

Will gestured to a folding stool, in no more mood for cards than talk.

"Let me guess," Hugh said, taking a seat. "Monckton and his minions have made another wrong move."

Will relived the heated moment over again, the storm inside him widening. "Governor Lawrence as well as Monckton want to detain us."

"Detain us? In truth, they want to be rid of us as much as they do the Acadians. They only put up with us because we do what they cannot, thrashing about in the backcountry. Those English regulars and officers revile us irregular Rangers."

"'Revile' is too tame a word."

Hugh lapsed into silence as if waiting for Will to elaborate. Finally, the captain said, "Word about camp is that Lawrence intends to keep our companies here till all the Acadians are loaded on ships and deported, which makes no sense as there aren't enough ships as it is."

"More transports are coming from Boston. Aged hulks that are hardly seaworthy." Will sifted through the harrowing details. "I told him we would by no means stay on, that General Braddock's orders are to return us to Ticonderoga, and any offer of transport is unnecessary as we have our own sloops waiting."

"I'm sure he did not offer you a brandy at that."

Nay. Monckton had been livid, his face nearly the scarlet of his uniform.

Hugh began shuffling cards. "My fear is that this foolish business will drag on till winter, a foul enough time to transport livestock, much less human beings."

Weary, Will sat on a camp chair, the lantern light buffeted by the wind. "None of these English officials have authority from the Lords of Trade in London to remove the Acadians."

"How many are there?"

"Some fifteen thousand souls." Will fixed his gaze on a tent peg as if it could somehow anchor him. "The Acadians at Chignecto and Chipoudy Bay will be first."

"Where will they be transported?"

Will was no longer listening, the unrest inside him was so intense. He'd stepped back to that moment when Sylvie Galant set down her milk pails and faced him. She had thought him one of the Resistance. He had let her believe the lie. In fact, he had fed it. And she would soon be rounded up and made to leave everything she'd ever known, along with the little girl dancing around the well with the striped cat on her heels—every last one of the Galants.

A sergeant ducked into the tent somewhat hesitantly after announcing himself, as if sensing Will's mood. "Your supper, sir."

Will couldn't—wouldn't—eat. His thoughts were crammed full of English arrogance and scheming, his throat so knotted he said nothing as the plate was set down atop the table before the sergeant retreated. Greasy beans and bacon and some sort of black bread. If it had been the finest fare, it wouldn't have mattered. With a whistle, Will sent the plate to the ground, and Bonami came through the tent's entrance to partake of what his master couldn't.

"As you've stated so oft of late," Hugh said, "it's one thing to fight those intent on your scalp but another matter entirely to wage war on a neutral people." He expelled a tense breath. "It's been a bungled mess from the beginning. These officers' monumental pride blinds them."

Will took a steadying breath. "Monckton wants one more foray. He's determined we bring in more Resistance fighters, especially the elusive Bleu."

Hugh frowned. "But the Resistance is now more deadly—and harder to detain—than ever, given all that is at stake."

"As I told Monckton, I'm done. My Rangers are done. He can take the matter up with Braddock if he so chooses." Will reached into his hunting shirt, withdrew the wolf's paw, and hung it from a tent pole. "There is no reason to stay on here—and no reasoning with the English's evil intent."

20

Reason is not what decides love.

Molière

Sylvie rued she spoke English. Every epithet she heard at Fort Cumberland's gates, every rebuff and insult, lodged in her heart and head like Mi'kmaq arrows. Never would she forget these merciless men and their cruelty. Day after day she and other Acadian women were met at the sally port but not allowed to enter. She stood on tiptoe, hoping for a glance of Père as guards took all they had brought, then emptied their baskets and haversacks into the dirt. Countless loaves of bread, vegetables, meat, and freshly picked fruit disappeared behind fort walls.

Would their men even get a taste? Or would the English consume it like everything else?

"Jean-Luc!" one woman cried out, trying to dart inside a narrow opening.

A cursing guard shoved her to the ground with such force Sylvie feared he'd snap her bones. As the Acadians rushed to aid her, Sylvie felt a hot, murderous fury pour through her. The woman was helped to her feet, and together they turned away from the hostility to begin the long walk home.

Nauseous and shaking, Sylvie kept to the rear. None of the women looked back to see if she followed, so profound was their distress. As misery overrode her usual good sense, Sylvie took a less traveled trail, favored by Bleu, that led home a different way. Alone and allowed her own pace, she watched the lush woods for any sign of the brother she'd not seen for some time. Was he now penned up somewhere like Père? Hunted down by the stranger who'd been so brazen at the well? She refused to think of the enemy as gallant.

How quickly the forest's summer splendor turned menacing with the enemy lurking. Oh, why had she left the company of the other women? Would she add to Mère's heartache by placing herself in harm's way? Beset by a dozen detestable possibilities, she quickened her steps till she was almost running toward the opening in the shadowed woods that spilled out onto a sunlit beach.

She was nearly to the light when a rustle in the brush spun her around. Just behind her lurked the wolf dog, regarding her as if she was raw meat. She wanted to bolt, but the thought of being pounced on from behind was worse than facing the trouble.

The creature suddenly dropped to the forest floor with a whine. Was it hungry?

Bread crumbs littered the bottom of her basket. She gathered them up and held out her hand, bracing herself for a snarl or a bite. But the creature—Bonami—ate gently, tickling her open palm. Chary, she sensed his master was not far, though she heard no footfall, not even the rustle of brush as revulsion rolled through her.

Out of the corner of her eye she watched William Blackburn come toward her noiselessly, clearly as surprised to see her as she was him. "Mademoiselle Galant."

Her heart beat hard beneath her sweat-stained shift as she met his eyes. Her taut tone was bitter. "What have you done with my brother?"

"Nothing. I have not been able to find him."

"Are you lying like you did at the well that day?"

"Today I have no cause to bend the truth." Wiping his brow with his linen sleeve, he rested the butt of his rifle on the ground. "I've not seen Bleu, though I have been charged to find him and bring him in along with other leaders of the Resistance."

He stood behind Bonami, an arm's length away, so close she could see sun lines crouched at the corners of his eyes. An insect bite swelled his right cheek, and numerous scratches marred his darkened skin as if he'd plowed straight through brambles.

"You shouldn't be here." His gaze shot past her to the surrounding woods. "It's dangerous with so many English soldiers hungry for more than victuals."

She took a step back, her face feeling fevered. He spoke the truth. Had Mère not warned her? Even Blackburn could harm her and none would know, nor would a scrap of justice be forthcoming.

Her fingers tightened round the basket handle till her nails bit into her palm. "Leave Bleu and the others alone. They are only trying to defend us. Our lives. Our lands. Would you not do the same if your own territory was being taken?"

"Aye." He stepped around her, gun in hand. "I'll escort you back."

More faux gallantry? "No."

Her refusal was met with a terse, "I insist."

Fighting tears, she started after him and Bonami as the trail wound down to the sand dunes and sheltered coves of the bay.

"You have other brothers," he said quietly over his shoulder.

How did he know?

"Where are they?"

She clamped her mouth shut, her distress over Pascal and Lucien's absence growing by the day. Though she sensed they hovered around their homeplace, ready to leap to their family's defense at a moment's notice, they remained out of sight.

"Answer me, mademoiselle."

She shook her head, trying not to cry.

Once they'd reached shore, he walked beside her atop sun-warmed rocks and sand. If she worried his focus was on her, she needn't have. His gaze never settled, as restless as her roiling insides. And it struck her hard that he was as much hunted as hunter. Anguish formed another knot inside her, tightening her chest and causing her to open her mouth to breathe.

"Tell them to stay away. Join up with the Mi'kmaq." His words seemed forceful as if he were issuing an order. "I'd advise you to do the same."

Tears blurred the path they trod. "And forsake my father, who is penned up in the fort?"

"He's soon to be penned up in the hold of a ship."

So the rumors were true. "Just the men?"

"All of you. Governor Lawrence and the English officers will stop at nothing till every Acadian is rounded up and transported." He expelled a breath. "Or killed."

"Why are you telling me this?"

He stopped and faced her. "Because you should know the evil coming against you."

"You are part of that evil—"

"Nay." His eyes shone with a convicting zeal. "When I accepted orders, I knew nothing about this. I want nothing to do with forcing peace-abiding people from their homes and lands, especially women and children. That makes us no better than savages."

"You are savages! That is the very word for all of you who deal so treacherously with a people who've done you no harm." She was crying now, her composure spent. "When you took our guns and then our men, you left us alone and defenseless." Her words came in winded bursts as she fought for control. "And now you—you will herd us all like sheep—onto ships. But where?"

"I know not."

"You care not."

"I care more than you realize or would believe." He reached inside his shirt and stepped toward her, passing her a handkerchief, before he began walking again.

She stared at the fine cloth, struck that it was the one he'd used to clean the milk from her sabots. It only fueled her wild fury. "I do not want your sympathy, nor your handkerchief," she shouted after him. "I want to be left alone!"

When he did not respond, she trailed after him, drying her eyes with the detested piece of cloth as they moved inland again through a stand of pine, summer's heat turned fragrant. A warbler sang on a low branch, so sweet it made her heart hurt all the more. She should be in the orchards picking fruit, birds all about her, the tang of apples sweet. Her thoughts leapt ahead to cider-making and all the stolen joys of autumn. A thousand beloved images assailed her, and she grabbed hold of them like a child did its mother's skirts, unwilling to let go.

Their homeland. Invaded. Thieved. Violated. Where would they be sent? What would she miss most?

Voice ragged, she flung a final question at him. "Do you English—"

He swung round to face her again. "I am not English."

She drew up short. "Do these English not fear God—His judgment?"

"They answer to no god but themselves."

She stared at him, meeting his eyes though she didn't want to. He spoke his mind. Not thin platitudes or sugared reassurances but the unvarnished truth.

"I'll go no farther. It wouldn't be wise for you to be seen with the enemy," he told her. "You'll not encounter me again. I sail with the tide." His eyes met hers a final time. "Bon courage."

She opened her mouth to thank him out of habit, then bit her tongue, knowing he no more expected her thanks than she was willing to give it. Without another word she left him at a run toward home, his handkerchief clutched in one fist.

21

Heat not a furnace for your foe so hot that it do singe yourself.

William Shakespeare

Unable to sleep, Will left the Fort Lawrence encampment at midnight to come down to the bay, where the Rangers' sloops lay at anchor with the rest of the fleet. Guards had been posted, but none looked askance at him as he commandeered a rowboat. Bonami remained on shore and gave a sharp yip of displeasure as Will rowed out to the *Constellation*, feeling more at home on it than the *Onondaga*.

He climbed the boarding ladder to the main deck, the full moon bright as a lantern. If he'd expected to leave his misery behind by changing locations, he was sorely disappointed. Bursts of laughter from the captain's cabin below his feet aggravated his angst. They were at cards, likely, rejoicing in an imminent sailing. Still celebrating Beauséjour's fall, full of rum and arrogance.

Was that how Sylvie Galant saw him?

He sat down on the top step leading to the quarterdeck,

turned away from the sight of the forts on the ridge and Galant land. His view was the starlit opening to Chignecto Basin, which, come morning, he and his companies would pass through to open ocean.

He was done with the British. Done with the Acadians. Done with—

A sudden, hard thud brought him to his feet. At the corner of his vision he saw a moving shadow, as if someone had been hiding in the rigging of the foremast and leapt to deck. His hand went to the knife sheathed at his side, every sense heightened. But the shadow was faster, flashing past him before delivering a stinging blow to his backside with such force it sent him to the deck. He rolled over, knife extended, to thwart another blow. The shadow was in front of him now, not phantom but flesh. Will scrambled to his feet, then lunged at his assailant before he could strike again.

Back and forth they stepped as if they had swords instead of hunting knives. Will pulled his tomahawk from his belt, both hands weighted with weaponry, the glint of moonlight shining off steel. And he knew to his marrow who his adversary was.

Bleu.

Will lunged and Bleu lost hold of his knife. It skidded across the deck's planking toward Will, who kicked it behind him. As Bleu raised his tomahawk, Will tackled him, dropping his own weapons to wrestle with the man who seemed a wall of muscle and sinew. After stealing the remaining weapon away from him, Will flung it into the darkness. They rolled painfully atop unforgiving wood, each of them gaining then losing the advantage in a furious, near-fatal contest.

Bleu was dripping wet and slippery as an eel but fought like a panther, no second wasted. Will's breath came hard as he tried to pin him down, to no avail. His enemy seemed driven by an uncontainable rage that pulsated in his every move and gave him extraordinary strength.

Bleu's choking neck hold seemed Will's inglorious finish.

Desperate to breathe, Will slammed an elbow backward into Bleu and broke his grip. Drained, he pulled himself to his feet and faced Bleu, who held himself upright though he seemed unsteady. They stood a few feet apart, chests heaving and visibly battered.

When the moon slipped free of a cloud, Will's soul stood still. He saw Sylvie Galant in Bleu's silvered features.

"For God's sake, end this!" Will spat out the words with blood running from his mouth. "For your sister's sake."

A second's hesitation, and then, with a move as fast and furious as the one that brought him onto deck, Bleu sprinted toward the stern. He dove over the side of the sloop, the splash of the bay his farewell.

Stunned and shredded of strength, Will made it to a barrel and sat down, the gash on his head stinging and his chest still heaving. He could hear Bonami barking from shore.

Two crewmen appeared from below, staggeringly drunk. And then an English voice shouted from shore, "All well, Major Blackburn?"

Will could not answer. All the fight had gone out of him.

22

The inhabitants, sadly and with great sorrow, abandoned their homes. The women, in great distress, carried their newborn or their youngest children in their arms. Others pulled carts with their household effects and crippled parents. It was a scene of confusion, despair, and desolation.

Colonel John Winslow

When the women went to the fort with food the next day, they found their men missing. They had been loaded onto transport ships in the bay, an officer said, his cobbled French barely understandable. But this was told them after the English took their goods, leaving them empty-handed and more empty-hearted. No one would inform them which men were on what ships, though they were told families would be kept together. Staring out at the entire hulking fleet crawling with English soldiers made Sylvie sink to her knees, overwhelming anguish forcing her to the sandy ground.

The next day the order came for all Acadian women and children to be at the waterfront to board the ships at dawn. A frantic despair gripped the Galant women as they decided what to take and what to leave behind. Mère was more concerned with people than possessions.

"Grandmère is hardly able to walk," she said. "We will have to transport her in the cart."

"I will fit it out for her, then," Sylvie said, carrying quilts and bedding to the barn where the cart waited.

Done with that, she woodenly turned the cows and calves out of their stalls, then let loose the pigs and chickens. She'd heard the enemy had taken and also destroyed much of the Acadian beeves meant for Louisbourg. Père's pride had been his large herd. She could hardly take in the loss.

Before dawn, the Galants stood before the only home Sylvie had ever known, the broken windows boarded up rather than replaced. It had become a shell without Père and her brothers. She looked about, willing Pascal and Lucien to come and say goodbye but knowing they would be in danger if they did. Still, it seemed yet another cruelty to be denied a parting with those they loved.

Sylvie managed the pony cart while a white-faced Mère and a tearful Marie-Madeleine walked with a large number of friends and neighbors to the waterfront, bringing their most needed possessions. Numerous longboats already plied the bay, carrying Acadians to the waiting ships. In the long line, Sylvie waited her turn with all the rest.

As she watched the soldiers with their bayoneted muskets poke and prod them forward like livestock, Bleu's oft-repeated words came to her.

Like lions, not sheep.

How could they be lions when all was mayhem and madness? Wailing and praying women. Screaming infants and terrified children. Even the skies wept, a hard, cold rain soaking them and turning their garments chill and heavy. Finally, someone began singing the old Acadian songs and others followed suit, though it brought little comfort to Sylvie and seemed only to aggravate the soldiers.

"Whatever happens, we must stay together," Mère said, as if tying an invisible cord around them with her words.

"Are we not on the same boat as Père?" Marie-Madeleine's confusion halted them for a moment.

"We were promised, oui," Mère answered. "But it would be a miracle if so."

They filled the longboats, packed together like dried, salted cod into hogsheads, most of their belongings abandoned on shore in the melee. Sylvie kept hold of Marie-Madeleine's hand and her own haversack as Mère and a cousin tried to help Grandmère from the cart into a boat, only to have soldiers intervene and take Grandmère away. The cousin ran after them while Mère turned toward Sylvie, tears cascading down her face like the rain.

"Come into the boat, Mère," Sylvie cried as it filled and left no room for her. "Quickly!"

As the vessel pushed off, Mère managed to climb aboard. Sylvie's heart thrashed so hard against her chest in relief she couldn't breathe. The haversack on her back grew heavier, Marie-Madeleine's hand tighter.

All around her came sobs and shouts. Rain beat down harder as soldiers began pushing and shoving the remaining Acadians into whatever cargo boats had room, separating families. Her soaked cap dripping into her face, Sylvie watched in horror as the fulfilling life they'd known shattered like centuries-old stained glass. Tearing her gaze from Mère and Marie-Madeleine's stricken faces, she took a last look across the pockmarked bay toward home. Did Pascal and Lucien watch from shore?

The *Dolphin* loomed ahead of them, unlike any ship Sylvie had ever seen, its high sides an impenetrable wall. As she was used to whaling boats and canoes, these immense transports lined her spine with ice.

Once on deck, the women and children were pushed below into the pitch blackness of the hold, so cold and reeking of flesh and fear that Sylvie's stomach nearly gave way.

And she realized again she knew not where they were going.

⌇

As time ticked by without them setting sail, Sylvie's unease grew. Allowed on deck but a few minutes each day, she tried to overhear what the soldiers assigned to the *Dolphin* murmured about. Was it that there were too few ships and too many Acadians? And too few soldiers and crew, only eight per vessel? When a few Acadians on another ship escaped, overpowering the enemy, it sent the *Dolphin*'s soldiers into a fury.

As they languished at anchor for days on end, sickness broke out. Denied light and fresh air, even a chamber pot, Sylvie felt her spirits plummet further along with those of everyone trapped below.

Mère spoke into the darkness when Marie-Madeleine slept. "There is no hope in this hold."

"I fear for us all," Sylvie answered. "We are said to be bound for the colonies, but we remain at anchor."

"I wonder if your père is with the imprisoned Resistance on another ship—or even Bleu." Her voice wavered. "I wonder about my own father and mother . . ."

Sylvie sensed the old and sick would not last long in such conditions, nor even the children. Their constant cries and restlessness rent her heart. Her own skin itched from lack of washing just as her throat grew parched from lack of water. Villainous pork and moldy bread were given to them, but the food was unpalatable even to their ravenous stomachs.

The weather worsened, and without heat, the cold sank to their bones.

With nothing to do but sit, Sylvie's limbs grew cramped. Only her mind was free to roam, and it took her dangerous places, circling back to those terrifying words.

You should know the evil coming against you.

The evil had come. It pulsated all around her, thick and black and unruly as a horde of gray wolves with no restraining hand.

What had become of William Blackburn?

She wearied of his name thundering through her thoughts again and again. From here on, she would push him away and think of him only as *the Scot*. So vile a man didn't deserve to be named. Even Le Loup was too good for him. The day he had walked her through the woods seemed long ago. He had been bent on leaving then. By now he must be far from here, his mission accomplished, returning to the war waging elsewhere.

The next day during her time on the upper deck, she saw great billows of black smoke from the direction of their habitations. Were their homes being destroyed to prevent their return? Smoke swirled above nearly every Acadian farm she knew, and her chest tightened so much she had to open her mouth to breathe. She could not bear to tell her mother or sister.

She realized the flint-faced Captain Hancock watched her in her brief walkabout. Did he not notice the horror of the two hundred in the hold? Their tears? Did he not feel remorse? She bit her lip till it bled to keep from crying out, rage and anguish warring inside her.

Hours later, without warning, they set sail in a frigid dawn. The convoy of transports navigated Chignecto Basin into Baie Française escorted by men-of-war, then moved out to the open Atlantic. Rough seas had them retching, the hold's putrid deck covered with more than excrement.

Sylvie half lay, half sat, too ill to get up or clean herself, though she did clutch Marie-Madeleine's limp hand. Her sister was not only violently ill but feverish. No fresh water could be had, and the hatch was kept shut because of foul weather, sealing them in utter darkness.

Soon they were six less than they had been, the bodies taken up and tossed overboard. The moans and cries of others pressed around her as the battered ship rose and fell in great shuddering surges that seemed like Hades itself.

I prefer death.

"Mère," Sylvie called as the ship lurched again and an eerie lull ensued.

No answer. Another heave and roll and Sylvie held Marie-Madeleine, who retched again, only there was so little in their stomachs there was nothing left to vomit.

Where was Dieu in such a storm? Why had He let such evil prevail?

Bon courage.

Was that what William Blackburn had said to her at the last? Would those be the last words she would remember before her own watery death?

23

After Confering 2 with Majr Murray it is agreed that the
Villages in our different districts be destroyed immediately.

From the journal of Governor Charles Lawrence

S nowflakes sifted down onto the main deck and turned
Sylvie's sabots to skates. No longer were they in a convoy. Since the storm, the fleet had been scattered. Some
ships were reported sunk. The grim faces of both sailors and
soldiers haunted her. Not knowing where they were headed
or if Père and other kin were alive or dead clawed at her along
with the vermin eating at her scalp and skin.

As weight fell from her once generous frame and her
parched throat grew more raw, memories of her family's
deep, cold well tormented her, as did the stubborn image of
the Scot drawing water to wipe her shoes clean. Oh, if she
could but go back in time . . . try to reverse the horrendous
present.

Mère refused to leave the hold for her few minutes of
fresh air, Marie-Madeleine in her arms. She stayed below in
the filth and stench, watching over her fast-fading youngest
daughter. They'd lost track of how much time they'd been

at sea, nor was any hope given them of when they'd make landfall. Life seemed measured in bodies thrown overboard and rough weather.

"She has not long now," Mère whispered one night, her voice breaking.

Sylvie set her jaw against the anguish of it all, fearing her teeth would crack. "You must sleep, Mère. God watches over her." But even as she spoke the words, she failed to believe them.

By morning, Marie-Madeleine was gone, wrapped in a soiled sheet and pitched overboard. Sylvie sensed Mère would be next, dying more from grief than hunger and disease.

"My life is over," Mère said. "Without your father and our home, what have I?"

"We have each other, Mère. We will try to return to Acadie and find Pascal and Lucien and Bleu—"

"Take my bundle—and your sister's." Mère was crying, but her lifelong practicality held sway. "You still have the gems, Père's money." She took a ragged breath as if the very life was leaving her. "I feel sick to my soul."

That night they slept, but it was a sleep torn by exhaustion and fear. Sylvie awoke to the groan of timbers and that deep, unsettling motion that only a fierce gale wrought. When frigid seawater washed into the hold, drenching them and turning them to ice, it seemed they were gripped by a watery hand so violent she knew it was un ouragan. A hurricane.

Eyes shut tight, she prayed for an end to their misery as every soul below but the most sick wept and cried out. Sylvie swallowed past the bile in her throat to do the last thing she felt capable of. Barely heard above the storm, she sang.

"A la claire fontaine . . . M'en allant promener . . . J'ai trouve l'eau si belle." *At the clear spring . . . as I was strolling by . . . I found the water so nice.*

She kept on till the last memory she had was of other voices joining in, strengthening her own.

Water. Water everywhere. Not fresh but salt. It tore off her apron and cap even as it washed down her throat. Her haversack was lashed to her back. Mère had seen to that in the darkness as her fumbling hands tied frantic knots. A wave knocked them down, and Sylvie struggled to stand, trying to hold on to Mère's slippery hands. But there was too much water, too much wind—and then a sudden, swirling blow to her head.

"Ici!" The masculine voice held an authority that brought her out of the blackness. "Help this one!"

Firm handling jarred her further. She began choking on seawater as hands turned her over to clear her lungs. Someone spoke kindly to her in French as time ceased and she was pulled from her pain and confusion to safety.

Too weak to sit up, lungs burning, she lay in another boat's bottom, aware of the sodden haversack poking at her bony back. Shadowy figures grew more distinct as dawn parted the darkness like a golden, sea-washed curtain.

Mère . . . Mère.

Sylvie's eyes opened and tried to focus. Other figures in the boat—faces she had rarely seen because of the hold's darkness—took shape. But not her mother's. The sea, so violent hours before, seemed to have spent itself and now lay flat as glass, reflecting the rising sun. She craved warmth, the hearth's fire of home, and her own closet bed.

English voices mingled with French as she was lifted and removed from the boat. Her head was cradled against a strong shoulder, so different from Père's bearish embrace. A light passed before her eyes, and then she was taken up steps and heard the squeak of door hinges.

Soothing voices took hold. Sylvie's sodden garments were removed by careful hands, causing her to reach in a panic for her haversack. There it was, so wet it sat in a puddle atop the plank floor. Firelight spread warmth over a small room that bore a bed and simple furnishings. An older woman and a girl moved the bed from the wall nearer the hearth, away from the chamber's cold corners.

"I'll bring up a tray of soup and bread straightaway," the woman said in English. "She looks to be nigh starved and has clearly been through more than the storm. The captain is trying to determine from whence she and the other surviving passengers came." She left, her step heavy on the stairs.

The girl took out a comb and began to untangle Sylvie's hair. "You're in need of a hot bath when you're strong enough, though I do wonder if you ken a word I'm saying."

Sylvie fought through the haze of exhaustion to answer. "I do."

"Are you able to tell me what brought you to our shore, then?"

Sylvie's eyes roamed the plain walls in confusion. "Where am I?"

"Indigo Island off the Virginia coast. Captain Lennox and his crew rescued you. I'm Annie, bound girl to Mistress Saltonstall here at the tavern. And you are . . . ?"

"Sylvie Galant of Acadie." She swallowed with difficulty, causing the girl to turn to the near table for a cup of water.

"Please, miss, say nae more till you've refreshed yourself."

Sylvie drank deeply, wondering if the island had a well or if she tasted rainwater.

The other woman reappeared, her manner brisk and practical. A tray was set down, the hot soup like the richest fare.

With Annie's help, Sylvie sat up, wobbly as a newborn lamb. The realization brought a razor-sharp pang as she recalled their herd of sheep and Marie-Madeleine's fanciful names for them. She reached for the spoon and swallowed some soup without sputtering, knowing she needed nourishment and strength for whatever was ahead.

"Only a few survived the shipwreck," Annie said quietly, looking toward the window as sun lit the panes. "The captain saw the *Dolphin* founder and helped all he could. Thankfully, by the time he and his men reached you and the others, the seas had calmed." She talked on as Sylvie ate slowly, answering her unspoken questions as if sensing all that lay beneath the surface. "They tried to rescue a child, but he drowned before they could. Some Frenchmen came in with you—and three women. For now all are here in Mistress Saltonstall's tavern. She's the woman who brought your tray."

Soup finished, Sylvie started on the bread, tearing off pieces of it and trying not to stuff it in her mouth all at once, she was so ravenous. She looked at her sodden haversack, unsure of what it still held and if it needed drying out.

Annie offered to bring it to her. "I can open it and dry out your belongings near the fire if you like."

Sylvie nodded, steeling herself against the rush of memories as Annie saw to the task. Careful hands pulled out the Lyonnais silk gown, bundled and tied with twine. Her one tie to Bleu. With a little murmur of appreciation, Annie draped it across a chair back, unfolding the petticoats to air out. Next came the pearls and garnets, none the worse for wear. The sewing kit and fur-wrapped scissors had survived. The bottom of the bag was weighted with Père's gold pieces, gathered in a small leather pouch blackened by water. How he'd saved and guarded them, securing them in a small crock in their cellar near the cider. The safest place, he'd said.

When the Scot's handkerchief appeared, Sylvie bit her lip. Why had she kept it?

With a look of sympathy, Annie set the empty haversack

aside. "'Tis best you sleep for now. I'll be near at hand should you need anything."

The next day the few Acadians rescued from the *Dolphin* gathered in the tavern's taproom downstairs. Though otherwise empty, it reminded Sylvie of the fête at Pont-a-Buot with the traitor Boudreau. Only there'd been no monkey in residence sitting atop a barrel near the flickering hearth. The creature cocked its head and yawned, baring its fangs. Sylvie almost smiled despite herself, but the tenor of the tavern was grim and her heart and body too battered for mirth.

Eyes down, she took a bench alongside refugees she did not know. Quiet introductions told her they were from Minas and Grand-Pré, a great distance from her family's habitation. As these Acadians rejoiced over being together again, their reunion sharpened her own loneliness. One by one they told their stories to the sympathetic yet stoic Captain Lennox and a few of his crew.

Sylvie realized anew the horror they'd lived through when so many had perished. She sensed to her marrow that Mère was gone, drowned in the storm when the *Dolphin*'s masts had snapped like sticks and sent them straight into the teeth of the hurricane.

When they'd finished, Captain Lennox leaned forward in his chair, hands clasped together. There was a straightforward intensity to his gaze that won Sylvie's confidence and at the same time reminded her of the Scot. "At present, we suspect other transport ships bearing Acadians are en route to our shores, likely part of the fleet that sailed south with you."

Sylvie digested this, hope taking hold. Could Père or any of her other family be among them?

"Unfortunately, Virginia Colony's governor claims he was

not apprised of your coming and is unwilling for any Acadians to disembark." The captain frowned, his French holding regret. "Once the ships are here, I'll meet with the captains and determine who is aboard and make you known to them in hopes of reuniting you with your kin."

A heavy silence ensued, rife with emotion.

"We thank you for all that you have done for us," one of the men said. "We did not want to leave our homes and lands to come here. We do not mean to stay."

"I understand." Captain Lennox looked to the monkey, which let out a frightful, nerve-rattling screech. "For now, I'll take you to the near port of York, where I'll lodge you before I go to the capital and meet with Governor Dinwiddie about the matter and await the other ships."

24

The superiority of chocolate, both for health and nourishment, will soon give it the preference over tea and coffee in America which it has in Spain.

Thomas Jefferson

By week's end, the few survivors of the *Dolphin* were ashore. In York, they lodged in a clean if spare tavern on Water Street with a view of the harbor. Eulalie Benoit of Grand-Pré shared her room and shed all the tears Sylvie could not, her own feelings wrapped in a tight ball of turmoil deep inside her.

"I'm thankful Captain Lennox is working tirelessly on our behalf, but it is so different here," Eulalie said when they walked about town. "How I wish I understood the English tongue."

"It's as if we've stepped into a different world," Sylvie said. Already she'd begun to think of Acadie as a sort of fairy tale. It belonged to the before. Now they were caught up in the after, which overflowed with strange, unwelcome sights and sounds and all the accompanying emotions.

Sylvie held tight to her haversack and looked up and down

160

Water Street. It was redolent of coffee and chocolate, fish and tar, a strange commingling. Her gaze fixed on a sign that swung about in the cold coastal wind. *Shaw's Chocolate.* Oh, to escape inside like the plum-gowned woman she'd just seen, while gentlemen came in and out of a coffeehouse next door.

Harsh English voices were everywhere, and the bustle and fuss all around them lent to her intimidation. Clad in the linen and wool garments Mistress Saltonstall had given her, Sylvie felt further at sea, though her feet were firmly planted on the dirty street, countless ships riding the water at her back. Did any of them hold newly arrived Acadian refugees?

Wanting to lift their spirits, Sylvie mustered the courage to enter Shaw's Chocolate shop. Eulalie hung back at first, clearly chary, gazing through the bow-fronted window that tempted with tall silver chocolate pots and pretty porcelain cups, sweetmeats and other confections.

The bell attached to the door jingled merrily as they stepped into a chocolate-laden world. A young woman greeted them, her colorful chintz gown drawing Sylvie's eye.

"What do you buy?" she queried with a smile.

Sylvie hesitated, wishing her French accent wasn't so pronounced. "We've come for a taste of colonial chocolate, if you please."

Understanding lit the woman's eyes, and she responded in French. "You must be among the French party Captain Lennox is concerned with." Surprisingly, her lovely smile did not dim. "A warm welcome, then. I am Esmée Shaw."

Sylvie dug in her pocket and placed a coin of Père's atop the counter, uncertainty seizing her. Did the English deal in such currency? "Is there enough for a small something?"

"More than enough," Esmée Shaw replied in French, returning the money to Sylvie. "As the chocolatier here, I invite you to anything your heart desires, free of charge."

Eulalie began to cry, heightening the tense if tender moment. Was she moved by this unexpected kindness, or was it simply hearing their own tongue spoken by an Englishwoman?

Sylvie murmured her thanks as a swarm of customers swept into the shop, sending the bell into a frenzy. Pressing a handkerchief into Eulalie's hand, Sylvie shrank back against one paneled wall. Eulalie composed herself, and they took in these genteel Virginians who bought coveted bricks of chocolate and all the accoutrements with which to enjoy them.

"Pardon," Esmée Shaw said once the shop emptied. She disappeared into a back room, then returned with two steaming cups in hand. "A chill day calls for hot chocolate, no?"

Cups brimming with the rich drink, Sylvie and Eulalie sat down upon an upholstered bench after expressing their thanks. As they sipped from glazed white mugs, the chocolatier began packaging sweetmeats and other delectables while another young woman who was clad more simply restocked their wares.

"Delicious, no?" Sylvie whispered, feeling the chill leave her bones.

Eulalie nodded and took another sip, then surrendered the damp handkerchief. "Tell me, where did you get such fine voile?"

Rent by the reminder of the man she didn't want to remember but couldn't forget, Sylvie looked at the linen square in her lap. It was woven in silk with a rolled hem, the initials WB embroidered at the top with a pattern of red stripes and black diamonds, as bold as its owner.

I do not want your sympathy, nor your handkerchief.

What would Eulalie say about her consorting with the enemy and having so personal a belonging?

At last Sylvie mumbled, "It belonged to someone I knew in Acadie."

Eulalie said no more, and they lapsed into a melancholy silence.

To their surprise, when they'd finished their chocolate, Esmée Shaw sent them away with enough confections to share with the rest of the Acadians lodging with them. That night they all gathered in the tavern's dining room to have supper and discuss what might happen next. They'd begun to rely on Sylvie, the sole English speaker other than Nicolas Surette, to inform them of any relevant news from the Virginia newspapers while they awaited Captain Lennox's return. In the waiting, they went round and round about their expulsion.

Why couldn't the Acadians have mounted a better defense and held their ground? Why hadn't Abbé Le Loutre stopped his incessant dike building and instead marshaled more Mi'kmaq and mowed the English down? Why had French military commanders capitulated so easily while the Resistance fought more fiercely?

A fortnight passed, allowing them to regain their strength if not their former standing. Captain Lennox even sent round a physician to tend to Nicolas's limp arm and the festering gash on Antoinette Laroche's foot.

Meanwhile, Sylvie perused copies of the *Virginia Gazette* for anything that might concern them, her heart stopping at one telling line.

Governor Dinwiddie warned Virginia's assembly that the very welfare of all the colonies on this continent was in jeopardy from the French and Indians.

And then came the news that more shiploads of exiles were at anchor.

Captain Lennox could not reappear soon enough.

The Acadians did not wait long before a wagon came, secured by Captain Lennox, to take them to the almshouse where the governor said they could seek refuge. Lennox's meeting with Dinwiddie had allowed them this, at least. The last thing they wanted was to be placed on a ship, even the Acadian ships at anchor, though they were hungry for news of them.

Sylvie bade the captain goodbye with a knot in her throat. He was doing all that he could for their comfort and safety. He even prayed for them, reminding them to let God be their foremost thought and refuge. It touched her and made her reconsider. Perhaps God had not abandoned them completely?

"I'll return to see how you're faring once I meet with the captains of the Acadian transports," he told them, shaking hands with the men. "As it is, the almshouse knows you're coming and has made preparations for you."

Sylvie climbed into the wagon with the other refugees, cape hood drawn close to her face as the wind rose and the skies threatened rain. The wagon's rocking made her queasy, a reminder of the ship, though there was plenty to distract her as they rumbled north along the wide York River.

Within a short time the almshouse chimneys were visible, spewing gray smoke into the leaden skies, and they were left before a shabby door. A few tents stood to the north of the clapboard buildings as if in readiness for them. In moments an unsmiling, heavy-jawed man greeted them, separating the men from the women and telling the men to go to the tents. Sylvie followed a matron upstairs to a room with several cots, one for each of the women with her. She felt another glimmer of gratefulness that the captain had forewarned them of their arrival.

Supper sent them belowstairs again to eat with a great many other women who spoke English in hushed tones and darted furtive glances at them. To Sylvie's surprise, the fare was palatable if odd, a thick beef stew and coarse-grained bread. The applesauce she recognized, accompanied by weak tea and dry cake. If the meal was any indication, they'd not starve nor have cause for complaint.

Sylvie returned to her room with Eulalie, wondering how the men fared outside in the tents with the weather worsening. Climbing atop her narrow rope bed, she pulled the thin blanket over her and closed her eyes. At home she'd always ended the day on her knees, but prayer seemed to belong to the before, not the after—to another less ravaged soul in another life. The Sylvie she'd once been was now a shadow. Sleep was not only needed, it gave her the refuge of oblivion she craved.

Sylvie had spent but three days at the almshouse before she was beset by memories of Acadie's autumns. By now she would have helped bring in the last of the harvest, back pinched from stooping, arms heavy but heart satisfied. Baskets of apples would overflow, along with cabbages, turnips, and onions from the garden. Cider would be kegged and chilled in the cellar, stored in reassuring rows as the snow pelted down, wrapping them in the snug cocoon of an Acadian winter.

But Virginia still showed signs of summer. In the courtyard where the women gathered for fresh air, a lone rose climbed up a wooden wall, its slender stems sending out frost-pinched, blush blooms.

When they weren't outside or at meals, the refugees were assigned simple tasks. Did the English assume that since most of them couldn't speak English, they could do no more than the most menial things? They tended fires, washed dishes, swept, and oversaw the orphans. These ghostly enfants, so different than her well-fed, well-loved family at home, tugged at Sylvie's heart.

Summoning courage, she sought out the unsmiling matron, Mistress Boles. "Madame," she began tentatively, "might I have a word with you?"

With a sharp raise of her brows, Mistress Boles peered more closely at Sylvie. "You know our tongue?"

"My great-grandmother was Scottish," Sylvie said, then forged ahead. "I saw a great deal of cloth arrive in a wagon this morning. Might you have need of a seamstress?"

Mistress Boles frowned, absently touching the chatelaine dangling from her waist with rheumatic fingers. "How skilled are you?"

"I can sew whatever is needed."

With a little harrumph, Mistress Boles looked askance at her. "Our latest benefactor recently requested new garments for every man, woman, and child housed here, though we are hard-pressed to get a willing, able hand to help. How quickly can you turn out a shirt or shift?"

"As fast as a mantua-maker or tailor, given the right supplies. I have my own scissors and sewing kit but will need thread foremost."

Mistress Boles led her to a room that required unlocking. It had the look of a workroom with a table and bench, bare shelves on the walls. Once inside, Sylvie eyed the piles of osnaburg and linen and wool in various colors, all new cloth. Through the sole window, sunlight poured like melted butter, warming the chair beneath it.

"Stack each finished garment on the shelves," the matron said. "If you lack anything, tell me and I'll see that it's gotten. Within reason, of course."

"I shall begin, then," Sylvie said, hastening to retrieve her supplies. "Merci—thank you."

Without another word, Sylvie was left alone, gloriously

alone. She sat down in the unfamiliar chair, eyes on the tools of her trade lying on the table. Since she'd been entrusted with so much, she wasn't about to disappoint.

By afternoon she'd turned out a woman's shift, a man's shirt, and two aprons. Mistress Boles came by and fingered the work, looking at it with a critical eye as Sylvie began a petticoat.

"Fine stitching indeed," she murmured through tight lips as if unused to doling out compliments. "Continue your work, Miss—what is it?"

"Galant, Madame. Sylvie Galant."

"A shame you refugees are considered enemies of the Crown and cannot hire yourselves out." She selected a finished apron and tied it around her spare waist. "But we certainly have need of you here."

She left wearing the apron, surely the highest compliment Sylvie could hope for in such circumstances. Enemies of the Crown, oui. But she kept on sewing, every tiny, even stitch worked with equal parts angst and determination.

 **25**

The robbed that smiles, steals something from the thief.

William Shakespeare

At week's end, Sylvie had a visitor. The chocolatier, Esmée Shaw, appeared in the doorway of the sewing room, a basket on her arm. She stepped into the sunlit chamber, giving Sylvie a better look at her than she'd had in York. Dark curls spiraled beneath a jaunty feathered hat, and the green velvet riding habit with its black buttons lent an air of elegance to their humble surroundings.

"Good afternoon, Mademoiselle Galant." Her soft voice had a musicality that beguiled, her eyes smiling. "I've been told you've set up shop right here and I shan't have to worry about the children being warm enough this winter."

Fingers slightly stiff from continuous stitching, Sylvie stood, abandoning her work and gesturing to an empty chair. "Please, sit down."

Esmée set the basket on the table before removing her riding gloves. "I've asked for tea to be brought. No doubt you'd like some refreshment and a respite."

As another almshouse woman appeared with two creamware cups and a large porcelain pot, Sylvie's thoughts were full of Madame Auclair and the Pandora and tea at Beau-séjour.

"Thank you, Hannah." Esmée reached into her basket and produced a finely embroidered handkerchief. "I heard you had a cold of late but hope you're feeling better. Perhaps this will help?"

"You're never empty-handed nor empty-hearted, Miss Shaw. 'Thank you' hardly seems enough." Hannah curtsied before shutting the door behind her, the gift pressed to her bodice.

Throat tight, Sylvie looked at this vision in green who seemed half angelic. "You're all but revered here for your many kindnesses."

"Oh? Any scrap of compassion assumes Goliath-like proportions to those used to hardship and harshness. I simply do what I can, which is not nearly enough."

"You've even begun teaching the Acadian women English," Sylvie said. "Basic words and phrases to help prepare them for the colonial world."

"Of which you need nary a lesson." Esmée smiled as she poured the tea with a steady hand.

"Your mother helped found the almshouse, Mistress Boles said."

"Years ago, before she passed away." She reached into the basket again and withdrew two chocolate tarts wrapped in a linen cloth, a supply of sugared almonds, and even a small chocolate brick wrapped in brown paper. "I can go nowhere without sweets, as you can see. My late mother left me Shaw's Chocolate, not just her almshouse endeavors. Both keep me busy, and my father, a retired admiral, doesn't object." Esmée slid the tarts and almonds across the table to Sylvie. "A reward for your labors."

"Thank you, though I must confess sewing is more pleasure

than work. I just never thought to ply my needle outside of Acadie."

Esmée took in the newly finished garments atop the sewing table with palpable pleasure. "I've long prayed for help with the residents here, especially the orphans." She took a sip of tea, her pleasure shifting to sadness. "Virginia, to its shame, cares little and does less."

Sylvie listened to the dulcet voice, not embittered but heavy with regret. If Virginia did so little for its own needy citizens, how could the Acadians expect anything, given they were the enemy French?

Esmée's gaze returned to her. "You've been through an unfathomable ordeal. The facts are just coming to light here in the colonies. You Acadians should never have been driven from your homeland." She poured more tea, the quiet in the room broken by the mewling of a cat outside the window. "Such cruelties will not go unpunished, I assure you. In the meantime, Captain Lennox has enlisted the support of my sister's husband, Lord Drysdale, a powerful ally in Virginia and elsewhere. Along with prayer, that may prove a potent combination."

Sylvie sampled the flaky tart without tasting it. She knew nothing of Lord Drysdale, but not even Dieu, she'd decided, could return them to the before nor be of much help in the after.

⟞⟝

That night after supper, Sylvie returned to her room to find her haversack gone. She'd left it beneath her corner cot, unsure of where else to secret it. Dropping to her knees, she searched beneath the sagging ropes that supported the straw mattress. A bedbug crawled up her arm and she shook it off, more frantic than repulsed. Why had she not kept her valuables locked up in her sewing room?

She sought out Mr. Boles since she couldn't find his wife. "We aren't constables, Miss Galant. Theft is commonplace among the indigents here. I suspect your belongings are now the property of some vagrant who happened by and has since departed."

"Can I not search for it?" she pleaded.

"And cause a disturbance? I think not." The firm shake of his balding head shot down the notion. "I'm sure you had little of value, destitute as you are."

Eyes smarting, Sylvie wrapped herself in a borrowed shawl and traded the almshouse for the twilight evening. Firelight glowed like fallen stars among the refugee tents, the York River a dark ribbon. A few newly arrived Acadian women stood about with the men, sharing their humble habitations. They had escaped one of the transport ships anchored up the James River, seeking their kin. Sylvie saw no one she knew, though she searched each face as she walked among them, making inquiries about her family and friends as she looked for her missing belongings. With no success, she had started back toward the almshouse when a man stepped out of the shadows.

"I am Sebastien Broussard. You are looking for something, mademoiselle?"

Drawing her shawl tighter against the chill, Sylvie felt helpless as a child as they made introductions. "My haversack has been stolen."

"What was in it?"

"A gown. Necklaces. Coin." Her voice nearly failed her. *All I have left of home.* "Héritages."

With a nod, he walked past her toward a tent at the end of the encampment. She followed, his purposeful stride reassuring her. Pausing at the opening of the tent, he called, "Adélard?"

A boy stuck his head out, answering in French.

"Bring me the haversack," Sebastien said.

"Bof!" came the reply as the boy disappeared back inside. In a trice, Sebastien had both the boy and her haversack in hand. Head hanging, Adélard murmured an apology and confessed to the theft.

"Stealing from your own," Sebastien said with contempt. "Such is a crime in Acadie as well as Virginia."

"Please, say no more," Sylvie said. "'Tis enough that it's now in my safekeeping." Clutching it, feeling the familiar weight of the contents, she guessed nothing was missing. "Merci."

Firelight called out the haggard lines of Sebastien's handsome face. "You are gracious."

"I still have my manners if little else."

His half smile was wry. "A favor for a favor, then." He reached into his weskit and withdrew a folded *Virginia Gazette*. "We must keep current with events. Can you read to me the news?"

"Of course," she said, also curious. She'd not seen a paper since York.

He gestured toward a tent where a lantern hung, a crude bench beneath it. They sat, and he held her haversack while she perused the paper's ponderously small newsprint warning of an impending war with France. She nearly rolled her eyes. Was it not plain to all they were at war already?

"Here is a speech from Governor Dinwiddie," she said as the lantern light waned. "'Our people are much alarmed and in great confusion in having any French among us . . .'"

Stoic, he listened as she read on, but she sensed their shared turmoil. When she'd finished the article, he urged her to continue, but all that remained was a boldface line in the bottom corner.

After a decade's service to the Crown, Major William Blackburn resigns his commission.

She recoiled as if struck. The Scot? Resigning when a declaration of England's war with France was expected any day? Where would he go? What would he do? She handed the paper back to Sebastien without reading further.

"Merci, mademoiselle," he said.

A cold rain began to fall, spattering the newsprint and making the ink run. Tempted to ask again for the paper and have answers, Sylvie raised her shawl above her head instead. "Au revoir," she called as she walked away, haversack dangling from one shoulder.

If not for the weather, she would have stayed to hear more of Sebastien Broussard's own story.

 **26**

The greater the obstacle, the more glory in overcoming it.

Molière

Captain Lennox returned as he had promised. Sylvie saw him standing amid the men's encampment, making her wonder if he wanted no listening ears from the almshouse. But he'd not come alone, and the man beside him claimed all her attention. Perhaps it was the contrast they made—the captain in his black tricorn and simple garments beside the shorter, stockier man dressed so divinely in a fine broadcloth suit with expertly tailored embellishments, brilliant paste-buckle shoes on his feet. His cocked hat even bore a white feather.

She walked faster, not wanting to miss a word, before coming to a halt behind the wide stance of Sebastien Broussard. Twenty-eight Acadians had gathered, so small a number when the deportation had been so many.

"It grieves me to not bring better news," the captain was saying, a document in hand. "But I'll deal with you honestly or not at all. You've had your fill of lies and deception, I'll warrant."

A great many nods ensued as the Acadians pressed closer.

"I have here a letter from Governor Dinwiddie to you that states, 'Virginia now has 1,140 Neutrals from Nova Scotia, which gives great uneasiness to our people. We have received them and now maintain them by my order and the governor's council, but whether the assembly will be prevailed upon to make some provision for them is very uncertain, and I complain of Governor Lawrence's not giving us some previous notice of their coming that we might be prepared to receive them.'"

"How many ships are now at anchor from Acadie, Captain?" Nicolas Surette asked.

The captain folded the paper and pocketed it. "The *Sarah and Molly* from Grand-Pré. Four vessels from the Canard and Habitant River regions—*Endeavor, Industry, Mary,* and *Prosperous.* The latest to arrive is *Ranger* from the Minas Basin."

How well he knew their business. Sylvie believed that if pressed, he could recall all their names too. Her admiration bloomed, crowding out her heartache if only for a moment.

"One of these vessels has been ordered to Richmond at the falls of the James River," Captain Lennox said. "Why, we do not yet know."

The finely dressed gentleman introduced himself as Lord Drysdale and said in steady, sympathetic tones, "Since we can do nothing for those aboard these accursed vessels as of yet, we intend to help you who've gathered here in the meantime. I speak for several Virginians who advocate on your behalf. Our time is short, so listen well." His gaze beneath his cocked hat was intent. "We want to prove that you are not a burden to this colony but an industrious people of excellent reputation. We invite you to leave the almshouse and join the working force of Williamsburg and York. We will try to match those willing to work to your skills."

Stay on? Her vision reached far higher. She wanted to return home. Wanted Governor Lawrence's actions condemned and considered an outrage so they could resume their lives and live in peace. The smoke and ruins she had seen when they sailed away from Acadie did not deter her. They would begin anew.

A chair and lap desk were brought from the almshouse while the willing Acadians formed a line. A few hung back, saying they would instead seek out their friends and relatives in the places Acadians were allowed to dock and disembark.

As much as she disliked the almshouse, what sort of employment could be had? She could not live long upon Père's coins, and the almshouse was only a temporary respite.

Though Acadians were considered enemies of the Crown and forbidden to work, somehow this powerfully placed man had gotten past that. And she sensed some merchants and businessmen would risk employing them if only to curry favor with Lord Drysdale.

Sebastien went ahead of her, giving her courage. She listened as his resonant voice answered their well-placed questions.

"Your full name, sir?" Captain Lennox asked in French.

"Sebastien Broussard of Grand-Pré."

"Former occupation?"

"Farmer. Dike builder."

"Married?"

"A marriage contract. My would-be bride was put on the *Duke William*. I know not where she is."

Sylvie heard the grievous lament in his voice. Had he not heard the *Duke William* was believed to have sunk soon after sailing? She hoped it was an unfounded rumor, though she had read its confirmation in the newspaper.

"Age?" the captain queried, the scratch of his quill trailing ink upon the paper.

"Eight and twenty."

Older than she. Sylvie crossed her arms against the cold. Snowflakes began to drift down, tossed about by a fretful wind, as Lord Drysdale asked Sebastien a few more careful questions in French.

Last in line came Sylvie. She looked from Lord Drysdale to Captain Lennox, still debating her course while the others were warming themselves around a bonfire, discussing what they'd just done.

"My name is Sylvie Galant," she began. Once her family's name was respected, even renowned. "I am unwed . . . six and twenty . . . a seamstress."

The captain and Lord Drysdale regarded her kindly. Would she be willing and able to work at something other than sewing? And would she kindly part with her wooden shoes?

Warmth engulfed her. Her sabots were all she had left of her Acadian garments, other than her Lyonnais silk gown. But here they were hopelessly out of place, sure to invite ridicule.

"We'll have you fitted for shoes and any other garments needed prior to your service," Lord Drysdale reassured her. "Merci, Mademoiselle Galant."

With the questions at an end, Sylvie turned away and walked toward the almshouse. She was in no mood to gather about the bonfire with the others, only rue what she'd just done.

⁓

Sylvie cried herself to sleep. It was something Marie-Madeleine had sometimes done over some trifling matter. Only in hindsight, nothing about it seemed trifling. Sylvie had thought herself too old for such things, but the unbearable pain in her chest must have relief, and missing her sister made the tears come faster and harder. Who would have ever thought Marie-Madeleine would meet a watery grave? And Mère? Then there was Père and Lucien and Pascal. Bleu. Not knowing their fate haunted her.

Their faces crowded into her consciousness as she'd last seen them. Marie-Madeleine shrunken and feverish. Mère frantically tying on the haversack during the hurricane. Père's profound disbelief at being duped into going to the fort and imprisoned there. Lucien and Pascal's bewildered sorrow at having to leave them and go with the Mi'kmaq. Bleu's fury and disgust over the Ranger William Blackburn. Grandmère being trundled away in the cart to another ship.

But that was all in the past, and the present loomed, demanding answers. Where would she be in service? To a mantua-maker? A milliner? Though French fashion was considered the gold standard, that did not apply to French Acadians. She sensed she would not be used in that way.

What, then?

She did not have long to wait. Three days later, as winter's cold choked the courtyard's last blooming rose, Captain Lennox and Lord Drysdale returned with the promised garments and further news.

27

A person often meets his destiny on the road he took to avoid it.

Jean de La Fontaine

However daunting the future, Sylvie was not sorry to leave the almshouse behind. Shod in new black woolen shoes, her haversack made heavier by her hidden sabots, she rode away from the York River to a place inland called Williamsburg. Jostled about in a wagon with her were other Acadians assigned service. They were a silent, grim lot as if going to the guillotine, though perhaps the worst was behind them, not ahead of them. The road was rutted, snow spitting in their faces.

At the last, Esmée Shaw had appeared, bringing knitted gloves and scarves. Sylvie noticed she and Captain Lennox seemed to know each other well.

"Williamsburg isn't far," Esmée told them, handing out blankets next. "Only a few miles."

Sylvie tried to keep her mind off the ships still at anchor, the surviving Acadians huddled without heat in the dark, filthy holds. Sorrow pressed hard against her, diminishing what little hope was left in her heart. She, who had never before left the land of her birth, looked out over frozen fields and woods, finding them cheerless and unhospitable in the clutch of winter. Her whole being cried out for the cliffs and pines and seascapes of home, an unforgettable palette of cinnamon and azure and jade in every season. The stark Virginia landscape seemed akin to her soul.

She looked past the thickset wagon master to Captain Lennox atop a bay horse, Lord Drysdale riding beside him on an equally fine mount. These men would introduce them to Williamsburg, and for that she felt a rush of gratitude.

On the town's outskirts she saw the spire of a church rising like chimney smoke as men and women went about their business despite the weather. Animals were being herded, and shopkeepers set out their wares. Signs hung above countless businesses, one advertising a milliner, a hat painted on the boards. A sparkling, bow-fronted window invited a longer look, filled with gloves and fur muffs she wanted to sink her hands into.

Down a cobbled main street they went. Their driver slowed the pace to deposit them before a tavern with a wide front porch. The captain and Lord Drysdale ushered them inside to a blue-painted foyer then a small private chamber.

Lord Drysdale ordered drinks to warm them, steaming pitchers redolent of ginger and spirits. All drank the flip as a hearth's fire crackled at their backs. It was then Sylvie remembered the note Esmée had given her before she'd gotten in the wagon, telling her to pocket it for safekeeping should she need it.

Sylvie dug it out now, finding English words scrawled upon it. *Lady Drysdale née Eliza Shaw Cheverton of Williamsburg.* She repocketed it, looking at Lord Drysdale, who spoke with Sebastien near the door. His wife?

In time several strangers appeared, all men save one

woman, a tavern keeper. One by one the Acadians signed contracts for their service. Sylvie's turn came and she put her name to paper. She turned toward the scarecrowish, black-clad man Lord Drysdale was introducing and to whom she was now employed.

Thomas Hunter, bookbinder and stationer of Williamsburg.

The next morning, Sylvie stood in the shop on Duke of Gloucester Street surrounded by endless shelves of books—more books than she'd ever beheld in her life or imagined could exist in one place. Not only finished books but books in various stages of production. The large, many-windowed shop pulsed with activity and smelled pleasantly of ink and leather, paste and vinegar. The workers hardly gave her a glance, so intent were they on their tasks.

One burly man stood wielding a mallet, smashing papers flat on a stone anvil. Another plied needle and thread in some sort of frame, sewing papers together. Still another stacked finished books in a press. One boy swept the shop floor while another replaced paper in cubbyholes along one wall. Someone barked at a little girl who had ventured from a back room. She wore a shift and tiny stays but not much else. Her feet were bare though a cap covered her curls. Sylvie hadn't expected to find any enfants in so busy a place. The little girl stared at her wide-eyed for a moment till a woman took her hand and snatched her from sight.

Overwhelmed by the bustle and fuss, Sylvie's mind stretched to take in the bookbindery as customers came and went, opening and shutting the front door with such force she feared for its hinges. Little wonder she'd been hired as a day laborer. What would be her piece in this complicated puzzle?

Mr. Hunter finally entered, hanging his cane and heavy black cape from a wall peg near the rear door before summoning Sylvie into the adjoining stationer's shop. A stout, middle-aged woman stood behind the counter, supplying customers with all kinds of stationery supplies.

"You'll assist Mrs. Webb till I determine how best to use you." Mr. Hunter stopped at the long counter's end, shrewdly assessing what was lacking before calling for an apprentice to fetch more Edinburgh inkpots and gilt-edged paper. "Starting out in the stationery shop will give you a solid foundation for the bookbindery."

Mrs. Webb eyed her, unsmiling, as Sylvie smoothed her apron and looked out the shop's front window where pale sunlight struck the cobbled street. "Best study the shelves and get your footing," the woman told her tersely before greeting another customer.

Sylvie did so, taking in inkstands and pounce boxes, vials of ink in varied colors, and reams of paper bearing such names as imperial, elephant, crown, demy, royal, and super royal, to name but a few. Could she commit them to memory? As she tried to familiarize herself with the strange and manifold merchandise, she listened to the English banter sometimes interspersed with Scots.

"Needs be I excuse myself for a moment," Mrs. Webb told her before disappearing and seeking the necessary behind the shop in one corner of a small, faded garden.

Left to face half a dozen customers alone, Sylvie was gripped by a paralyzing bewilderment when a bewigged gentleman stepped up to the counter. "Three black lead pencils and a merchant's blank book, please." When she darted a look at the burgeoning shelves, he pointed a finger to what was needed. "You're new here, obviously. I've not seen you before."

She climbed a small ladder and fetched what was wanted,

wishing Mrs. Webb back. "I've no notion what to charge you, sir."

He chuckled. "I pay in tobacco credit, Miss . . . ?"

"Galant," she replied, trying to subdue her accent while wondering what tobacco credit might mean.

At last Mrs. Webb returned, and Sylvie watched her record the transaction in a large ledger. The rest of the morning was spent shadowing her and trying not to allow the woman's sour mood to scare her.

At midday Sylvie was given leave to go into the back room or rear garden and eat. She had nothing nor knew where to get food, so she simply sat and digested the garden's tidy geometric design, which promised a riot of color in spring but held no lingering vegetables she might scrounge.

Stomach rumbling, she shifted on the hard bench, eyes on the lane behind the shop where the stables stood. Peering at her through the fence along the lane was a creature with a black-striped tail and huge feet, its white coat marbled brown and sable.

In a trice her empty stomach was forgotten. Light-headed, she blinked as her whole being roared *no*.

Bonami? Could it be?

If so, his owner could not be far behind. Shrinking down on the bench, Sylvie drew her cape hood tighter. As if catching her scent, Bonami whined. Then a distinct whistle stole his attention, sending Sylvie off the bench and back into the shop, as nauseous as she'd been hungry moments before.

28

Ah, if you knew what peace there is in an accepted sorrow!

Madame Guyon

Will took a Williamsburg back street, avoiding Duke of Gloucester's crowded thoroughfare, which stayed chaotic except for the Sabbath. New to Virginia, he rented rooms nearer the College of William and Mary, but business often brought him to the heart of town. Today he sought a daybook these Virginians were so fond of. He'd not frequented the stationer's yet, and he needed to visit the bookbindery as well.

He looked down the bare-treed lane, curious as to why Bonami lingered by a paling fence. The caped woman hunkered down on a back bench? A whistle brought the dog to heel, and he loped by Will's side as they rounded a corner and neared the bookbindery, then obediently waited by the steps while his master went inside. Several customers were ahead of Will, none familiar but one.

"Major Blackburn," came a loud voice, followed by a hearty clap on Will's back. "What brings you to town?"

Will faced Baird, the James River planter he'd met a month before. "I'm hoping to find a Fry-Jefferson map, to start."

"And well you should, as William and Mary's newly appointed surveyor," he replied, his smile nearly reaching his ears. "Congratulations! This calls for a toast, surely. Shall we adjourn to the Raleigh after our business here?"

Will nodded, suspecting more to the invitation than a celebratory tankard. Baird was more businessman than planter, intent on acquiring additional acreage that needed surveying, likely.

"Aside from surveying," Baird said, "is there any truth to the rumor the *Bonaventure* carrying your new publication has just docked in York? A finely tooled leather volume of frontier exploits with a first printing of several thousand in London, or so I've heard. At six shillings a copy, it won't deprive the middling man."

"Of which I am one," Will replied with a wry smile. "As for the journals, I'd not heard, nay."

Chuckling, Baird stepped up to the counter and summoned a clerk to inquire about a prior order. "Have you finished lettering Pope's works in nine volumes and binding the Anglican prayer book for my wife?"

As an apprentice dealt with Baird, Will eyed the crammed shelves that looked hard-pressed to accommodate more books. He couldn't deny a beat of excitement about news of his own humble contribution begun at Fort Saint-Frédéric. Would anyone want to read about his military career, especially his former one? He certainly didn't. Since he'd resigned his commission, he'd faced harsh criticism in the face of a declaration of war, not only from his superiors but from citizens. Yet Acadie had convinced him he was finished. Ever since he'd left those unforgettable shores, it had required continual work to not let bitter memories hinder his present fresh start. Lord willing, he'd make restitution for his part in the debacle somehow, some way.

Seeing the stationer's empty, he retreated there. An older woman dusted shelves while a younger woman, her back to him, replaced reams of paper. He studied the inkpots and powders, deciding on blue sealing wax and wafers. Taking them in hand, he knocked a quill pen to the floor, which sent him and the young woman stooping to retrieve it. His hand shot out as hers did, but he was faster, an apology ready. Standing, they faced each other, and Will nearly spilled all he held.

Sylvie Galant recoiled from him like he was a venomous rattler while he stood turned to stone, oblivious to any who looked on. Their eyes locked in stunned silence. Why was she here? What were the odds? Will steeled himself against the change in her. Her once lush contours had thinned to sharp peaks and angles, her pronounced cheekbones a startling counterpoint to angry blue eyes.

A dozen defenses reared up in his jumbled thoughts.

I wanted no part in this war.

I've left the independent company of Rangers because of it.

I've demanded answers from port authorities about the Acadian ships at anchor.

I've prayed for you.

I never thought to see you again.

Finally the older woman asked him his business as Sylvie moved away from him.

He managed to murmur, "I've need of a few supplies."

With a curt nod, she tallied the cost, her smile appearing when he paid in coin, not credit. He returned to the bookbindery, his pulse ratcheting harder than in any Indian ambush.

Sylvie's stomach pitched like she was still at sea at the height of the hurricane. Fearing she might cast up accounts, she hurried to the rear door a second time without a parting word to Mrs. Webb, uncaring that the woman looked at her in disdain as if she was shirking work.

Trembling within and without, Sylvie all but stumbled out the door into the cold afternoon air. Her breath formed a cloud as she stared unseeing at the necessary with its prim pyramid roof.

How was it possible the Scot was here? He was nothing but an ill-timed, barbed reminder of all the heartache of before, while she was trying to navigate the after with its clashing sights and sounds and customs, so opposite of everything she knew and was. Questions beat about her brain, giving her an instant headache.

Why had he come so far south? Why had he not returned to New England?

"Miss Galant, are you well?" Mrs. Webb's aggravated voice was at her back, returning her inside.

There was no escape. Not from Williamsburg. Not from Mrs. Webb. Nor the Scot.

At day's end, Sylvie was charged with seeing the children fed—the shop boy who'd been pushing a broom and his wee sister confined to the back room. Hunter's gruff explanation rattled around in her benumbed brain like a marble. The parish had apprenticed these two orphans to the bookbindery the previous summer, though they were too young for the work. Childless, Hunter's wife had urged him to take them, but she'd recently died and an enslaved woman took care of them at night. For now, Hunter tasked Sylvie with tending them, at least for supper.

"Mrs. Scott, the tavern keeper, is expecting you. I've made

prior arrangements." He seemed relieved when she quickly took the enfants in hand and agreed to his directions to sup with them across the street. Both children eyed her curiously, clearly skittish about this new arrangement.

"You must tell me your names," Sylvie said, trying to smile.

"My sister is Rietta," the lad told her with a lisp.

Henrietta? Sylvie regarded the tiny girl, who looked up at her with eyes the hue of violets, before turning back to the lad. "And you are?"

"Nolan." His face wrinkled in concentration as if he couldn't recall his surname. "Nolan . . . Lawson."

A sense of dread overtook Sylvie as she looked about warily. No sign of the Scot. Relegating him to the trash bin, she crossed the street, holding tightly to the children's small hands as carriages and horses clattered atop the cobbles from all directions.

Once safely inside the tavern, they sat at a long pine table with other diners and ate cold ham and fowl and a most curious bread that turned to fine crumbs in Sylvie's mouth.

"Hoecake," Nolan told her, partaking of his with gusto across from her.

Henrietta couldn't seem to get enough either, shunning her meat and potatoes to have more bread. Round as a drum, she scooted near Sylvie on the bench as if afraid she might lose sight of her, her table manners dainty despite her youth.

Why were these children bereft of their parents, and how had they avoided the almshouse? The better question was, what sort of life would they have underfoot at the bookbindery? Sylvie's heart tugged so hard at their plight she nearly forgot her own.

When they returned to their quarters above the shop, Sylvie spied two cots in the room across from hers. A tall woman stood in the doorway, greeting the children by name and gesturing for them to come inside. Stoic, she averted her gaze till Sylvie asked her, "Are the children in your keeping?"

A curt nod. "Since Mrs. Hunter died a few months back."

"I'm Sylvie Galant. And you are . . . ?"

"Eve. Just Eve."

Sylvie looked on as Henrietta took a crude doll from a wooden crate and Nolan took a bag of marbles. Clearly disinclined to talk, Eve went inside the room and shut the door.

Retreating to her own quarters, Sylvie took stock of the narrow room. Tucked beneath the gables of the attic, it was cheered by a warm fireplace, the dry wood sending sparks up the chimney as the fire spread yellow light to the dark corners. A window framed the scarlet sunset, the very hue of the detested British uniforms.

Which brought her mind round again to the Scot.

Only he hadn't worn the usual uniform but had been dressed as a woodsman and Indian, at least when in Acadie. In Williamsburg, a far more civilized clime, he was now a man about town in his fawn-colored breeches and dark frock coat, a creamy cravat about his suntanned neck. The change was confusing, even jarring. Did he think a change of clothes meant a change of character?

This southern colonial town was the last place she'd expected to find him, short of Hades itself.

29

Tho' these people are very poor, yet they seem very cheerful.

William Byrd on French Huguenot refugees

Will studied the surveyor's license, his commission from the College of William and Mary as surveyor of King William County. He'd just returned from being sworn in at the county seat, but any pride in this marked achievement faded in the harsh light of encountering Sylvie Galant.

Since coming to Virginia three months before, directly after resigning from the Rangers, he'd found one open door after another, confirming his decision to venture south. If he'd hoped to get away from any notoriety here in Virginia, he'd been sorely mistaken. At every turn he was besieged by requests to tell of his exploits, demonstrate his marksmanship, and join the militia. The *Virginia Gazette* printed news of his arrival, thereby destroying any anonymity he hoped to have by changing location.

His past be hanged.

He'd begun to suspect he'd been awarded his surveying commission based on his reputation and little else. Disgusted, he opened the front door of the brick house on the west side of Palace Green where he lodged in the home of law professor Judge Kersey and his niece. The foyer was empty, a pine stair winding up one blue-and-white-papered wall. Two other young men who read law under the house's owner-attorney also rented rooms here.

In the formal parlor a case clock tolled five times. No one was home yet, and for once he wished they were. He needed a distraction like cards or chess. Since he wasn't a drinking man, at least to excess, the town's taverns held little appeal. He couldn't drown his woes in heady pipes of madeira or potent bowls of arrack punch.

With a heavy tread, he climbed the staircase to his bedchamber on the second floor as the front door opened below and a familiar voice filled the echoing space. "Major Blackburn."

He paused on the landing and looked over the balustrade. Spencer Roane.

"Great luck to find you here so early in the evening, Major." After removing his cloak, Spencer shed his cocked hat. "Care to join me for some Caribbean rum? I've gleaned fresh news of the Acadians since you've been away on surveying business."

Will turned round so sharply it seemed more a military maneuver. Once down the steps, he followed the law student into the front parlor, where a fire cast cheerful light about the elegant room. He stood at one end of the hearth as a servant brought the requested drinks. Taking a chair, Spencer leaned back and took a sip while Will waited on tenterhooks.

"To the governor's great displeasure, another ship carrying Acadians has arrived and been ordered to the falls of the James River."

Will wanted to curse. "Which makes five Acadian vessels at anchor, upwards of a thousand souls sent to Virginia alone, not to mention the other colonies. The burning question is what is to be done with them."

Spencer winced. "Dinwiddie is being pressured to accept them and to house and feed them by a minority of powerful Virginians, but public opinion has reached a fever pitch. Most Virginians are adamant these Neutrals not disembark since many of that nation have joined with the Indians and are murdering and scalping our frontier settlers."

"These Acadians are peace-loving people, at least those not with the Resistance." Will thought of Bleu and wondered what had become of him. "The majority of them aren't guilty of any crimes in the homeland they've been deprived of. They speak French, but that is their sole commonality with France. They swear neutrality and take no oath of allegiance to either nation."

Spencer paused to take a long drink. "You know Lord Drysdale is spearheading Acadian support. He and Captain Henri Lennox are said to be working tirelessly to that end."

"Lennox the privateer?"

A nod and a half smile. "Lennox, aye, who's just as renowned as you but on sea, not land. When he's not on his island, you'll find him about town. I've heard he may return to sea, so his support might be short-lived."

Will absorbed the news, glad two respected men were leading the charge. "If admitted, these Acadians would make as industrious and law-abiding settlers as the French Huguenots in western Virginia who were once exiles themselves. They've strengthened Virginia's frontiers with their prosperous farms since their arrival fifty years prior. They often intermarry with their English neighbors."

"You have the makings of a fine attorney, not just a surveyor. Few could argue, aye." Spencer watched as Will added another log to the fire. "I'll play the devil's advocate. Port inspectors say sickness abounds on these vessels, many of them unseaworthy. Naturally the governor's first concern is that these Acadians don't bring disease to Virginia."

"The blame lies entirely with Governor Lawrence and his minions in Canada. I was there and watched it unfold, at least in the beginning. Countless lives were lost even before they'd left Nova Scotia due to abominable shipboard conditions."

He wagered hopelessness accounted for as much death as fever and dysentery. He'd seen the emptiness in Sylvie's eyes at the bookbindery. Emptiness and anger where there'd once been light and liveliness.

"Dinwiddie insists on meeting with the governor's council to determine the Acadians' fate—"

A commotion in the hall halted their conversation. A young woman was complaining to a housemaid about the weather. Kersey's niece, Will guessed. Clad in red and yellow, she had the look of an autumn leaf blown in by the wind.

"Gentlemen." She smiled, entering the parlor like she owned it. "I suppose I shall make conversation with the two of you till my uncle returns, seeing as how this is my home now too."

Spencer stood and gave a little bow, as did Will. He felt stiff as a ramrod doing so, but here civility ruled. Spencer struck up a conversation so skillfully that Will felt little need to join in, but after a few minutes Miss Kersey seemed determined to draw him out.

"Sometimes I feel your stealth has followed you off the frontier, Major Blackburn." She looked askance at him with something bordering on a smile. "You are very adept at listening and observing, but surely that serves the woods better than a Virginia parlor."

"I'll let you know if I have anything worth saying," he replied with an affability he was far from feeling.

"I, on the other hand, say more than a southerner should,"

Spencer said, his ruddy color deepening. "Would that I owned a little of Blackburn's reserve."

"We born-and-bred Virginians are never at a loss for words—though perhaps we should be," Miss Kersey replied as a maid brought tea. She took a seat on the sofa and arranged her skirts before reaching for a cup. "Here you are, Major."

Will declined, almost amused at her ensuing astonishment.

She kept on, coquettish. "Do you not care for so refined a custom, then?"

When he didn't answer, Spencer reached for the cup. "I have no such reservations."

"Very well." She added sugar to her own. "Might I ask what you drink, Major, if not tea?"

"Cider." Will hated the memory it wrought. Sylvie by the well. Sylvie believing him to be an ally. Sylvie—

"Cider? 'Tis so . . . boring. We must convert you." She settled back against the upholstered sofa, tea in hand. "So tell me, how is my uncle's recovery from that cold and racking cough? Were my rum-soaked cherries any help returning him to health?"

"Rum-soaked cherries cure a great many ills," Spencer told her with a chuckle. "He seems much improved. I believe he's at the Raleigh right now, making up time lost."

"He was there when I left an hour ago," Will confirmed, looking toward the stairwell and wanting to make an escape.

"Uncle Elliot has been like a father to me since my own parents passed last year. I do worry with him working such long hours. When he's not at the college he's at the tavern. I hope my moving in here might change that."

"Has Cloverwell sold, then?" Spencer asked.

She frowned. "Our plantation now belongs to the Carters. It's been a hard parting, as I was raised there and taught how to manage staff and dependencies. I shan't know what to do with myself here in town other than play hostess to my uncle's boarders."

"I daresay that will disappoint. He doesn't care to entertain, does he?"

A sigh. "Just you lodgers on occasion. Perhaps I shall change that, though I can't possibly enliven this place like you lodgers do. Uncle lives to talk law and politics and land. Sadly, we women merely serve as ornamentation oftentimes."

"That you do quite well," Spencer said, giving her a lingering look. "Something tells me you won't stay a miss for long."

"Which brings me to the ridiculousness of 'Miss Kersey' and 'Major Blackburn' and 'Mr. Roane.' We must simply be Liselotte and William and Spencer, please." She smiled at them over the rim of her teacup. "I'll not lie to you. Father had many debts, and I lack a dowry. I have in mind something other than marriage, if that's what you're thinking. Many of Williamsburg's taverns and businesses are operated by women. I don't mean to be idle."

So she decried marriage? With Spencer listening raptly, Liselotte continued to talk of Cloverwell and all that she would miss. Excusing himself, Will went upstairs, hearing her uncle come in shortly after and join them.

Restless, he went to a window and looked down on a back street with its litter of autumn leaves. Rain rent the crisp air. He could smell a storm a day distant. Below, within a picketed fence framing the garden, Bonami lay in a soft bed of frost-bitten woolly betony. Lamb's ears, the gardener had told him. Good thing Kersey tolerated dogs, as did his gardener, at least in the colder months.

Suddenly his view, this room, all of Williamsburg shifted. His new world widened to accommodate the woman he thought he'd left behind. Their chance meeting clawed at him and refused to quiet, a great many questions clamoring for answers.

Was she one of the Acadians whose ship had foundered off the Virginia Capes? He'd read newspaper accounts of the storm, but there had been few survivors and he'd never imagined she would be among them. The almshouse had a small refugee camp, though he'd not yet been there. In truth, the storm might have saved her. Better to be on land than rotting in the hold of a prison ship with little hope of liberation.

And here she was, by some miracle, working at the bookbindery and stationer's. Only she didn't belong there. She needed to be free of this French-hating town. Free like he longed to be. Already the constraints of Williamsburg were wearing on him. He had his mind on the Rivanna River one hundred miles west. His surveying was but a means to get him there.

 **30**

When men are employed they are best contented.

Benjamin Franklin

B y week's end Sylvie had been introduced to the entirety of the bookbinding trade during long, foot-aching, mind-whirling days. And in that span of time she'd come to realize she had no one but herself to rely on. Her future, unwelcome as it was, was in her hands. She must forge a life in this new, alien place with strangers on every side and unceasing demands to be met, including the care of two petits enfants.

Shoulders squared and focusing on her many tasks, she was able to distance herself from the Scot . . . though she nearly held her breath each time the shop door opened and another customer entered. As this was the only bookbindery and stationer's in town, where else would he shop?

Mr. Hunter, she learned, was one of the most successful merchants in town. Work never ceased. The paper mill near Williamsburg endlessly supplied them, and the bookbindery sold more daybooks than any other merchandise. Sylvie soon learned the most bound book was the Bible, followed by the

Anglican prayer book. Pocket almanacs were wildly popular, especially in the New Year. As if those weren't enough, each time the Virginia assembly met in Williamsburg, the session laws had to be printed in bulk. Simply put, these Virginians delighted in paper.

Looking taxed if pleased, Mr. Hunter informed them a James River planter's library needed replacing after being lost at sea, necessitating an extra flurry of work and the signing on of two more indentures.

"And we've this just in from London," an apprentice announced, opening a crate with more than his usual zeal. "The factual, never-before-published *Journals of Major William Blackburn.*"

Quoi? The bottom dropped out of Sylvie's stomach. She could only stare at the stack of leather-bound books authored by a name she knew too well.

Mr. Hunter took one, cracking open the flyleaf. "Customers have been clamoring for this ever since we received word of its first printing. And now it's in its—what?—fourth edition, so London says. We're lucky to have gotten any at all."

"I'll place two in the front window," the apprentice said, gathering an armful. "But I'm willing to wager they'll soon be sold."

"Don't forget those who've reserved their copies and have been waiting," Hunter said before returning to the press. "I've already requested another shipment through my agent."

Did the Scot write of Acadie in his journals? Sylvie had little time to wonder as a rush of customers drove away any idle thoughts.

Though Mr. Hunter had first placed her in the stationer's side of the shop, Sylvie was soon back in the bookbindery. Had Mrs. Webb complained? Here she folded sheets of paper into different arrangements with an ivory blade, creasing them into printed sheets. Next she worked at the stitching frame, sewing sheets together to form book pages with sturdy thread and needle, then moved on to trimming and gluing edges before squaring stacks of finished books in the standing press. It was the stitching frame where she felt most at home. A buttonhole stitch was all that was required to affix the leather headbands to the book's spine.

"A book should no more be seen without headbands in a library than a gentleman should appear without a collar in public," Hunter half shouted amid the hustle of the shop.

So intent was Sylvie on her sewing that at first she didn't realize the noise had dimmed and everyone from apprentices to master—and even Mrs. Webb—had encircled her.

"Jolly dogs!" one apprentice exclaimed when she paused to rethread her needle. "You've outstitched the rest of us, even those who've been here for years."

Scratching his chin in a bemused sort of way, Mr. Hunter finally said, "Miss Galant will continue at the stitching frame henceforth. The rest of you will be hard-pressed at your own stations to keep up with her."

Sylvie felt a flare of confidence. Though the wages were small—seventeen shillings and sixpence a week—her board and bed were paid. As she climbed the stairs to her room after supper each night, her fingers pinched from repeated stitching, her back and feet sore from standing, she tried to hold on to hope even as she held tightly to the hands of Henrietta and Nolan.

When she was especially tired, bittersweet memories rushed in like Baie Française's tide. Now, at week's end, she pushed the past back as best she could, but she was no aboiteaux. Biting her lip, she added another log to the dwindling fire as Eve came and relieved her of the children's care. But Henrietta ran back and buried her head in Sylvie's ink-stained apron, her plump arms wrapped around her knees.

Nolan watched from the doorway, his face shadowed.

"Rietta's lonesome for our mother. Sometimes she cries herself to sleep."

Weary as she was, Sylvie settled the child on her lap, wishing she had a sweet or a toy to soften their good night. All she could do was sing. "Frère Jacques, Frère Jacques, dormezvous? Dormez-vous? Sonnez les matines! Sonnez les matines! Din, din, don. Din, din, don."

Her soft song seemed to settle Henrietta, much as it had done Marie-Madeleine years before. As she recalled the sweet memory, Sylvie's voice cracked then smoothed. Better to remember her sister as she was long ago, full of joie de vivre, than she'd been aboard ship, so broken.

"Come along, child," Eve said softly when Sylvie's singing stopped. "Miss Galant needs her rest, same as you."

The door shut behind them, and Sylvie sat alone by the fire, a curious thudding at her temples. Removing her tight woolen shoes, she thought longingly of her sabots hidden beneath the bed. If she could but bathe before she slipped between those linen sheets . . . Her hair was a mass of dirty, limp strands, and she seemed to have become one with Williamsburg and its stench. Her senses were assaulted wherever she went. Did these English not bathe but simply smother themselves in pomades and perfumes? She would not be like them.

Taking soap and a towel, she left her lodgings, seeking a small, secluded millpond at the edge of town. Never mind that it was nearly winter and heavy frosts had set in. Not even January had stopped Bleu from bathing in Baie Française. With as much stealth as he, she got the deed done, skin and hair scoured, before hastening back to Duke of Gloucester Street.

Once in her nightclothes, a plain linen gown that seemed paper-thin against the encroaching winter, she pushed her narrow bed nearer the hearth. At last she lay down, drawing the woolen blanket up to her chin, hoping the thunder in her head would quiet. But even the bedcovers failed to stop her shivering.

The next morn she awoke to her windowsill lined with snow, snowflakes pressed against the glass pane. It was the Sabbath. Carriages hurried by, their usual noise muted. The Anglican church was not far. She'd wanted to see where these English worshiped, but the pain in her head was still there and the room tilted when she sat up.

If she just could get to the tavern and settle her stomach with tea and toast. Across the hall came the sweetness of children's voices. Should she take them to breakfast? Slowly she dressed in her clean garments from the almshouse, missing her striped skirts and colorful, beribboned waistcoats of before.

When she knocked on the children's door, there was no answer. Slowly she made her way downstairs and out the bookbindery's side entrance. Pressing mittened fingers to her temples, she willed her headache away. Snowflakes struck her heated cheeks, seeming to sizzle rather than melt. Had she a fever? The apothecary was not far, but its shutters were closed.

She took another step, light-headed again, her mouth bone-dry. And then her white world narrowed to a tiny pin-prick of light as her knees buckled and she pitched into the frozen street.

31

The LORD is nigh unto them that are of a broken heart;
and saveth such as be of a contrite spirit.

Psalm 34:18

At last Will returned from King William County. His
first successful survey had evolved into a second, the
days blurring. A snowstorm had kept him confined
to an outlying ordinary with his surveying party when they
were done. Chafing at the delay, he finally rode into Williamsburg and nearly went straight to the bookbindery, but
surveying was not a tidy trade. His garments were so mud-
spattered it looked as if he'd returned to Rangering.

He sought his lodgings at Kersey's, hoping for a welcoming fire and a sizzling tankard of flip if only to warm him.
Liselotte was at the milliner's, a maidservant said, and her
uncle at the college with the law students.

An uninterrupted hour later, Will emerged from the townhouse, all the better for soap and a razor. Despite the heavy
weather, Williamsburg brimmed with people going about
their business on a Monday afternoon, sound and movement

at every turn. The shops were open, and Will had need of items that could be had in town.

As usual, the bookbindery and stationer's were crowded. He waited his turn, taking stock of everyone who came and went, his heart knocking about his chest in anticipation of seeing Sylvie again. Nay, anticipation was not the right word. Dread, mayhap. She caused such a stew of his feelings he could not possibly sort them out.

"Greetings, Major Blackburn," Mr. Hunter said, stepping away from tooling a cover to face him. "What brings you out this dreary day? If you've come to see how your journals are selling, we've sold out."

The journals were the furthest thing from Will's mind. "A word with you in private, if I may."

Raising an eyebrow in question, Hunter ushered him to the back room.

"I'm looking for the Frenchwoman I saw when I was last here."

"Miss Galant?" Hunter sat on the edge of his disorganized desk. "She arrived over a fortnight ago from the almshouse, accompanied by Lord Drysdale and Captain Lennox. I know little about her except she is willing to work and I'm in dire need of hands. That she sews like an angelic being is no small matter."

Did she? Somehow Will felt cheated he didn't know. "But she's not here today."

"Nay. She's fallen ill and is confined to her room. George Pitt—the apothecary-surgeon—has been treating her."

"What is her malady?"

Hunter looked at him as if weighing his New England Scots bluntness. "The seasoning most newcomers suffer upon arrival here. Fever, chiefly."

Fever could mean a host of ailments, none of them good. Will hadn't weathered such maladies, but he was a colonial, after all. He reached into his waistcoat and withdrew a small notebook he'd carried while in Acadie. Bereft of a Bible on campaign, he'd written down a few Scriptures he'd committed to memory. Perhaps it would be of use to her too, if she could read English as well as she spoke it.

"Give her this, if you will." Will tempered his intensity, wanting to keep the door open should he need more information. "With my concerns about her health and my prayers for her recovery."

"Very well, Major." Surprise softened Hunter's severity. "I did not realize you knew her."

"In another time and place." With a tug at his cocked hat, Will turned and left the bustling bookbindery, though his concern about Sylvie wouldn't budge.

A woodsy fragrance woke Sylvie. Part pine, part spice, it threaded the cold chamber and seemed to settle about her still form. Somehow it carried the scent of home, of her cozy closet bed with its deep feather paillasse and hanging curtain, her own beloved nest. Contentment cocooned her till she opened her eyes to the gaping emptiness of the present.

Snow still limned the window, and the hearth's fire was robust, fingers of light flickering over the worn floorboards. Scraps of recent memory came back to her. She'd fallen ill. A man she guessed was a doctor came and went through the haze of her fever. When he wasn't there, Eve was. But no longer was she burning hot, nor was her tongue thick or her head heavy. She had not cared much if she lived or died, but here she was, still alive, and even more bony. Her stomach cramped in complaint. How long had she lain abed?

Below, the bookbindery hummed like a hive. She could feel its workaday pulse even from above and heard the continual thud of the shop's door.

Pushing herself up on one elbow, she took stock of her room. All was just as she remembered it save the bedside table. There rested a little book, no bigger than a pack of playing cards, bound with a leather tie. The doctor's? She reached for it, finding the scuffed cover worn smooth. Laying it on the bed, she looked up as the door cracked open and Eve appeared, her dark face creased with concern.

"You hungry, Miss Sylvie?"

Abandoning the book, Sylvie sat up. "Oui—yes."

"Dr. Pitt says to eat all you can hold." Eve set the tray down on her lap. A porringer of thick, steaming ragoût was filled to the brim, and a pewter plate bore more sliced bread than she could possibly eat in a sennight. Beside it were small pots of what looked like preserves and butter. Even cheese.

"Won't you join me?" Sylvie said, moving the tray from her lap to rest atop the coverlet. Eve was even thinner than she. Sylvie held out the spoon, but Eve shook her head in a sort of horror. "I must thank you in some way for helping take care of me."

Tentative, Eve sat on the end of the bed as Sylvie sampled the fare. Salty and rich, the stew called for another bite, but Sylvie surrendered the spoon and buttered the bread instead.

"You're a curious sort of white woman," Eve murmured, taking a tiny bite. "I fear what Mr. Hunter would do if he found me partaking of your supper."

"Where do you usually take your meals?"

"With the other servants at his house behind Wetherburn's."

"How are the children?"

"Right now Rietta's napping and Nolan's playing with his toy soldiers." Eve poured cider from a pitcher, and Sylvie could smell the apple tang as she passed her the cup.

One sip and Sylvie nearly spat it out.

"You look like you swallowed pepper vinegar instead."

Eve took a sip from the pitcher. "It ain't rancid, just a mite green."

Sylvie set the cup down with a shudder. Whatever it was, it paled next to the apples pressed from home. Were the Galant orchards still standing? Scuttling the thought, she slathered another piece of wheaten bread with butter and peach preserves to counter the taste. Suddenly ravenous, she ate everything. When nothing but crumbs remained, Eve disappeared with the tray.

Sylvie returned to the little book. Had the doctor left it behind? If so, she had no wish to pry into his business. She shut it gently, but a flower pressed flat fell out, its dried blueness startling against the linen coverlet. A lacy fern followed, its faded green still lovely. She stared at them, breath held and eyes filling. Chicory, with its periwinkle hues and saw-toothed edges, fluttered to the bed next, followed by pale pink wild rose. And then a fragile lady's slipper. Flowers of Acadie, all.

A rap at the door sent her carefully gathering up the dried flowers and returning them between the pages before setting the book aside and swiping at her eyes with the sleeve of her shift.

"'Tis Dr. Pitt, Miss Galant." He entered in, looking pleased to find her awake. "You're on the mend, then. Eve said you've eaten and are talkative. Good signs for a recovering patient." He set his satchel on a table. "You didn't need to be bled, but you do require some strengthening, either Turlington's Balsam or Freeman's Cordials. Mr. Hunter is anxious for you to return to the shop, but I urge caution."

"How long have I been ill?"

"Nearly a sennight, but a mild case, it seems. Many don't recover but succumb completely. Slight as you are, you seem made of sterner stuff." He extracted a bottle, eyeing it with spectacles on.

"Is this yours, sir?" Sylvie asked, extending the leather book.

"Nay," he replied. "Mr. Hunter brought it up to you just yesterday, saying it originated from a man named Blackburn."

He talked on, turning to medical matters, but she heard nary a word. He left a bottle of Turlington's Balsam on the table and gave instructions on how to use it, but she was lost in the book, discovering a treasure of more pressed flowers between the pages . . . and then heavy black ink, some of it smeared as if caught in the rain, the words still distinguishable. She read slowly and thoughtfully, marveling at the fine penmanship and her own opposing thoughts.

The Lord is my shepherd; I shall not want.

Oh, but she did want. The before gnawed at her day and night.

He maketh me to lie down in green pastures: he leadeth me beside the still waters.

But the waters had engulfed her, and there were no green pastures here.

He restoreth my soul: he leadeth me in the paths of righteousness for his name's sake.

Her soul was in tatters, rent like the ship's sails in the storm. She felt battered still.

Yea, though I walk through the valley of the shadow of death, I will fear no evil.

Yet she'd feared blatant evil in red-coated men who'd stolen their land and lives.

For thou art with me; thy rod and thy staff they comfort me.

She felt akin to a sheep without a shepherd. Where was comfort?

Thou preparest a table before me in the presence of mine enemies.

This gave her pause. Enemy English surrounded her. Yet there were also those like Captain Lennox and Esmée Shaw and Lord Drysdale. As for the table, had she not just partaken of abundance on a tray?

Thou anointest my head with oil; my cup runneth over.

She felt no anointing. No overflowing. Only a deep, abysmal emptiness.

Surely goodness and mercy shall follow me all the days of my life, and I will dwell in the house of the Lord for ever.

Eyes smarting, she dashed her tears away with the back of her hand.

Goodness and mercy belonged to the before, not the after.

32

[It is] a magnificent structure, built at the public Expense, finished and beautified with Gates, fine Gardens, Offices, Walks, a fine canal, Orchards, etc.

Rev. Hugh Jones on the Governor's
Palace in Williamsburg

Since Sylvie's coming, Will felt as though he was on another reconnaissance, another foray, as a Ranger. He looked for any sign of her, often passing by the bookbindery on foot rather than horseback to see if she'd returned to work. Glancing up at the second-floor windows in hopes of catching a glimpse of her availed him nothing.

Might he have erred giving her the book? Or had she grown more ill?

The empty place where the book once rested against his chest was a continual reminder that it was now with her . . . unless she'd tossed it into the hearth's fire or thrown it down the necessary. He winced. She clearly didn't covet his company. Her reaction in the stationer's reminded him of that, driven into his memory like a surveying stake.

Yet his stubborn heart refused to take heed.

The snow soon melted but the cold remained, stealing the

last of the leaves from the trees in colorful, windswept bursts and snatching hats off heads. Will walked toward Wetherburn's for a supper meeting with burgesses who needed surveying done, Bonami by his side. He climbed the wooden steps to the tavern that just happened to be opposite the bookbindery but for once reined himself in and refused to give the latter a long look.

His supper companions hadn't arrived, so he stood in the candlelit foyer along a paneled wall as diners entered and exited. A bill of fare hung nearby, and his gaze left it as two children hurried in, a cloaked woman behind them. The lad looked up at him, the tiny hat he wore with its colorful cockade amusing in miniature. The sight of the linen-capped girl who reminded Will of the little sister he'd once had tugged at him, even as she tugged at the hand of the woman who was none other than Sylvie herself.

God be thanked she was well again. Relief washed through him.

Their eyes met—hers more surprised than angry this time—and then she whisked the children into the dining room as if it was a regular occurrence. The noise was rising, hungry diners taking their places at long tables. He and his expected company had reserved a private room, but for now he was very much preoccupied with the public area. It didn't escape his notice how attentive she was to her small charges, which left him wondering who they were in this increasingly complex puzzle of her being here.

She looked up at him across the crowded room. He concentrated on the handbills and notices pinned to a near wall. One of them caught his eye, and he tore it free.

> Seeking instruction by way of classes in the art of fencing, dancing, and the French tongue. Inquire within at the Raleigh Tavern.

Sylvie kept her eyes down though her hackles were raised, hardly lending to her appetite. But she must be a good example to the children, even remembering to bow her head and say grâce au bon Dieu. But in English, not French. Henrietta seemed reluctant to release her hand, but Nolan was already passing dishes as they came his way as expertly as any grown-up.

"Miam!" Henrietta said, tasting the creamed ham.

Sylvie smiled, unwittingly having taught her the French word. When with the children, she sometimes forgot herself, slipping back to the easy rapport she'd had with children in Acadie.

Nolan craned his neck to look toward the kitchen. "See any ratafia cakes?"

"I smell gingerbread," Sylvie told him, eyes on her plate, wanting no excuse to look up and meet the Scot's gaze again. "Perhaps with the lemon custard you're so fond of."

As for herself, she ate without tasting, swallowing the sour beer she found so distasteful but these Virginians couldn't seem to get enough of, and listened to the robust conversation all around them. At last, her plate empty save the coming gingerbread, she dared to look up.

The foyer was empty.

Her mind veered to the little book in her room, capable of softening her heart with the pressed petals between its pages. Why had he given it to her? What did it matter to him that she was here? Was she not a barbed reminder of all that had been? No matter where he was—or she was—he remained the enemy. Pondering it, she built back the wall around her heart that had started to crack with his gift.

Yawning, Henrietta picked at her gingerbread with tiny fingers while Sylvie gave hers to Nolan. Grinning his thanks, he devoured it, and they made ready to leave. Outside, street-lamps were being lit as the day's light was snuffed by the gathering darkness.

"Is that a dog?" Nolan poked a finger toward one side of the tavern steps. "Or a wolf?"

"A wolf dog," Sylvie said, and the creature raised its sleek head to look at them. "Bonami."

"Is that its name?" Nolan dropped to one knee and ran a hand over the brindled back. "How did you know?"

"He belongs to a man I know."

"He needs a bone," Nolan said as Bonami wagged his plumy tail. "Our old dog liked bones."

"His master is in the tavern. Perhaps he'll bring him some scraps." Sylvie wished they had something to give him too. "Let's be on our way, as the wind is chill and we have no fur like this patient creature."

At the top of the bookbindery stairs, Henrietta told her, "I'm cold. May I sleep in your room?"

Sylvie bent down and picked her up, dismayed at her shivering.

"She used to share Mama's bed when Papa was away soldiering." Nolan's voice wavered then stiffened. "Before they both got sick and died."

If only she could take away the sadness that seemed to trail a boy so small. "You must miss them very much." She hadn't asked about their past. Let them tell her in their own time and in their own way.

And then there was Eve, waiting patiently for them at the doorway of the children's room, making Sylvie wonder about her past too.

"I see no reason you can't keep warm with me," Sylvie told Henrietta. "I have two thick blankets, so you can give yours to Nolan. He can sleep in my trundle bed."

Henrietta gave a joyful little laugh, throwing her arms around Sylvie's neck. "Can I bring Tabitha, my doll?"

"Oui, otherwise she might be cold too." Try as she might to say *aye* or *yes, oui* repeatedly found its way forward.

Sylvie set Henrietta down, and the girl rushed down the narrow hallway past Eve.

"You sure about this, Miss Sylvie?" Eve asked.

"I'm glad of their company." Sylvie looked at the woman who said so little yet did so much. "And you deserve a peaceful night, Eve."

Eve looked away, her face in shadows. "I don't recollect the last time anyone fretted themselves about that."

33

Now I know myne owne ground and I will work when I please and play when I please.

Anthony Johnson, free Black, Virginia Colony

Will sat upstairs in the Bruton Parish Church gallery, crowded with William and Mary students, while Lord Drysdale sat in the pew below reserved for him and Lady Drysdale. The sermon was long but to the mark, and aside from refusing to pray communally for the English king, Will left church in a better frame of mind than when he'd arrived. He half expected pealing bells to rend the December air, but there was no bricked belfry here like in so many New England churches.

Despite the cold, the day was sunny and Palace Green had more than a few people walking about. He nearly took a step back as his gaze fastened on one in particular as easily as his surveying compass found magnetic north. But in a town of only two thousand souls, he was bound to keep coming across Sylvie Galant.

She was walking toward the Governor's Palace, the children he'd seen with her at supper in hand. Beside them walked a Black woman he'd noticed about the bookbindery. Owned by Hunter, likely. Half of Williamsburg was enslaved. He decried it, and his stance had earned him enemies since coming to Virginia. But a few shared his views, some of them members of Bruton Parish Church, including Lord Drysdale, who'd invited him to the morning service.

To clear his head, Will turned down Duke of Gloucester Street to avoid Palace Green. The shops were closed, the Sabbath hush at odds with the agitation inside him. He was expected at the townhouse to join Kersey for dinner at two o'clock, but he was no idle Virginian, sitting and smoking and imbibing till then. A long walk would do him good.

Sylvie walked faster, trying to keep up with the children. They were cooped up like chicks in the bookbindery for long days, and now they frolicked like spring lambs in the wintry air and darted away from her. Eve had knitted them mittens and hats, and their rosy cheeks and noses turned them into winged cherubs. Sylvie was soon out of breath, not quite recovered from her recent malady.

Palace Green stretched languorously in the sunshine and seemed to lure everyone outside. Sylvie lost count of the fine carriages that lumbered past—chariots, these Virginians called them—some with liveried servants, their occupants adorned in silks and velvets. Churchgoers? Eve didn't gawk like she did but kept her eyes down.

"You're quiet today, Eve," Sylvie said, hoping to draw her out.

"I don't talk much, Miss Sylvie," Eve replied. "I just . . . do."

"We don't know much about each other beyond our names. I count you a friend and would learn more."

"Friends?" A lengthy pause. Eve never spoke in haste.

"That's a mighty strange word to call somebody like myself. Besides, my place isn't to ask questions, just answer them. The quieter I am, the better." Her slender face beneath her cap was stoic, the faint lines about her mouth the only indicator of her age. "Mam always told me so."

"Is your mother here in Williamsburg?"

"She's out a ways from town at Carter's Grove."

"I've not heard of it."

"Fancy that." Eve chuckled, a rare occurrence. "Then you'd be the first. Burwell Carter is known far and wide just like his grandfather, King Carter, used to be."

"Why is your mother there and not here?"

"When I was small, we were separated. Sold. Mam went to the plantation, but Mr. Hunter bought me at auction on the steps of the Raleigh Tavern when I was no bigger than Rietta here."

Sylvie schooled her revulsion. To shackle a child, to own a fellow human being . . . The enemy's evil was boundless. Eve knew a different sort of bondage, a far greater one than Sylvie, who was free even if she felt chained to her circumstances. She could quit Mr. Hunter, but Eve never could.

"There aren't any slaves where you're from?" Eve asked quietly.

"Black sailors, mostly." Sylvie's thoughts stretched back. "I recall a few dark-skinned people when I went to convent school at a place called Ile Royale. But I didn't know much about them or how they came to be there."

"We hail from Africa mostly, on slave ships. Some Blacks come from the Caribbean. I know a few free Black jacks from Captain Lennox's crew."

"Have you any freedoms at all?"

Eve's forehead knotted. "We ain't free to go to church or marry. If we don't mind our place, we get pilloried or whipped or worse. We ain't allowed to learn or be schooled.

Can't carry a weapon or defend ourselves. Striking a white man or woman means death." She frowned, eyes on the cobbled street. "So many laws keep us bound up, but I've never known any different."

"Can you earn your freedom?"

"Rare as hen's teeth, freedom. Slaves don't get wages, understand. Masters provide for our living, or are supposed to. Now, Mr. Hunter's better than most. I get victuals and a bed—and he leaves me be."

Sylvie had seen light-skinned Black children in town. Could this be what she meant? Or did he simply not whip her?

"We Acadians simply have to be inside before dark," Sylvie said, having broken this rule already. "If we venture to another parish, an armed escort is needed. We're not supposed to be employed since we're considered wards of the parish, though some powerful Virginians are testing those limits."

They walked on, turning down Nicholson Street, a back road that housed the public gaol. The place, full of pirates and convicts and the insane, left Sylvie sorrowful and disturbed. She could hear their cries and shouts past the barred windows. They took another right, onto Waller Street behind the pompous, brick capitol building where these English governed. And there she came face-to-face with the Scot. Again.

She simply must escape Williamsburg.

She slowed, her awkwardness plain. Eve shot her a questioning glance before taking Henrietta and Nolan in hand.

"Mademoiselle Galant." His words were deferential, his gaze direct. "Un moment, s'il vous plaît."

She balked, but how could she ignore a man who had come to a complete halt in the middle of the street?

"Please go on without me, Eve," she said softly. "The children are growing cold."

Eve hastened her steps, Henrietta and Nolan in tow, though they looked back at Sylvie questioningly.

She nearly sighed as she met his eyes. "You needn't address me in Française."

"You needn't be ashamed of who you are," he replied in French.

Sylvie looked about, continuing in English, "Where is Bonami?"

He persisted in French. "In Kersey's garden on Palace Street."

Was that where he lived, then? She fell silent, the wind toying with her wool cape and sweeping dried leaves across the street more briskly than any broom. He took something out of his coat pocket and handed it to her, though the wind tried to snatch it away. She looked down at an advertisement of sorts, struck by its wording. So, instruction was needed in the art of the French tongue?

"What a riddle you English are." She couldn't keep contempt from her tone. "You revile us yet covet our language, our fashions and cuisine, even our dances."

"I'm Scots, remember. A world away from the English. And I only covet your conversation."

She faltered, chastising herself. Rarely was she unkind, and it seemed especially unbecoming on the Sabbath when he was so civil. "I am already employed."

"You aren't indentured but a day laborer," he continued. "At liberty to do what you will with your free hours, including teaching your native tongue."

"And why would I?" The question came softly as she met his eyes, finding them a gleaming silver like the wares of Williamsburg's silversmith.

"You'd be surprised by how many colonials want to be fluent. It's a mark of gentility, a way to keep up with learned Londoners and the rest of Europe."

She allowed herself one curiosity. "How did you come to speak it so well?"

"I was locked in a French fort for months on end with little to do otherwise. But that's a story best saved for another day."

Surprised, she pocketed the paper lest it fly away. She wished *he* would. They were teetering dangerously close to what felt like a confidence. A forbidden familiarity. But he made no motion to leave, and since it was the Sabbath and the street was mostly deserted, he had no reason to move from where he stood.

"I'd rather hear about you," he said, again in French. "What happened aboard the *Dolphin*?"

She hesitated as a couple strolled by arm in arm. Their high-spirited talk and laughter rankled. She waited till they'd passed to answer. "We were at sea more than three weeks before foundering in a storm. Prior to that, many aboard the vessel sickened and died." To the end of her days she'd believe more perished of heartbreak than disease. "I lost my mother and sister. I don't know what became of my father and brothers or the rest of my kin."

Though she kept her voice free of emotion, she saw unchecked sorrow in his face. It chipped dangerously at her composure, so she changed course. "And you? Why are you here and not in New England?"

He ran a hand across his clean-shaven jaw, reminding her of how bewhiskered he'd been in Acadie. He was even more saisissant—striking—than she recalled, and she hated that she noticed. Hated that she still felt that same infuriating, inexplicable fascination for him as she did at first.

"Acadie changed everything for me," he said. "I wanted to get away from the war. Virginia seemed a new beginning."

"But you must have family in the northeast."

"Nay." The terse word led to a pause so prolonged he had

her full attention. "My family was massacred by French and Huron when I was a boy. I hid in a hayrick and watched it happen . . . then I ran."

Massacred?

She stood mute, mind whirling. Horror and bloodshed and mutilation leapt to mind. Tears blurred her vision, her heart so rent she couldn't speak.

Stepping away, he touched the brim of his cocked hat. "Adieu, Mademoiselle Galant."

34

I sincerely hope your Christmas . . . may abound in the
gaieties which that season generally brings.

Jane Austen, *Pride and Prejudice*

The Rivanna River was one of the comeliest watercourses Will had ever seen. Cradled by foothills sloping down to timberlands, it cut an icy finger through
his newly surveyed territory a half mile wide in places. He
stood, breath pluming, wishing the cold away and longing to
canoe clear to its watery end at the foot of the Blue Mountains. Come spring, the land would be glorious, thick with
redbud and dogwood, bluestem and spicebush. For now he
felt satisfied he'd carved his initials into the trunks of mas-
sive oaks and elms at the land's boundaries.

This place matched the image in the vision, the one that
had come to him long ago.

This was his land, the acreage patented in Williamsburg,
the deed locked away. Two thousand acres of frontier once
owned by a Virginia burgess whose debts and death led to
a quick, fortuitous sale. Though it had sat empty for a few
years, the handsome house was well-built and sturdy, the

well sound, the many dependencies still standing. An old Indian trail cut behind the barn, overgrown but still traceable, though the Monacan tribe had long since moved farther west.

He'd quickly seen all that was needed. The river itself begged a ferry and both grist- and sawmills. Solid, dependable ones like those he'd seen in the northeast. Cleared of debris like rocks and snags, the Rivanna would be navigable, and he spied a fine fording place not far from the old, overgrown orchard. Twisted trees still stood in neat rows, some enormous, their gnarled branches upraised like bare arms. Fallen, half-frozen fruit lay about like forgotten treasure.

He reached into his pocket and withdrew a small sack of Acadian apple seeds, a reminder of Sylvie. Not Sylvie as she'd been on Waller Street, heartbroken and defiant, but the warm, winsome woman untouched by tragedy, endearingly befuddled at first meeting.

He started toward the biggest apple tree, then froze when a cardinal shot out from a low branch and careened over his head toward the river. His pulse beat a hard, breathless rhythm, steady as a military drum. Would he never heal from the feeling of being hunted, a target? Every shadow, every turn still seemed to conceal the enemy or some potential pitfall. It had helped make him a wary child then a watchful Ranger, but now as a civilian . . .

At least the murderous rage that once burned in him since his family's massacre was banked, the fire out. For that he could be thankful. The Almighty had saved him before he'd taken more lives or had his taken, his eternity in question.

For now, he put away the seed packet and turned back toward the place he'd call home, a far cry from the roughly chinked cabin he'd known in childhood. The solid stone-and-brick house before him would still be standing a century hence, its neglected grandeur making the surrounding dependencies shabbier still. If only he had a company of Rangers ready to farm and rebuild. Barring that, he knew a few Acadians who needed the work.

As Noël neared, Sylvie's thoughts were awash with the past. It was the time of croque-cignoles and midnight mass, of clan gatherings and snowfalls and plans for the New Year. In Louisbourg merchants celebrated by opening their shops on Christmas Day. On the Aulac Ridge, Fort Beauséjour once fired its cannons with a celebratory clamor heard all over Acadie. What she'd give to gather with her family and sing "Est Né Le Divin Enfant" once more by candlelight.

Adrift, she tried to maintain ties to the other Acadians in Williamsburg. Eulalie was now working at the Governor's Palace, Antoinette at the apothecary, and Sebastien at the blacksmith's down the street. Sylvie was unsure about the others but wanted to see if they could somehow arrange a time to meet. Busy as she was in the bookbindery and with the children, it seemed an impossibility, but Mr. Hunter shuttered the shop for the English celebrations extending from Christmas to Twelfth Day in January. Here the holidays were a time not only for churchgoing but for merriment like masquerade balls and fox hunts, a mix of piety and pleasure.

Mr. Hunter had even hung mistletoe above the bookbindery door. One of the apprentices informed her it was meant for kissing. She dismissed his long looks, hoping he'd turn his attentions elsewhere in time, though she credited him for being undeterred by her Frenchness.

The next Saturday, restless after a long day at the bookbindery, she left Eve and the children, all three nursing colds, in the attic. Bundled up in her cape, she walked the back streets as the cressets were lit, the hanging iron baskets full of fatwood keeping a steady flame around town. The sharp tang of woodsmoke and comely squares of golden light framing countless windows was now familiar.

She ventured toward the stately brick house she now knew as Kersey's, intent on the second floor. Which room was the Scot's? She'd not seen him lately around town, nor had he come into the shop. Since his shocking revelation on that windy Sabbath, he seemed to have vanished. Did he watch her now from a window? The possibility hastened her on, his words still haunting.

My family was massacred by French and Huron when I was a boy . . .

This startling exposé had somehow shifted how she regarded him. He was no longer the marauder in her mind but among the wronged and wounded. His hard beginnings seemed a world away from the feared and revered Ranger he had become, but they had surely shaped him into pursuing the military path, much as Bleu's mother's death at the hands of the English had shaped him into becoming united with the Resistance.

At the end of the street, Bruton Parish Church dominated one corner, an arresting, circular window above an arched doorway, the interior laid out like a Latin cross, or so she'd heard. A graveyard with frosted tombstones gave her pause, and then she turned up Nassau Street, where genteel homes and geometric gardens held sway. A few late flowers still bloomed, making her somewhat disbelieving it was December.

She walked on, sunk in thoughts of home as she'd last seen it, full of fire and fury. Now in winter it would be naught but ashes under sullen skies, bereft of music except the eternal murmur of Baie Française against long stretches of sandy shore.

Her heart twisted anew, and she hurried north to the Governor's Palace to visit Eulalie, avoiding the scrolled iron gate at the forecourt to seek a side entrance. A liveried servant pointed to the kitchen when she asked for Miss Benoit.

"She's working in the big house now," he replied. "A housemaid was needed more than a kitchen maid."

In minutes she'd gained the palace itself and was ushered to a small chamber reserved for visitors. A low fire burned in the hearth, and there she waited and warmed herself. As she heard the tap-tap of heels coming her way, she hoped Eulalie would be genuinely glad to see her.

"Sylvie!" Tears stood in Eulalie's eyes, removing all doubt, and they embraced long and hard before bursting into effusive if whispered French.

"I have been wondering about you," Eulalie said, drying her eyes with the hem of her apron. "Noël is almost upon us."

"I am hoping we can gather for a veillée. None of us will be working. We can at least share a meal. I can let Sebastien and Antoinette know, though I'm not sure where others of us have gone."

"Gabriel and Lucas are at the cabinetmaker's and Nicolas the cooper's. Louise was moved to the chandlery from the cobbler's. Some of our older men were taken to plantations to work the tobacco, including my cousin Antoine."

Sylvie looked about the elegantly paneled room. "How is it here?"

Eulalie pushed a strand of fair hair beneath her cap. "I confess I am more mouse than maid. The upper servants shun or belittle me, but the lower servants are more peaceable. I try to do my work, say nothing, and hide my Frenchness."

You needn't be ashamed of who you are.

The Scot's insistent words returned like a rogue wave, only she was more inclined to agree with them now than when he'd first said them.

"How goes it for you at the bookbindery?" Eulalie asked, pale features pinched with concern.

Sylvie lifted her shoulders in a shrug. "I stay quiet and work hard like you so that no one can fault me. Save the Sabbath, I help care for two foundlings who are too young yet to apprentice."

"Your hours are full, then." Eulalie's half smile became a sigh. "How are we to make a life of our own, always working for someone else?"

Sylvie tried not to look ahead. The weight of each day was worry enough. "Perhaps if we all meet for Noël we can consider that together."

⌒

Sylvie found Sebastien Broussard at the blacksmith's. Despite the cold, he was seated outside on a bench, smoke from his clay pipe curling into the chill air, much as his breath did when he spoke.

"Bienvenue, mademoiselle," he said, unsmiling.

"Merci," she replied, not wanting to intrude on his quiet time even as he gestured to the bench beside him. Sitting down, she clasped her mittened hands in her lap, coming straight to the point. "I have been to see Eulalie at the Governor's Palace, and we hope to gather with you and the others at Noël."

He nodded. "There is little to celebrate, but I am willing to gather, oui."

"We hope to enjoy each other's company if nothing else," she said softly, looking at the forge's fire without wanting to. It cast her back to Pont-a-Buot and the doctor-spy. "How goes your work here at the smithy?"

A shake of his head withered her hopes. "Alas, I am a farmer, not a blacksmith."

The lament returned her to verdant fields and dike lands and the richest of grains. The Broussards had been renowned farmers and cattlemen, not only Resistance fighters. Turning back to him, she spied a burn on his right hand, fiery and blistering. "I can bring you some salve for your wound. The apothecary is not far—"

"All the salve in the world would not help me. Let the burns be a reminder that I cannot get comfortable here among our enemies."

No, never comfortable. She clasped her hands tighter. "You want to return home, as I do, but we cannot."

"No, we cannot. I've heard the enemy is even now giving our homeplaces to the Anglais."

This was the ultimate insult and humiliation. Was there no justice? No restitution? For a time they lapsed into a mutual, miserable silence.

When he broke it, his voice was so low and grieved it was nearly lost to her. "Why do I feel like a jilted lover, spending my life and labor on lands that will now go to another?"

A fair comparison.

He took another draw on his pipe, then blew out an agitated breath. "To lose all that we love—all those we love. They seem to hover endlessly as if their souls can find no rest."

Was he thinking of his betrothed? Realizing they should have been wed by now, welcoming winter as a couple? She studied him in the last of daylight. He looked more than hurt. He looked haunted. Perhaps she did too.

"I want to believe we are blessed to have survived, but . . ."

"Blessed?" he said. "Once I knew the word, but no longer. Is it not utter torment to wonder what has become of our loved ones? To ponder those still at anchor in Hampton Roads and elsewhere?" His jaw clenched. "I have no rest, no peace. It is all I can do to stay standing."

Was it not the same for her, as she continually pushed back the harsh memories of before to try to stay atop the challenging, baffling after?

"This place stifles the soul."

This she understood. They were made for wide-open spaces and endless waters, not landlocked English towns.

Reaching out, she put a hand on his sleeve. "Will you come to our small Noël fête?" she asked gently. "At least for a few minutes?"

"Perhaps," he said without looking at her. "But I cannot promise you any jollity, Sylvie Galant. I am completely bereft of celebration."

 **35**

So help thyself, and heaven will help thee too.

Jean de La Fontaine

Sylvie prepared for Noël once the shop closed for Christmas, wondering if Sebastien would come or if anyone could possibly enjoy their small celebration bereft of chapel and mass and all the usual trappings. The pine boughs and laurels she'd found behind a near tavern, the money she'd spent on candles, and the strange confections she'd bought at the bakeshop would have to suffice. But it seemed a pitiful echo of a bygone time.

Still, Mr. Hunter had offered the back room of the bookbindery for their use. As he was brusque and barked at the slightest shop infraction, she'd not thought he had such kindness in him. Marveling at this allowance, she wanted to make the occasion as welcoming and warm as she could. It touched her that the children wanted to help, their unfeigned delight bolstering her spirits. She invited Eve too, and came up against Virginia's strict social order.

"Miss Sylvie, white folks don't mingle with Black folks," Eve said, clearly taken aback.

"The English, you mean," Sylvie replied. "We Acadians are different. We welcome others and learn from them. We even marry and have families. My own brother is part Mi'kmaq."

"Fancy that." Eve regarded her curiously. "What do you call this gathering?"

"A fête—a celebration of Noël."

"Christmas," Eve said as Sylvie adorned the room with the greenery she'd found. "Seems you need music. I can ask my brother, Noah, to come play. His master's the cooper and lets him fiddle around town once the work is done."

"Would you?" Sylvie asked. Though the room was small, they might dance, or just sit and listen.

When the time came, Sylvie lit the candles while Nolan tended the fire. Henrietta sampled a pastry, hiding shyly behind Sylvie's skirts as guests arrived. To their surprise, the first to appear was Lord Drysdale and a servant. Unaware of their meeting, he stayed long enough only to inquire after them and wish them well, then left money gifts for them, including pipes and tobacco for the men, gloves and lace for the women. Before Sylvie could inquire about Lady Drysdale, Captain Lennox, and Esmée Shaw, he bade them farewell, not wanting to intrude on their plans.

As Noah tuned his fiddle in a corner, Eulalie entered, making much of the children and complimenting Sylvie on her decorating. In her basket was a wealth of sweetmeats gotten from the Governor's Palace kitchen, the remains from last night's masquerade ball. Surprisingly, Sebastien appeared next, carrying a small keg of cider. Others arrived, some Sylvie recognized and some she didn't, till the chamber held more than twenty Acadians, all who labored in and around Williamsburg.

As the music started, cider was served and the table seemed to swell with fare, including cold Virginia ham and smoked fish, cheese wafers, and the coveted figs and walnuts.

"Even pork pies like our tourtière," Nicolas said in approval, taking seconds.

Sylvie was glad of the bounty and those who ate heartily. She herself could hardly manage a bite, making sure everyone was comfortable and enjoying themselves as much as they could. A fragment of the Psalms the Scot had written out for her wended through her thoughts again.

Thou preparest a table before me in the presence of mine enemies.

For a few seconds she felt somewhat satisfied.

Eve hovered, pulling out a chair for Sylvie to sit. "Rest yourself. The merriment ends all too soon."

Though the room was too crowded for dancing, Henrietta and Nolan amused them all by trying to step a jig in a corner. Toward midnight the music dwindled along with the rest of the feast. When Noah put his fiddle away, the conversation continued, and Sylvie listened, warmed by the English Yule log burning in the hearth.

"Have you any news of friends and family?" Etienne broached the question uppermost in all their minds. "Anything at all?"

A somber hush ensued. Would that not be the best Noël gift of all?

"Nothing substantial, only that more Acadians have escaped the ships at Hampton Roads and farther up the James River," Sebastien said. "They are fleeing Virginia to go north and south to find family and friends."

"I would jump ship too," Eulalie said. "Why is the governor taking so long to decide what to do with our people still aboard in such miserable conditions?"

"The governor is at the mercy of the council." Nicolas spoke with the gravity of a judge. "Though a few good men champion us, we have many adversaries here, and the powers that be bicker among themselves as to our fate."

"Once I have enough funds, I am considering leaving to seek my own family where ships have landed in colonial ports," Jacques-Rene said. "Perhaps buy passage on a ship if I cannot go far on foot."

Louise shuddered. "Never do I want to be at sea again."

Several nodded in agreement, Sylvie included.

"Williamsburg isn't the place for me," Sebastien murmured. "Though Mr. Houghton treats me decently, I am no blacksmith, nor will I ever be."

Nicolas shook his head. "Nor am I a cooper, which brings to mind a curious offer made by a man named Blackburn. He approached me several days ago and said he is looking for men to work his acreage on the Rivanna River. He wanted me to tell all of you if you are interested."

Blackburn again? Sylvie snapped to attention, Henrietta asleep on her lap.

"A planter, then?" Thibault asked. "Why doesn't he buy slaves like most Virginians?"

"He isn't Virginian. He's from the north, a former soldier. He prefers to contract indentures—or employ free men like ourselves," Nicolas told them.

"Free? I do not feel free." Jean-Luc grimaced and poured himself more cider. "Working another man's land is no better than blacksmithing when you need to be working your own."

"Are you considering?" Sebastien asked Nicolas.

He nodded. "I have no choice but to work for another until I earn enough to buy property or go in search of my family. Besides, Blackburn makes a fair offer. He promises a good wage, bed, and board. He needs an abandoned plantation he bought at auction restored. He has seed, tools, and all that is necessary."

"The Rivanna River?" Béatrice asked. "I don't suppose he is wanting women to work? To cook and tend gardens and orchards?"

"I shall ask him," Nicolas replied. "He lodges here in town while he prepares to move to his land."

"How does he come by his money for such a proposition?" Skepticism threaded Sebastien's tone. "An ambitious, even dangerous endeavor, partnering with us outcasts."

"He has the backing of a few influential Virginians besides being a newly appointed Crown surveyor," Nicolas answered. "He founded Ranger companies in the British army till he quit them after our forced removal, and he has recently published a book of his exploits in an attempt to further his plans."

Eulalie looked horrified. "Major William Blackburn of Blackburn's Rangers?"

"Oui," Sebastien said with thinly veiled contempt. "Le Diable Blanc."

Nicolas continued, undaunted. "He was in Acadie at the last, searching for leaders of the Resistance, but was not told of the English's plan to remove us until it unfolded before his eyes. He then resigned, creating something of a storm when he is most needed in this ongoing conflict."

An outburst of comments ensued, but Sylvie paid no attention, she was so overwhelmed with details she hadn't known. Crown surveyor? Plantation owner? William Blackburn had not told her this, though he might have, had she been more willing to listen.

"We'd be wise to consider both sides," Jean-Luc was saying. "What sort of man would willingly employ those of us called the 'mongrel race of French papists'?"

"A brave, bold one," Etienne answered, "who is unafraid of what ungodly men devise."

Sylvie sighed, and Sebastien's gaze turned to her.

"Will you go to the Rivanna River?" he asked her.

She tried to tamp down her curiosity to no avail. "How far away is it?"

"Nearly a hundred miles west of here. Frontier, formerly Indian land stolen by the English."

Jean-Luc expelled a breath. "Wide-open places, and fewer people would be welcome. Farming is what I know best. Though I am older than most of you, I am not afraid of hard work."

"Blackburn warns that it will be rough," Nicolas said. "Raw land and former fields need clearing, in addition to roadbuilding and river navigation—not unlike what met our great-grandfathers in Acadie."

"But it is work we know, wrestling with the land," Thibault mused, lighting his new pipe. "I would hear more from this Blackburn."

36

I have more memories than if I'd lived a thousand years.

Charles Baudelaire

A sennight had passed when Sylvie realized something was afoot that might end her tenure at the bookbindery. Someone had lodged a complaint about her with Mr. Hunter, an apprentice confided. Sylvie wasn't surprised, certain her being Acadian rather than her work performance was at the heart of it. Mrs. Webb refused to speak to her, and over the next few days Sylvie felt a growing tension in the shop though she kept to her work, sewing more headbands at the stitching frame than ever before. It was then she remembered the advertisement about classes in the art of the French tongue.

Once the workday ended, Sylvie postponed supper with the children and hastened to the Raleigh Tavern, where the notice had originated. A maid ushered her into a back room, where she waited, her prayers interspersed with window gazing as wealthy gentlemen left coaches and saddles to converge in the popular Apollo Room.

At last the tavern's owner appeared, looking slightly flustered, his spotted spectacles in need of cleaning. "The French tongue, you say? That advertisement has since been filled." Sylvie schooled her disappointment as he continued, "But I have it on good authority that a French tutor is needed for Governor Dinwiddie's daughters, if you've the courage to apply at the palace."

Dare she?

Out the door she went, lamenting her plain clothes and scuffed shoes. Then she remembered the Lyonnais silk gown. And Bleu. Sorrow clouded her thinking as she made her way back to the bookbindery to take the children to the tavern.

Upstairs, Eve met her with a frown, her usual reserve missing. "Miss Sylvie, I overheard Mrs. Webb tell Mr. Hunter she would up and quit if you stayed on."

"But why would he listen to her?" Sylvie's dread deepened. "He's the owner, she's the help."

"She's his sister," Eve returned. "And sour as Caribbean lemons."

Sylvie sank down on the end of her bed as the children rushed in, clamoring for their supper. How she would miss them and Eve! Henrietta buried her face in Sylvie's aproned lap, but Sylvie's thoughts were rushing ahead to what she might do to spare both herself and Mr. Hunter a confrontation.

Quieting the children, she explained this new turn of events and confided to Eve, "I have a gown that might suit the palace." Though it had traversed leagues in the dank, reeking ship's hold, rimed with sea salt and wrinkled, it hadn't lost its luster. "But I'll need your help pressing it and making it presentable."

"The silk I cleaned for you a while back?" Eve started for the iron. "I'll set it to rights while you have your supper. Never you mind Mrs. Webb. This is bound to be more blessing than curse."

The Governor's Palace, always grand and forbidding, was never more so than when seeking employment. Sylvie met with Eulalie beforehand, telling her the plan. With a conspiratorial air, Eulalie brought her through a back door into the grand entrance hall that boasted a great many weapons and a black-and-white-tiled floor, including a royal coat of arms. Sylvie wasn't the only one beseeching the governor's favor. The forecourt and stone steps overflowed with people awaiting a meeting.

Eulalie whispered in the butler's ear why Sylvie was there, so her wait was not long. She was soon ushered into a small antechamber, where a clerk entered her name in one of the large leather books the bookbindery sold. Then she waited again, taking in the rich wallpaper and furnishings, especially smitten with the tall, narrow windows sparkling with English crown glass.

"Mademoiselle Galant." A liveried footman beckoned for Sylvie to follow, and she was led upstairs to what she guessed were the family's private rooms, her silk skirts whispering on the dark wooden steps. The gown hung a bit loosely now, but Eve had helped her pin it becomingly in place, so she held her head up, feigning confidence. Eve had done a fine job erasing every wrinkle and even found Sylvie a bergère hat so stylish in Virginia, trimmed with a bit of silk ribbon.

Another clerk led her to an upper middle room and introduced her not to the governor but the governor's wife. Mrs. Dinwiddie was a small, plump woman, heavily powdered and sporting a beauty patch on her right cheekbone. She entered the chamber, her eyes on Sylvie's garments and not her face. Did she find the silk favorable, or was it too grand for Sylvie's mission?

"What is your purpose, mademoiselle?" Mrs. Dinwiddie asked her.

"I've come seeking an appointment as French tutor to your daughters."

With a gesture inviting Sylvie to take a striped silk chair, Mrs. Dinwiddie sat across from her, her bejeweled hands folded in her lap. "Your credentials and character references?"

"I am simply French born, newly arrived on your shores, and lately in the employ of the bookbindery." Sylvie grasped for more to embellish this slim proposition. "I've fallen on hard times, and if not for the kind assistance of Lord Drysdale and Captain Lennox—"

"Ah, two such esteemed gentlemen. Say no more, mademoiselle." Mrs. Dinwiddie switched easily into French, conversing loquaciously with Sylvie for a half hour. "We've been in Virginia for four years but find proper education lacking for genteel females. Our former tutor has returned to England, and we've been in search of a replacement. I have high hopes for my daughters, you see. But enough about Rebecca and Elizabeth—you must meet them." With a smile, Mrs. Dinwiddie pulled on a bell cord. Two girls came into the room so quickly Sylvie wondered if they'd been listening at the keyhole.

Before her gaped two mademoiselles, one Sylvie guessed to be Marie-Madeleine's age. The comparison pinched, but the pivotal moment allowed for no melancholy. Clad in lovely shades of mint and rose, they looked to be miniatures of their mother. Standing, Sylvie gave a small curtsey. Good manners were never amiss, were they?

"These are my lovely daughters who are in need of mastery of the French tongue." Mrs. Dinwiddie surveyed them fondly as she introduced them to Sylvie. "Girls, meet your newest tutor, Mademoiselle Galant. I forbid you to speak English with her, only French."

"Like they do at Versailles?" the younger, Elizabeth, asked with a childish lisp. "In the court of Louis the Beloved?"

Sylvie felt a qualm. This mademoiselle knew more than she about French affairs across the water. Smiling past her nervousness, Sylvie reverted to her native tongue. "Comme je suis heureux de vous rencontrer." *How happy I am to meet you* was an overstatement, but what else could she say?

Elizabeth smiled while Rebecca looked on with a chilly hauteur. "Where shall Mademoiselle Galant live, Mama?"

"Here in the palace, of course, along with the upper servants."

"When will lessons begin?" Elizabeth asked so eagerly Sylvie was touched.

Mrs. Dinwiddie looked to Sylvie. "Mademoiselle?"

"As soon as you wish," Sylvie replied, hardly believing her turn of fortune.

"Day after tomorrow, then. We shall make arrangements."

The four Acadian men gathered in Kersey's townhouse looked out of place and uncomfortable. Even though Liselotte Kersey, acting as hostess, tried to put them at ease, they stood stiff as scarecrows in the ornate grandeur of the chamber, which was made only slightly warmer by the robust hearth's fire.

"At your ease," Will told them, inviting them to sit.

Sebastien Broussard took an upholstered sofa, the others following suit, but on so cold a day Will was sure they'd rather keep to the hearth. Their curiosity was apparent as steaming drinks were brought in large tankards, redolent with spices and spirits. Had they never had flip? From the looks on their faces, nay.

Nicolas, clearly the spokesman for the group, nodded his appreciation. "We're here to learn more about the work you offer on the Rivanna River."

Liselotte stood at a side door as if asking if Will needed anything more. She was attentive of late, more than a little interested in the Rivanna purchase. With a slight shake of his head, he bade her close the door for privacy's sake.

He thanked the men for coming, letting them enjoy their drinks as he gathered his thoughts. Having returned from a short survey the night before, he'd been surprised when he'd learned several Acadians had been to the townhouse seeking him.

As they emptied their tankards, Will laid out the terms of employment per contract and did not hide the fact that the endeavor would entail strenuous work. But he'd witnessed these Acadians laboring among their aboiteaux, harnessing the strongest tides he'd ever seen—strength that was wasted on blacksmithing and chandlery. These were men of the earth. Farming was what they did best, and he would treat them as he had his Rangers, fairly and generously and with respect. He felt a profound regret that they no longer inhabited their homeland.

It did not hurt that he spoke to them in their native language, even calling them défricheurs d'eau, which spoke to their ingenuity and strength and made them smile.

"Oui, I am a water clearer, soon to be a land clearer," Nicolas told him. "When do we begin?"

"The first of March, by my reckoning," Will answered. "I have indentures on the Rivanna working ahead of your arrival, preparing your dwellings as I amass more provisions and tools."

"Can we begin sooner? We fear that in so English a town, we might well be rounded up and exiled like before, to places unknown," Jean-Luc said as their expressions hardened.

"That remains a threat, aye." Will would not mislead them like he had Sylvie. "But as you know, Lord Drysdale and Captain Lennox continue to act on your behalf—and I'm just as committed to giving you another opportunity."

"Have you need of any women workers?" Thibault asked.

"Are any willing?" Will replied.

"One mademoiselle asked about cooking and gardening," Sebastien told him.

Not Sylvie, Will guessed, though he wished otherwise. "If she can withstand the remoteness and conditions, she's welcome to join us."

They nodded, seemingly undeterred. Their dislike of Williamsburg and close proximity to the English were clear enough.

He himself felt hemmed in like a fox before hounds. With anti-French sentiment at fever pitch, and the ribald public times when the courts convened in the capital approaching, the Rivanna seemed a sort of haven.

"You've no doubt heard of the French Huguenots in King William County," Will told them. "Though they're Protestant, they began as exiles and refugees, laboring and gradually acquiring land of their own, marrying, and having families. The Rivanna settlement is patterned after them as I've studied their successes and failures. It will take time, but all solid endeavors do."

"You are now a Crown surveyor if not a soldier," Nicolas said. "How often will you be at the Rivanna settlement?"

"As it stands, I'll continue my surveying work. But I consider the Rivanna my permanent home and I'll continue provisioning it as needed, in my absence or otherwise."

More flip was served as he explained his vision, answering their questions and thereby confirming his plan might well work. Less risky than going into battle, it would still be a battle nonetheless.

He fell quiet, letting them talk. Relaxed by the fire and the mellowing flip, they spoke freely of their time in Williamsburg and their ties to those who had escaped both the ships and the almshouse with the help of Lennox and Drysdale.

"We had a small gathering at Noël," Etienne said, "at the request of Mademoiselle Galant. Though we are far from feeling celebratory, it was still good to be together."

Will added another log to the fire. "And how is Mademoiselle?"

"She has exchanged the bookbindery for the Governor's Palace," Sebastien told him.

Will turned away from the hearth, his stoicism slipping. "The palace?"

"It seems the governor's daughters covet French lessons." Etienne's half smile was wry. "And at a most opportune time."

Jean-Luc nodded and swallowed more flip. "There was some upset in the bookbindery that necessitated her leaving, but I'm certain Mr. Hunter was loath to lose her, especially since she helped care for his orphans."

"So, she's now living at the palace?"

Lifting his shoulders in a slight shrug, Nicolas regarded him with undisguised amusement. "Something tells me, Major Blackburn, that you will soon find out."

37

All battles are first won or lost, in the mind.

Joan of Arc

Sylvie's head spun with all the changes. After so many shattering events, she seemed to have stepped into a fairy tale. Yet she was chary, never forgetting for a moment that she was still among the English who had routed her from her homeland and took it as their own. Though a Scot, Robert Dinwiddie decried Acadians being in Virginia to begin with.

Thankfully, Mrs. Dinwiddie did not question Sylvie further about her origins. The very names of Drysdale and Lennox seemed to convey a sort of magic that was almost amusing. Spared the drudgery of the bookbindery and the malevolent presence of Mrs. Webb, Sylvie felt great relief, though she missed Eve and the children.

With Mr. Hunter's blessing, Sylvie moved her few belongings into the palace, granted a small chamber near the daughters' rooms. Far grander than her attic quarters, it boasted a marble hearth and blue-papered walls that bespoke a calm elegance. She peered more closely at the trompe l'oeil pattern of a green meadow with a picturesque watercourse. Though the little book full of dried flowers and a few Scriptures was in her knapsack, one irrepressible line leapt to mind.

He maketh me to lie down in green pastures: he leadeth me beside the still waters.

Her soul stilled. Might her being in this room be not by happenstance but by design? Perhaps the Lord was leading her in ways she hadn't planned or preferred, but still *he leadeth.* There was little room to ponder the possibility, nor spare a moment's thought for the Scot who somehow, against her will, had simply become William Blackburn in her most private thoughts.

Since the Dinwiddie daughters had fallen ill with severe colds, lessons were postponed. This gave Sylvie a chance to return to the heart of town to purchase what she needed, including suitable garments from a mantua-maker. The remainder of Père's money lay heavy in the bottom of her haversack, along with her final wages from Mr. Hunter. As the door to the marchande de modes jingled, she entered the shop she'd only admired from the street. At once she was enveloped with the scent of cologne and newly imported fabric.

"Good day to you." A young seamstress sewing by a window greeted her, her keen eye no doubt dissecting Sylvie's humble woolen garments right down to her shoes. But she was tidy, at least. And clean.

In an hour Sylvie had left the shop with an armful of shifts, stockings, petticoats, and two dresses that befit her new station. She took a back street to avoid notice, sought the servants' entrance at the palace, and went up a back stair. Hanging her new clothes in the mahogany wardrobe that hugged one papered wall, she still felt disbelieving and, despite her luxurious surroundings, even more uncomfortable than she'd been at the bookbindery.

She closed the wardrobe just as Eulalie knocked, her smile

wide. Their rapid French volleyed about the small chamber, warm and effusive.

"Who would have thought we'd both end up in service at the finest residence in all Virginia?" Eulalie whispered as she dug in her pocket. "I've snuck you some of Cook's marzipan. The governor's butler, Mr. Gibbs, told me to tell you that you'll dine with the governess and the upper servants at meals, though I'll serve you tea right here at four o'clock."

"Serve me?" Sylvie asked as Eulalie passed her the sweets hidden in a linen napkin. "Can't you join me?"

"I'm merely a housemaid, a lower servant. There's a strict standing in the palace."

Yet another hurdle, then. Sylvie preferred to eat and keep to her room. Would they mind her Frenchness? What if they were no better than Mrs. Webb?

"There's frightful gossip here amongst the servants high and low, and all are abuzz about your arrival." Eulalie started for the door with a warning look. "We've a few varlets here, as the English say. Avoid Tristan, a footman, and Richard from the stables. They're all hands and gawking and take frightful liberties."

"Varlets," Sylvie echoed. Suddenly their elevated surroundings grew tarnished. "You don't sound content—or safe."

Eulalie lifted linen-clad shoulders in a shrug. "'Tis better than the almshouse . . . for now."

The upper servants gathered around a long table that evening, terse introductions made before a silent serving of soup, then a tasty chicken fricassee with vegetables and bread, followed by more marzipan. Eyes down, Sylvie ate, feeling her presence put a damper on what she guessed was usually a more garrulous gathering. Dread knotted her middle. How she wished she and Eulalie could simply share a simple crust of bread and some broth in her room.

"Mademoiselle Galant," the governess finally said at meal's end, "Miss Rebecca and Miss Elizabeth will soon be well enough to resume their lessons. Before they do, I'd like to meet with you in the schoolroom."

Sylvie forced a smile and nodded her agreement, only to wait twelve tense hours till Eulalie led her to the designated meeting place the next morning. Rain streaked the window-panes and the room was cast in shadows, though stacks of books and papers and writing implements were visible enough. A bird sang in a gilded corner cage, stealing Sylvie's attention. She pitied the poor creature. Did she not feel a little like that here in this gilded palace?

"I wanted to have a word with you about our charges," Mrs. Oliver began, looking dour in her gray garments, finely tailored though they were, an elaborate chatelaine dangling from her waist. "I see you admiring Lady Rebecca's canary. She's only diligent when it comes to playing her serinette to train Otto to sing."

A trained bird? Sylvie studied the box on the table—a bird organ? She had read about such things but never thought to see one. Something about it stifled the spirit. She was continually baffled by what amused the gentry in this colonial town.

Mrs. Oliver continued in methodical tones. "Rebecca is a bit willful and feels she is too old for lessons, preferring to gad about town. She has her father's sternness and can be quite forbidding. Elizabeth, however, is all roses and rainbows, more like her mother. At ten, she is still eager to please and devours her lessons like the songbird does seed."

Sylvie listened, determining not to be cowed by the glowering Rebecca. Elizabeth reminded her of Marie-Madeleine, and she felt an instant sentimental fondness for her.

"I wish you the best of luck with both. Should you have any concerns, please report them at once. Mrs. Dinwiddie has other matters to tend to and leaves overseeing the education of her daughters to me." Mrs. Oliver turned toward a glass-fronted bookcase and took a large daybook from the shelf. "Here is where you'll keep an account of your lessons—what was learned each day and any failures or successes. I peruse them regularly, as does Mrs. Dinwiddie and sometimes the governor himself."

With that, she gave Sylvie a skeleton key to the schoolroom, which was kept locked outside of lessons. Heavy and cold in her hand, the key seemed to unlock a door to her future. Her new position was unwanted but essential to her survival.

The first day of lessons dawned bright despite Rebecca's downcast countenance and her plea to return to her room. Sneezing into her lace-edged handkerchief, she pouted at Sylvie's refusal, and Sylvie counted it to her ill health rather than ill temperament. Or so she hoped. Elizabeth, on the other hand, beamed up at her like the rising sun, giving Sylvie a glimmer of hope.

Sitting down with them at a small round table while the songbird sang sweetly in its corner, Sylvie took a breath. Remembering not to speak a word of English, she began slowly in French, "Mightn't we play a word game? It will help acquaint me with how well you know the French tongue."

Rebecca nodded glumly while Elizabeth's amber eyes flashed in anticipation. Sylvie tossed a number of French words out, enunciating carefully, unsurprised to find that Elizabeth translated them faster than her sister. Next they penned the words with ink and paper, saying them together till the pronunciation was flawless. Though they were not fluent, they could converse adequately if slowly.

Sensing she was losing Rebecca's attention based on her frequent looks out the window, Sylvie withdrew the magazine à la mode she'd gotten from the bookbindery, along with a charming children's book of French verse with colorful illustrations.

"May I look?" Suddenly rapt, Rebecca all but seized the fashion magazine and paged through to the gowns.

Leaving her to look at her leisure, Sylvie turned her attention to Elizabeth, who read aloud from her book in halting French. When Rebecca gave a little gasp, Sylvie turned toward her in question.

"Oh, to have a gown like this for my father's next assembly!" she said, losing her reserve and turning the magazine toward Sylvie and Elizabeth. "Have you ever seen the like?"

"Robe à la française?" Sylvie noted the gown's box pleats at the back, with fabric trailing at the floor. Especially fetching were the ladder-like bows decorating the embroidered stomacher. "With an echelle?"

Enraptured, Rebecca seemed transformed. "Rose and cream are my colors. I simply must have a gown such as this. The Grande Pandora Mama bought me is ready and waiting for such a creation."

This time it was Sylvie's turn to be surprised. "En grande toilette?"

Rebecca nodded, still gazing at the magazine. "My sister has Petite Pandora in her bedchamber en déshabillé."

Elizabeth turned conspiring, snapping the book shut and getting to her feet. "We must make introductions!"

Rebecca did not protest but hurried to the door, Sylvie following. Up a stair they went to the daughters' private chambers, where Sylvie came face-to-face with a life-size Pandora along a damask wall in the boudoir.

Rebecca stood by it, still beaming. "She is my twin, is she not?"

The wax creation wore a vivid parrot-green gown that failed to have the allure of the one in the magazine, though her coiffure was a masterpiece of curls and pearls.

"Look at mine, mademoiselle." Elizabeth touched Sylvie's arm. "She is so lifelike I sometimes want to chat with her."

In a corner was the second Pandora dressed in a shift, stays, stockings, and garters but awaiting a gown. Once again Sylvie schooled her astonishment. For a moment she was cast back to the small Pandora loaned her by Madame Auclair that Marie-Madeleine had coveted. The memory seemed dusty and faded, though the pain was still sharp.

"Alas, Mama is cross with the Williamsburg milliner," Rebecca said in low tones. "She is always late with our gowns and has exhausted our patience. I am in need of a new ensemble, but . . ."

Sylvie felt excitement kindle, knowing the Dinwiddies enjoyed the finest imported cloth and embellishments. She fairly itched to stitch again and needed an ally. "If your mother agrees, I can begin sewing a dress for you at once, provided I have all the materials and it shan't interfere with your lessons."

"Oh, it shan't, Mademoiselle Galant!" Elizabeth all but danced with delight. "We shall work even harder for you!"

Rebecca regarded Sylvie more deferentially. "You first came here clothed in one of the most stylish gowns we'd ever seen. Can it be you are as skilled with a needle as you are speaking French?"

"I began sewing as a child and count it among my favorite pastimes. It would be an honor to create a gown for you if your mother approves."

"Oh, I'm sure Mama will have no objections." Elizabeth sniffed, swiping at her nose with a handkerchief. "Will you make me one too?"

Hands on panniered hips, Rebecca snorted in an unlady-like fashion. "As the eldest and most marriageable daughter, I come first."

Elizabeth's wan face fell, eliciting Sylvie's sympathy and a smile. "I sincerely hope, petite mademoiselle, that you and your Pandora shall have your gown in time."

38

Strange to the world, he wore a bashful look, the fields
his study, nature was his book.

Robert Bloomfield

At last Will had a reason to seek out Sylvie. He'd gone
to the bookbindery for stationery supplies, asking
about her if only to get confirmation she was no
longer employed there. The lad Will had seen Sylvie with
was pushing a broom while the little girl was confined to the
back room. Will was glad of Sylvie's good fortune to trade
this frantic place for the palace. Though industrious, the
shop hummed like a hive full of discontented bees.

Mrs. Webb, in a rare fawning mood, showed him the latest
shipment of his journals in the bay-fronted window. He was
polite, wondering all the while if she was the reason Sylvie
had quit the shop.

Mr. Hunter, always harried, stopped long enough to hand
him a letter. "This came earlier today," he said, pointing
out the elegant seal on the back. "Please deliver this to Miss
Galant if it's not too out of your way, as I haven't the time
nor the help to spare."

"My pleasure," Will replied, tucking the letter into a waistcoat pocket.

The day was fair, emboldening him. Bonami loped alongside him, the winter air frosting their breath. He'd been to the Governor's Palace once of late, to a reception of sorts for the newly appointed surveyors to Virginia. He'd been struck with Dinwiddie's forthright Scots manner and the elegance of the rooms that seemed an echo of England.

Will moved into the forecourt and up the stone steps to stand in line, possibly the only visitor *not* awaiting the governor. He was admitted to the circular foyer without much of a delay, the chamber lined top to bottom with a blatant show of British military strength intended to awe and intimidate. But the truth was most of these munitions were outdated, and none of them were as capable as his trusted rifle. He felt a marked relief he'd left Rangering behind.

"Your business, sir?" the bewigged butler asked him.

"To see Mademoiselle Galant," he replied.

With a lift of his heavy brows, the man ushered him into a side chamber while a maidservant sent for Sylvie. At the room's center, a clerk scratched his quill across a ledger of names, including Will's. Servants came and went, giving the impression of a genteel, efficient household, while more people piled into the foyer.

At last Sylvie came. She took one look at Will and quailed like a doe before a wolf. He nearly cursed beneath his breath, a stubborn, unregenerate habit he hated. Giving a stilted little bow, he wondered who had penned the letter to her, holding on to the distant hope it might carry news of Acadie.

"Monsieur Blackburn." She spoke with clipped courtesy, hiding the winsome smile he remembered.

"Step into the adjoining meeting room," the clerk told them, gesturing to yet another small chamber where they had complete privacy.

Will shut the nearest door, hemming them in completely, though Sylvie looked like she might flee out the half-shut door at her back. "Mr. Hunter asked me to give you this," he explained, relinquishing the sealed letter.

She took the paper and pocketed it after giving it a cursory glance. She wouldn't make this easy for him, then. If he had any sense, he'd let the letter be the sole reason for their meeting and then flee himself, but something pushed him past any reticence.

"How are you faring here?" he asked, his gaze lifting to the ornate ceiling before returning to her.

"Well enough." She clasped her hands together at her waist. "I suppose I have you to thank, as the advertisement for French lessons brought me here. It's a better arrangement than the bookbindery, though I am unsure how long I'll stay."

"Why is that?"

"Is it not obvious?" she continued softly. "I am right beneath the nose of the governor, who may well put me on board another ship to ports unknown."

"He'll have to exile me first," he said without thought, still drawn to her despite all that was against them. "The letter isn't the only reason I'm here. There's to be a courthouse ball in a fortnight. I'm hoping you'll accompany me."

Her lip-parting surprise made him realize the futility of his asking.

"A ball." She looked down at her clasped hands. "You are brave, Major Blackburn."

"Call me Will." What made him so bold? So determined? "It might help take down the wall between us."

Again that flash of surprise. At least he wasn't predictable, however she felt about him.

"A fortnight?" She turned her face to the sun streaming through the tall window, unwittingly accenting her lovely profile. "I would have to ask my employer."

"Your time outside of work is your own, Sylvie. As I've said before, you aren't enslaved like so many here in Williamsburg. You're a free woman . . . free to refuse me."

Wariness lit her eyes. "There must be plenty of Williamsburg mademoiselles who would leap at the chance to have you escort them."

"But there's only one Sylvie Galant."

Her pale features pinked. Had she never been courted in Acadie? She'd kept company with Bernart Boudreau, but he'd wager their tie had been as shallow as the doctor himself. Still, not knowing raised a roaring curiosity inside him.

Still flushed, she met his gaze, her reserve slipping a notch. "I will attend the ball with you, then."

It was his turn to be surprised. Nay, *elated* was the better word.

39

Surely a pretty woman never looks prettier than when making tea.

Mary Elizabeth Braddon

The invitation Will had brought lay upon the writing desk in Sylvie's bedchamber. She'd perused it several times, thinking how kind, if surprising, to be invited to a lady's townhouse for tea. Lord and Lady Drysdale lived around the corner from Bruton Parish Church, not far from Will himself. In preparation, Sylvie readied her second-best dress, saving the Lyonnais silk for the ball.

The January jollity and Twelfth Night were now over. Winter set in with a vengeance, and when Sylvie visited Eve and the children she learned that Mr. Hunter and one of his apprentices were ill.

"Don't rightly know what their malady is," Eve told her, "but we'll find out soon enough."

Hoping Eve and the children wouldn't succumb and promising to see them the next Sabbath, Sylvie tried not to dwell on the tea or the ball to follow.

"You've been invited to Lord and Lady Drysdale's?" Rebecca Dinwiddie's shock nearly rivaled Sylvie's own. "I was at their townhouse over Christmas, and their hospitality is unsurpassed!"

"I do wish we could go with you," Elizabeth chattered in French, following Sylvie down the back stairs. "Perhaps you'll be served their celebrated punch!"

Lady Drysdale had kindly offered to send a coach round, but Sylvie balked at anything so grand. Besides, the bracing weather helped sharpen her wits ahead of the visit, though there was no help for her skittishness. Having tea with deux belles dames was not something she was accustomed to.

She slowed her pace near the Kersey townhouse. It sat back from the street, its stalwart bricked lines as sturdy as Will Blackburn himself. He didn't seem the sort of man who would lodge at another's residence for long.

As she thought it, the front door opened and an aging, stout man appeared. A lovely young woman in a lavender gown and deeper purple fur-trimmed cape was on his arm. Miss Kersey? Sylvie quickened her step, but to her dismay, they followed her a short distance before crossing the street and paying a call at another residence.

As soon as she mounted Lord and Lady Drysdale's stone steps, the door opened. A butler admitted her into a grand world of silk walls and English furnishings—and an enceinte hostess dressed just as sumptuously in sapphire silk. Esmée, however, was clad as simply as Sylvie.

"Mademoiselle Galant." Esmée greeted her with a smile so warm Sylvie's nerves settled. "This is my sister, Eliza Shaw Cheverton—Lady Drysdale—though we refer to her privately as Eliza."

Sylvie gave a small curtsy, which seemed to amuse Eliza. "Enchanté! You must make yourself at home and dispense with all formalities. Please warm yourself by the parlor fire. Hot chocolate and Hyson tea are coming—or punch if you prefer. I trust the palace is meeting your needs adequately. I shudder to think how Governor Dinwiddie's Scots frugality might be!"

It was Sylvie's turn to smile. The Dinwiddies did fret about finances except when it came to dressing their daughters.

At Eliza's bidding, they sat around a lacquered tea table in front of the hearth, Eliza's bulk touching the table's edge. "Pardon my girth," she said. "This babe is due any day, but I refuse to slow down till my lying-in."

Esmée began serving in her sister's stead, pouring dark, rich chocolate from a tall silver pot. Sylvie took a sip from her porcelain cup, thinking of the servants' simple creamware at the palace, struck by how delicious the chocolate was. Porcelain plates were heaped with a tempting array of delicacies she had no name for.

Noting her perusal, Esmée explained, "Jumbles. Queen's cake. Chocolate almonds. And Eliza's favorite, chocolate tarts."

"This babe is turning me into a hogshead," Eliza exclaimed, reaching for a tart. "And my dear husband, Quinn, has begun calling me Fubsy."

They chuckled, and Sylvie took a bite of cake. Buttery and rich, it paired well with the hot chocolate. A far cry from the pine needle tea and molasses bread of before.

"Tell me, how are you doing here in Williamsburg?" Esmée said gently. "I was distressed to hear you'd been ill."

Her marked kindness and concern always struck Sylvie as genuine. "I was feverish for several days but had good care from Dr. Pitt. Newcomers are not always so fortunate, no?"

"Newcomers succumb in frightful numbers here, sadly, but I firmly believe those who are spared serve a special purpose," Eliza told her. "Should you need another doctor, I can send mine round. For now, he's attending some of your people farther up the James River at the request of my husband."

"Your concern is heartening," Sylvie said. "Lord Drysdale has been especially helpful—and Captain Lennox."

Eliza looked sagely at Esmée. "Speaking of the renowned captain—or shall I say, my sister's renowned captain—"

"Nay, you shall not," Esmée exclaimed, smiling nonetheless. "He is no more mine than is the Prince of Wales."

"Nonsense!" Eliza took a second tart. "Mademoiselle Galant should know—"

"Please, call me Sylvie."

"Very well, I shall." Eliza took another bite, brushing a crumb from her vermilion lips. "Sylvie is such an unusual name. What does it mean, by chance?"

"Spirit of the woods."

"Lovely," Esmée said.

"I agree," Eliza continued seamlessly. "As I was saying, Sylvie might be interested in hearing about your adventure as lighthouse keeper on Indigo Island."

"Indigo? The place I came to after the wreck of the *Dolphin*?" Sylvie looked at Esmée, vaguely remembering talk of a lighthouse at the island's opposite end.

"The very same." Esmée set down her cup. "Captain Lennox and I have long wanted to have a light there. And now the lighthouse, finally finished, needs a keeper."

"Sister is to be one of the first female lightkeepers in the colonies, but not the last, I'm sure." Pride warmed Eliza's voice. "I hope that she pens her exploits like Virginia Colony's newest surveyor."

"Major Blackburn?" Sylvie asked without thinking.

"Yes, do you know of him?" Esmée looked at her in question. When Sylvie hesitated, she said quietly, "But of course. He was lately in Acadie before Virginia . . ."

"I was surprised to find him here. He seems to be doing well," Sylvie nearly stuttered. Was she imagining it, or did Eliza leap on the words like the Persian cat at her feet would a dish of cream? "He brought me your gracious invitation. It came to the print shop, but I was at the palace."

"Ah, I did wonder how it finally found you," Eliza said with a sly smile. "And might the major have more on his mind than mail delivery?"

"And what if he does?" Esmée said gently by way of apology, casting Sylvie a sympathetic glance. "'Tis none of our concern."

"Well, I've always had a weakness for romantic intrigue." Chuckling, Eliza took another sip of chocolate. "And I'm quite curious about the major's memoir of his time commanding the Ranger companies."

Esmée nodded. "His popular journals?"

"I sent a maid to the bookseller's for a copy"—Eliza shifted in her seat, looking uncomfortable—"but it has sold out again, not only here but in England and on the continent, the newspapers say."

"I'm glad to hear it," Esmée said, looking at Sylvie again. "You're probably aware that with his publication Major Blackburn is raising relief for Acadians displaced by the British government, at least those in Virginia."

He—what? Sylvie's lips parted, but no words came.

"A very worthy endeavor." Eliza's admiration faded to a frown. "Meanwhile, Dinwiddie and the sloth-like general assembly continue to dither, while more practical, enterprising men move forward with establishing a settlement on the Rivanna River."

"I pray they succeed." Sylvie felt hope take hold. "Acadians desperately need a home if Canada is denied us."

"Major Blackburn has nearly twenty-five Acadians willing to establish or revive the plantation he's recently acquired. Some men, like my husband, have given additional acreage to aid that vision. Several thousand acres, all told. And Captain Lennox is more than generous with his prize moneys."

So William Blackburn would surround himself with Acadians? Sylvie finished her drink, mulling the prospect, almost afraid to hope it would be successful for all.

"Have you given thought to your future, Sylvie?" Esmée poured more chocolate. "I can't imagine how hard this is for you. Have you any word of your family?"

Sylvie stared absently at the bouquet of dried everlastings at the table's center, weighing her answer. "I wish I knew what became of my family, my father especially. I lost my mother and sister aboard ship. I'm sure my grandparents perished on other vessels as they were in poor health. As for my brothers, I don't know."

Esmée was visibly moved, her eyes bright with tears.

Again Sylvie thought of William Blackburn. And Bleu. Somehow the two were inexplicably linked in her mind.

"We plan to invite other Acadian women like you here, but for now we want to know if there's anything you need that Eliza and I can see to," Esmée said. "Not only you but any Acadians about Williamsburg. Anything at all?"

So many needs, few of them material. A cure for heartache. Loneliness. Homesickness. Despair.

"Please pray for me," Sylvie finally said. "Pray for all my people."

40

There were more Dancers than the Room could conveniently hold, which is enough to constitute a good Ball at any time.

Jane Austen

They were indeed in need of a little levity, Sylvie admitted. The doldrums of January were considerably brightened by a ball. And yet after all that had happened since autumn, it seemed wrong to make merry. In truth, there was little joie de vivre left in her soul and little among her fellow Acadians. But she had promised William Blackburn she would go.

And he'd asked her to call him Will. Would she ever be able to? She drew up short at the thought, yet she couldn't deny she had already taken his full name if not his first name to heart. Oui, to heart. Slowly but surely he had somehow wooed her since first meeting, and she had failed to distance herself no matter how hard she'd tried. When she thought of him it lent to the flutter in her stomach, which was becoming more a flame of late whenever she recalled how boldly attractive he'd been in the palace antechamber. He might have shed his Rangering, but he'd lost none of his resolve.

With the Dinwiddies away visiting friends, the palace was quieter save for the servants. The steady stream of visitors and officials seeking the governor's favor came to a halt as if frozen, the foyer and meeting chambers empty.

"Ah, that silk is such a lovely color on you," Eulalie said, winding faux pearls through Sylvie's hair as she sat before a small dressing table. "My borrowed gown is rather bright, especially for a winter fête."

"The scarlet color suits you," Sylvie reassured her.

Eulalie sighed. "It reminds me of the English army uniforms."

This Sylvie couldn't deny. "Perhaps we could soften it with a lovely fichu. I have one from Mère that would be perfect. She wore it on her wedding day and saved it for my trousseau."

"You would let me wear such an heirloom?" Awe touched Eulalie's tone. "I would be honored."

Sylvie took the creamy lace from her wardrobe, then reached for a silk rose she'd made and pinned it to the fichu's bosom knot, turning it especially fetching. "Voilà!"

"So very bonne, merci." Eulalie studied herself in the looking glass. "I confess I am rather half-hearted this evening. Sebastien has been especially despondent given the recent confirmation his betrothed drowned on a ship bound for South Carolina."

"Un cauchemar," Sylvie murmured. *A nightmare.* "You care for him."

"To no avail." Eulalie shook her head. "There can be no affection in a man's heart when love for someone else resides there."

"Perhaps in time."

Eulalie pulled a handkerchief from her sleeve and dried

her eyes. "On the other hand, Major Blackburn seems more than ready to pledge himself to a demoiselle like you."

Staring at her own reflection, Sylvie saw her color was so high she had no need for rouge. "Perhaps it is simply to assuage his conscience."

"Bon sang!" Eulalie turned to her, indignant. "You delude yourself. He is a man of honor, and his affection for you is untainted, I am certain. He deeply regrets his past in Acadie as well as his service to the English. He abhors what happened to us as much as he does the fate of his own people, the Scots."

"How do you know all of this?"

"Nicolas has spoken at length about it with him. He has full confidence in Major Blackburn and is counting the days till he can join his Rivanna River settlement."

"Will you leave the palace and go too?"

"I would rather serve my people there than stay here. So, oui, I hope to join them." She looked at the clock on the mantel. "For now, we mustn't be late lest the men wonder what's become of us."

They left out the servants' entrance, finding Will standing just outside the palace forecourt with Sebastien. Blazing cressets lit the short distance to the courthouse, the high notes of a fiddle beckoning. Tongue-tied, her head full of Eulalie's upbraiding, Sylvie said little as they made their way, glad Eulalie bantered with Sebastien as if determined to lift his spirits or at least distract him.

With Will by her side, Sylvie stepped inside the crowded courthouse and immediately relaxed. Here it did not matter if she and the others were French Neutrals. The music was so loud none could even hear their accented English.

Clad in their finery, a press of people she'd never seen jostled them on all sides, if not gentry then the best of the middling class. Cheeks still hot, she was aware of her escort's admiring eyes as he removed her cape. Others were equally well clad, even powdered and painted, though she and Eulalie were not.

As for her escort, he won both her eye and her admiration with a handsome suit almost Quaker plain but finely tailored, making her realize he needed no outward adornment. Freshly shaven, his glossy hair caught back with black ribbon, and standing a head or more higher than any man in the room, he was such a presence she wasn't alone in her admiring glances.

"May I have the pleasure of your first dance, Mademoiselle Galant?" Will gave a little bow, his silvery gaze holding hers for one meaningful moment.

She extended her hand, aware of the callused warmth of his. Warmed, too, by that same undeniable allure she'd first felt at the well that long-ago day.

Though the music was different from that of her homeland, these colonials knew the same dance steps. As for her partner, he was unsurprisingly lithe on his feet, and no sooner did he release her than another man took his place and then another. Soon the room was awhirl with color, the crush of revelers necessitating the opening of the courthouse doors. Some even danced outside, the spirit of gaiety as strong as the perfumes and unwashed persons.

Sylvie spied Eulalie and Sebastien near an enormous punch bowl along one long wall. Without her asking, Will brought her a cup, and they stood near an open window. A draft cooled her neck and stirred loose tendrils of her hair even as her heart still skipped as if she'd not stopped dancing.

"So what do you think of your first Williamsburg ball?"

His simple question returned her eyes to him. "These Virginians dance admirably . . . and one New Englander I know."

His half smile turned him roguish. "You thought I knew more about Indian round dances than quadrilles."

"I honestly don't know what to think." She took another sip of punch, savoring the citrus and ginger on her tongue and trying to reconcile who she thought he was with who he really was. "Though some sing your praises. Lady Drysdale, for one. She is keen to read your memoir, as she calls it."

"Memoir? A fancy name for an unadorned account of my time in the wilderness."

"I should like to read your journals too."

"Hardly the literary merit of *Robinson Crusoe* or *Gulliver's Travels.*"

"And yet Mr. Hunter cannot keep it on the shelves." She swirled the punch in her cup. "I heard you're giving the publishing profits to my people for resettlement."

"Aye, but the publication contains nothing about Acadie, if you're wondering. My resigning the Rangers spoke to that."

His words fell heavy. Did he think she still blamed him for being a part of the expulsion? Something simmered between them, a tangle of attraction and hope, ruminations and regrets.

As she turned toward him to reply, a rumpus erupted across the room. A portly man grabbed hold of the punch bowl to drain the last of its contents only to be tackled by another drunkard, which sent the bowl to the hardwood floor. Though the glass didn't break, their scuffle ended the dancing and brought a sheriff running.

Taking her arm, Will led her outside into the starlit night, then returned inside for her cape before reappearing. "These Virginians seem overfond of their whistle belly and bogus and rattle skull or whatever it is that turns them surly." He draped the garment over her shoulders.

She thanked him, eyes on the stars. "I've not tasted those,

but syllabub is quite refreshing. The palace kitchen serves it often."

They stood facing west, their backs to the courthouse. The fiddling resumed, but it seemed distant, her awareness centered on the man beside her and the security she felt near him. She'd not felt safe since the English sailed into Baie Française, though at the moment her mind was filled with the present, not the past.

She looked up at the pale crescent moon, wondering about the place that he'd said nothing about yet wouldn't let her be. "Tell me about the Rivanna River settlement."

He hesitated. Had she taken him by surprise? "It's little more than a vision for now, a former plantation auctioned to cover a dead man's debts."

"Does it have a name?"

"Greenmount, on account of the house on the hill." He passed a hand over his jaw, a mannerism she recalled in Acadie. "It begs renaming."

"I've heard you have indentures there already repairing habitations, and lumber enough for a mill, even fallow fields ready to be sewn with clover, corn, and wheat." She took a little breath, remembering all Eulalie had told her. "The soil is richer there, not so sandy but loamy, the air better for one's health."

"Do you want to come with me, Sylvie?"

"I-I don't know what I want." Had he read the longing in her words? To be far from here, surrounded by fields and forests again, even a river, with a view of the distant mountains? Her whole being seemed to cry out for that. "It's a hundred miles west of here, is it not?"

He studied her, his gaze almost caressing in the darkness. "A hundred miles west, aye, and a hundred times better." His voice held a rare tenderness she'd not yet heard, almost as if he wasn't talking about land but a woman.

She looked away from him to the sky. "Is there any danger from Indians?"

"Not any longer. Sometimes peaceful Cherokee delegations pass through on an old Indian trail en route to Williamsburg to meet with the governor. It skirts the orchard."

She forgot all about stargazing. "Is it a large orchard?"

"Eleven hundred bearing apple trees, as well as cherry, peach, pear, and quince—and several bee skeps."

She couldn't imagine it. Their own orchard hadn't been half so large. "Of all my old tasks, I miss orchard tending most."

"I have some Acadian apple seed, though I don't know the variety. You might."

Was he dangling seed in front of her like the caged songbird?

"There's more to the place than it seems. I don't quite know how to say it . . ." He looked off in the distance. "Long ago when we were burned out—after the French and Huron struck—a place came to mind, like a painting on a parlor wall. It appeared at odd times, usually when I was in danger, like a door to another, better life. When I came to the Rivanna River, it seemed to merge with the picture in my mind. It seemed I'd found that place. It feels like coming home."

His honest words fell between them like a rarely told confidence, raising a knot in her throat. Home. Were they not all looking for home? A place to call their own? Even such a man as Will?

They fell silent as the fiddler struck another tune. She prepared to return inside for more dancing, but an Englishman came out the door nearest them with an intrusive step.

"Major Blackburn? I have a question about your Rivanna endeavor."

With a word to Will, Sylvie returned inside and was claimed by Sebastien for a quadrille.

41

The smallpox was always present, filling the churchyards with corpses, tormenting with constant fears all whom it had not yet stricken, leaving on those lives it spared the hideous traces of its power.

T. B. Macaulay

The Dinwiddies' gowns were almost finished, the Pandoras sumptuously clad and awaiting the daughters' return. Their absence gave Sylvie ample time to do little but sew. As she stitched, her every thought returned to Will, whom she'd not seen since the courthouse fête a week before. The time stretched long after the excitement and color of that evening. Though she'd managed to forget her uneasy circumstances for a short time, the unknown future was waiting for her afterward, a reality she couldn't dodge. A reality that made the Rivanna River endeavor seem a sort of refuge.

A knock at the door brought Sylvie's head up, her needle stilling. Eulalie swept in with a tray, reminding Sylvie it was teatime. From somewhere in the mostly empty palace a case clock tolled the hour. Rain spattered the window glass, dusk not far behind.

"I'm glad of the company," Sylvie replied with a smile, setting the petticoat aside.

Eulalie's face was grave as she set the tea tray on a small table. "I bring de mauvaises nouvelles."

Bad news? Sylvie all but held her breath. Would they all be exiled again?

For once, Eulalie did not just leave the tray but sat down across from her. "There's sickness in Williamsburg."

"Sickness?" Not exile. Sylvie's mind raced to Will before veering to Eve's recent confidence that Mr. Hunter was ill.

"Apparently the malady is now sweeping like fire through town. All the doctors have their hands full and are talking of quarantine." Eulalie poured the tea with an unsteady hand. "I fear yellow fever or smallpox. I hope and pray we escape both. You know how it is with us newcomers, privy to all sorts of colonial maladies."

Sylvie added sugar and milk to her cup, for once the sweetmeats on a pretty dish far from tempting. "I've had neither. And I wonder about the Dinwiddies."

"The governor has decided to remain in Maryland for the time being, though he may return if the sickness abates and leave his family behind. As for me, I've decided to go to the Rivanna River settlement with Major Blackburn."

Sylvie felt a sudden loss. "How soon?"

The relief in Eulalie's face was unmistakable. "On the morrow."

"But Governor Dinwiddie—the butler—"

"They've given permission due to the circumstances. Shops and businesses are closing their doors while we Acadians who've cast our lot with Major Blackburn are already packing."

All but Sylvie.

The loneliness that was now so familiar deepened. The question Will had asked her the night of the fête seemed to echo with a resounding shout.

Do you want to come with me, Sylvie?

Eulalie's brow creased. "There's a place for you too. It's not too late for you to change your mind. We're stronger together, not scattered. Major Blackburn knows the wilderness and has the means to sustain us, at least for the time being. It's a chance for us to make a home, a new life, and escape the sickness besides."

How welcome it sounded, full of hope and possibilities if not the life of before.

Eulalie continued between sips of tea. "There we won't be spat upon in the streets or made fun of in the palace."

Though Sylvie had borne the brunt of curses and comments herself on occasion, the kindness of others had muted it somewhat. If not for Esmée Shaw and Lady Drysdale and their men . . .

"You're leaving the Dinwiddies at the best possible time." Eulalie looked at Sylvie's sewing with a sharp eye. "They'll return here to beautiful new dresses. What better adieu could you give them?"

Sylvie's mind veered to Eve and the children. Eve wasn't free to leave. And Henrietta and Nolan, so small, were especially vulnerable. She recalled one redcoat at Fort Cumberland marveling at how many Acadian children lived past childhood and how free of disease Acadie was. But here in this crowded, reeking town . . .

"I've no doubt Major Blackburn wants you to join us." Eulalie drew her shawl closer about her shoulders, shivering at the room's chill even as Sylvie got up to add another log to the hearth's fire. "He cares for you. I see it plainly. You didn't have a beau in Acadie, did you?"

"No . . . never." She was cast back to that day when the

270

English ships came and she'd been dreaming of her future husband on her beloved overlook. Might it be Will?

There no longer seemed a taint of their expulsion about him. In hindsight she realized he hadn't lied to her in seeking Bleu. Perhaps she'd just fallen victim to her own confusion. Alone with him lately, she'd felt an almost unbearable sweetness of being.

"Please consider his offer if not his courtship," Eulalie urged, eyes pleading. "If you stay here, you are in more danger of deportation and now this unknown illness. Williamsburg has little to offer us."

Will sat back in his chair as the supper dishes were cleared away by Kersey's housekeeper and after-dinner drinks were served. Liselotte and Spencer kept up a lively conversation by the hearth, having traded the table for the fire's warmth.

"So, you're leaving with certainty on the morrow?" Kersey looked less than pleased. His eye trailed to his niece before returning to Will. "I've pledged my support to your endeavor, Major, but I have another proposition in mind as well. I'm wondering if you wouldn't benefit from having Liselotte at the settlement for a time."

Will swallowed his brandy, schooling his reaction. Could Kersey sense his surprise—and reluctance? "Does she speak French?"

"Nay. But that shouldn't get in the way of the work. She's been brought up on a small plantation, as you know, reared to manage the dependencies you have waiting—weaving house, kitchen, laundry, dairy, and so forth. Matters best left to the women with the men in the fields. And I understand you have few women going to the Rivanna, at least this early."

"Seven women," Will said. "And eighteen men."

"My niece would make the eighth, then. And I can assure

you that she is able to do the work of two women and manage all the rest."

"Is this her idea or yours?" Will asked. A burst of laughter from the hearth assured him Liselotte and Spencer weren't listening as the law student recounted a joke.

"She approached me to approach you."

A bold move. Still, it didn't endear Will to the plan. "The Acadians are industrious people and likely need little management. In fact, after all they've endured, they might resent it."

"I've heard of their dike lands and their crop yields. They are renowned master farmers and cattlemen. Still, Liselotte might be a steadying influence on the women. She's at loose ends here, grieving the loss of both parents and plantation. I'm little help, being away so much at the college. Perhaps, given time, she won't care for the Rivanna and will return to town, but I hope you'll be willing to let her attempt it."

"On a trial basis, then." As much a trial for Will and the Acadians as it was for Liselotte.

"This will always be her true home, of course. But sometimes in the midst of grief, a diversion is needed. A change of scene."

Will couldn't argue with that. Had he not felt the same? "Would she be willing to leave tomorrow?"

Kersey chuckled and cast a fond glance at his niece. "She's already packed and ready, waiting for your consent."

⌒

Sylvie stood with Will in the palace's small antechamber adjoining the butler's pantry. Her heart caught at the sight of him and his half smile as if he was unsure of her. His silver eyes seemed steely. He was clad in a wool greatcoat with a turned-up collar and attached cape, silver buttons marching up the deep-blue front. He was not only well dressed for travel, he looked more a menace than the wintry weather.

"Sylvie, consider what you're saying." He spoke with remarkable calm, though his eyes retained their quicksilver ferocity. "Smallpox is spreading and you've not had it. Even if you shun my personal attentions, consider your safety. Your very life."

She hesitated, knowing Eulalie and Sebastien and other Acadians were even now filling wagons and saddling packhorses to begin the journey west. Will was doing a merciful thing, taking them early to try to evade more calamity.

She studied his handsome face but found no pockmarks, only a faint scar or two. "Are you immune?"

"I survived it at Fort Saint-Frédéric that long winter." He looked down at the cocked hat in his hand. "I was at ebb water, weakened by winter and a long, bitter march through the wilderness. I nearly died but for the efforts of a French surgeon."

She felt one burden lighter, at least, though she continued to worry about Henrietta and Nolan. "Please don't worry about me. I should be safe here. The butler forbids us to leave palace walls, at least those of us staying on."

Even as she said it, she realized how foolish it sounded. Someone delivering food to the kitchen or hazarding an outside meeting might be their downfall. Was he thinking it too?

"I'm more worried about you, Will." She let slip the intimacy of his name, struck by the possibility she might never be allowed the privilege again. "Aside from the smallpox, it feels like the weather is about to worsen."

He looked toward the window, his features tight with concern. "Though it takes time to reach the Rivanna and the weather isn't in our favor, every step forward is a safeguard from disease."

Unless one of your party has it but doesn't know it yet.

Feeling the terrible tick of time, she reached for him and took one of his hands between both of hers. His face did

273

not register surprise, but she sensed it as his gaze softened. Rough as river rock, his tanned, callused skin reminded her of Bleu's. As she thought it, he brought her hand to his lips and kissed the backs of her fingers, wiping his gallant gesture at the well from her mind. She was one step shy of throwing herself into his arms and leaving all behind to go with him into an unknown future.

With effort she resisted the wild impulse and said, "When will you be back?"

"I don't know, Sylvie."

Hard, cold facts stared them in the face. He could leave and die himself, if not by pox then by some other malady or accident. She could stay on and succumb. The dire possibilities were endless.

Long-banked emotion rose inside her like the tide, choking her and making a proper goodbye impossible. With one last look at him, she pulled free and fled upstairs.

42

No man dared to count his children as his own until they
had had the disease.

Comte de la Condamine

A fortnight passed, the longest and possibly the qui-
etest of Sylvie's life. Though she wasn't supposed
to leave the palace quarantine, her mounting worries and questions had her sneaking away after dark. Not
knowing how the children were faring was a miserable exis-
tence given they were so near.

When Eve opened the attic door, both children rushed to
greet Sylvie with such welcome she was nearly bowled over.

"Where've you been?" Henrietta asked, burying her face
in Sylvie's petticoat.

"I'm at the palace now, teaching the governor's daughters French and sewing pretty dresses, remember?" She'd
explained it before, but young as she was, Henrietta only
understood that Sylvie had left the bookbindery attic—and
them. Another loss in her little life. What toll were all these
griefs taking?

"Will you sew me a pretty dress?" Henrietta asked, her wide hyacinth eyes almost pleading.

Sylvie hugged her close again. Why had she not thought of it before? With Will gone and the Dinwiddies still in Maryland . . . "A pretty gown with bows and lace in abundance." Sylvie kissed her curls missing a cap. "What color do you prefer?"

"Butter."

Eve chuckled. "I suppose she means yellow."

Nolan squirmed out of Sylvie's embrace. With a downcast look, he retreated to the fiery hearth to play with his toy soldiers, saying over his shoulder, "Mr. Hunter's still sick and Mrs. Webb's buried."

Sylvie looked at Eve, who nodded in confirmation. "Have the children been around them?"

"Nay, Mrs. Webb couldn't abide children," Eve whispered as Henrietta went to retrieve her doll before returning to Sylvie's lap. "And Mr. Hunter had little to do with them, busy as he was. I'm not sure how he'll fare. Dr. Pitt said he's nearly as sick as his sister."

"I'm sorry to hear it."

"Half of Williamsburg and the rest of Virginia is sick to death too. But enough about the rest of us." Eve's eyes darkened with concern. "Why didn't you leave out with Major Blackburn? Everybody knows he gathered up the Acadians like some sort of Moses at the exodus—all but you."

Sylvie almost smiled at the comparison but for the hole in her heart. "I felt like I was abandoning the children."

"They aren't yours to abandon, remember." Eve let out a breath. "If they keep well, they'll be bound out to somebody else if Hunter passes. Or they'll return to the almshouse."

"What about you, Eve?"

"I belong to Hunter and, if he dies, his kinfolk. Or I'll be put back on the block and sold."

Sylvie nearly shuddered as Eve tended the fire. Plates and cups sat empty on a table, a few bread crumbs left over from their supper. But the room was tidy, even if they'd been holed up beneath the eaves like trapped squirrels.

Sylvie shifted in her chair. "Is Henrietta still having nightmares?"

"Betimes." Eve jabbed the fire with a poker, and the logs settled into an orange morass. "And Nolan frets me lately. He needs to be outside these walls, doing chores and running free like a child should, not pushing a broom."

"They need a true home." Sylvie weighed all that was lacking. "At the very least Henrietta needs a new dress."

"You have enough fixings for that?"

"I'll use the silk and fripperies the Dinwiddies gave me to do with as I wish."

"Silk like that fancy gown you wore to the courthouse ball?" At Sylvie's raised brows, Eve continued, "I happened to be on an errand for Mr. Hunter when I saw you on the arm of Major Blackburn, walking down Palace Green. I half expected Miss Kersey." Eve was in an oddly garrulous mood. The quarantine was clearly taking a toll. "You know what's said about her, I reckon? That she's set her bonnet for Blackburn?"

"Oh." Sylvie's stomach twisted as she stroked Henrietta's hair. "I've not met her, but I once spied her coming out of their townhouse."

"I have kinfolk who work in the kitchen there." Eve began to wipe the table clean. "I was surprised to hear Miss Kersey went west with the Acadians."

Had she? Her stomach dropped. Shock widened to alarm. "Miss Kersey doesn't seem made for the Rivanna but for town."

Eve chuckled. "Women are fools for love, rich or poor."

Fools, indeed. And Sylvie was the worst of them, so seized with a sudden, writhing jealousy she couldn't speak. Was this not evidence of her strong feelings for Will? Feelings she'd tried to conceal from everyone until lately—including herself?

"Blackburn has one foot in town and one out of it. He'll keep his ties to Williamsburg on account of his being a Crown surveyor. As a landowner he'll go to his acreage too, like privileged Virginians do." Eve sat down and clasped her long, bony fingers together. "I hear he has a proud house over in Albemarle County fit for a bride."

Greenmount. The name had threaded like green ribbon through her consciousness. All her imaginings about the place had painted too pretty a picture, surely. And now she had Liselotte Kersey to contend with. Suddenly weary, she stood and placed a sleeping Henrietta on her bed, then removed her shoes and covered her with a quilt. She took a last look at the girl's pale, pure skin and smoothed a hand over her jumble of curls.

Returning to her stool, Sylvie broached the subject she dreaded. "We never knew much sickness in Acadie. Tell me about the smallpox, Eve. You've had it. I see the scars on your skin."

"As a child, I took it and it stole my pappy away at the same time." Eve's eyes glittered. "Dr. Pitt said it takes four forms, the worst being the purple. Nobody recovers from the purple. That's what carried off Mrs. Webb. I fear Mr. Hunter may be next. If you survive it, you're safe, but it takes a frightful toll."

"So there is a rash? Blisters?"

"First comes a fever, raw throat, and aching head. Then the sores. You can even rally for a time and get relief, only to die right after."

Sylvie looked again at Henrietta, fast asleep, and Nolan, who showed no sign of needing rest. The both of them were so vulnerable it made her heart hurt. "Thank you for taking such good care of the children."

Eve eyed Sylvie with such concern it seemed foreboding. "I'm most worried about you, Miss Sylvie."

43

Love begins with a smile, grows with a kiss, and ends with a teardrop.

Augustine

Will clutched the latest edition of the *Virginia Gazette*, bereft of its usual news, the headline dedicated to the contagion sweeping Virginia and elsewhere. "A True State of the Small Pox" was in boldface, the names of Williamsburg's stricken inhabitants beneath. Standing in a cold circle of winter sunlight on Greenmount's porch, Will scoured the list of names among the recovered, dead, sick, and not yet taken. His breathing grew heavier as dread gained the upper hand. Sylvie's name was missing, but one prominent name was not.

Lord Drysdale, carried off by the purple.

He read it a second and third time, cut by disbelief.
God, help us.
His main ally in Virginia—tall, stalwart, unflinching—felled without warning like the finest tree in the forest. It

seemed the noble's hand had been in every facet of Virginia life. The House of Burgesses. The governor's council. The Bruton Parish Church vestry. He had even been justice of the peace and a highly respected barrister. And he was now gone. Nothing had been printed about his wife and child.

Stunned, Will was cast back to Kersey's parlor, where Lord Drysdale had declared his outrage with British officials and pledged his unswerving support to the Acadians.

Who would stand in his stead?

His remaining ally, Captain Lennox, was on a cruise at the request of the colonial government, his return uncertain. It left Will feeling alone. Adrift. On such a clear, sunlit day it was hard to believe anyone could be ill or mourning.

He looked at the newsprint a final time, a small announcement at the bottom catching his eye. Future issues would be suspended till further notice. His gut wrenched again. With that terse stroke, his tenuous tie to Sylvie seemed suspended too.

The raucous banging of a loose shutter in the wind turned his attention upward. The shutter hung precariously from the second floor, and he made a mental note to nail it down. All around him were sounds of life, labor, even laughter. It seemed almost a miracle he'd gotten the Acadians out of Williamsburg without one of them falling ill, as if Providence wanted to spare them more misery. Aside from a few good-natured squabbles among themselves while settling in, they'd set right to work, even Liselotte Kersey, who seemed determined to show him she well knew how to manage a plantation.

He didn't want to be disappointed with this venture, and he didn't want to disappoint them. He kept short accounts with his workers day by day, overseeing their labor, listening to their ideas as he sought to make his venture more about the common good than his own personal stake in the matter, which was suddenly and irrevocably more complicated.

He folded the gazette, secured it in a coat pocket, and looked toward the river, its silver sheen leading to distant places rife with bloodshed and battle. Virginia's back settlers were taking a beating from the Indians and their French allies. Where and when it would end, Will didn't know. He prayed for peace, yet peace seemed naught but a dream.

For now, he focused on what was within his control. To the east stood newly inhabited mud- and stud-frame buildings that had the look of a small village. Most of the Acadians lived there, half-hidden by a towering stand of chestnut trees. A kitchen house stood near a well at one end of the muddy lane. Gray smoke purled from the kitchen's twin chimneys, mingling with the aroma of baking bread. A paddock and stable were nearest him, even a small if empty coach house. He could see women passing from smokehouse to spinning house to kitchen and dairy and stillroom, Liselotte foremost, a brisk efficiency to her step.

Craving solitude, he turned toward his own front door. By Virginia standards his dwelling wasn't grand, but to him it seemed a palace with six generous rooms and a gabled attic. Well-built right down to the mahogany door with its brass knocker, it held an austere elegance he favored. His footsteps echoed on the foyer's pine floor, as there was little furniture that hadn't been auctioned. A bucket and basin and a linen towel sat atop a bench where he washed. Candles and a few tin lanterns were scattered throughout.

Though bare, the house bore details that bespoke a prior woman's pleasure. Sash windows with crown glass. Brass sconces on painted plastered walls. Corner fireplaces with carved mantelpieces. Even a bake oven in the kitchen. A fine place for a family. His hope was to let his bride fill it with the things she wanted. In return, all he wanted was *her* presence.

Was he a fool focusing on a woman who remained unsure of him?

A knock on the door he'd just entered cut short his reverie. Nicolas stood outside on the bricked steps, hat in hand, his weskit dusted with wood shavings from the carpentry shop. "Since it's the end of another successful workweek, we thought we'd celebrate," he said.

"You've earned it," Will returned, stepping onto the porch and shutting the door behind him.

"Won't you join us?" Nicolas's expression, markedly different from when he'd been laboring in Williamsburg, seemed so satisfied Will couldn't help but turn from his melancholy over Lord Drysdale, if only for a moment. "The women have promised a feast, and Thibault has stood watch over the fire pit and has pronounced the meat almost done."

"I'm not one to shirk an invitation, especially when the kitchen is involved."

"Even Mademoiselle Kersey has put her apron on."

They walked toward the tumbling river, the drooping sun spreading yellow light over its eastwardly rush. Talk and laughter could be heard at a distance. The Acadians seemed to thrive on being together, and tonight seemed evidence of their recovering spirit. Trestle tables with benches offered enough seating for all of them inside the kitchen house. The roast pig had been carved up by an expert hand—Acadians were very fond of pork, Will had learned—and several side dishes along with an endless supply of both Indian and wheaten bread covered the table.

As early evening swept in, the chill shadows were chased away by a roaring bonfire on the riverbank. No one seemed to mind the cold. A keg of cider was rolled out, and Will looked toward the extensive orchard that would bear apple saplings in time. Most of the Acadian seed he'd brought here had sprouted, awaiting planting, which turned his thoughts again to Sylvie. But it was Liselotte he spied walking toward him when the meal was over, a briskness he was becoming used to in her step.

"Did you enjoy your supper, Major Blackburn?" she asked as she whisked his empty plate away.

"I can't fault the cooking," he replied, taking out the clay pipe Kersey had given him upon his leaving. "But I'm still making peace with Virginia's Indian maize."

"It improves with butter," she replied with a smile.

They stood outside the circle of Acadians who'd gathered to sing as they sat on the benches they'd used during the meal. One of them even had an old fiddle and another a hautbois, a reed instrument crafted in the settlement's carpentry. Their ingenuity in exile continued to surprise Will.

"When do you leave on your next survey?" Liselotte asked over the music.

"I'm awaiting word of that. For now, the time is better spent right here."

"You've accomplished a great deal already. I expected a run-down farm, but it's very much like Cloverwell, my former home."

He didn't miss the lament in her voice. "You're doing admirably here. Your uncle would be proud."

"I want to make you proud, Major. I know how much this endeavor means to you."

He looked at her through the smoky darkness as she drew her shawl closer about her.

"Something seems to be weighing on your mind, if you don't mind my saying so," she said. "You were in high spirits earlier."

Had his usual reserve slipped, or was she more insightful than he'd thought? "A post rider came earlier with the latest news from Williamsburg, none of it good." He still felt numb with disbelief. "Lord Drysdale has died of the pox, for one."

"A shame. My uncle will count it a great loss, and it's surely a blow to your endeavors here. Is it true Lord Drysdale introduced a measure to exempt the Acadians from payment of all public and county levies for seven years?"

"Before Candlemas, aye," Will said, struck by both grief and gratitude.

"My uncle also told me you and his lordship convinced Mr. Carter of Corotoman to sign over a tract of fifty thousand acres bordering this plantation. Is that true?"

"Sixty thousand, of which each Acadian is allotted fifty acres in return for their work here."

"Let's hope the generous Mr. Carter stays standing, then," she replied. "What we need is a church. Perhaps these French Catholics would be viewed more favorably as converts rather than as Virginians' enemies, with their hatchet waving and conspiring with the Indians and the like."

"At the moment, politics and religion are the last thing on Acadians' minds. They're solely concerned with survival."

"But in time they'll need a place to worship. And all Hades will break loose if they ever raise a mass house."

"My plan is to build a chapel. Till then I'll hold worship services in the main house for any who want to join me."

"Even papists?"

"God has no such divisions, last time I checked."

"Tell that to this very parish, who I'm sure would bar their doors to them."

"Middle Church and any prejudices you mention are quite a distance from here."

Frowning, she turned back to the music. "Do you know what they're singing?"

He listened to the refrain, recognizing it at last. "An old French ballad."

"Rather pretty if strange." She turned to him again. "Won't you teach me their tongue, Major Blackburn? I feel a bit left out at times, especially when you converse with them in French."

"Best ask the women, as you're with them the most." He took a long draw on his pipe, wondering at her motives. "It's not a language easily mastered."

"Indeed, I've only picked up a few words and phrases." She made a face. "Gâteau. Jardin. Eau. Rivière Rivanna."

"A fair start." He gestured to Bonami, who'd finally appeared after a roam in the woods. "Chien."

"Dog?" She laughed. "Chien."

He knelt and knocked the dottle out of his pipe, then ground the remains with the heel of his boot. The last thing he needed was a fire along the Rivanna. "Au revoir, Mademoiselle Kersey."

Looking amused and perhaps a tad dismayed at his going, she met his eyes before he turned and went up the hill to the house, Bonami trailing. His breath plumed bitterly, the mud beneath his boots more ice. He craved spring and lambing and a finished gristmill and ferry, to name but a few.

And Sylvie. Always Sylvie.

Leaving Bonami on the porch, Will went inside, weighing the wisdom of locking the house at night. Traversing the foyer and staircase in the dark, he was overcome that this was now his. Each step. Each brick. Every crevice and corner. If not for his change of direction and the Lord's provision, where might his hard-heartedness have led him?

He readied for bed, turning away from the washstand that stood between two upstairs windows. He could see the dwindling bonfire and hear distant singing, a reassuring sound after the emptiness he'd experienced when he first set foot here. He sought solitude as often as he could, but the gaping emptiness of a place that needed habitation was a different matter. He felt that emptiness in this house bereft of a woman's presence. But not just any woman.

Shuttering any thought of Sylvie, he lay down in the big, unfamiliar bed with its smooth linens and quilted coverlet gotten in Williamsburg, expecting a sound night's sleep. It was nearing midnight. The case clock in the foyer below tolled with a resounding echo.

Strange what came into a sleepless man's mind in the endless dark. Stranger still why he'd rise long before dawn in the dank cold and stumble sleepily to the stable to saddle Braddock, then ride such a distance for anything other than surveying or securing supplies. It seemed some unseen hand was urging him forward and unraveling his plans for the day to lead him somewhere else entirely.

And he was willing.

By noon he'd made it as far as the fall line of the James River, Braddock showing no sign of strain. Fine Virginia bloodstock, capable of going the distance. Bonami kept up with him as if it was all a lark.

In hours the weather turned, hurling hail and sleet from leaden skies. At last, saddle sore and feeling lamed himself, Will rode into a much-changed Williamsburg, signs of mourning everywhere, with shops still closed and streets too open.

He slid off Braddock's back and handed the reins to a groom before entering the Kersey residence by a side door, relief filling him.

44

I love thee, I love but thee! With a love that shall not die
till the sun grows cold, and the stars are old.

Bayard Taylor

Sylvie sewed by her bedchamber window, ignoring
the pinch in her back. A great many garments were
finished for the palace servants, the evidence of sitting so long. With the Dinwiddies still away, she plied her
needle nearly nonstop. The tediousness of her task left her
mind free to roam. So quiet was the house that she heard the
caged bird singing in the closed schoolroom below. Despite
the gloomy weather, it trilled and warbled as if celebrating
the coming spring. They were firmly entrenched in an icy,
melancholy March, disease and death everywhere. Like a
tightening noose, the circle of those still well was shrinking.

She was now reeling from the news that Lord Drysdale
had succumbed. His widow, sick herself but recovering, had
gone to Indigo Island in the care of Esmée, who'd taken the
baby soon after birth. The loss shook and saddened Sylvie.

Mr. Hunter had long been buried. After another nighttime
visit to the bookbindery attic, Sylvie found it locked, Eve and

the children gone. Where, Sylvie did not know, and no one was available to tell her. Sick at heart, she'd returned to the palace, barely evading the sheriff and night watch on their quarantine rounds. There was no one to share her worries with since Eulalie and the other Acadians were long gone, safely ensconced on the Rivanna.

She hadn't needed to consult the calendar in the shuttered schoolroom to know Will had been away more than a month, long enough to realize again and again what a fool she'd been to let him go without her. Every missed opportunity, each cold, careless word she'd ever spoken paraded before her, leaving her riven with regret. Liselotte Kersey had been the wise one, as ready as Sylvie was reluctant. Had she by now made inroads into Will's heart? A warm, willing woman near at hand could easily dismiss from a man's mind a cold, careless one at a distance.

In between the layers of regret lay yearning. All the little details about Will she'd refused to entertain returned and made her heart stand still. His long, thoughtful looks. That endearing affability around her that faded to a stoic reserve with others. His patient persistence and unflinching fortitude. The risks he took. Williamsburg seemed empty without him. She was empty without him, even more than before.

Biting her lip, she bent over her work, a tear spotting the linen shirt she was making him—if they saw each other again. Surveying was dangerous work. Starting a settlement had its own risks. And by choosing to stay here, she might die here—of disease or heartbreak, both seeming to war over which would claim her first. Of late she'd felt that same nightmarish foreboding as when the English ships came into Acadie, before all their lives unraveled.

What did the future hold?

Trading her needle and thimble for a handkerchief only made her more emotional. It was Will's handkerchief, one she'd used too often of late. Abandoning her sewing, she dried her eyes and went to the window. On the top floor, it offered a splendid if rain-streaked view. She pressed her forehead to the cold glass, more tears mingling with the rain. As she stared at Palace Green, so still it resembled a painting, a flicker of movement caught her eye. Who would dare step out on such a wet, windy day with contagion roaring around them?

Her heart stilled.

Will.

He was on foot, leading a dun-colored bay horse, Bonami loping along. Was he headed west toward the Rivanna and Greenmount, far beyond her reach again?

She whirled away from the window and ran toward the door. The back stairs were steep, and in her haste she nearly stumbled. Once out the side servants' entrance, she was hit by a blinding blast of weather, but it hardly slowed her. As the wind snatched her cap, she hitched up her petticoats and abandoned any pretense of modesty, sleet soaking her to the skin in seconds. And then, just as suddenly as he'd appeared, she lost sight of him.

"Will!" Her voice held a frantic echo, bouncing about the deserted street.

She raced on, careening through puddles rather than dodging them. There he was at the corner. Slowly he turned toward her. He waited, his hat dripping water, his buckskin leggings a sodden black and nearly as dark as his blue woolen coat.

"Sylvie."

Oh, the low, tender way he said her name. It left her half melting. With no thought, only a forlorn, lost feeling, she flung herself into his arms, breathless with relief and longing. Cheek pressed to his wool coat, she shut her eyes. Her crying came as hard as the rain, the thawing she'd felt since his leaving flowing out of her like Acadie's rivers into Baie Française.

He held her for long minutes without saying a word, his jaw resting against her bent head. The silence settled around them with that security he wrought, the longed-for peace she'd not known for so long she forgot it was even possible. It made her never want to let go.

"Don't go, Will. Don't go without me—please."

The woman who looked up at him seemed a stranger. Gone was the cool pride and simmering resentment he'd grown used to. Sylvie Galant was now all entreaty and tears, her eyes pink from weeping, the dark hollows beneath telling. Somehow the immense change softened her and made her more beautiful. He forgot his dripping hat and Braddock's reins and that Williamsburg was watching from countless windows.

He placed a cold yet gentle hand against her damp cheek, but at his touch she seemed more undone. He felt that pull to hold her close, to shelter her and chase the world with its fractious cares away. He wanted to do more than hold her. He wanted to kiss her. Kiss her long and thoroughly till the wet street was obliterated and she kissed him back.

But common sense prevailed. Without another word, he lifted her to the saddle, then reined toward Palace Green. Within minutes they were inside the Kersey townhouse, dripping water onto the pine-board floor. Sylvie's eyes lifted to elegant papered walls and paneling as Will spoke to a wide-eyed maidservant.

"Take Miss Galant upstairs and lend her one of Miss Kersey's dresses. I'll wait here."

At the maid's urging, Will moved into the parlor to stand by the blazing hearth, his sleeplessness overtaking him, his plans for the day unraveling in the best way. Kersey was at the college though it was not in session, and he'd given Will the run of the house when in town, a boon given the taverns were now closed.

It took time before the maid returned Sylvie downstairs in a dress that looked like spring, the floral chintz as bright as the day was dark, her wet hair combed and pinned up beneath a borrowed cap. Liselotte was smaller in stature and the gown fit snug and short, but Sylvie was dry, at least, and more composed than she'd been on the street.

Once she entered the parlor, the maid closed the door, sealing their privacy. Sylvie's concern now seemed to be him in his sodden state. "Do you not want to change?" she asked softly as she took a seat on a near sofa.

"Nay, I'm on my way to the almshouse and can't avoid the weather. With Hunter buried, the children are there."

Her hand went to her bodice. "I wondered where they'd gone. I went to the bookbindery but couldn't find them."

"Kersey, as executor of Hunter's estate, arranged for me to take them as their new bondsman."

Tears glazed her eyes again. "A merciful, generous act."

"Not entirely." His voice held humor. "I have other motives."

Her gaze lightened, then grew shadowed again. "Oh?"

"I am in need of a caretaker."

"Oh, Will . . ."

Their eyes locked, and in that poignant hush she gave him her answer.

He could hardly speak for the rush of emotion he felt. If he'd not been sleepless, if he'd not heeded that midnight urge to ride . . . "We'll leave once the weather clears. For now I'll go to the almshouse and make arrangements."

Sylvie met with the butler once she returned to the palace, hardly believing that life could take a blessed turn in so short a time.

"Yes, Miss Galant?" He sat at his desk where papers and daybooks were piled high, testament of his overseeing palace staff.

"I've come to give notice, sir, and I hope you'll pardon the suddenness of my doing so."

He studied her, this florid-faced man in livery, looking understandably weary and not at all surprised. "Meaning you are leaving town posthaste, I suppose."

"As soon as the weather clears." She wouldn't share the details. She wasn't even sure of them herself. He likely didn't care and had far weightier concerns than her future. "I've finished the dresses for the Dinwiddie daughters and left a note bidding them adieu. And I'll bring down the garments I've finished for the other servants."

"Very well. We shall miss your needle." He drummed his knuckles atop the table. "As it is, we've no word on when the governor and his family shall return. Though you've spent your time well in their absence under quarantine, I don't blame you for seeking service elsewhere."

She thanked him and returned upstairs to pack. A small chest soon held her few belongings, including her sewing kit and scissors. She'd started on Henrietta's garments but so far had cut out only the pattern, finding more enjoyment in this diminutive dress than any she had made as she simply anticipated the child's delight.

Her last hours at the palace flew past, leaving her looking out the window toward Kersey's townhouse and wondering when Will would reappear. A niggling fear remained . . .

Mightn't something happen to prevent her and the children from leaving after all?

45

Come live with me, and be my love, and we will some new pleasures prove of golden sands, and crystal brooks, with silken lines, and silver hooks.

John Donne

Sylvie hefted her small chest and met Will beyond palace walls at dayspring, as he called it. True to his word, a wagon and team waited outside, the bed filled with supplies and tools, even a hogshead. He took her chest and secured it behind the seat, then helped her up to sit beside him.

Other than a rather gruff greeting, he hadn't said a word. Nor had she.

The damp and the quiet would likely have magnified any talk, perhaps even awakened residents to their activity. Williamsburg remained a melancholy town even beneath a misted, rising sun, and she hoped within a few miles the feeling would lift. For now, the team trod slowly down Duke of Gloucester Street where the staccato clip of hooves announced their leaving.

Through the mist, Sylvie saw Eve waiting outside the bookbindery, the children in hand. A slightly bigger chest than Sylvie's own rested at their feet. At the sight of the wagon, Nolan began jumping up and down while Henrietta held tight to her raggety doll, face solemn.

"God bless Judge Kersey," Will remarked beneath his breath, slowing the team and setting the brake. "He even made arrangements for Eve to ready them for today."

Without waiting for him to help her down, Sylvie jumped to the ground in her eagerness. She embraced Eve, saddened beyond words she wasn't coming too.

"Don't pay me any mind," Eve whispered, drawing back. "I'll likely stay on right here in town. But I'll rest easier knowing the children are in good hands."

Will arranged blankets for the children to sit on in the wagon bed directly behind Sylvie. Eve had dressed them warmly in hats, scarves, and mittens, and Sylvie covered their woolen-clad legs and shoes with more blankets.

"Where are we going now?" Nolan asked Will, worry in his pale, freckled face.

"To a better life. A place you've never been, where you can learn to hunt and fish and farm," he answered, casting a look in Sylvie's direction. "Miss Galant will be near, as will I."

Seemingly satisfied, Nolan leaned back against a sack of grain while Henrietta kept hold of Sylvie's hand, making her wonder if she shouldn't climb into the wagon bed after them. To the children's delight, Bonami jumped in and settled down between them, adding to their warmth.

Sylvie faced forward as Will took the reins in hand. She'd envisioned this moment but hadn't expected it to be atop a wagon with the children.

The road was mud and rock beyond Williamsburg, the day nearly blinding with its brightness. The sun climbed higher, warming their backs as they rode west, shimmering off every frozen blade of grass and leafless branch. At intervals, Will had them walk to stretch their legs and lighten the team's load.

By late afternoon, it dawned on Sylvie that they'd have to overnight somewhere. The farther they traveled, the fewer people and habitations she saw.

Finally, at a crossroads, a stone building appeared along the frozen road like a figment of her imagination. Two stories of gray stone and a sloping roof crowned a long porch running the length of the building. The George Arms.

"We'll overnight here," Will told them.

Once they were inside, the innkeeper assigned them lodging and made assumptions. "Major Blackburn, you and your wife and children should rest well in our best room—the only one left given the hour. Now that your bed is settled, your board awaits." He pointed them in the direction of the public room. "Supper should serve your family well, as my wife and daughters are able cooks."

Will didn't correct him, only thanked him and turned toward the clink of cutlery and conversation. A few guests crowded round the hearth or occupied tables filling the large, low-ceilinged room. Seeking a corner, Sylvie and the children took a bench with Will across from them. Stiff from sitting in the wagon and cold to her bones, Sylvie felt relieved to have left town but was unsure of Will. They'd not talked much on the road, as if both of them were giving the other time to adjust to their shifting circumstances.

Amusement stole past his stoicism when she said, "So, Husband, it seems you've managed well for us tonight."

"Sylvie Galant Blackburn does sound almost poetic." He winked as a tankard of ale was set down, along with hot cider for her and the children. "And given there's only one available room . . ."

That flush only he was capable of raising rushed in, and she focused on the fare, her suddenly swaying stomach at odds with the feast before them. Roast fowl and game pie were served alongside heaping plates of fried potatoes and

pickled vegetables, applesauce, bread and butter, and preserves. The children ate heartily, gladdening her further.

"Who cooks for you along the Rivanna?" she asked him,
wondering where Liselotte Kersey fit into this new endeavor.

"Eulalie Benoit and Antoinette Laroche."

Both women she'd be glad to see again. "And the others?"

"Liselotte Kersey has a hand in overseeing the women and
any concerns or needs that arise. Sebastien Broussard and
Nicolas Surette are in charge of fieldwork and roadbuilding. Soon they'll be plowing, as we're bringing plow points
and other needed tools with us. The other men, including
indentures, rotate fieldwork while some repair the gristmill.
Work will start on a ferry after planting."

"Ambitious." She put her arm around Henrietta, who
yawned even as she stuffed more bread into her mouth. "I
hope your wheat crop is flourishing."

Will chuckled and continued eating, making her wonder
at his thoughts. Such high hopes she now had after having
none at all. She wanted to think no further than right here,
yet now all the unknowns crowded round her, chipping away
at the pleasure this hard-won moment wrought.

When she put down her fork and looked up, his eyes were
on her. "What made you decide to come with me?"

How lost she became in his steady, silvered gaze. For a
moment she forgot his careful question. "I need to let go of
the past and live in the present." Her voice stayed steadfast,
though she still felt like a sentimental puddle. "All I have is
this blessed moment. There's no promise of a future with
the political situation and the smallpox."

"You have a future, Sylvie. With me. And the children."
He set down his fork. "The Lord didn't bring you this far
otherwise." He looked like he wanted to say more but pushed
his empty plate away, ending the matter. "When you're ready,

go on up to the room and get settled. You three take the bed. I'll sleep in the barn near the wagon."

She felt a sudden dismay. "In this cold?"

His half smile said her concern was unwarranted. "Given I've weathered a howling blizzard or two, the barn will be warm. Nor do I want any pilfering of wagon or provisions."

This she understood. Bidding him good night, she got up from the table reluctantly while he sat alone to finish his ale.

"I feel sick," Henrietta told Sylvie as they washed their hands and faces at a washbasin in their room.

"You ate even more'n I did," Nolan said from the window where he stood watch. "I counted you had five buns. Pa used to call you Little Piggy, remember?"

"Nay," she said softly.

Sylvie pressed a hand to Henrietta's forehead and found it blessedly cool. "You're simply tired like me."

Heavenly Father, let that be all it is.

The plea, earnest enough, felt empty after so much prayerlessness.

"I'm not tired," Nolan boasted, squaring his small shoulders. "I want to sleep in the barn like Mr. Major."

"Perhaps you can keep him company another time," Sylvie said, tucking Henrietta beneath the covers. Though the hearth's fire danced with amber light, the room stayed cold. "Best ready for bed so you can help Mr. Major in the morning."

With that, Nolan climbed into bed and was soon asleep even as Henrietta burrowed closer to Sylvie. Snug, eyes closed and arms around the children, Sylvie felt a tendril of contentment take hold. These were not her children nor was the man downstairs her husband, but for now, on this frozen night, she was somewhere safe with those she loved, and that was enough.

46

Love was as subtly catch'd as a disease. But being got, it is a treasure sweet, which to defend is harder than to get; and ought not be profaned, on either part, for though 'tis got by chance, 'tis kept by art.

John Donne

Sylvie had not expected so much forest. Dogwood and redbud, oak and hickory and maple, poplar and towering pine. Will named what she didn't know.

At last, limbs numb from riding so long and faces pinched with cold, they reached the Rivanna. It was a comely river, only a mile wide at the most, so different from the rivers of before.

Père's weirs, teeming with sturgeon, shad, and salmon, sprang to mind. "What fish are here?" Sylvie asked.

"Shad and rockfish foremost—and herring, which you call gaspereau," Will told her, holding the reins loosely. "When we tire of hunting, we fish."

After another hour they came over a slight rise to see the distant settlement she'd tried to envision. Her eyes roamed everywhere at once, finding the land bleak beneath pewter skies. Trying to imagine it dressed in spring, Sylvie searched for any sign of the orchards. "I'm glad I'm in time to see the apples blossom. I'll help tend the orchards if you like. I can teach the children to tend them too."

"Children will be good to have here. They bring life and laughter to a world marked with hard work."

From the bed of the wagon, Henrietta and Nolan clamored to walk, tired of riding.

"Another mile yet," Will told them.

Down the rise they rolled, the team plodding at a slower pace. Log outbuildings dotted cleared woods, along with small timber-framed houses nearer the river with what looked like a lane between them. Smoke wafted from a dozen chimneys, and Sylvie could see people going to and fro. Some men worked in outlying fields and others on roadbuilding. All bespoke careful planning and long hours. This was now home to Will, matching the picture in his mind he'd carried since childhood. Somehow knowing that imbued the place with poignancy for her too.

"This is your vision, what Virginians call a plantation," she said, having never seen one. "Hard to believe it was abandoned and auctioned—and now thriving."

"Mostly because you Acadians don't shirk work." They were at the edge of the settlement now, but Will swerved to a road beyond it. "We're restoring what was left or lost. See the rebuilt mill farther downstream? One day there'll be a bridge rather than a ferry to reach the north bank." She followed the swing of his arm as he pointed out various sites. "Two warehouses stand on the south bank, and there's another half-finished near the mill."

Her appreciation grew as her gaze moved to a house on the hill, tucked in a stand of trees. A marvel of brick with no less than four chimneys that seemed deserving of town. "Who lives there, set apart from the rest?"

"The fool leader of this endeavor."

Surprised, she turned back to him, losing the reserve of the last hundred miles. "You're far from foolish, William Blackburn."

"Holy Spirit driven, mayhap inspired." His gaze touched hers before returning to the house. "As opposed to the White Devil of before."

They came to a stable, where they left the team to an indentured man she'd not met. From there they walked through woods where the river wended like a horseshoe, a sandy beach in one winsome bend. The children ran toward it, leaving mittens and scarves in their wake. Sylvie swallowed down the caution she felt, but they'd been so good on the journey she didn't want to spoil their high spirits.

In the shadow of the big house, farther down the hill, sat a small cottage with a narrow front porch surrounded by hemlocks that reminded her of home. Hers?

"You've not endured a Virginia summer yet," Will said, stepping onto the porch ahead of her. "You'll be glad of the shade trees come June."

"This place is so private. Set apart."

"Greenmount's farm manager once lived here, but it's been empty for years. The women cleaned it ahead of your coming. I had it in mind for you from the first, though I wasn't sure you'd ever see it."

Overcome with all she might have missed, she darted a look at him. His pride in the place—and in her being here—was plain even though he wasn't smiling.

In back of the cottage sprawled a gnarled, forsaken orchard overgrown with blackberry vines and weeds. Did he sense her dismay?

"Give it time," he told her, apology in his tone. "There's a great many varieties there—Hewe's Crab and Taliaferro, the best for cider, and Newtown pippin and Spitzenburg, best saved for dessert. Even Acadian seed that's already sprouting."

He opened the door, then stayed on the porch to keep an eye on the children while she stood on the threshold, clasping her hands together in wordless delight. She'd expected earth floors and chinked logs, not plastered walls and pine planks, nor twin hearths with wooden surrounds and deep-seated windows of gleaming glass. In one room, three beds bore linens and coverlets, and in the other were four chairs around an oval table. A washstand graced with a pitcher and basin stood between two windows.

In moments the children rushed in, drawing up short in wondrous bewilderment as she had. Will began kindling a fire in one hearth, sending Nolan back outside for wood, while Henrietta slipped her hand into Sylvie's as they passed into the other room.

"Is this our house now?"

"Oui, and a fine house it is."

Henrietta patted the bed's colorful coverlet. "Très belle."

Sylvie smiled, delighted by her joy. "Oui, très."

Will started a second fire in the bedchamber, then took Sylvie outside to show her the well beyond the back door. What looked to be a wild rose wound about its base, a promise of spring. She wondered at its color. All here was stillness and peace, unlike the other end of the settlement that seemed the equivalent of a hive. The memory of the teeming, reeking town was already receding. She took a deep, bracing breath of clean, frosty air.

"You'll need to be apart from the others for a time—you and the children," Will said. "Dr. Pitt recommends at least a fortnight."

"Of course." She felt a sudden contentment, a newfound freedom despite these light restrictions. "The last thing I want is to carry any sickness."

"I'll bring your belongings in and tell the others you're here." He reached out, the backs of his fingers grazing her cold cheek. "Expect supper at dusk."

As promised, Will reappeared, carrying a heavily laden tray. The humble task touched her, and they sat down together for another meal graced with both his presence and a prayer. Joining freshly washed hands, they bowed their heads.

"Father, we give Thee endless thanks for bringing us safely home," Will said. "Prepare our hearts to serve Thee here and elsewhere all our days. Amen."

Home. Did he already think of Greenmount that way? How had he come to have an endearing humility when he'd once been so formidable a soldier? Somehow it removed her further from the Ranger she'd known in Acadie. He'd become something more, a new man with only hints of the old one about him.

Could she somehow move beyond her own grievous past and become a new woman in turn?

"Do you live here too, Mr. Major?" Nolan asked, spooning his stew with gusto once they'd set out dishes.

"I'm in the brick house up the hill," he replied. "You're welcome to visit."

"Can I come too?" Henrietta asked with a rare forthrightness.

"Anytime you please, aye." Will shot a look at Sylvie. "The same goes for you."

"If you're not here," Nolan continued, reaching for more cheese, "I promise to keep her and Sister safe from coons and cougars and the like."

Will agreed. "You'll need a slingshot. I'll see if the carpenters can whittle one for you or teach you how. And a fishing pole."

"Take care with the river," Sylvie cautioned. "It's deep especially in spring, and you might—"

"Drown." Nolan frowned and nodded. "Pa used to tell me the same."

"If you respect the river, it's less of a threat." Will poured them more cider. "When you're a little older, we'll team up and carve a canoe for you."

"An Indian canoe?"

"Huron, aye."

Nolan's eyes rounded.

Henrietta wouldn't be left out. "Miss Sylvie's going to teach me to sew," she said proudly, looking at Sylvie for confirmation.

Will winked. "If you sew as well as you speak French, she'll be hard-pressed to keep up with you."

With a giggle, she hid her flushed face in her apron, making them all laugh.

"We'll be quite busy here making a new home." Sylvie stroked Henrietta's hair and looked at Will. "Once you bring me the bolts of cloth you mentioned, I'll start sewing. I don't mean to be idle even if we're isolated."

When supper was over, as the children played with their toys, she went to her trunk and took out the shirt she'd made Will. She'd not tell him of the tears she'd shed over it, nor how her heart had seemed to shift and soften stitch by stitch and seam by seam, leading to this tender moment.

He took the garment she held out, pleasure flickering across his face in the firelight. "I've never owned a finer shirt."

The compliment left her eyes awash. She'd meant it as a token of her gratitude, but the words wouldn't come even if the tears did.

"I waited nine months to see you cry, and now you can't seem to stop." His words came low, not in censure but in a sort of wonder.

Setting the shirt aside, he reached for her and pulled her onto the bench by the hearth where he sat. She seemed to melt into him as his arms encircled her, so quietly the children didn't stop their playing. They clung together as if they'd been apart years, not weeks. Each of them was in need of different things, or so she sensed—he her softness and scent, she his strength and purpose. Her head rested on his shoulder, the romance of the firelight lending to their intimacy.

Amused, she whispered, "Père would not approve of me nearly sitting on your lap."

"He would if he knew my intentions were honorable," he murmured against her hair.

Her eyes closed as the exhaustion of the day took over. In time the mantel clock she'd noticed earlier struck the hour. How long had they sat there as if they were the only two in the room?

Slowly, Will shifted as if awakening her and stood her on her feet.

Mère seemed near, somewhere in the shadows, her words a soft echo across time and place.

The sweeter the moment, the faster it flees.

47

I was long a child, and am so yet in many particulars.

Jean-Jacques Rousseau

A fortnight to themselves at the cottage helped Sylvie and the children settle in. Will left on a survey, so early in the morning Sylvie missed his going. But he'd left a note for her, assuring her of his return and telling her to seek out Nicolas if she had any questions or concerns. He made no mention of Liselotte Kersey. Bonami lay on her porch as if at his master's command. He wagged his tail as she greeted him in French, touched that Will had left him behind as if to help ensure their safekeeping.

"Mon ami!" The familiar voice halted Sylvie as she gathered firewood stacked at one end of the porch. Eulalie, obviously tired of waiting for Sylvie's quarantine to end, appeared on the riverbank. Looking a tad exasperated, she took a seat atop a boulder on the horseshoe beach. "Major Blackburn said you were here but that you weren't to be disturbed. I'm eager to know why you refused to come with us at first but have now appeared."

"I had a change of heart," Sylvie said, walking to the end of the porch nearest Eulalie.

"Well, I'm overjoyed you've joined us. And what a pretty cottage you have! I wondered who would take up residence here when I cleaned it ahead of your arrival."

"Remember the quarantine," Sylvie said, hiding a smile. "We cannot be in the midst of the settlement in case we sicken."

"A needless precaution. I think there is more to it than that. You are all the nearer Major Blackburn." Eulalie's laugh boded well. Not once had Sylvie heard her laugh before now. "I am glad to see you again at last."

"And you," Sylvie returned. "How is everyone else?"

"A few have fallen ill of the ague, but most are well. We have an infirmary of sorts here and ample medicine, though no doctor save Monsieur Dubois, who pretends to be one and is quite good at dosing us with tisanes and whatnot."

"So everyone has settled into their work? I'm trying to do my part sewing garments for the settlement."

"I expected nothing else. I doubt you are missing those fancy Pandoras at the palace." Eulalie rolled her eyes in good-humored exasperation. "We are in need of your needle. Farming is hard on garments, and those of us in the kitchen house fare no better."

"Well, I've no complaint about your cooking, and I'm even becoming fond of Indian bread. Tomorrow ends our isolation, and we'll join you for supper."

"I look forward to it. I'd best return to the kitchen lest Miss Kersey comes looking for me." Waving, Eulalie disappeared through the woods. "Till tomorrow, then."

Late the next afternoon the dinner bell clanged, easily heard at their cottage. Freshening up at the washstand, Sylvie tied on a clean apron and pinned a cap in place before washing the children's hands and faces. Taking them in hand, she simply followed the scent of baked bread as they walked to the kitchen house farther downriver.

"Sweet potato buns," Nolan said. "Don't you eat 'em all, Rietta."

"Shush!" She held a finger to her lips, expression stormy.

"We'll use our best manners," Sylvie told them, almost as shy as Henrietta at joining the others after so much solitude.

Releasing her hand, Henrietta skipped ahead of them. "Where's Mr. Major?"

"Surveying, remember?" Sylvie looked up the hill to the handsome house, the setting sun burnishing the brick red-gold.

Nolan summed up what Sylvie felt in spades. "He's been gone too long."

Sylvie found herself listening for Will's voice, willing him back among them. Would he often be away like this? Even if they were to marry? Though he'd only teased her about being Sylvie Galant Blackburn, she sensed the serious undercurrent beneath, and it was not one-sided. But he'd not yet kissed her, not yet wiped away the taint of Boudreau's clumsy kiss.

Leaving the woods, they approached the eastward half of the settlement. Men and women, both Acadians and inden-tures, gathered about the kitchen house entrance, forming a line of sorts. At the door stood Liselotte Kersey, her fair hair pinned beneath a lace-edge cap, her dress more genteel than their linen and wool garments. Pinned to her waist was a chatelaine, giving her an officious look as if she held every key to the settlement. Strong and unlined, she was in marked contrast to the Acadian women who'd suffered much. Yet she'd lost both her parents and her own home in the recent past, Will had said. There was little time to dwell on it as Sylvie's fellow Acadians greeted her and made much of the children, who, for all their flushing, seemed to delight in being the center of such warm attention.

"I thought we might not cross paths again," Sebastien said, his usual solemnity softened by a smile. "But you have escaped both Williamsburg and the smallpox. And quite timely too. We are in need of your sewing, as you can see." Raising an arm, he revealed a rent in his sleeve. "In exchange I will try to do some service for you."

How good it was to be among her people again and hear their tongue spoken freely. No hiding or dissembling here like in Williamsburg.

"What are they saying?" Henrietta asked her as they took a seat at one of the trestle tables.

"*Bonjour* means 'hello,'" Sylvie told her. "And what means *au revoir?*"

"Farewell," she answered, toying with her spoon.

Sylvie looked about, feeling she should be serving, not sitting, but Eulalie and Antoinette seemed to have all in hand. Wooden platters of meat were passed alongside heaping bowls of cabbage and root vegetables, even applesauce—and endless rounds of Indian and wheaten bread.

Nine women sat at one smaller table while more than thirty men occupied a larger table, benches serving as seats. At Nicolas's invitation, Nolan joined the men, which made him puff out his chest with a pride no one missed. Laughter and talk ensued, the men's robust conversation almost drowning out the women's. They spoke of their work and plans for the morrow, not a dissenting voice among them. Were they always so congenial?

"I'm tempted to ring the bell to quiet them," Eulalie said with a chuckle. "But they work so hard, let them have their mealtime merriment."

Liselotte ate with eyes down, saying nothing. Could she speak no French? Over the hubbub, Sylvie introduced herself.

"At last an English voice!" Liselotte looked relieved. "It's been rather difficult making myself understood, indentures aside. I have only learned *merci* and *s'il vous plaît* and so forth. I asked Major Blackburn to teach me more, but understandably, he lacks the time."

"La langue Français can be rather complicated."

"*Rather* is an understatement." Liselotte made a face. "Major Blackburn speaks it well. And your English is only slightly accented. I'm afraid my accent would be atrocious."

"I'm not as fluent as I wish to be, though our languages share many common words."

Liselotte sighed and gave a small shrug. "So, how do you like the farm manager's cottage?"

"It suits the three of us well," Sylvie said, helping Henrietta butter her bread. "And you?"

"I occupy what was once the overseer's cottage at the settlement's opposite end, near the wheat fields. Being here reminds me of my former home along the Rapidan River. We've accomplished a great deal since we first arrived, and Major Blackburn works as hard as the rest of us when he's not surveying. It won't be long before the fields are ready for harvest." She added sugar to her coffee after Antoinette served them from a large, steaming pot. "I saw you in the orchard the other day when I was there with an indenture looking over the bee skeps."

"I've been working there when I'm not sewing." Sylvie tried not to be discouraged by how large and unkempt the orchard was. "There's much to do, but the children are a help. Nolan carts pruned branches away in a wheelbarrow—"

"And I pick up old apples for the pigs and horses," Henrietta said between bites.

Sylvie smiled down at her and said in English and then in French, "We three work well together. Soon we'll have enough apples for cider and tarts."

Eulalie nodded. "We've a fine stone cellar here with plenty of room for apples."

"We've a spinning house too," Antoinette said. "And a rather stubborn flock of Hog Island sheep."

"And a dairy that's clean and fresh as can be," another woman joined in. "I mind the cows and their calves and make crocks of butter and cheese."

"You should see the garden," Eulalie told Sylvie. "Bigger than ours in Acadie and sewn with the most peculiar vegetables—okra and cowpeas and gourds. We've even watermelon, though I don't know what it is."

Sylvie sensed Liselotte's frustration as the conversation continued in French, so she translated what she could. She was happy to return to the quiet of the cottage once the meal ended.

In the days following, it didn't take Sylvie long to learn the rhythms of the Rivanna and who worked the hardest and the least, who avoided whom, and who was smitten with whom.

All the while she waited for Will. He often appeared unexpectedly, Liselotte said, slipping in and out without fanfare. He would surprise them by turning up at a meal or meeting, only to be gone surveying again. Though he'd wisely placed other men in positions of authority, there was no doubt who was in charge, as Liselotte often reminded them when it came to debated matters and differences of opinion.

In Will's absence, the big house sat empty. No one appeared on the wide, pillared porch or strolled through the brick-walled pleasure garden in back. Sylvie went uphill with the children, Bonami trailing, to admire the work of the gardener, an indenture who'd once traveled to Holland and France to study their flowers. A Scotsman like Will, Archie Chisholm came from Inverness. A knot garden had begun to take shape beneath his capable hands, a recovered ornamental cherry tree at its heart. Such beauty here. Such peace.

Archie was showing them the roses he'd uncovered beneath

a tangle of ivy when the supper bell rang. It sang across the settlement, signaling a close to the workday.

Sylvie and the children returned to the cottage to tidy themselves, then made their way to the kitchen house, the March day so warm they went without their usual wraps. Nolan joined the men while Sylvie sat down between Antoinette and Henrietta, and they bowed their heads to say grace.

When Sylvie looked up, she saw Will come through the open doorway, and her heart's sudden leap left her breathless. But she wasn't the only one glad of his return. Across from her Liselotte stared openly at him, leaving no doubt as to her own feelings.

Greeting them all, Will took a seat with the men, his garments gray with dust, his face bearded. Fork suspended, Sylvie drank in the sight of him, wishing he'd look her way.

"So, how is the sewing coming?" Antoinette asked her, returning her to the women's conversation. "I, for one, will be glad of a new petticoat."

"I should finish those on the morrow." Sylvie cut bites of smoked beef for Henrietta and then herself. "Then I'll move on to the men's shirts."

"I'm weary of wearing wool," Eulalie said. "Linen will be a welcome change."

Liselotte sent another look to the men's table then to Sylvie. "Monday is washday. These men muddy clothes so, laboring like they do. There may be mending for you also."

"I shall be glad of it, then," Sylvie answered.

The children were yawning, worn out from all their outdoor play. As she slipped out a back door with them to return to the cottage, Will remained behind, talking with the men and Liselotte. How she wanted to stand as prettily by his side, greeting him openly after his lengthy time away, not riddled by shyness, unsure of herself—and him.

To bolster herself, she dwelled on the little routines that formed the fabric of their days. Tomorrow was the Sabbath, a day of rest along the Rivanna. On Saturdays after supper she took the children to the river to bathe. The current was slightly sluggish in the horseshoe bend, the water remarkably clear and waist-deep. The children shivered and shouted at the cold, and Sylvie promised them in summer it would be warmer.

Once they were clean and in their nightclothes, she tucked them into bed after prayers. Sitting beside them like Mère used to do with her, she talked to them softly and sang the old French songs till their even breathing told her they slept.

Quietly she left the cottage and went through the orchard farther away from the settlement. The moon, free of clouds, offered just enough light to guide her. Clad in her shift, she waded into the water with the bar of Marseilles soap the Dinwiddie daughters had given her, a little luxury and a reminder of Bleu, who'd brought fancy soap from French traders. Its pleasant wintergreen scent was a far cry from the soft soap stored in barrels in the settlement's warehouse.

The river was as sharp and cold as Baie Française, where she'd taken her first swim long ago and pretended to be a mermaid. Ashiver, she pulled herself free of the water, wet hair hanging to her hips. Along the bank a whip-poor-will piped a sweet, repetitive song. She turned in the bird's direction, rocks pinching her feet, and startled as her gaze fell on a figure in the shadows.

There along the bank sat Will in breeches. Chest bare, his naked feet firm upon the sand and his own wet hair hanging free to his shoulders, he extended his arms to her. The bird continued chanting, but she hardly heard it. Unable to ignore the sudden tumult inside her, she left the water and all but ran toward Will with the abandon she'd been denied in the kitchen house.

Gently, he wrapped her towel around her and took her in his warm, castile-scented embrace. She shivered but not from the cold. Pressed together, as close as two unwed people had a right to be, they still seemed not close enough.

Her words were a bit breathless. "How long have you been here?"

"I'd just gotten out of the river before you got in."

"I stole your bathing place."

"You stole my heart, Sylvie Galant, the moment I wiped milk off your shoes."

That day. Once sore, the memory now shone bright as candle flame. "You came looking for Bleu, but now I wonder if, in some mysterious way, you came for me instead."

"I don't doubt it." His lips brushed her forehead. "You're the only thing I don't regret about Acadie."

"And here we are in the moonlight at long last, having a private moment in a settlement that never lets you alone."

"I've thought of little else since I left." His hands, warm and firm, spanned her waist. "Betimes you seemed a dream, and I half feared you'd not be here when I got back."

"I'm no dream, Will, and I'm not leaving, at least not of my own free will."

She placed her hands against his chest. He felt startlingly new—unsafe and unmapped—yet still like a homecoming. He made her feel . . . lovely. Not wounded or unwanted. Not scarred. His mouth met hers with all the need and sweetness she'd hoped for, removing every trace of Boudreau's unwanted kiss.

"Nothing seems to matter except that you're here." His silver eyes, so dark and full of feeling in the fading light, shone like damp onyx. "That you're mine."

"I'm yours completely, Will. You don't just belong to my past, painful as it is, but my present—and my future."

"Our future, Sylvie."

The stars came out, tiny pinpricks around a moon as bright as a Spanish silver dollar. He kissed her again, and the world spun away. It was just the two of them in this breathless moment, a simple man and woman who'd somehow fallen in love despite their foremost reservations and intentions.

48

Few planters but that have fair and large orchards, some whereof have 1,200 trees and upward bearing all sorts of English apples . . . of which they make great store of cider . . . likewise great peach-orchards, which bear such an infinite quantity of peaches.

Thomas Glover

Morning painted the room with soft yellow light. Nolan snored softly while Henrietta mumbled in her sleep. Yawning, Sylvie pushed back the covers, then lay still as Will and the river meeting rushed back. There'd been so many kisses and whispered endearments she'd lost count. She'd wanted to reach up to the heavens and pin the moon in place. Stop time with all its sweet fleetingness.

The Sabbath passed as quietly as Saturday had set the riverbank ablaze. Will's day was spent with his farm managers and at his desk while Sylvie and the children kept to the cottage. But by Monday's first light, the settlement came alive again, the ring of an axe underscoring a return to work.

As Sylvie left the cottage with the still-sleepy children, a basket of dirty laundry on her hip, her gaze traveled uphill to the house she'd not yet been inside. Curiosity gnawed at her. She longed to step onto the wide porch and enter through that handsome front door. Since the house's contents had been auctioned, her homesick heart dressed it in her imagination, adorning every bare place. For one, she'd set chairs and benches on the porch, making it a hospitable house. A welcoming home.

Henrietta noticed her gawking. "Where's Mr. Major?"

"Perhaps he's already at the kitchen house," Sylvie told her. "Look for Bonami and he'll likely not be far."

They walked on, and Sylvie weighed the wisdom of doing laundry when the skies shifted fitfully, heavy with gray clouds. But Liselotte had designated Monday after breakfast as washday, and downriver was the designated place, split-rail fences serving as drying racks. Everyone ate hurriedly as if mindful of the weather, Will's absence giving them no reason to linger.

Liselotte was the first back outside, lending to Sylvie's admiration. She possessed an ability to do many tasks well, overseeing the dependencies with an uncomplaining, competent if unbending hand.

"Bonjour," Sylvie greeted her, setting down her basket.

"Good morning to you. Or so I hope." Liselotte poured hot water into a washtub and cast a glance at the glowering sky. "The weather's changeable as a maiden's mood."

"Is that thunder in the distance?" Sylvie began scrubbing the children's soiled clothes while they waded in the water.

"Thunder usually means lightning." Liselotte paused. "Will—Major Blackburn—has ridden out to the west boundary to repair fences. He doesn't need the aggravation of a spring storm. After that, he'll be leaving on another survey, which doesn't bode well with foul weather either."

Sylvie scrubbed harder, trying to dismiss her sudden hurt

at hearing secondhand. Liselotte, she knew, met with Will and the farm managers frequently. Naturally she'd know his comings and goings. But his laundry? Sylvie took a second look at the clean clothing Liselotte was draping over a fence. The shirt she'd made Will was easily identified, but his other garments were unfamiliar. Liselotte handled them with a practiced ease, turning a routine task intimate.

Other women joined them to wash, half a dozen scattered along the riverbank, talking and laughing among themselves as the distant drum of thunder sounded again.

"I'll not rest till he's back," Liselotte murmured as if to herself. "He drives himself so. He needs a helpmate and family to keep him here." Turning away from the fence, she gave Sylvie a half smile as she continued in low tones. "My hope is to make this my permanent home, not a temporary situation. The major may not realize it yet. Men can be so . . . preoccupied."

Again Liselotte marked some invisible emotional boundary as if driving home a surveying stake. Sylvie was at a loss for words.

"Of course, we'd have to journey to Middle Parish for that. I do feel sorry for Béatrice and Thibault, wanting to wed but forbidden to do so."

"Forbidden?"

"No clergyman in Virginia or elsewhere will wed papists like yourself, nor join in holy matrimony a Protestant and Catholic, for that matter." Liselotte spoke with an authority that Sylvie couldn't naysay. "Your religion is considered treasonous and is treated as such by Virginia officials."

Sylvie knew Catholics were loathed, but did that extend to marriage too? Will hadn't told her. Surely he knew the laws.

"My uncle is a judge, remember." A touch of pride emphasized Liselotte's words. "I'm well versed in matters concerning you and your people."

The Acadians were at the mercy of these Virginians, a law-abiding people who didn't want them. If not for Will—

"Miss Kersey?"

Another woman approached and asked a question, which Liselotte answered with her usual skill. Finished with washing, Sylvie toted the wet garments and called to the children to return to the cottage as feeble sunlight speared the wooded path.

Did Liselotte fancy Will cared for her too? True, he had a singular way about him, making each of them feel valued. Never dismissive or arrogant, he gave them his undivided attention when the moment called for it. Evidently Liselotte misconstrued that attentiveness for something more.

Pondering it, Sylvie went about her tasks under the still-grumbling sky, sewing and minding the children before collecting the clean garments from the fence.

Henrietta and Nolan were the first to see Will coming through the orchard toward their cottage. He scooped Henrietta up, tucked her under one arm, and tickled her while he gave Nolan Braddock's reins with instructions to lead him to a water trough then take him to the stables.

Setting the laundry basket on the porch, Sylvie hastened to meet Will as he set a giggling Henrietta down. Reading the weariness in his face, Sylvie hurried to bring him water from the well. He drank it down, handed Henrietta the empty cup, and asked her to return it from whence it came. She scampered away, and Sylvie had him to herself, savoring the feel of his hands as they clasped hers and then raised them to kiss the backs of her fingers. Her heart did a little dance even as her stomach felt awash.

"I came in ahead of the rain." He looked down at her, his eyes holding hers in a way that felt as intimate as a kiss. "Mending fences is much more agreeable when I find you waiting for me."

She flushed and confessed, "Thoughts of you sweeten the most mundane tasks. In truth, I hardly know what I did."

His wink made her nearly forget Liselotte's startling revelation. "And what did you do?"

"Washed clothes. Sewed. Lost my thimble then found it again." She flinched as a flash of lightning lit the sky in back of him. The rumble that followed nearly drowned out the supper bell, though it set Henrietta's face alight as she returned.

"Tater wagons rolling, Mama said."

"Tater wagons, aye. A whole army of them." Will picked her up again and started through the woods toward the kitchen house. "Can you smell the coming rain?"

"The rain smells like"—Henrietta looked skyward—"a mud pie."

Will's chuckle was buried beneath another boom as they sprinted through the woods ahead of the downpour and arrived as the heavens opened. Sylvie looked about for Nolan but faced Liselotte instead. Standing by the door, she glanced at Will in admiration then at Sylvie in unmasked irritation.

"I hope you enjoy the meal. With Antoinette taking the grippe, I lent a hand in the kitchen," she said to Will, who thanked her before taking a seat.

Sylvie's hunger vanished as she took a place upon the bench. Rain pelted the roof with such a vengeance she feared leaks. Grace was said, but Sylvie barely heard it over the tumult of rain and wind. Helping Henrietta, she felt all thumbs when she dropped the knife to the floor.

"Really, Miss Galant, you're as clumsy as the child." Liselotte's barbed remark slipped beneath the side conversations all around them. "Have a care."

Stung, Sylvie picked up the knife but made no comment. A burst of masculine laughter raised her gaze. She warmed to Will's presence. She wanted to continue hearing that deep, sonorous voice for the rest of her life. Though he preferred to listen, he was a skilled storyteller when he wanted to be, telling of a recent survey that had his party chased by bears and then a cougar.

"I believe they were in league together, determined to drive us out . . ."

Sometimes the men would tell of life in Acadie as if determined to keep the memories alive, while the women listened or talked of more mundane matters. Butter that wouldn't set. Seed that wouldn't sprout. The spinning wheel that needed repair. What remedy was best for sour stomachs and blisters.

"I do wish you women wouldn't patter on so in French." Liselotte's face grew colder. She pushed the food about her plate as if she'd lost her appetite.

Sylvie longed to sit down for peaceful meals with Will and the children in the house on the hill. She ate a few bites, finally giving what remained to Henrietta.

Watching, Liselotte frowned. "The child eats like a farmhand."

"A tribute to your cooking, perhaps, if not your conversation," Sylvie replied tartly, unable to endure her insolence a second longer.

At this, Liselotte left the table, and Sylvie all but exhaled in relief. She smiled at Henrietta reassuringly, hoping she hadn't heard her unkindness or, if she had, wouldn't remember it.

Eulalie watched Liselotte's abrupt departure with a shrewd eye. "I know enough English to say this is not at all about Henrietta or being clumsy. This is about Major Blackburn."

"Oui, entirely." Sylvie looked again at Will, who was listening to Thibault tell of the so-called spirit bears in New Caledonia, the white-coated creatures that reminded her of Bleu. Bleu had nearly revered them and refused to hunt them.

Eulalie continued on in a whisper meant for Sylvie alone.

"Miss Kersey is making a fool of herself for a man who doesn't seem to give her more than a polite glance."

Sipping her cider, Sylvie wondered where Liselotte had gone. "I've wondered why a genteel woman would agree to work alongside outcasts in a settlement."

"Well, now you have your answer. Major Blackburn is the prize. And in her mind, once she marries him, her labors will cease. She will retire to the big house and from there boss us without mercy."

Sylvie took a steadying breath, trying to fight any unforgiveness taking root. "I must admit she is skilled at managing a plantation. And she is Anglican, not Catholic, a woman who knows far more than we do about life here. She's less likely to fall ill, being Virginia born and bred. Even her uncle is well respected and an investor in this settlement—"

"Bon sang! Will you talk yourself out of loving him?"

"No." Sylvie smiled despite herself. "It is entirely too late for that."

49

But times do change and move continually.

Edmund Spenser

Will walked down the hill from the main house, moonlight illuminating his steps. He'd trod this way so often the grassy path was now well trammeled, a telltale sign of his devotion. Sylvie's cottage glowed golden with candlelight, an unspoken invitation on this rain-streaked night. He stepped onto the porch and saw her through a window, sitting by the children's beds, their hands folded in prayer. He waited till they'd finished before tapping quietly at the door.

Sylvie answered, stepping onto the porch and into the security of his open arms. "You're leaving soon?"

"Before first light." Partings were hard for her, he knew. He sensed they always would be. She'd lost too much. "I go to Williamsburg after the survey. I don't know when I'll return."

He already felt the ache of leaving her, fragile as their circumstances were, circumstances he wouldn't apprise her of until he'd sorted fact from fiction.

"I'll miss you every moment." She squeezed his hands. "And I'll pray you home."

The soft, almost reverential way she said "home" filled his mind with a dozen different images. Children gathered around the table and running up and down stairs. Muddy footprints on the porch and handprints on glass windows. Shared whispers and talk and laughter. Things he vaguely remembered and missed most from his fractured childhood.

"I want you to feel this is your home, though it may take time."

"My spirit is more settled here." She smiled, further reassuring him, her expression less haunted. "I never felt that in Williamsburg or anywhere else since leaving Acadie."

"You'll be more at home once you're on the hill." Together they looked to the big house, a stalwart promise of the future in stone and brick, a sole light flickering like a star in an upstairs window. "It won't be home to me till you are."

"It needs a woman's hand."

"Yours."

Her gaze turned wistful. "I've not set foot in it yet."

Nay? He felt a fool not realizing it. "Come with me now, then."

She brightened, eager as a child. "Let me make sure they're sleeping."

In moments they were up the hill and on the wide porch with its territorial view, moonlight spilling silver across its smooth planks. Will gave a push to the front door and it opened to the foyer, where a single sconce shone upon a paneled wall and a stair wended upward. Sylvie stepped inside, and even the shadows couldn't hide her delight. It made him feel a pride he couldn't really own in a house he hadn't built, just occupied. He regretted it was so unadorned.

His voice seemed to thunder through the barrenness. "For

now it echoes with emptiness. But once you begin making it ours and the children are here, it will come to life."

She touched the carved pineapple finial atop the newel post in a sort of awe. He followed her as she climbed the stairs, one hand on the oak handrail. She paused at the tall window on the landing to take in the walled garden below, its painstaking restoration kinder by moonlight. The twig trellises and the bell jars used to cover fragile plants seemed to hold an odd enchantment in her appreciative company.

"I'm no longer just in love with you, Will," came her whisper. "I'm besotted with your house."

"Then be its mistress, Sylvie." He stood behind her, breathing in the clean scent of her upswept hair. "Marry me. Be my bride and settle here with me till my life ends, or yours, or the both of ours." She turned toward him as he continued, "Mayhap we can wed when the apples bloom in the orchard."

She drew back a bit as if thunderstruck. "How did you know?"

"Know?" He held her face between his hands.

"Since I was small I've wanted to wed during apple blossom time. I always thought it would be in Acadie . . ." Her voice faded then strengthened. "But apple blossoms are the same here as there, and I couldn't have a finer groom anywhere."

"Is that an aye, then?"

"There could be no other answer." She touched his cheek. "I am yours completely, heart and soul. I sensed it from the beginning though everything was against us."

"I feel the same, though it might take time to find a pastor."

Her face lost its light. "Can you find one willing?"

"I'll find one, aye. He'll not be Catholic or Anglican, rather

Baptist or Presbyterian. It will be honorable and legal, and you'll never have to worry about home again."

"You're sure, Will . . . about me?"

The soft entreaty rent his heart. "I was sure before I left Acadie, Sylvie, though I didn't ken the why or the end of it."

Her arms went round him, holding him as tightly yet as tenderly as he held her. They stood there, wed in spirit already if not by clergy and contract.

~

Sylvie missed Will sorely and found her gaze traveling up the hill again and again. He'd said little about his work, though she was becoming familiar with the tools of the trade—his chains and markers, the field book often tucked under one arm, and the ever-present compass. Twice his surveying party had come by, made up of woodsmen like himself as well as several Indians, even an African. Their presence created quite a stir about camp, as did their horses, which gravitated toward the river and the greening grass at its edges.

When a light flashed from an upper window after only one week, she gave in to her curiosity. Had he already returned? Anticipation lent wings to her steps, and she fairly flew up the hill after an especially trying day of Henrietta's crying, a shortage of linen thread, and the lingering burn of Liselotte's words.

Rain slicked the grass, soaking her shoes and making her shiver. She hugged her shawl closer with one hand while fisting her petticoats in the other to keep her hem dry. Around the back of the house she went, aware she might be spotted if she used the front entrance.

She glanced at the garden gate, wanting to linger and peer over the ironwork. Archie Chisholm had cut back all the remaining overgrowth with a shovel, then carted weeds and thistles and vines to a burn pile behind the bricked enclosure. His cottage was dark, but she spied him inside smoking his pipe.

The rear door of Will's house was more modest than the front door, with a few stone steps that climbed above the grass and dandelions. She gave a knock, her heart in her chest nearly as loud. She craved Will's nearness, the security of his arms. The place seemed to hold his scent, his very presence. Had she only imagined that light?

Slowly, she opened the back door beneath the staircase and heard another door closing. An intruder? The thought chilled her and propelled her forward all at once. Will did not lock the house, only his study. If someone wanted to break in, little would stop them, lock or no lock. He had little to hide whether he was home or not.

Wishing for a light, she felt her way through the house. "Will? Are you home?"

She started up the staircase, one hand caressing the hand-rail's smooth wood. Daylight was fading fast, denying her the details she loved. Will's bedchamber door was open, inviting her in. A canopied bed draped with mosquito netting dominated the room. One corner was adorned with a fireplace, its ornate mantel a work of art. His shaving stand stood between two spun-glass windows that overlooked the river and her cottage. For a moment she forgot her skittishness, lost in the pleasure that Will might have stood here watching her.

A sudden footfall spun her around. Sebastien stood in the doorway, a scarecrowish silhouette.

Disappointment gave way to confusion then fear. But Sebastien wouldn't hurt her, surely, even if he'd come into the house uninvited.

"I saw a light and thought Major Blackburn might be back," she said.

"I snuffed my lantern when I heard you." He regarded her in silence for a few tense seconds. "I wonder if you're not searching for what I'm searching for."

His cryptic words spiked her fear. Shaken, she put a hand on a bedpost.

"Do you have the keys to his study? The door is locked, and I don't have the tools to take it off its hinges, let alone unlock it."

"Why would you?"

"I've heard he's received correspondence about what is to become of us Acadians. I'm searching for evidence of such."

Sylvie grappled with the implications. "Major Blackburn isn't one to dissemble or hide the truth. I'm certain he'd tell us any news straightaway."

"I have begun to wonder. He has the ear of powerful Virginians I mistrust, the governor and his council foremost. I've just returned from farther downriver getting supplies. Word is this settlement will soon be disbanded and we'll be forced onto ships like before and sent to places unknown."

She stared at him in horror, the thought of being hunted down again too much to bear. She couldn't take another ship, another separation—

"Our only recourse is to flee." Sebastien rubbed his bearded jaw. "I've heard Fort Duquesne on the three rivers in Ohio territory is a refuge for our people."

"Fort Duquesne . . . in the middle of the wilderness?"

"There we would be firmly in French territory with fellow Acadians, perhaps even find family and friends. We would not be outcasts like here, dependent on the goodwill and generosity of a few benevolent men, one of whom is dead of the pox."

Stunned, she sat down on the window seat, wishing Will would walk in and make things right.

With a labored breath, Sebastien turned away and started

for the stairs. His tired tread mirrored her sinking spirits. She heard him go out, shutting the door behind him, hopefully heading to his own quarters in the twilight.

Near tears, Sylvie turned away from the window to survey the room a final time. A large Bible rested on Will's bedside table. He carried a smaller one in his saddlebags. Seeking comfort, she returned to the window seat that framed the last of the sunset and paged through the heavy tome till coming to the Psalms. Her eyes lit on a line that held her heart still.

Thou tellest my wanderings: put thou my tears into thy bottle: are they not in thy book?

Her heavenly Father, the creator and sustainer of the universe, a tear keeper?

Will faced Lady Drysdale in her elegant Williamsburg parlor, steeling himself against the change in her once beautiful face. The pox had ravaged her delicate features, the scars slow to heal, but it seemed not to have daunted her spirit. She was now a grieving widow, but her eyes were clear and she studied him unflinchingly when he said, "I lost a powerful ally in Lord Drysdale."

"Indeed you did." She paused as a baby's cry came from abovestairs, that quieted just as suddenly. "But his purposes didn't end. It now falls to me to carry on his work and legacy. I am determined, with the Lord's guidance, to do all that I am able and then some." She gestured to a sofa facing the fire. "Please, Major Blackburn, join me for refreshments. I believe you enjoyed the flip I served you last time when my husband was here."

"Aye," he said and sat down, adjusting to the emptiness without his host's presence.

"As you know, my husband had the utmost respect for

your endeavors with the Acadians, and he was"—she arched her brows—"rabidly interested in your recent publication."

He reached inside his waistcoat and produced a signed copy. She took it with obvious delight. "The success of the Rivanna settlement is largely dependent on Lord Drysdale and Captain Lennox." He left off as a maid appeared with steaming ceramic mugs, turning the air redolent with ginger and molasses cream.

"Speaking of that, not long ago I entertained a lovely young Acadian woman in this very parlor." Lady Drysdale balanced her mug with pale hands and breathed in the steam. "You must tell me how Mademoiselle Galant is faring along the Rivanna." A smile snuck past Will's stoicism, and she continued, "Ah . . . I'm guessing she is quite well, which surely has something to do with you."

"We're hoping to wed if I can find a willing, unprejudiced clergyman."

"Felicitous congratulations to you both!" Smiling, she raised her flip in a sort of toast. "I would recommend a Baptist, then. They are among the bravest and boldest dissenters, years ahead of their time. In fact, I know the very one. He happens to be in your parish, an itinerant preacher, if you will."

"I'll tell Sylvie and seek him out, then," he said. "Thank you."

"But your nuptials aren't the only thing on your mind, I'm sure." Her face clouded. "No doubt the Acadian hurricane, as it's being called by colonials, is worrisome, though I doubt any other ships will arrive in Virginia or any other colonial port this late. A great many Acadians were lost at sea, and it's thought half perished on those criminally ramshackle transports."

"I'm most concerned about the fate of the Acadians still held at Hampton Roads and farther up the James."

She frowned. "Since I returned from Indigo Island, I've been keeping a close eye on those developments and am doing all that I can to prevent those shiploads of refugees from being sent out of Virginia Colony. At the very least, I'm using everything within my power to ensure your Rivanna settlement—and every Acadian there—is left alone."

Will felt some of his burden lift. He'd come here alarmed by reports of an imminent deportation in April. "I've seen your petitions and heard that you even addressed the burgesses in their chambers."

"Yes, and like you, I've also personally met with the governor and his council about the matter, given the Acadians are being denied repatriation. It behooves these colonial officials to right a matter gone grievously wrong. If they do not, I shall appeal to Parliament and my allies in England while withdrawing my support of Dinwiddie and his council here."

"I have a meeting with Dinwiddie this afternoon and pray it's in the Acadians' favor."

"Feel free to tell him you've met with me as well. It might reinforce that you aren't alone in this undertaking."

Will knew her late husband had wielded considerable influence in the colonies and abroad. Thankfully, Lady Drysdale knew how to use that not only to her advantage but to others' as well. "You are as strong an ally as your late husband, Lady Drysdale."

"I mean to be. And when Captain Lennox returns from his cruise, he'll join us in our commitment to see right prevail. As Scripture says, a threefold cord is not quickly broken."

50

To endure is the first thing that a child ought to learn, and that which he will have the most need to know.

Jean-Jacques Rousseau

Sylvie watched the road coming from Williamsburg for any sign of British soldiers as much as she did for Will's return, fear forcing her into corners she'd rather not consider. If she saw those detested scarlet coats, should she grab the children and run into the woods like so many Acadians had done when the English arrived? Had their fleeing done them any good?

She sought the company of others rather than risk soldiers overtaking her alone with the children at the cottage. In the spinning house, the wheels whirred with a routine contentedness and work played out all around her, yet she knew everything could be upended in seconds. Still, she plied her needle and placed newly made garments on the shelves as if she had no other worry than Liselotte's continual counting and inventories and surliness.

"Miss Sylvie, I hurt." Henrietta was at her side, holding up a finger with a thorn embedded in the pink flesh.

"I'm sorry, Rietta. Here, let me look." Sylvie set aside her armful of shifts, sat down, and took Henrietta gently onto her aproned lap. Try as she might, she couldn't free the thorn.

"I saw her plow straight into the sticker bush." Liselotte's voice sounded from the doorway, an odd mix of concern and condemnation. "Come here and I'll take care of it."

Henrietta squirmed off Sylvie's lap and ran to the other woman, who, in seconds, relieved her with the help of some tool on the chatelaine dangling from her waist.

"Thank'ee," Henrietta said, casting Sylvie a backward glance as she hurried out of the spinning house.

Sylvie watched her go reluctantly. Will had advised her to not tether the children so tightly in a bid for their growing independence and to quiet her mother-hen nerves. Nolan was even helping the men in the fields of late, and she felt a motherly pride, especially when two indentures remarked how well behaved and polite the children were. Still, she worried, and Liselotte seemed determined to fan those fears.

"Next the little hoydens will be snakebit," Liselotte said, watching Henrietta return to her doll beneath the eave. "Or drown themselves, as they play so near the river."

Biting her lip lest she give a saucy reply, Sylvie walked around Liselotte and out the door, craving a drink of well water as much as quiet. To her dismay, Liselotte followed.

"We're in want of a dozen wool petticoats ahead of winter. And if you've need of any supplies, come to me, not Major Blackburn. He shouldn't be concerned with such trifles."

Sylvie saw through the ruse of her words. She wound the bucket to the well's bottom and back up again, then took a gourd dipper of water to slake her thirst, trying to keep in mind the good of the settlement. "I can begin knitting stockings and caps if you're thinking of winter. I'll just need wool and knitting needles."

"I'll manage the knitting myself." Liselotte shook her head when Sylvie offered her water. "For now my hands are full helping Antoinette in the kitchen and Lucie in the garden since Eulalie is ill."

"Ill?"

"She's feverish as of this morning and confined to the pesthouse." Liselotte grimaced. "Major Blackburn calls it an infirmary. Mr. Dubois has seen her, but what we need is a bona fide doctor. How I detest the role of nurse. Whatever her malady, time will tell if it's a mortal illness."

Mortal? But not the pox, surely. Eulalie had been away from Williamsburg and the contagion for weeks now.

Calling for Henrietta, Sylvie left Liselotte standing by the well, intent on the infirmary. Set apart farther down the riverbank, the building was empty of all but Eulalie now that several of the men had recovered from a recent ague. She lay atop a pallet near a window, asleep, the light showing her high color. Bending over her, Sylvie gently placed a palm against her alarmingly hot cheek.

In minutes Sylvie was back at the well, relieved to see Liselotte had gone. After drawing an entire bucket of water, she returned to the infirmary, Henrietta in her wake, her doll dragging in the dust.

"Play here on the stoop, mon chou," Sylvie whispered.

"*Chou?*" Henrietta looked up at her with all the offense of a budding four-year-old. "I am *not* a cabbage."

"No, you are much prettier." Sylvie knelt down, looking into her remarkable eyes. "How about *ma fille*? It means 'my girl.'"

At that, Henrietta's arms snuck around her neck, and she gave Sylvie a hasty kiss before sitting down, digging in her pockets, and producing acorn cups and leaf saucers for her favorite pastime—a pretend tea party. Sylvie wished she had a confection or two to sweeten the fête.

Toting the bucket inside, she found Eulalie awake and looking relieved to see her. "I miss home especially when I am ill," Eulalie said. "How I wish for our old remedies. Elderberry foremost."

"I've brought a few things from the Williamsburg apothecary," Sylvie reassured her, not wanting to ask Liselotte to open the stillroom. She gave Eulalie a long drink, then poured water into a basin and took up a clean cloth. She cooled her friend's brow while searching for something to say amid her suffering. "Do you know what I just learned? That God Himself collects our tears and stores them in a bottle."

The words fell into an uneasy silence.

"Why would He?" Eulalie frowned. "Where did you hear such fancies?"

"I read it in the Holy Word," Sylvie continued. "The Psalms. God takes note of our suffering. It is no light matter to Him. I find that . . . comforting."

"There is no bottle big enough for Acadie's weeping." Eulalie's eyes closed, but a tear trailed down her flushed face. "Where was God when we were robbed of our homeland and so many perished? When we live in a continual bewilderment about all that has befallen us and wonder where our loved ones are?"

Those questions had been her own, asked on the long wagon ride with Will coming here. She could only echo his response back to Eulalie now. "God was there in our midst. He is right here, right now. And He is no stranger to death or separation or evil. He gave up His own Son." The memory of the crucifix in their former chapel had never seemed so significant.

Eulalie's eyes fluttered open. "What if I die? There's no priest, no last rites here."

Sylvie's mind clouded with all the things she had no answer for. "You're going to recover, Eulalie. You've come through so much and are bonne santé."

"No. I am guilty of living when so many perished. I wish that I had died too." Taking a breath, she rambled on in a fever of misery and remorse. "I should have done more to help my family . . . I should have fought for us to stay together . . ."

Sylvie felt near tears herself, for had she not often regretted the same? "You have reason to live. You can make a new life, have a family, a home of your own in time. There are many men here who need a helpmate."

"But not Sebastien. He is intent on leaving before les Rosbifs come against us again." Her eyes closed again, her tone resigned. "I tried to tell him how much we depend on him here, but he's obsessed with reaching the French fort—I forget its name."

"Duquesne."

"Oui, on the frontier, a hundred leagues distant."

"So far." Sylvie felt weary even pondering it. "And so very dangerous, given the Indians and French are fighting the English there."

"The war seems so close . . . Are we not in enemy hands here in Virginia as much as before?"

"Shush. You need to rest. I'll see what I have from the apothecary in the meantime." After giving her another long drink, Sylvie left her to sleep, praying her fever would break.

Outside the infirmary she met Sebastien, the earliest of Virginia's wildflowers in his gnarled hand. "How is she?" he asked.

"Resting." Touched, Sylvie admired the petite bouquet. "In need of your prayers."

"Prayers." He spat into the dust. "I curse more easily than I pray."

She looked from the flowers to his face. "You've not yet recovered your strength from the ague."

"My malady always returns." He passed her the blossoms, wiping his brow with his sleeve. His high flush seemed akin to Eulalie's, but it was his mental state—his mood—that most worried her. "If I were to leave this place I might be well again."

She bit her lip, wondering if it was true that the ague, once taken, often recurred again and again. If so, it seemed especially vicious. "I have cinchona, the Jesuits' bark. You're welcome to more of that if you need it."

"I need more than cinchona, Sylvie."

Though she wanted to return to her work lest Liselotte accuse her of sloth, she motioned him out of the sun beneath an eave. They sat on a bench, the forgotten flowers lying between them. Calling for Henrietta, Sylvie asked her to bring Sebastien a dipper of water.

Henrietta skipped away and soon returned, eyes on the dipper. "I didn't spill a drop!"

"Merci, princesse," Sebastien said with a smile that sent her blushing into Sylvie's arms. Sylvie kissed her forehead and straightened her cap before Henrietta returned to her playing.

Sebastien drank deeply, his smile fading. "I am a sick man—and a restless one. The future holds little for me since I continually suffer another malady for which there is no cure, one that affects not only the body but the mind and spirit."

This homesickness she couldn't deny. But how would they survive unless they sought the good?

"I know this isn't what we know, nor will it ever be," Sylvie said, "yet you have a future here, a guarantee of your own acreage in time. You're working the land again and benefiting all of us till then."

"I'd gladly go into the wilderness and face the enemy if I could regain what we have lost."

"Did you not see the burning? The destruction? That life is lost to us forever," she replied so matter-of-factly she surprised herself. "And we have no choice but to begin anew."

"You would stay here rather than search for family and friends?" He regarded her with something akin to disbelief. "I remember the Galant reputation across Acadie. As fine a name as Broussard or Melanson or Belliveau. What would your father and brothers say to see you now? A servant among servants, laboring for a former English soldier. You should be ashamed, Sylvie Galant."

Ashamed? No. But wiser when she'd once been naive. She wouldn't say that she felt her family had perished. How did one explain the bone-deep sense that they were no more? That searching would be futile and more heartrending?

"I cannot rest till I try to find the others," he said.

"And if you survive the journey to Fort Duquesne, what then? You still have no home, no prospects. Here there is hope and promise, though it may not be what you envisioned."

"You have made peace with being here?"

"Not entirely. But I am learning to not compare the past with the present and let discontent cloud my days."

He spread one hand in entreaty, his reddened palm a crust of calluses. "I want to do the same, but . . ."

"Please, Sebastien. Give it more time. You're needed here. Few farm as well as you. You are made for the land no matter where it is."

He seemed to consider this, a light in his eyes. Then, with an apologetic half smile, he showed her yet another rent in his shirt. "And you and your needle are just as necessary."

"See? We must all work together."

"There's another matter . . ." He regarded her with sunken eyes. "Will you tell Blackburn I was in his house?"

"It isn't my place. You tell him. I was also trespassing, remember, and need to confess that."

He expelled a breath and a chuckle. "Something tells me your trespassing shall sit better with him than mine."

She almost smiled. "Wait here and I'll bring you salve for your hands—and a new shirt." She rose from the bench and started toward her cottage. "And a vase for Eulalie's lovely flowers."

51

The bee that hath honey in her mouth hath a sting in her tail.

John Lyly

O vernight the weather turned humid, swarms of insects clouding the air, seeking bare skin and even the bedding of the Rivanna settlers. When one of the men found and killed a rattlesnake near the necessary, Sylvie patrolled her own cottage and the paths she and the children trod, axe in hand. She even fancied she saw an Indian lurking in the woods, but it turned out to be a lone white hunter following the river's course.

Will had been away three weeks, and she missed him with a physical ache. Their moonlit tryst on the staircase returned repeatedly in all its sweet clarity. Others missed him too. Lately around the supper table, talk centered on troubles that beset surveyors in the backcountry. Did the entire settlement sense Will's absence spelled something dire? Snakes could strike and kill in minutes. Roaring rivers, both salt and fresh, sucked a man down like Old Sough's deadly whirlpool in Acadie. Dysentery and a host of other ailments, not to mention tumbles off horses and tussles with Indians, added to the conjecture.

A great deal had happened along the Rivanna with Will away. Eulalie was better, but an indenture had been injured by a fall from a horse. There were weevils in the wheat and a spell of rain that did more harm than good, even a return of the ague for Sebastien and others, pulling them from fieldwork.

One twilight, Sylvie waited for the settlement to quiet and the children to fall asleep before she went up the hill, looking longingly at the bare porch that begged for benches and company. A rosebush at the rear garden's entrance had been ravaged by deer, and the wrought-iron gate gave a slight groan as it opened. Within, the walled greenness seemed to expel a cool breath. Dirt paths had been pebbled and more plants coaxed to new life.

Of all the Acadians and indentures along the Rivanna, the gardener seemed the most content. But who could blame him? Being a well-read man, he had a quote each time she saw him, his last easily remembered.

God Almighty first planted a garden. And indeed, it is the purest of human pleasures.

Seeking beauty and stillness, she took a graveled path, the sultry air threaded with the scent of earth and early blooms. She came here often of late. This was the place that bespoke hope and a promise of the future, a living embodiment of how a tangle of weeds and thistles could be tamed and a thing beautified and restored little by little. Much like a life.

The snap of a twig turned her round.

"Sylvie."

She startled as Will stepped forward, rifle in hand. He leaned the gun against the brick wall by the garden gate, his hat hanging from its upturned barrel. Catching her up in his arms, he lifted her off the ground. "I went to your cottage, but you weren't there. When—"

She silenced him with a fervent kiss rife with as much relief as passion, her arms tight about him. He smelled of pine and leather and long days in the saddle, but she didn't care. He ushered in that astonishing sweetness of being, found solely in his presence.

"You missed me."

"It seemed years, not weeks."

"A decade, aye." He gently righted the cap he'd ruffled, twining his fingers in her hair. "At least dusk allows us a private homecoming not to be had by day."

"You're well?" She looked at him searchingly. "And all went well?"

"Well enough. The survey is finished, though I lost some valuable papers when a canoe overturned, and one of my Indian guides took a fever. But I've news from Williamsburg. Good news." He kissed her furrowed brow. "But all that concerns me at the moment is you. And the children."

Good news? All the tension left her. "Nolan has grown an inch since you left. I marked it on the doorframe. And Henrietta is learning to sew on buttons. But enough of us." She bit her lip. He was likely tired. Famished. "I'll go to the kitchen house for your supper if you'll lend me a key."

"Come into my study and I'll show you the cupboard where the keys are kept." He took her hand, giving the garden an appreciative glance. "Then I'll meet you here for supper after I wash in the river."

Hastening downhill with the key, Sylvie sought the kitchen house. The settlement was sleepy, a few Acadians smoking and talking in hushed tones beneath the eaves of their lodgings. Before she'd turned the key in the lock, she felt shadowed and was dismayed to see Liselotte emerging from the stillroom opposite, a jar in hand.

"What brings you to the dependencies so late?"

Sylvie faced her before opening the door. "Major Blackburn has returned and is in need of supper."

"I suppose he gave you the key." At Sylvie's nod, Liselotte frowned and followed her inside, shutting the door after them. "He should come to me instead."

Sylvie took a clean trencher from a shelf and went to the hearth, where Indian bread and a rasher of bacon remained from supper. Enough ragoût covered a bowl's bottom. Not hot but satisfying.

"He's becoming a prominent man here in Virginia, not just New England and elsewhere. A surveyor of merit, not only a former commander of a company of Rangers and new plantation owner." Liselotte set her jar down hard on a table. "You'll do nothing but sully his reputation."

Sylvie reached for a fork and a cup, her voice quiet. "Obviously, Will thinks otherwise."

"Will, is it? He may be infatuated with you now, but in time he'll come to despise you and all you represent. I suspect he feels sorry for your plight as an Acadian and that has corrupted his reasoning." Her tone grew more venomous. "Don't think for a minute that by currying his favor or even taking his name you can change your detested papist French roots. I pray he comes to his senses. The entire settlement depends on it."

The joyeux homecoming of minutes before sullied. Sylvie left the kitchen house, the plate and cup in her trembling hands. She'd not easily forget such bitter words, nor would she burden Will with them.

⁓

The next morning, Sylvie stood and watched from her cottage as the children rushed to greet Will the moment he set foot on his front porch. Before he'd come halfway down the hill, Nolan emitted something resembling a battle cry while Henrietta followed his mad dash up the hill on stout legs. Will caught her up in one arm while wrestling Nolan with the other, never slowing his pace.

"Will you come see the tree fort I made?" Nolan asked him while Henrietta played with a button on his shirt.

"If your button is loose, Mr. Major, I shall sew it on for you," she told him with a shy smile. "Miss Sylvie taught me how."

"There'll be time for forts and buttons after breakfast," he replied, setting her down as the bell sounded for the meal. "Eat heartily, the both of you. Fresh supplies are due any day."

Men and women swarmed the tables, ready to break their fast, glad to see Will. He fielded questions about the survey, then asked questions in turn about what had happened in his absence. There was always a comfortable camaraderie among their group when he was present, especially with Liselotte missing. She appeared late, eyes reddened. Couldn't they just get along and keep the peace? Sylvie wanted no trouble with anyone.

As the men left the kitchen house for the day's work, Will called a meeting with the farm managers. Sylvie watched him leave with Sebastien and Nicolas, wondering when she'd steal a private moment with him again. Last night he'd been so tired she hadn't pressed him about the good news he'd mentioned from Williamsburg. She'd simply taken his supper dishes to the kitchen house then returned his key, trying to ignore Liselotte's scathing words.

Taking Henrietta by the hand, Sylvie emerged into fresh air and sunshine and walked the short distance to their cottage. On the porch they resumed their sewing, a small pile of buttons and scraps of linen in front of the little girl.

As she began cutting wool for petticoats, Sylvie began a lesson. "When you are asked what your linen is made of, answer . . ."

"Hemp or flax," Henrietta said without a pause.

"Both are plants, whereas woolens are made from . . ."

"Sheep!" She shifted on her stool. "An animal."

"You're learning quickly. I'm proud of you and your work. When I was small I learned my lessons and how to sew too."

Henrietta's lips pursed in concentration as she tried to thread her needle. "I want to sew as good as you."

"We shall get you a thimble soon. Would you like that?"

She nodded so vigorously her curls bounced. "My fingers get sore from being poked. Will Mr. Major bring me a thimble from Williamsburg?"

Mr. Major. The name never failed to amuse, yet Sylvie longed for her to call him *Papa*. "We shall ask him. Or maybe a peddler will pass by, bringing what we need. Remember the last one with his jangling bells and wagon?"

Henrietta laughed. "His dog tickled my face with his tongue but barked at Nolan."

"I remember," Sylvie said with a smile.

"I'd like a pup or a kitten to play with."

"Oh? I had a chaton once that grew into a big chatte." The memory of their belled barn cat was vivid. "Her name was Papillon, French for 'butterfly,' because she used to chase them."

"I would name mine something pretty too." Henrietta finished sewing a button and passed it to Sylvie to knot the thread. "What became of your cat?"

"I wish I knew. We had to leave our home and Papillon behind."

"Like us. We had to leave our dog, Willis, behind too when Mama and Papa died. But then we met you—and Mr. Major."

Sylvie smiled. "And dear Eve, who took good care of you."

In hindsight, Sylvie saw kindness and mercy at every turn.

 **52**

At 9 [we] went to another house where the French were convened, had a dance and spent the evening in jollity.

Reverend William Drummond

That evening, Will arranged for a small fête with roast beef, sweetmeats he'd brought from Williamsburg, and plenty of ale from one of the Rivanna warehouses, a favorite beverage of the men. All seemed in high spirits, especially when he put their minds at ease over the matter of their being forced to leave Virginia.

"After this last survey, I went to Williamsburg and met with the governor." Will's voice reached far into the bonfire-lit stillness. "He has promised exemption from deportation for all Acadians in the Rivanna settlement. Much of that has to do with the efforts of the late Lord Drysdale and his widow, Lady Drysdale, who has pledged her continuing support to us here. Captain Lennox is at sea, but once he returns he wants to journey here and see our work firsthand."

As cheers erupted, Sylvie was taken aback at such generosity. Privately, Will had shared with her the details she'd been wondering about. Williamsburg was slowly reopening as smallpox cases dwindled, Dinwiddie and his family had returned, and Will had seen Eve, still in the bookbindery attic.

At the first notes of a fiddle, couples moved onto a grassy place cleared for dancing. Sebastien partnered with Eulalie, raising Sylvie's hopes. Increasingly moody, Liselotte did not dance but stood with arms crossed on the outside, resembling a powder keg waiting to ignite.

When Will sought Sylvie out for a second branle, he whispered in her ear, "Meet me in the orchard at dusk."

Despite the rousing music and motion, the minutes ticked by as slowly as an Acadian winter. At last Sylvie noticed Will missing and managed to slip away herself after asking Antoinette to watch the children. She nearly ran through the woods to meet him. The orchard held a hundred shadows, none of which carried any terror because he was there.

Something gold glinted in his palm. He took her left hand and slipped a ring on her narrow finger.

"Oh, Will . . ." She stared down at it in the moonlit dark. A perfect fit, not too loose or too tight. How had he gotten it right?

He kissed her ringed hand. "The engraving says 'Cert a mon gre.'" *Certainly my choice.*

Did he truly feel she was more bride than burden? Liselotte seemed to shroud the tender moment, feeding her insecurities.

"Without a doubt." He held her gaze. "The question is, are you sure of me? Our future together?"

"There's no man I'd rather spend my life with." They lapsed into French, which they sometimes did when the conversation took an intimate turn. "If we can find someone willing to wed us . . ."

"There's an itinerant Baptist pastor in this very parish. All I need to do is find him."

Could it be that easy? In Acadie there had been a formal

marriage contract. Women even kept their maiden or family names. As she pondered it all, her hands slid from his weskit to her sides. "Aside from that, do you truly want me, Will, when I—my people—are considered the enemy and the papers say a declaration of war is at hand? Wouldn't it be wiser to choose a wife without taint? You could have a lady of good standing from a family of merit to replace the one you lost—"

"I choose you, Sylvie."

His eyes darkened in question as she hurried on, wanting to silence Liselotte's barbs and accusations for good. "At this very moment, perhaps, but someday mightn't you look back and regret it? Even a few years from now, will you wish for something—someone—different?"

Surprise flared in his eyes—and something else. She'd wounded him with her words, but did the truth not hurt? All her shortcomings were ever before her, begging an airing before they took this monumental step.

"I have no one, Will. No family to call my own. No dowry. Since Acadie's loss I am not even a well woman but a broken one. I don't know that I'll ever be whole again. How can I be or give my best to you and our future children?"

He took her in his arms. "Who has been filling your head with such nonsense?"

She wouldn't say Liselotte—or even Sebastien with his doubts and complaints. She could not blame them entirely. Hadn't she been bullied by her own fears from the first? Whatever the source, the ongoing emotional storm inside her left her unutterably weary.

"None of us are whole till heaven, Sylvie. Let God begin a healing work here."

Tears stood in her eyes as the truth of his words encircled her like the ring on her finger, somehow strengthening her and giving her courage.

"If I could give you back Acadie, I would. But I can only offer you a secondhand farm along a distant river that most people have never seen or heard of."

The humility in his voice touched her. "It's more than I deserve, Will. You're more than I deserve. And it's more than enough."

Will walked up the hill to the house once he and Sylvie had returned to the fading fête to collect the children for bed. Tomorrow was the Sabbath, and all could rest from their labors. He trod the sagging porch steps, their creak a reminder of another needed repair. Before he opened the front door he took a last look at her cottage, still surprised by her impassioned queries. Had he left any doubt in her mind that she was the bride he wanted, the mistress of this house, and the future mother of his children?

He chafed at having to delay the wedding, but he wanted what she wanted—and when. Their union glowed like a star on a darkened landscape of crop failure, signs of drought, recurring illness, and persistent fears of deportation. He'd breathe easier when Sylvie bore his name, further safeguarding her from anything these war-minded Virginians might devise.

Taking the candle from the foyer's sconce, he sought his study. An hour passed as he sorted through the collection of papers and correspondence he'd brought from his Williamsburg address, intent on anything resembling word about the Acadians, the Galants particularly. He'd written to a few of his former Rangers encamped near Fort Duquesne as well as elsewhere, seeking information about Sylvie's family. One contact confirmed that Bleu was serving the French at the Forks of the Ohio as interpreter and guide. Will hadn't told Sylvie, as he didn't want to raise her hopes then disappoint her. She'd endured too much.

But if he could reach Bleu and eventually reunite Sylvie with her brother, he'd feel victorious after months of rabbit trails and dead ends. And yet the reunion brought risk. Bleu might object to their marriage. He might even persuade Sylvie to stay with him or return to Acadie or elsewhere. A large remnant of the Acadians were now seeking asylum in French-held Louisiana at the behest of Governor-General Vaudreuil.

He unrolled the map of his latest survey and anchored it at the corners with iron paperweights. Bonami sniffed around the open door, refusing to lay down as he often did. The room was stuffy, so Will got up and opened a rear window, letting in fresh air along with the last of the fiddle music from the fête.

Sitting back down, he poured himself some well water from a pitcher, his eye on the dog who rarely left his side. "I suppose, Sergeant Bonami, that your habitation will be the porch as soon as Mademoiselle Galant becomes Madame Blackburn."

Bonami cocked his head a bit pensively, seemingly understanding every word, as his master returned to the survey and field notes till the candle guttered. Will finally went upstairs and readied for the night, then snuffed the candle and climbed into the tester bed, which groaned beneath his weight. The linens felt freshly washed and held a trace of lavender. Sylvie's doing?

He shut his eyes, the weariness of the trail catching up with him even as Sylvie threaded his dreams. Sylvie belonged in this house, the children down the hall, the emptiness filled. He'd thought it when he'd first set eyes on the Rivanna orchard.

Will was barely aware of Bonami's odd whine at the door. Had he forgotten to let him out . . . or were they still on a scout? For a moment the big, comfortable bed beneath him seemed hard ground till he turned over, feeling the fragrant linen against his skin. Sleep tugged at him . . . and then the press of something dry and cold against his bare leg tugged back.

At a sudden coiling beneath the covers, Will jerked awake. Bonami leapt atop the bed as Will left it, nearly colliding with the corner mantel in his haste. He backed up as Bonami began digging at the bedcovers, and then, in the pitch blackness, something thudded onto the plank floor. Will flew downstairs to his study and worked to ignite his taper from the hearth's embers, his heart hammering. Once it was lit, he hurried back to his bedchamber and halted in the open doorway.

The candle cast macabre light about the chamber. Bonami had a snake between his wolflike jaws, shaking it so ferociously Will couldn't watch. He looked to his own bare legs, sure he'd been bitten.

In moments Bonami's frenzied shaking had torn the snake to pieces in the chamber where Will sensed he'd never rest easy again. Used to serpents of all kinds in the woods, many venomous, he'd never seen one the size of this.

No longer a threat now, the snake needed disposing of. Had Bonami been struck?

With a whine, Bonami dropped what remained of the snake before coming to Will. Overcome by revulsion and relief, Will leaned into the doorframe before going below to await daylight.

53

It is easier to forgive an enemy than to forgive a friend.

William Blake

Before morning, Bonami sickened, the bite wound on his hind leg testament to the copper snake's venom. Lying on his side and panting on the porch, the creature looked more miserable than Will had ever seen him. He applied whiskey to the wound, so intent on his faithful companion that at first he failed to see Sylvie behind him on the stoop.

"What happened?" she asked softly, holding the breakfast he'd missed.

"Copper snake," he said tersely, standing up and taking the plate and cup from her. Snagging a strip of bacon, he offered it to Bonami, but the dog wouldn't eat.

"Snake?" Sylvie looked about in the grass warily before stepping up onto the porch to stand beside him. "Where?"

"In my bedchamber last night."

Horror leeched the color from her face. "Are you hurt?"

"Nay. Somehow the snake got entangled in the bed linens. It slid to the floor and then Bonami shook it to death."

She stared at him in disbelief as he sat down, gesturing for her to do the same.

"I wondered where you were at breakfast. I feared you were ill." She looked to Bonami, her face so full of pathos his own heart twisted. "Snakes don't oft climb into beds, Will."

"They do get into houses on occasion but are unusual bedfellows unless you're sleeping on the ground, aye."

She stared off into the distance, where the settlement enjoyed a sleepy Sabbath. "I don't want to cast blame, but I found Sebastien Broussard in your house when you were gone Saturday last. I saw a light and thought you'd come home. He was intent on your locked study. He said he thought you were withholding information about our people and Virginia's plans for us."

"I withhold nothing of substance," he said with a terseness sharpened by a sleepless night.

"I don't doubt you, Will, but I am becoming fearful of Sebastien."

He tasted the lukewarm coffee. "Why, exactly?"

"He has the temerity to search your house. He may have returned again with the snake." She lowered her voice to a whisper. "He's increasingly discontented here and frequently ill but believes all will be well if we reunite with our people at Fort Duquesne. His hope is to return to Acadie in time." She looked at him entreatingly. "He may have meant you harm with the snake."

"It's the time of year when snakes come out of their dens and are more easily trapped. If he meant harm, he succeeded." He looked toward Bonami again, raking his mind for a remedy. "I've sensed Broussard's restlessness, his doubts about being here. He's an able laborer, but his attitude suffers. His misery is evident—and understandable."

"He's grieving the loss of his betrothed. I'd hoped he and Eulalie . . ."

"Eulalie? Nay. Nor do I believe it's another woman he's mourning." Will took another drink of coffee, the rest of his untouched breakfast near Bonami. "He's smitten with you, Sylvie."

She turned to him, clearly astonished, even speechless.

"He watches you and goes out of his way to speak to you. If not for me, he'd have declared himself by now."

She went scarlet. "Like Liselotte."

It was his turn to feel heated. "Aye, though I've not encouraged her."

"I've not encouraged Sebastien," she said quickly. "I've merely been kind, as one friend to another."

"I don't doubt it, but the sooner we marry, the better for all concerned." Still pondering the snake, Will looked over at Bonami, who had ceased his panting and lay still. Too still? He lay a hand on the dog's soft undercoat, feeling his uneven breathing.

Sylvie bent her head and closed her eyes. Was she praying for his faithful companion or their matrimonial knot tying?

"Major Blackburn." The gardener's thick Scots burr sounded from the side of the house. "A word with ye, if I may, about the pleasure garden—and your missus too."

⁀

Sylvie's thoughts were on anything but the matter at hand as they stood in the walled garden. Her thoughts tumbled back to the last time she'd talked with Sebastien. Was Will mistaken that his feelings were more than friendship? The unwelcome possibility paled beside the very real danger of his wanting to harm Will.

"Miss Galant, what do you prefer?"

Sylvie's gaze wandered from the thriving narcissus and tulips at her feet to Archie Chisholm. "Pardon, monsieur . . . you were asking about roses?"

"Roses are always a lady's preference, even in the wilderness." He pointed to a number of pots. "These are bulbs—white tuberoses—from Mr. Custis's garden in Williamsburg. Would you like them at the front of the garden or the back?"

Feeling the mistress of the manor, Sylvie smiled. "Please plant some at the back by the Apothecary rose you uncovered in the southeast corner. But save one or two for the garden's entrance."

He gestured to a leggy, vigorous bush that promised an abundance of blooms. "Here, by the Gallica rose? Consider it done."

"Merci." Sylvie turned slowly, taking stock of his work from every direction. "You've transformed what I never believed would be a garden again in mere months. Perhaps because you find joy in working, even on the Sabbath."

He chuckled. "It hardly qualifies as work when you'd rather be here than anywhere else. I had ten gardens to tend in Williamsburg but wanted only one like this. There's no better master than Major Blackburn."

Sylvie looked to Will as Archie left them, carting a wheelbarrow. For a few moments they were left alone as the sun beat down on their backs and left Sylvie wishing for her straw hat.

She looked toward the settlement with a little sigh. "Do you ever wish it was just the two of us . . . and the children?"

"I won't lie to you and deny it," he admitted. "This morning especially."

"Will you talk to Sebastien?" she asked.

"Aye." He took her hand and led her back to the front porch where Bonami lay. "But I'll pray about matters first."

54

Solitude sometimes is best society.

John Milton

Will left Bonami in Sylvie's care, the children hovering, while he went down the hill. The Sabbath was blessedly quiet. Too quiet. Again, he expected a bell's tolling. If Middle Parish wasn't so far, he'd take Sylvie and the children to worship there. He knew the Acadians missed their priests and chapels, and he felt they should be allowed to practice their religion as they pleased. As it stood, he was unsure how well received a Protestant cleric would be, though a spiritual presence was needed beyond his usual reading from Scripture on the Sabbath.

As he made his way to the kitchen house with the breakfast dishes, he kept an eye out for Sebastien. Several men were fishing downriver while women gathered by the well to talk. A few courting couples walked about in pairs. The sight lifted his spirits. Future weddings—and families—made the settlement seem less temporary and more permanent, but finding someone willing to marry them was as much a hurdle as their being willing to wed without the blessing of a priest.

Antoinette greeted him and took his dishes as he passed out of the kitchen house to a warehouse. There he took stock of supplies before moving on to the fields to survey the work done in his absence. Nicolas, his ablest farm manager, fell into step beside him.

"I've been wanting to give you a report on the planting and yields before your next survey."

"Glad to hear it," Will replied as they passed a split-rail fence that bordered a field. "I can see the season has been bad for wheat."

"The weather was too dry at first to bring it up, then too wet so we could not roll it."

"And the riverside corn?"

"Hardy, like the oats. We've since sown clover seed at twelve pounds an acre, finishing thirty acres at four bushels to the acre. I can't yet decide if sandy river soil is a bane or a blessing."

"Mayhap both." Will came to a stop on a small rise that overlooked acres of hard labor, greening plants overtaking brown ground. "Difficult to turn a profit with a dearth of rain."

Nicolas nodded. "For now, we're resting the plow horses and making use of the fluke hoes. And petitioning the Lord Himself for a change of weather."

"Prayer, aye," Will replied. "We well know who is in charge of the elements, and it's not us. If the wheat fails, we'll buy it from neighboring farms."

After discussing the lambing, Nicolas turned back and Will walked on. His thoughts veered to Sebastien, whom he'd not seen since last night's merriment. How did one approach a man with suspicions of snake planting? Mayhap he'd better settle the fact of his prior trespassing instead.

Or was the entire matter best left alone?

"Major Blackburn."

Will turned to find Liselotte behind him. His thoughts again veered to Bonami, who would have alerted him with a little yip as to any who approached. She was dressed in her Sabbath best as if going to church, and he greeted her, his gaze rising to the house on the hill.

She looked around. "Where is your trusty companion?"

"Snakebit and on the porch."

She looked so alarmed he ruled out her guilt in the matter. "I'm sorry to hear it, though the wolf in him frightens me."

"He's supposed to frighten, just do no harm."

Warily, she stepped away from a thicket. "The climate here is a haven for snakes. I saw one curled up by the milk house door the other day." She shuddered. "Will the cur live?"

"God only knows," he said and resumed walking toward the heart of the settlement, so choked with sadness he couldn't continue. Bonami had been with him a long time, through endless wilderness journeys, and had even preserved his life a time or two.

She kept pace with him. "I've come to ask something rather personal."

"Speak plainly, then."

"Might I accompany you to Williamsburg on your next trip there?" She smiled up at him, as coquettish as Sylvie had accused her of being. Or was he imagining it? "I've a list of things to buy that I can't entrust to anyone else."

"The next time I leave the settlement will be to summon a pastor to wed myself and Miss Galant."

She halted so abruptly it seemed he'd struck her. "Mademoiselle Galant?"

With a nod he walked on, bypassing the smithy and stables. When she caught up with him, she said in a rush, "Are you certain, Major Blackburn? I suppose I should offer my congratulations, though I only feel condolences are appropriate. I've seen her with Sebastien Broussard so frequently that I thought—"

His stern look stemmed the accusation. Then another voice joined in from behind, coming from the infirmary.

"Major Blackburn, sir." Dubois approached, his interruption timely. "Your Irish indenture—Kilgore—is down with the ague. I checked one of the warehouses for medicines but cannot locate the last supply. Cinchona is best, though valerian powder works well in its stead."

"It's in the stillroom, likely," Will told him. "Miss Kersey can show you where if we have any. How severe is the attack?"

"Fever and chills. A sharp headache. The first bout is often the acutest."

"See that he's well watered and kept at rest." Will rued Kilgore was ill, as he did any in his employ. They'd not had a death yet, though there was an old burial ground west of the orchard. "No need to have him up and in the fields before he's recovered."

"Agreed, sir."

Dubois disappeared with Liselotte into the stillroom, leaving Will to consider what warranted checking next. As he started for another warehouse, an indenture waylaid him.

"Major Blackburn, sir." Concern wrinkled the older man's features. "Sebastien Broussard seems to have gone missing. I thought he might be farther downriver fishing as he's sometimes wont to do on the Sabbath, but all his belongings are gone too."

"He wasn't at breakfast?"

"Nay. And two horses are missing from the pasture."

A costly loss. Will opened the warehouse door with a key. "Horse thieving is a hanging offense. Especially in horse-besotted Virginia."

"Maybe the horses simply cleared the fence and Broussard will return." The man heaved a sigh. "But I have a bad feeling about this."

Will stepped into the warm, humid confines of the smallest warehouse, intent on the task before him, awash with an odd mix of relief and loss at the news. "Should Broussard reappear, I want to know as soon as possible."

55

She who adores not your frowns will only loathe your smiles.

William Blake

On the cottage porch, Sylvie worked on her wedding trousseau, small though it was, sewing a pale blue ribbon as embellishment on a nightgown. What had become of her dower trunk? She couldn't remember all it held now that time and distance blurred the details. At least the task before her assuaged her somewhat, as did Will's parting words and embrace at first light.

"I won't rest till we're reunited," he'd told her. "Once we're wed, I'll be here more than I'm away. I know my leaving goes hard on you though you never complain."

"You are a discerning man, Major Blackburn." She touched his bewhiskered jaw, committing to memory every endearing thing about him before he walked away. "I'll be quite content here finishing your wedding suit."

"No worn buckskins or ragged linen, my usual trail attire."

"No, though you're the handsomest man I've ever beheld no matter what you're clad in."

"Will you wear your Lyonnais silk?"

"For you, oui."

"When do you want to tell the children and the rest of the settlement?"

He was being so patient, letting her lead, making sure this was what she wanted as much as she wanted what was best for him.

"For now, let's keep it a secret. Ours and the children's." She felt a moment's qualm that Liselotte already knew their plans. "We'll save this lovely ring for the wedding."

"Not too much longer now. I have in mind going to the coast afterward. Enjoying our first days together far from here without work and interruptions." His voice was low and reflective as if he'd given it considerable thought. "We could go to York, mayhap Indigo Island. The captain offered his cottage there before he sailed."

"Oh? How gracious." She smiled, trying to envision it. No more separations or stolen moments like this. Just the two of them for a few blissful days alone on the water. "La lune de miel."

"Our honeymoon, aye," he echoed. His pleasure faded to concern. "Pray for our safety." He kissed her hand where the posy ring rested. "No delays or rough weather. A speedy return with a pastor to marry us."

"A willing pastor, oui."

"In the meantime, consider what to call this place." His lips brushed her hair. "This is your home now—our home—and as such it deserves a new name."

They had both agreed Greenmount belonged to the past, but she'd yet to come up with something new or unique in its place. Rivanna Rise . . . Blackburn Farm . . . Orchard Hill . . . As the possibilities wound through her head, he'd kissed her a final time, long and lingering, and then gone to meet his chain men and markers at a rendezvous place.

Remembering that kiss, she finished with the ribbon embellishment, watching as Henrietta stitched on her sampler. The girl looked up suddenly, heart-shaped face alight. "When you and Mr. Major marry, can I wear the pretty dress you made me?"

"Bien sûr!" Sylvie leaned over and kissed her cheek. "With apple blossoms in your hair."

"Nolan says marrying makes you our mama and our papa."

"We want to be, though we can never replace your own parents, who I'm sure loved you very much and were sad to leave you."

"I only remember Mama was sick and Papa was always away on a ship." She stopped her stitching. "I am glad Bonami is well again but sorry Mr. Major had to go."

And not only Mr. Major. Sebastien, too, had not returned. Sylvie looked toward the fields, more troubled than sad, though she understood his reasons for leaving. But to have taken two valuable horses . . . She couldn't quite bring herself to think of him as a horse thief. And while Will had been spared confronting him about trespassing, Sebastien's lack of an adieu was hurtful, especially for Eulalie.

"I expected it," she'd said resignedly, "though I doubt he'll be any happier wherever he's going, even if he survives crossing so treacherous a frontier. One's contentment has more to do with one's outlook than one's circumstance, my mère used to say."

"We must remember him in our prayers," Sylvie said, wondering if they'd ever know his fate. "Perhaps he'll make his way west and find joy somehow, somewhere."

That afternoon, Sylvie watched Henrietta splash along the river's edge as the sky rippled with mare's tails, as Nolan called them. He was out of sight helping in the orchards.

Would she and Will be blessed with children in time? They'd been given a felicitous start with these two. Soon all four of them would move up the hill into the house, into the very rooms she'd chosen. Henrietta's had a charming tiled hearth and windows overlooking the walled garden while Nolan's overlooked the orchard and had a closet. Will had promised Sylvie a chance to purchase furnishings on their honeymoon. As she held close his reassurance of being home more, her heart sang.

The supper bell rang, so she made her way to the cottage with an armload of linen from the spinning house while Eulalie took Henrietta to the kitchen house. Stepping free of the wooded path near the cottage porch, Sylvie spied Liselotte coming out of the orchard. Rarely was she at this end of the settlement. The unexpected sight was as jarring as it was unwelcome.

"Come quickly!" Alarm scored Liselotte's pale face. "Nolan's been stung by a great many bees!"

Dropping her linen onto the edge of the porch, Sylvie hitched up her skirts and ran. The bee skeps were at the very back of the orchard where the apple trees gave way to cherries. She'd cautioned Nolan to stay clear of the bees, but his boyish curiosity often got the best of him. As she all but galloped over the uneven ground, myriad remedies buzzed through her mind.

Crushed mallow or plantain leaves? Whiskey or a clay poultice?

Winded, she reached the heavily leafed cherry trees, Liselotte on her heels.

But where was Nolan?

The skeps looked undisturbed, a haze of bees around them. Confused, Sylvie turned around in question. Someone seized her arms and pinned them behind her with such force she felt a sudden burning. Trying to jerk free, she cried out, but Sebastien bound her mouth with a cloth and silenced her while Liselotte worked feverishly to bind her wrists with hemp rope.

Two horses waited, clearly skittish at the commotion. When Sebastien hefted her into the saddle, Liselotte came forward with a sack and tied it onto the pommel. Bile backed up Sylvie's throat, worsened by the tight gag, and she started slipping from the saddle. With bound wrists, she struggled to keep her balance.

Sebastien thrust a pistol so near it grazed her temple. "Do not cross me, Sylvie Galant. I don't want to harm you."

Something hard and desperate in his tone convinced her the threat was not idle. He was not well. His mind was as unsound as his body. She'd often thought it, but never before with such clarity. Chary, intent on escape, she regarded him with rising terror as he mounted the horse ahead of her, a rope tied between them as he led out. Liselotte stood watching, a look of triumph on her face.

Shocked into numbness, Sylvie glanced back at the settlement, all gathered for supper and utterly unaware of the turn of events in the orchard.

56

I have so much of you in my heart.

John Keats

Will bid farewell to his chainmen and markers at the forks of the Rivanna, turning toward home. Home.

It had taken a while before he'd felt in his spirit that the settlement was home. He'd been rootless and roaming for so long he'd begun to think he'd never attach such a sentiment to any particular place. Sylvie had helped change that. But only God Himself could have arranged for such a fine house, even a garden, as if to make up for their rootlessness. Will couldn't have provided Sylvie with anything better, and she had the company of her fellow Acadians too.

As he rode through open fields that Indians once set fire to for planting, he wondered what had transpired in his absence. Had Sebastien returned? Aside from that, hope and a hard-won happiness lightened the journey. If he kept a steady pace, he'd not have to overnight again in the woods. Bonami loped alongside him, fully recovered, always at his best running free in the open.

By midafternoon a hard, punishing rain slowed him, lightning slashing sky that had been blue an hour before. Continuous thunder turned Bonami nervy. As they took shelter in a hollow sycamore to keep his gunpowder dry, Will waited, chafing till he remembered the crops in need of a drenching. When the weather worsened, he dozed, waking at what he reckoned was nearly four o'clock in the morning. Yellow glimmered on the eastern horizon. Since the trail was sodden and muddy, sure to slow him, he sought higher, drier ground.

At last he smelled the smoke of the settlement and heard the ring of a blacksmith's hammer. In the distance, men worked the fields and women the kitchen garden. Bonami gave a sharp bark as if alerting the settlement to their return while a beat of expectancy quickened Will's movements. He dismounted near the stable, seeking Sylvie, but only Dubois met him. His downcast expression told a woeful tale.

"Needs be I speak with you in private, Major Blackburn," he began.

Wary, Will left his horse to a stable hand while they went up the hill, his pulse thudding in his ears like distant thunder as he pushed open the front door and led the way to his study. Cool and shadowed, the house felt emptier than usual.

Dubois pulled something from his weskit pocket. "I'm sorry, Major, to greet you with this."

Will took the paper. A letter?

"I found it on the table in Mademoiselle Galant's cottage soon after she left."

"And when was that?"

"Ten days ago."

Ten days? A sudden coldness gripped him. He opened the paper and began reading as Dubois went to stand by a window, granting him privacy. He studied the looping, inked words, dread welling in his belly. It struck him hard that he'd never seen Sylvie's handwriting before.

Dear Will,

Forgive me for leaving without warning. I couldn't tell you face-to-face.

The Rivanna settlement is not the home I am looking for. I have cast my lot with Sebastien now and desire to find my loved ones, wherever that might lead. Do not attempt to find me. Eulalie can help with the children.

Thank you for all you have done for my people along the Rivanna. I pray it goes well for you.

Sylvie

He blinked, disbelief giving way to a welling pain that clawed at him so savagely it felt like an assault. He forced himself to read the letter a second time as if it could somehow lessen the blow. But the sick sense of all that had happened in his absence remained.

How had they parted?

In the garden they'd said a temporary goodbye, counting the days—nay, the minutes—till his return. She'd been sewing his wedding suit, her head and heart—and his—full of orchard blooms and their wedding. Their future.

Where had *that* Sylvie gone?

Pummeled by exhaustion, Sylvie rode on a plow horse unaccustomed to the wilderness. Soaked by rain and scorched by the sun in turn, she stared at her soiled linen garments that seemed to rub her sunburned skin raw. Even her scalp seemed on fire. In the melee of her departure, she'd lost her cap, though strangely, a few of her belongings were gathered into one cumbersome sack.

How had it been when the settlement found her gone? What lies had Liselotte told? What had the children thought?

Her heart twisted. They'd suffered enough loss in their short lives. And Will? Had he returned from his survey to find her missing? Would he not come after her?

Sebastien turned more brooding, so moody it scared her. His countenance was as dark as storm clouds. With every league they traveled, the more disturbed he seemed.

Her pleading with him had been for naught. Seemingly deaf to it, he trudged on, and then the second night, when they'd both collapsed atop the muddy ground, he looked at her from where he sat, chewing on a piece of dried meat she had no heart to eat. Someone had supplied him well with jerked beef. Liselotte? She had a key to the kitchen stores. Sylvie looked away as a flicker of fury burned through her.

"Your brother will be glad of your coming."

She looked back at him, exhaustion sharpening her temper. "What do you know about my brother? I have more than one." Or did have.

He shrugged. "I am a Broussard, remember. And all Acadie knows of Bleu."

Hearing her brother's name spoken after so long was startling. Under any other circumstance she would have smiled. Truly, Bleu was well known by many, both enemies and allies. How many times had she thought of him, remembering his words to her at the last? Like Will, Bleu had known what was coming and tried to warn her and her entire family before the great evil had been done, scattering them all to the winds.

"I would give almost anything to see Bleu again. But it shouldn't be this way, Sebastien." She marveled at how calmly she spoke when she was so wretched, dirt caked into every crevice, light-headed from lack of water and nourishment, her sunburn like a fever.

"You will see him when we get to the Forks of the Ohio. I discovered he is working for French officials there."

"At Fort Duquesne?"

"Oui. It is the howling wilderness, but it will be worth the distance."

"Some hundred leagues or more?" She stared at him in disbelief. "And what happens if we meet English soldiers like the ones who turned us out of Acadie?"

He shrugged. "We will make up a story of how we are man and wife, trying to find our way home."

His simplistic reasoning was but one of the concerns she had about him. "And what if we encounter Indians instead?"

"My scalp is hardly worth having, but yours . . ." His eyes slid to her loose braid a-tangle with twigs and leaves.

In that instant she felt his strange attraction for her. Will had duly warned her. What if Sebastien acted on that? Revulsion took root as she looked down at her tattered petticoats, torn from the hazards of the woods and revealing her pale, scratched legs. She waved a fly away, desperation building to a wide, frantic ache inside her.

Soon that dullness overtook him again, and Sebastien simply turned on his side, a saddlebag beneath his head, and went to sleep. His low snoring gave rise to how she might escape. But she was not Bleu, who seemed to have been born with a compass inside him. Other than the sun's trail, she knew not which direction to go. With night gathering them up in dark, sultry folds, she'd be completely helpless if she ran.

For now, her hands blessedly untied, she slapped at insects intent on devouring her. Images of the Rivanna tumbled through her mind, one after another. She missed the children with a growing ache. Was anyone tucking them in and kneeling for prayers? Was Henrietta's skinned knee better? And the sore on Nolan's lip? Such small matters loomed large in her absence. She was engulfed by a homesickness she'd not known since Acadie. That world was gone, but the Rivanna house and garden were vivid and real, not stolen or ravaged.

Unable to keep her eyes open, she lay down on her blanket, tormented by an incessant thirst. When she slept fitfully, she dreamed of Will. Will and Bleu.

Father God, please let them find me.

57

In the deepest night of trouble and sorrow God gives us so much to be thankful for that we need never cease our singing.

Samuel Taylor Coleridge

Days began to blur, Sylvie's hopes for rescue plummeting as time ticked on. Was it April? Or was it May? The heat pulsated around them like a living thing, slicking her with sweat and weighting her lungs. When they came to a wide, rushing river she wanted to gulp from it till her belly ached, then jump into its cleansing depths.

Sebastien rode up and down the rocky south bank as if deciding the best fording place. But the river rushed furiously past, a frothy white and ice blue. Indecision crossed his tanned face. Sylvie watched him closely, sensitive to his temper, fearful he might try to cross this impossible water that looked as unsettled and angry as he.

"We'll camp in that stand of trees and bathe in the river tonight." Jerking his head toward a huddle of pines, he led the way to their shelter of boughs and bark. At least it provided refuge from the hot sun skimming the treetops in its descent.

She made a makeshift bed away from him, using the blanket he'd given her the day before. In the sack of her belongings she'd found a clean linen dress, even a scrap of soap wrapped in linen. Liselotte's doing? Somehow she'd overlooked it in the misery of the first days. The sight of it resurrected the ugly memory of Liselotte standing smugly by at the last.

Saying nothing, she took the clean dress and soap in hand, walking away to find a private place to wash the grit of the trail away. She could feel Sebastien's eyes on her. He seemed to understand she would not run away, for she'd made no secret of how lost she felt, finally convincing him that tying her hands was unnecessary.

Sinking to her knees behind a boulder along the riverbank, she drank from her cupped hands before she stepped into the water. The cold raised goose bumps, but she sat down in the frothing river up to her shoulders and grabbed handfuls of sand to scour herself. Her hair she washed as best she could, though she had no comb.

At last she got out, envisioning the copper hip bath in Will's fine house. Huddled behind a rock, adrip and towel-less, she dressed in the sole clean garment left to her, wondering how long the dress would last in the wilderness. Her shoes were muddy and a heel was loose, but she was grateful for the Williamsburg cobbler who'd made them sturdy.

When she stepped into the open, she saw Sebastien leaning against a tree, arms crossed. Heat drenched her. How long had he been watching? She walked past him, head down, leaving her ruined garments on the riverbank.

"Très belle," he called after her.

Pulling her skirts free of a sticker bush, she plunged into the brush, sensing he was on her heels.

Oh, Will, where are you? Won't you come?

Before she reached the pine shelter, Sebastien caught up

with her. His hard hand fisted her petticoat from behind and stopped her. Panicked, she yanked the linen free of his grasp, tearing it in her haste.

"Why do you run away from me, mon bijou?" His endearment hung harshly on the sultry air.

"I am not your jewel, Sebastien." She faced him, chilled though the day was still hot. "I have pledged myself to another who will surely come after me, who I feel is even now on the trail to find me and bring you to a reckoning."

"Oh?" The same smugness that had marred Liselotte's features suffused Sebastien's. "Not when he reads the note that forbids him to search for you, saying you ran off with me of your own free will."

She stared at him. "Quoi?"

"Mademoiselle Kersey is very clever. She left a note in your name, making sure we would not be followed."

Mon Dieu, non. The tendril of hope she'd nursed through days of turmoil snapped. Clever? Nay, unutterably devious. And enough to deter Will's coming after her and ruin his estimation of her forever. Nausea rolled through her as she realized he had never seen her writing hand and had no way to refute the note's lies.

"Blackburn belongs with her. You belong with me." His gaze hardened. "I have been waiting for you to come to your senses about the matter. Why would you align yourself with a man who is not Acadian? Who is, in fact, the very enemy of our people?"

She studied him, searching for a glimmer of reason. Had they not been over this before? Truly, the ague was so virulent it affected the mind, not only the body.

"How could an enemy of our people establish such a settlement? He has even riled many Virginians intent on putting us on another ship to another land to live amongst people who revile us, who feel we are no different from the Indians and French waging war on this very frontier. How can you be blind to that?"

"It is you who are blind, Sylvie." He came closer, so close she could smell his fetid breath. "I risk much taking you with me, even stealing horses for your comfort." Taking a strand of her wet hair, he curled it around one filthy finger. "Bleu will reward me for my efforts once the only family member he has left is returned to him."

She stepped back, pulling free of him. "Bleu will not be so forgiving if you mistreat me or take advantage in any way. If you are intent on Fort Duquesne, I am depending on you to see me safely there."

He said no more as she sat down on her blanket, preparing for another long night. Weary as she was, she couldn't close her eyes till Sebastien slept. She did not trust him, nor did she trust these woods teeming with bears and snakes and wildness. She had no way to defend herself save One.

Father God, be my defense.

Snatches of Scripture had been returning to her day and night, oftentimes only a few words but enough to keep her from falling to the ground when she thought she could go no farther. Cicadas droned around her, and she could hear the horses tearing at the brush, famished after so much travel. Sebastien's horse seemed lamed, but she'd save that worry for another day. As she prayed for Will, wherever he was, to be discerning amid all the lies and confusion, a thought flitted across her consciousness like a dragonfly across a millpond.

What if he didn't find her?

The next day dawned clear, the cloudless sky mirroring the irascible river. Sebastien left camp briefly to find a fording place, but the look on his face once he returned was ominous.

"This river is deep and the current is swift," he told her,

securing the saddlebags. "The horses may not make it across, but to continue we have no choice but to chance it."

Sylvie ran a hand down the tangled, burred mane of the creature who'd miraculously not failed her other than stumbling and spilling her to the ground a time or two. Sebastien's mount was a bit more high-spirited, even unpredictable.

Once they broke camp, they rode along the riverbank into a day already as warm as a bake oven. Squinting, Sylvie once again rued her missing cap and straw hat. Her skin had begun to peel, blistering in places, her scalp sore. But better that than a tomahawk and scalping. Not one Indian had they seen, nor another white man. But in so vast a wilderness it was hardly surprising.

"Ici!" Sebastien's shout crested above the noise of the brawling river. Without waiting for her to respond, he kneed his horse into the current.

Skittish, his horse balked then moved forward at Sebastien's insistence. Sylvie's own mount resisted, but she coaxed her on into the icy tumult even as she fought against her own breathless terror. Water encircled her waist, and she clung to the mare's neck as the frightened animal strained against the powerful flow, its foamy spray blinding. She could feel the mare's hard kicking as its hooves left the slick bottom in an attempt to swim.

At once the horror of the hurricane swept over her, the wrenching loss of Mère and Marie-Madeleine thorn sharp and threatening her resolve. All was overwhelming white water and cold and terror, dragging her down and drowning her last hope.

Fixing her eyes on the opposite bank, Sylvie heard a hoarse cry. Her gaze swung to Sebastien as he lost his balance. His frantic voice would forever echo in her ears as he and his panicked horse were swept away.

58

And in to-day already walks tomorrow.

Friedrich Schiller

Shaking and benumbed, Sylvie reached the opposite shore. As she slid from the mare's sodden saddle, her legs gave way. Sand and rock bruised her knees as she hit the ground, and her heart seemed to pound through the linen of her bodice amid a breathless realization.

Mon Dieu, You have saved me once again.

Pulling herself to her feet, Sylvie ran on wobbly legs down the bank, searching for sight of Sebastien. But the river had claimed him, and deep in her spirit she sensed he'd drowned, his horse with him. The river's sharp bend swept out of sight, stretching on in its furious race to the west.

Bending over to catch her breath only to have it snatched away as she wept, she mourned the man who'd lost his way in countless respects. Her horse stood stone-still nearby, dripping and weakened by the fight with the water. She fumbled in her pocket and withdrew Will's handkerchief, worn from repeated washings. Somehow it assuaged her and left her riven all at once.

Dropping to the sand again, she sat, arms around her legs, head on her bent knees. The sun beat down, drying her dress and all the rest of her, as things became clear. She was alone. All the provisions had been swept away with Sebastien. She had no idea which direction she should go, either to the Rivanna settlement or to Fort Duquesne. She didn't even know how many leagues they'd traveled, though Sebastien had seemed confident of his course.

The mare nickered, returning her to the unwelcome present. Gathering her wits, Sylvie got to her feet and put her arms around the horse's warm, damp neck, grappling with gratitude and fear and the dilemma of where to ride. Should she follow the river? Settlements—even lone settlers—sought rivers upon which to build their lives.

Once in the saddle again, she let the river lead her.

Days passed in a haze of heat and insects and one long, rattling snake that slithered out from beneath a rock and reminded her of Will's fright in the bedchamber. She was growing weaker, light-headed from hunger that gnawed continually at her insides, though with the river near, she never thirsted.

Heavenly Father, I must eat.

In time she stumbled on wild sweet strawberries, so juicy they left a scarlet trail down her chin. She pressed on, the endless river shifting and turning in bewildering ways, but not one soul did she see. Had the newspapers lied about that too? Was the frontier war a fiction?

That night, sore from so long in the saddle and shaking from hunger, she lay down on the blanket she'd tried to clean with the last of her soap. When she slept, dreams of Will haunted her. Strange, twisted dreams that left her more worn out. He was not coming. He'd given up on her. He'd chosen Liselotte instead.

A warbler woke her. She shifted on her blanket, the pine boughs beneath poking her. Flat on her back, she opened her eyes and saw six dark faces peering down at her, moccasins edging her blanket.

Indians.

She shot upright, the fear of the river crossing no match for this new terror. For a moment she just sat as if turned to stone, and the Indians froze where they stood. Nothing moved, not even a breath of wind. And then one tall, half-naked man poked a finger at her braid as if ascertaining she was flesh, not spirit. He smiled, saying something to his fellows, who looked around as if making sure she was alone.

A lean, coppery hand extended, helping her to her feet.

"Merci," she whispered.

A volley of strange syllables followed, and then an older man, bald but for his colorful feather headdress and silver hooped earrings, gestured for them to be silent. In seamless French, he said, "Who are you and where are you going?"

She took a tremulous breath. "I am lost—alone. My brother's name is Bleu Galant, said to be at Fort Duquesne. I have come from the Rivanna River settlement of Major William Blackburn."

He studied her for a time as the other men looked on. "You are between both places. Where is your heart?"

The question touched her. *Where, indeed*. Torn. Wanting to be both places at once.

"Home." The word spilled out on a sob. Clenching her teeth, she willed herself to show no weakness even if it was warranted.

"You are hungry?" he asked.

"Oui." Her stomach growled in answer.

A pouch was opened. Jerked meat and something like crushed corn. Famished as she was, it seemed the richest fare. Slowly her strength returned as she ate, her stomach cramping after being so long denied. Someone thrust a canteen at her like the one she'd seen Will carry. When she uncorked it, she smelled spirits. Rum? She tasted it, swallowing a bracing if medicinal mouthful, before handing it back to him.

Another man mounted her horse and pulled her up after him. His leg bore a festering gash. Was that why he rode? The rest of them walked, striding through the brush like they knew every nook and cranny of the wilderness, and finally veered away from the river and all its harrowing memories.

⁓

Where were they taking her?

It dawned on Sylvie that she might now be their captive. Having been raised alongside the Mi'kmaq, she felt a lessening fear, though these Indians spoke a strange tongue and dressed more strangely, their weapons threatening. Sharp, shiny scalping knives and tomahawks hung from elaborately beaded belts, a reminder they were warriors foremost. But for the older man who spoke French and seemed to possess a love of finery, she would have felt more alone, though each of them treated her kindly, even respectfully. Sometimes the French speaker asked her questions. Did she have a husband? Children? Was she aligned with le français or Anglais?

She answered truthfully, telling him of Acadie and their expulsion, which he seemed to understand. Was their fate so different? These Indians were fighting for their lands, their way of life. At least that bound them if little else did.

They crossed another river, this time in canoes concealed in the woods near the water, confirming her suspicions that these men often traversed this vast territory and but for them she'd likely have perished. She grew less chary, sleeping more soundly and eating what they carried, though she longed for fresh meat and bread. She did not ask where they were going, for she sensed it would not matter. They seemed intent on a destination, and nothing she could do or say would alter it. Still, she wondered and prayed.

Would their journey never end?

When they crossed a great meadow speckled with wild-flowers and then yet another river, she felt hope take hold. The river reminded her of the Rivanna. Again they plunged into the woods and halted only at sunset when she felt she could not take another step. Here the horse was left to graze as the men made camp.

The last of daylight speared the surrounding trees, gilding the scene like a finely framed painting. Momentarily she forgot her weariness, the beauty and peace of the place overwhelming her. A waterfall splashed its way down a rocky draw and spilled into a creek that swept past like the blue of a painter's brush.

He maketh me to lie down in green pastures: he leadeth me beside the still waters.

She knelt at the waterfall and drank deeply, finding it sweet. She wet her hot face and neck, uncaring that her skirt was damp. A soothing wind rustled the leaves all around her, and she stood facing its direction, eyes closed in a moment colored with gratitude and grace.

When she opened her eyes, she saw Bleu.

59

What will not woman, gentle woman dare, when strong
affection stirs her spirit up?

Robert Southey

Bleu caught her up in the same hard, breathless embrace she remembered, lifting her off her feet and
twirling her in a smooth, sure-footed circle. One
worn shoe dangled, then fell off, but she hardly noticed or
cared.

"It has not yet been a year, but it seems like an eternity," he
whispered in her ear. "I have become something of a religious
man, praying for you. Praying for our reunion." He stood
her on her feet and stepped back, his dark gaze sweeping her.
"You are too thin—and brown as Virginia tobacco—but still
my beloved sister."

She wept then, hiding her face in her hands. His own face
shone with tears.

For a time they just sat together on a hollow log, the creek
a stone's throw away. They were alone now, the other Indians
gone. It seemed Sylvie had dreamed them up entirely. How
had they simply vanished?

"Allies of the French?" she asked.

Bleu nodded. "They patrol up and down the frontier, carrying messages . . . raising havoc where they will."

"On English settlers in the backcountry, you mean, as well as British troops."

"You have entered the ring of fire, as it's called. A very dangerous and destructive territory."

"How did you find me?"

"I heard you were in Virginia's largest town."

"From whom? When?"

His half smile bespoke much.

"Major Blackburn?"

His eyes sparkled. "I doubt that is what you call him."

She laughed, then flushed beneath his scrutiny. "You're right. I call him Will."

"His letter relieved then piqued me. I roam far but not so far south as Virginia, nor the Rivanna and the English towns beyond it. That is firmly settled ground, no longer contested."

"But I am safe with you. Far safer than I was when alone or with Sebastien."

"We must keep clear of the warpaths. I won't let my guard down for a moment, ma chère sœur, though I want you to be at rest."

Somehow his reassurance and his company seemed enough. Sylvie was content to just savor the security of his presence and surrender all that had happened since leaving the Rivanna. Bleu seemed to sense it, saving further conversation till she was stronger.

The next morning as they shared bread and meat from his pack, she told him about the shipwreck, losing Mère and Marie-Madeleine, and coming from the almshouse to Williamsburg and then the Rivanna settlement.

His face was so grieved it hurt her. "May God grant Mère and our sister peace."

"As for the others, I fear Père and our grandparents were on the ships that sank soon after sailing."

"Oui, I can confirm it."

"But I want to go on believing they went farther south to that territory on the southern waters."

"The land of no winter. La Louisiane."

"I hear it is even hotter there than here." Sylvie slapped at a mosquito, trying to recall what she'd read in the Virginia papers. "Thick with insects and snakes and something called bayous."

"All of those things, oui. But a haven for those who need it, as long as the French remain in control."

"Have you any news of our brothers?"

"Pascal and Lucien are with the Acadian militia and have gone to Restigouche at the head of Baie des Chaleurs."

So they were on the run. Still, they remained in their homeland if not at home. "With other Acadians?"

"A small remnant, but the English are ready to strike there, if they haven't already." Bleu shook his head. "They have no home, nor a hope of making one. English settlers are now poised to take our lands—the habitations that were not burned and are still standing across Acadie."

"Have you been back?"

"Oui. There is little left. Not even our orchard is standing."

She fell silent, so sore-hearted she couldn't speak. The destruction went deep. All the years she'd spent in their orchard, the trees growing up alongside her, seemed a part of her family, her heritage. Living things fashioned by the Lord's own hand, offering beauty and shade, every tool and furnishing, even food and drink through countless seasons.

That world was gone.

Bleu continued, "As for the traitor Boudreau, he has changed his name since fleeing Acadie and is at the Hôtel-Dieu de Québec."

She'd not thought of the doctor in so long it no longer mattered. "What of you, Bleu?"

He smiled that inscrutable smile she had missed yet never understood. "I have come down to the territory of the Yankees. The current battle in Canada is lost. For now, I am with the French at the Forks of the Ohio and Fort Duquesne. I was on my way to Virginia after learning you were there from Blackburn. Several of the Broussards work out of Duquesne, but I had no inkling one of them would attempt to bring you west. Shawnee scouts discovered your trail and we intersected."

"I'm so thankful. Sebastien was . . . unwell." The sight of him and his horse being swept away would never leave her. "He drowned in a river we should never have crossed."

"It is a miracle you survived, then. Even now you look quite undone." He studied their surroundings, so lush with the ripeness of spring. "All that you've endured makes me want to camp beside this waterfall a few days longer."

She could not argue. She was so very weary—and bewildered. "I have lost all sense of time . . ."

"It is early May." He stood, regarding her with the concern of a brother who knew her well. "What you need is a feast of buffalo. The marrow bones are a particular delicacy and will help restore you before we continue our journey." He gestured to the makeshift bough and buckskin shelter he'd made her. "Go rest, ma chère sœur. I'll return soon."

With a nod, she stood up too quickly then swayed a bit. His hand shot out to steady her as she gave way to a fresh fear. "Promise me you'll be back."

His eyes, so fiercely blue, softened. "I promise."

By late afternoon he'd returned with a young buffalo and roasted the meat over a fire, the smoke risky in so fraught a territory, surely. But Bleu was wise in the ways of the woods, reminding her of Will over and over again, and she trusted in that.

Marrow bones were indeed tasty, as was their broth, boiled in the buffalo's stomach overnight. She longed for a bit of bread, so they made corncakes from the pouch the Shawnee had left them. Bleu seemed more than a little amused when she wolfed them down, forgetting her manners.

He ate sparingly as if wanting her to have the lion's share. He even brought her more wild sweet strawberries and tender greens from the woods, reminding her of salat in the Rivanna's kitchen gardens.

"Your color is better," he told her, stretching out before the fire's embers. Smoke blew about in a light evening breeze, keeping the insects away.

"I feel stronger already. I hate to think what might have happened if the Shawnee had not found me."

"You sound like Mère with your worrying."

"She's never far from my thoughts. Nor are the others."

He reached into his pocket, brought out a pipe, and lit it by the dwindling fire. The scent of tobacco returned her thoughts to Will, only this tobacco was more fragrant, like the forest itself.

"Bearberry—kinnikinnick—from my Lenape friends," he told her, offering it to her.

She declined, though many women smoked. "I am content to watch you enjoy it." Her mind was finally clearing, though she grieved Sebastien's death, those dark days alone with him lingering.

"Major Blackburn sent a letter to the commander at Fort Duquesne, who happens to know us both." Bleu's eyes danced with amusement. "Imagine that. Two men who are supposed to be at odds corresponding like civilized messieurs—and over my beloved sister to boot."

"What did his letter say?"

"Si romantique." He winked, a sudden boyishness lending to his charm. He reached into his linen shirt and withdrew a paper. The blue wax seal was familiar, as was the bold, scrolling handwriting, dated several months before she'd even joined the Rivanna settlement.

Your sister, Sylvie Galant, is currently in Williamsburg, Virginia Colony. She is well but bereft of her family. I am writing to determine whether you are at or near Fort Duquesne as has been reported. It is of the utmost importance that she hear from you or meet with you in person.

Major William Blackburn

Tears stung her eyes. How enduring Will was, not only loving. He'd been working on her behalf early on even when she'd spurned him at every turn. Had she ever apologized to him for that? She could not remember, and suddenly it seemed so important.

"You must tell me the rest of the story." Bleu blew a purl of smoke between white teeth. "I still have questions of my own."

She looked down at the well-worn letter in her hands. "I will. But I want to know what happened between the two of you in Acadie at the last."

"Before our people were put aboard the ships?" He looked to the trees fading from green to black as nightfall encroached, his watchful gaze swinging wide. "Blackburn was on my trail, determined to hunt me down for the English, when he had a surprising change of heart."

"What do you mean?"

"I surprised him aboard his ship the night before he sailed, determined to take his life or at least teach him a lesson. We got into a furious fight, neither of us the victor. He spoke your name, and I realized you had played some part in his forsaking his duties and eventually resigning his commission."

Trying to imagine that fight, she folded the letter and held it out to him, but he waved it away. "Enough about me. You are my sole concern now. Tell me how it stands between you and the major."

And so she did, from her and Will's fractious beginnings in Williamsburg to his bringing her to live along the Rivanna, honorably and at no small trouble. "He asked me to marry him earlier this spring. But he didn't tell me he'd written you. Perhaps he is seeking your blessing."

"I thought the same."

"I hoped he'd come after me, but now I wonder." She stared into the fire as it shifted, sending out a spray of sparks. "What if he believes I had second thoughts and ran away?"

A firm shake of his head shot down the notion. "The Blackburn I know would have none of that, not after you pledged yourself to him, though perhaps he is wanting to offer you a final choice of staying with me and fellow Acadians or remaining with him. It is only fair, no? The decision is yours and yours alone."

"If he doesn't come for me, I could go with you."

"The life I lead is no life for a woman such as yourself. Always on the move, never settling, never home."

Though she'd been along the Rivanna only a short time, the house and garden had begun to feel more a home than a safe haven, a refuge. More than that, she'd moved past her fear and heartache to imagine she could be happy there, rooted again and not rootless, able to make Will Blackburn a competent wife.

Still, he had not come. And the reasons for this circled through her head, harassing her as she tried to make peace with his absence in so great a wilderness. Perhaps he had never questioned her love. Perhaps he could not yet find her or had started after her only to be waylaid by some accident or enemy or the kind of calamity that claimed Sebastien. What a torment to wonder and be beset once again by a wild restlessness that couldn't be quieted.

60

Every question was like the snapping of a little thread about my heart.

Dorothy Wordsworth

They could not stay here by this lovely waterfall in the woods forever, rustic and dangerous as it was. And yet somehow this place where Sylvie spent time with her beloved brother had become a needed interlude, an occasion that might never come again. Bleu said nothing about leaving, but she had regained her strength and there was no longer any reason for them to tarry. A decision must be made to push farther through the wilderness to French territory and Fort Duquesne or return her to the Rivanna.

As time ticked on, Sylvie prayed for Will, wherever he was. Her heart tugged her toward the Rivanna, but the return trip there was daunting even if she wanted to reunite with Will. She was at a crossroads, one of the most momentous of her life.

Sylvie and Bleu began packing up their belongings without communicating why. She rode her horse while Bleu led out on foot in a direction she was unsure of, taking a lightly traveled deer trail. Beneath the canopy of trees, not a single shaft of light shot through. She felt no fear yet realized their silence was wise as the wilderness unfolded on all sides of her. That night they left the trail and camped on a rise so high it seemed the world lay at their feet.

"I've not decided whether I favor sunrises or sunsets," Bleu told her, sitting cross-legged on a rock ledge while she dangled her petticoat-clad legs beside him. "When you were small, you used to say the gold of the rising sun was God's kiss good morning—"

"And the rainbow His smile." The bittersweet memory opened the door to others. "For a time I forbade myself to think of home—to remember. The hurt I felt overshadowed the beauty. Now I can't recall just how big Baie Française was. How blue. I can no longer remember how far the forts or the Pont-a-Buot tavern were."

"Time and distance are thieves."

"We mustn't forget family. What matters most."

"The future matters. This moment."

The sunset seemed made for adoration, the gilded horizon layered with lavender hues that reminded Sylvie of the Rivanna's fragrant walled garden.

"Where are we going?" she finally asked him.

"Home."

"But not Acadie."

"Eastern Virginia."

A rush of gratitude faded before a fresh worry. "And if I marry this man? Will you think me a traitor to our people like Sebastien Broussard did?"

"The Broussards are scattered to the winds," he said quietly, "but Blackburn is still a force to reckon with."

At that, Bleu lay down atop his blanket and soon went to sleep, while Sylvie, despite her bone-deep weariness, felt she'd be wide-eyed all night. Slowly the lavender leached from the sky and stars glittered like silver thread.

Oh, Will, mon bien-aimé, where are you?

⌒

Bleu seemed tireless on their journey while Sylvie grew tired of her own weakness. How far had they come? It seemed a thousand leagues, the distance daunting.

On the fourth day he drew up suddenly, his finger to his lips in warning. She bent low in the saddle, her heart beginning to gallop even as the mare came to a sudden, shuddering halt. She let loose the reins as Bleu took her to the ground in one grand sweep.

They lay facedown, concealed by brush yet aware of a steady tread, at first distant and then chillingly distinct. Indians? Or soldiers? Gooseflesh covered her like insect bites as savagery stormed her thoughts. A tomahawk could slice through the stillness at any second, splitting her head like a melon. Captives were oft burned at the stake. She'd heard the stories since coming to Virginia, nor could she forget Will's harrowing family massacre.

Beside her, Bleu stayed so still he seemed not to breathe. Lowering her head, she let the forest floor cradle her, breathing in its rich, earthy scent.

In time, the awareness of others in the forest faded and the skitter of squirrels and birdsong resumed. Bleu stood cautiously and led her another direction.

The next evening found them beside a stream, heat pressing down on them like a blanket. Sylvie knelt by the water, splashing her face to freshen herself, when the deadly cock of Bleu's rifle brought her to her feet. Wide-eyed with alarm, she started toward her brother as a great crashing of the brush made her look back over her shoulder. In seconds a great furry creature bounded straight toward her. Tail wagging, Bonami seemed more her rescuer than the man who appeared next.

Numb, Sylvie stared at Will as he came to a halt a stone's throw away. He, too, looked at her as if seeing an apparition, his own rifle dangling from one hand.

"Can it be?" she breathed, woozy all over again.

"You made it somewhat harder, wisely keeping clear of the main traces," Will replied with an appreciative nod at Bleu. "But I've no complaints to find you in one piece."

Bleu set his gun aside, a look of relief and amusement on his face. With manners that would have made Mère proud, he said, "If you'll excuse me, I have other matters to attend to," and disappeared with a rustle of brush.

Overcome by a bewildering shyness, Sylvie knelt on trembling legs and petted Bonami, whispering French endearments as he licked her flushed cheek.

"The orchard's blooming," Will finally said.

She looked at him then, tears in her eyes.

"Are you coming?" he asked quietly. "Or going?"

She stood as Bonami bounded after a squirrel. "I'm coming back to you, though I was beginning to wonder if I'd ever see you again." She gestured toward a mossy log. "Please sit down and I'll bring you something to eat and drink."

"I'd rather talk, Sylvie."

They lowered themselves to the log, an awkward space between them when all she wanted was to throw her arms around him. She stole a glance at his tight features and saw relief there and, she hoped, the same longing she herself felt. Still, they both had questions.

"I hardly know where to begin . . ." Taking a breath, Sylvie looked down at her scuffed shoes. "Though I didn't know it till too late, Sebastien and Liselotte were in league together. I went to the orchard after Liselotte told me Nolan had been stung by bees, only to have Sebastien tie my hands and put me on a horse. I tried to fight back, but he had a pistol and threatened me. I always feared his changing moods, which seemed to worsen the farther we traveled."

He nodded, taking a paper from the fold of his shirt. "This was found in your cottage. I realized you couldn't have written it, but since I'd never seen your handwriting it gave me a start at first."

She read the letter, the audacious words carefully penned in crowded, hurried script. "It's not from my hand—nor my heart, Will. That's Liselotte's doing. She wished me ill."

"I've already sent her out of the settlement. I had reservations about her from the first."

Reassured, she reached for his hand. "Glad as I am to be reunited with Bleu, I want to return with you as soon as we can."

He looked in the direction Bleu had disappeared. "You've no desire to go with your brother to Fort Duquesne or New France?"

"No."

He turned back toward her, his eyes tender and stern all at once. "You're sure?"

"This ordeal has affirmed it, Will. The longer I was away from you, the more I missed you. And the children." She squeezed his callused hand. "I belong nowhere but with you."

In halting words, she recounted to him that terrible moment at the river when Sebastien had drowned and the long, desperate days after when she'd been alone, trying to find her way.

"I think I was just going in circles. I felt so lost." Her voice wavered. "I sometimes think those warriors were angels in disguise. They showed me the utmost kindness and courtesy despite their weapons. And then came Bleu. And now you."

With Sylvie beside him, Will began to ease. The long, questioning days on the trail, his mind battered with one too many gruesome images from childhood, began to recede. He'd half expected to come upon her lifeless body at some point, but here she was, tears of gratitude in her eyes as she held tight to his hand. For a moment he couldn't speak.

He wished them back on the porch or in the garden along the Rivanna, already wed, far removed from these forbidding woods. "We need to leave out at first light, if you can manage it," he told her, thinking how far he'd come and how far they had to go. "I have a horse hobbled half a mile back. Your mare looks spent."

"Spent but still faithful." She smiled, reassuring him. "I want Bleu with us, to witness our wedding."

"He's willing?"

"Though he'd never say it, he's in need of rest in a place free of warfare where he doesn't have to watch his back. I want him to meet the children and see the Rivanna too."

He set his rifle down and took her in his arms, overcome with all the Lord had done to bring them together not once but twice, against nearly impossible odds. Surely that boded a hope-filled future.

She kissed him with all the breathless sweetness and longing he remembered, and he returned it, not wanting to let her go. But he needed a meal and a bath, and the noise of the near creek promised the latter while Sylvie saw to the former.

Bleu returned, calling them lovebirds, his smile removing any remaining doubt from Will's mind how he felt about the matter.

61

When I was at home, I was in a better place.

William Shakespeare

Returning to the Rivanna took time, so much time that Sylvie feared the pink and white blossoms would be lost till next apple season. Silly, she reasoned. What mattered most was being together.

To her surprise, Bleu accompanied her and Will. She'd not had to coerce him. Was he tired of all the patrolling and danger? Of shadowing and being shadowed? Whatever his reasons, she reveled in the company of the two men who mattered most, watching the slow unfolding of their unlikely friendship as they traveled southeast.

When she thought she could go no farther, she detected smoke—just a faint whiff—before she spied the distant orchards, the very place she'd been lured to the month before. Despite that, a deep sense of homecoming suffused her as they passed through the apple trees that scattered pink and white petals in the warm wind as if in welcome. They adorned her hair and tattered garments and carried the scent of spring. Her soul, shuttered for so long, seemed to swing wide and take in the beauty of the place she'd once thought lost to her forever.

Was there anything more beautiful than the Rivanna River in the month of May?

For once the lushness of spring crowded out comparison and longing. She was here. She was home. She never wanted to leave it. Bleu's admiring gaze was not lost on her, nor was Will's apparent pleasure—or was it more relief? They walked side by side, the horses trailing, beneath the shady canopy of branches that shook forth more blooms.

"Belle terre," Bleu murmured. "I suppose I am in enemy territory."

"Blackburn territory. Neutral ground," Will replied, reaching up to pick an apple blossom. "Home to you whenever you want it to be." Turning to Sylvie, he tucked the blossom behind her right ear.

She smiled as she pushed a limp strand of hair into place. "It's nearly June, but we'll have our orchard wedding."

Will nodded and gestured east. "There's a Baptist preacher in our parish a few miles from here. Just say the word and I'll send for him."

"And my ring?"

"On the washstand in our house."

She smiled and sighed all at once. "These apple blossoms won't wait much longer, and neither will I."

⌒

Sylvie sewed Bleu's wedding suit in the orchard. There the light was kind, and her brother sat beneath the spreading branches, not in a chair but on the thick grass. Henrietta had taken a fancy to him and was never far, a bit piqued that he was fashioning a bow and arrows for her brother.

"A war bow!" Nolan exclaimed with pride.

"A hunting bow," Bleu corrected. He whittled in that patient way that reminded Sylvie of Pascal by hearth light a lifetime ago, shavings at his feet.

"Are the arrows sharp?" Henrietta asked, sidling up to him.

"No, blunt till he knows better than to shoot at you."

She giggled, and the children returned to their playing while Sylvie stilled her needle and studied Bleu. The lines in his tanned face had eased, and his leanness wasn't so pronounced after a week of kitchen house fare.

"You could always move into my cottage once I'm on the hill," she said quietly, gauging his reaction. For now, he slept outside in the orchard when he wasn't helping in the stables or barns.

A half smile softened his features. "Can you see me in the cottage, ma sœur?"

She returned to her sewing. "Not in the least."

"Still, you would try to tether me."

"Try, oui."

"Some men are made for war, and I am one of them."

"I don't believe that. I see how you are with the children. How peaceful you seem here."

"And who would you marry me to?"

"Louise, perhaps." She'd seen the second glances of the Acadian women since his arrival, Louise foremost. Had he?

"It's a rather unpleasant time for settling down. This war seems to have no end. In fact, it seems to have not yet officially begun."

"Hush about the war. You are all the family I have left. I doubt I'll see our brothers again. Is it any wonder I try to tame you?" The teasing in her tone belied her heartache. "I sense your restlessness, though I believe your roaming nature can be quieted."

"I am in British territory. Somewhat amusing, is it not?"

"We are all in enemy territory except for Will and his

indentures, though it feels less so here along the Rivanna."
She looked toward the road Will had taken, hoping he'd materialize at any moment. He'd gone to summon the preacher
who'd marry them, and she looked east. "At the very least I
hope you'll come back here again and again."

"I am considering returning to Acadie. To see if I can find
our brothers or anyone else we know."

Stanching her surprise, she finished a sleeve, wondering
whether to let Henrietta sew on the death-head buttons once
she'd finished the buttonholes. "It's too dangerous."

"Since when has danger stopped me?"

"Will you be courting danger and still roaming when
you're Père's age?"

"Fifty winters? I am but thirty."

"I can't help but notice the same rheumatism in your
hands."

He set down his knife and the unfinished bow. "Nothing
that a little devil's claw can't cure."

"Forget devil's claw. I have another, better remedy." She
looked at him, wondering if this was the picture of him she
would have in mind when he left. "You should take la voie
douce, the gentle path. It leads home."

"And home is now here, at least for you. Have you decided
what to call this place?"

She smiled and lifted her shoulders in a slight shrug. "I
am still pondering it."

Inside her cottage, Sylvie dressed in the Lyonnais silk,
wondering if Bleu remembered bringing it to her that December day when she'd stood on the snow-swept bluff above
Baie Française. Through the open window, she could hear
the coming of wedding guests to the orchard. Voices floated

up to her, even laughter, as the sun shone down on a clear Virginia afternoon.

Bonami's sharp bark pulled her to the window. She spied Eulalie coming down the hill, a freshly picked bouquet from the walled garden in hand, as Henrietta and Nolan played ball in the side yard, dressed in their best. Henrietta resembled a fashion baby, clad in a dress of yellow-striped taffeta with a wide sash at her waist, while Nolan's suit was slate blue and twin to the groom's . . . wherever he was.

Was Will ready? As ready as she?

Sylvie took a last glance in the looking glass, hardly recognizing herself. Her gown gave a delicious rustle as she moved toward the door to answer the knock. Opening it, she found Bleu. She touched the fine broadcloth sleeve of his suit, noting the buttons Henrietta had finished so proudly. "You nearly look the groom!"

"I am merely the escort," he replied with a rare shimmer in his eyes. "Une très belle mariée."

"If I am a beautiful bride, it is because of your silk and my own happiness."

They stepped onto the porch, where Eulalie passed her the bouquet. Sylvie brought the blooms to her nose, a few apple blossoms tucked in, and breathed in the delicate scent as Will appeared on the main house's front porch. Their eyes met, and her heart gave a leap. He stepped off the porch and started down the well-worn path, his gaze never leaving her.

She moved toward him across the grass, her step light, the sun warming her as it fell across the orchard in its westward slant. Behind him, the main house was framed in light, its gilded outline well deserving of the name that had come to her on the way back to the Rivanna. A place of beauty and peace and possibilities. A promise of the future with a whispered reminder of the past.

Orchard Rest.

Author Note

I've long been fascinated by French history and the French language, so that is where this novel began. But like many people, I knew little of Acadie. Somehow, the epic poem *Evangeline: A Tale of Acadie* by Henry Wadsworth Longfellow, which brought this tragic history to light in the nineteenth century, bypassed me. I often felt overwhelmed while researching and writing *The Seamstress of Acadie*, hardly believing an event of such cruelty and magnitude happened. It's a testament to the Acadians' enduring spirit that a remnant survived such a tragedy and built new communities like those in Louisiana and elsewhere.

Sylvie Galant's journey asks a timeless theological question. Where is God in the midst of suffering and tragedy? I'm reminded of Canadian singer Gordon Lightfoot's lyrics from "The Wreck of the *Edmund Fitzgerald*": "Does anyone know where the love of God goes when the waves turn the minutes to hours?" To which we can answer, "Nor height, nor depth, nor any other creature, shall be able to separate us from the love of God, which is in Christ Jesus our Lord" (Rom. 8:39).

William Blackburn's character is based on the real-life historical figure Major Robert Rogers, founder of Roger's Rangers, who has influenced the US Army Rangers to this day. His renowned Battle on Snowshoes actually occurred later than referenced in these pages but was so extraordinary that I included it in the novel's time frame.

You'll find characters from my novel *A Heart Adrift* within *The Seamstress of Acadie*. Quinn and Eliza Shaw Cheverton, Esmée Shaw, and Henri Lennox's response to the Acadians was what should have happened historically. Sadly, few exiles were met with anything but hostility and hatred wherever they landed, even from those within the church.

As for the snake scene in chapter 52, this actually happened to an apprentice in eighteenth-century Williamsburg, Virginia. I came across it in my research and thought it served the story well.

For other novels related to Acadian history, I recommend Janette Oke and T. Davis Bunn's Song of Acadia series, Genevieve Graham's *Promises to Keep*, and Cassie Deveaux Cohoon's *Jeanne Dugas of Acadia*. There is a wealth of nonfiction about Acadie's history as well.

Special thanks to Stephanie Rousselle of Gospel Spice Ministries for her gracious help answering questions related to the French language. Any mistakes therein are my own.

For readers who have been to Nova Scotia, once Acadie, I hope you feel you've returned there in the novel's pages. For those who haven't been, I hope you visit to truly experience what a simple novel can't convey in words.

Laura Frantz is a Christy Award winner and the ECPA best-selling author of fifteen novels, including *An Uncommon Woman*, *Tidewater Bride*, *A Bound Heart*, *A Heart Adrift*, and *The Rose and the Thistle*. She is the proud mom of an American soldier and a career firefighter. Though Kentucky will always be home to her, she and her husband live in Washington State.

MEET

LAURA FRANTZ

Visit LauraFrantz.net to read
Laura's blog and learn about her books!

f   enter to win contests and learn about what
Laura is working on now

𝕏   tweet with Laura

◙   see what Laura is up to

℗   see what inspired the characters and stories

"A deeply atmospheric story of ***faith, love, and sacrifice*** that is as captivating as it is enthralling."

—**Sarah E. Ladd**, bestselling author of The Cornwall Novels

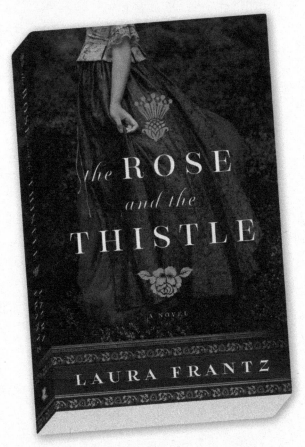

Amid the Jacobite uprising of 1715, an English heiress flees to the Scottish Lowlands to stay with allies of her powerful family. But while castle walls may protect her from the enemy outside, a whirlwind of intrigue, shifting allegiances, and temptations of the heart lie within.

Revell
a division of Baker Publishing Group
www.RevellBooks.com

Available wherever books and ebooks are sold.

"This tale of second chances and brave choices *swept me away.*"

—**Jocelyn Green,** Christy Award–winning author of *Shadows of the White City*

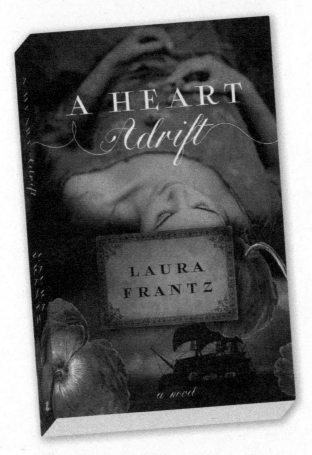

A colonial lady and a privateering sea captain collide once more after a failed love affair a decade before. Will a war and a cache of regrets keep them apart? Or will a new shared vision reunite them?

R Revell
a division of Baker Publishing Group
www.RevellBooks.com

Available wherever books and ebooks are sold.

EIGHTEENTH-CENTURY VIRGINIA
Comes Alive in Frantz's Novels

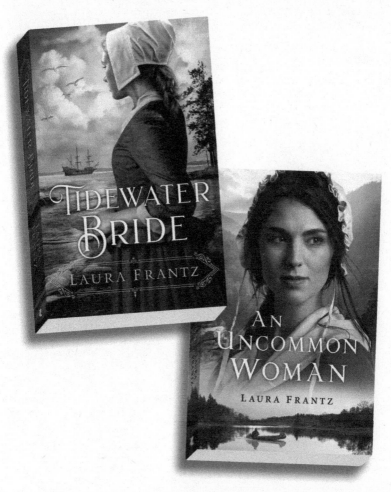

"Laura Frantz transports readers to a setting she has mastered, the eighteenth-century mountain frontier. Sensory-rich descriptions bring the landscape to life."

—**Lori Benton,** Christy Award–winning author of *The King's Mercy*

If You Liked This Book,
PICK ANOTHER TRANSPORTIVE HISTORICAL NOVEL